OPERATION AMETHYST

A NOVEL

LEESA WRIGHT

CONTENTS

CHAPTER 1

South Vietnam, Mid-January 1968.

ELYSE BOOKER FELT the chopper shudder from the heavy spray of gunfire as the crew chief and gunner returned fire. Bullets whizzed by, some striking the windshield and other parts of the aircraft. The pilot and copilot fought to maintain control of the helicopter in what was supposed to be a quick trip from Huế City to the Khe Sanh military base.

After a bullet hit the engine, it began to go down in heavy jungle, churning out of control. Elyse hung on to the bars of the chopper for dear life. The chatter from the pilots and gunners screamed through her head along with her own screams of terror. The crew chief took a bullet and his lifeless body slumped over his weapon. One more spin threw her to the doorway of the chopper. In a selfless act of desperation, the gunner used his foot to push her out the door before the chopper hit the ground. The thick jungle foliage cushioned her body as she rolled away. The chopper crashed on its side in the sickening grind of metal meeting metal as it continued to roll and spin before bursting into flames.

An hour or so later, Elyse opened her eyes. She laid on the ground looking up at the sky. Curious formations of white, fluffy clouds floated by, mixed with the fading plumes of thick, black smoke as a pounding headache started just behind her eyes.

Oh my God. My head. She rolled to her knees as confusion took over. *Where am I? What happened?* Confusion was soon replaced by the terrifying memories of the chopper and it's sickening spin. Elyse spotted the burned shell of the chopper about two hundred feet away from where she sat on her knees. All on board were dead, and a sob caught in her throat. *Those poor men. The gunner… his eyes…* his beautiful eyes had mirrored the terror she had experienced as he pushed her out the door.

Excited voices speaking in Vietnamese filtered through the jungle to where she knelt. They were too far away for her to make out the words but close enough to warn her that danger was approaching. Elyse was not ignorant of the war; it was one of her father's main concerns when calling her home. She knew how dangerous it would be if the North Vietnamese Army (NVA) or the guerilla forces, Viet Cong (VC), caught her. Run.

The foliage was thick, lush and so tall it blocked her view of the sun at times. Since she was using the sun as her compass, she was frustrated by the thick growth both on the ground and overhead. The sounds of insects, monkeys, and birds calling to each other added to the exotic hum of the jungle. She did not know exactly where she was, but she knew to move eastward toward the South China Sea.

Elyse did not know how far or how long she had walked. She had survived two long, hot days and two terrifying, sleepless nights filled with bugs, the pitch blackness of the jungle, and the sounds of night creatures. She was exhausted again, and it would soon be time to stop and rest, but first she searched for water and food. Finding large curled leaves of jungle foliage with small pools of water in the center, she drank the water. After many attempts, she mastered her technique so not a drop was wasted. She had found berries the day before, but they were bitter and left a foul taste in her mouth as she spit them out. Not that hungry, she halfheartedly searched for something to eat and found some small green berries. She had seen these before in the outdoor markets of Huế City. There weren't many on the bush, but she ate them savoring their exotic flavor.

She played back the last telephone conversation with her father in her mind, the argument that ensued as he told her to notify the South Viet-namese Royal Ballet of an emergency at home, pack all of her things as a chopper was already on the way to pick her up from the American compound where she lived in Huế City.

"Daddy, Why? Why do I need to come home? What's going on?"

"Elyse, please don't argue with me. There is no time to explain. I need you home as soon as possible."

"I have responsibilities here. I have two performances next week."

"I'm sorry, you need to do as I say."

"Why are you always ordering me about? I'm a grown woman." The call was breaking up, and soon, all she heard was the crackle of static on the line.

"You're," more static, "danger," then the dial tone as the call disconnected.

It was not a good way to end her last conversation with her father and Elyse was racked with guilt, wondering if she had heard him correctly. *Did he say danger?*

The afternoon heat was oppressive, and the humidity hung thick in the air as she stopped to pin her hair back up again. She looked down at her bare feet for the hundredth time, unsure if she had lost her shoes during the crash or in the jungle. Her simple, orange muslin mini dress was torn and ragged from the jungle, and her feet bloody, dirty. She was hot, sweaty, thirsty, and miserable. Slapping at another bloodthirsty mosquito, she sighed and moved on, determined to make it as far east as she could before nightfall.

Leaning against a tree to rest, Elyse brushed the hair from her eyes and adjusted a bobby pin to secure her bun. Noticing the bark of the tree, she thought, *that looks like banana bark.* She looked up. *Bananas, sweet.* The tree was immense, tall and thick. *No Problem.* Pulling her dress up to her waist, she began the climb, scooting herself up inch by inch, foot by foot until she reached the very top of the tree. The large leaves drooped over the fruit as she reached out to brush them away.

A small brown hand reached out from the leaves and slapped at her. Screeching, Elyse almost lost her hold on the tree, but her thighs held firm, gripping the tree. A small monkey pushed its way through the leaves and bared its teeth at her, daring her to touch the forbidden fruit.

"Come on, I just want one," Elyse said, as she reached again for the bananas. The monkey screamed and slapped at her hand again, then it leaped at her causing her to lose her hand grip as she fell backwards.

Elyse dangled upside down high above the jungle floor, her legs firmly wrapped around the tree. The monkey hung from her hand screeching in terror. That's when she saw them, VC, creeping through the jungle below her.

Cold dread filled her as she almost lost her grip on the squirming monkey. If the animal fell, the VC below would see her. She swung it so it landed on the tree, and it scooted back up to hide within the large leaves. Gracefully and silently, she pulled herself up so she was again hugging the tree with both arms.

Watching the VC guerillas now directly below her, she counted eight of them. She held her breath, heart pounding in her chest, as they stopped to rest and quench their thirst, their voices quiet and muffled.

The monkey again bared its teeth and handed her half an unpeeled banana before it jumped from the tree with a screech to land in another tree. Elyse gripped the tree, hanging on for dear life, all the while, praying that the men didn't look up. Eventually, they moved on and she stayed in the tree for another ten minutes watching for movement in the jungle below. Stuffing the banana in her mouth, she chewed the fruit before she scooted herself down and headed east through the jungle away from the VC guerillas.

She came upon a small village and watched from the jungle for a few minutes. Children played, and women weeded the small vegetable gardens, but there were no men. Stepping out from the jungle vegetation, she slowly walked up the pathway into the village. The huts with their grass roofs, the chickens and ducks waddled aimlessly about, the goats and other livestock in their neat little pens, all spoke of a poor but functioning village.

The children spotted her first, chattering amongst themselves. The women stopped their work to stare at her as she made her way to the center of the village. Women with infants in their arms and children gathered around her as a small boy of nine or so reached out to touch her hair, exclaiming in awe at her hair of fire. Smiling at him, she paused and waited for the elders in respect of their customs and culture. An old man, bent with age and years of hard labor, walked toward her as the crowd of women and children parted to let him pass. Elyse, having been raised in Vietnam and fluent in the language, addressed the old man with respect as she asked for water to quench her thirst. He signaled to an old woman, who Elyse assumed was his wife, and the woman brought a cup of water to Elyse.

"Are you American?" he asked.

"Yes."

"We are a peaceful village. We do not want trouble with the Americans or the VC."

"I do not mean to bring trouble to you. I am lost and need to find my way home."

"Do the Americans search for you?"

"I do not know."

"You are not safe here. The VC come through here to take our food to feed their men. We will feed you and point you in the right direction to find the Americans, but you must leave."

"I understand. I am grateful for whatever help you can give me."

Elyse sat on a stool outside, near the center of the village, as the children gathered around her, touching her hair and skin, pointing at her amethyst eyes, and asking a thousand questions. She patiently answered each one. A gaunt young woman with a babe at her breast handed her a bowl of rice. Elyse was hesitant to accept the food and take what little they had, but the woman urged Elyse to take it and eat. A girl of three with big eyes and a body too tiny for her age watched as Elyse took a small handful of rice. Unable to eat in front of the hungry tot, she put the handful of rice into the toddler's hands. The little girl called her "Toc chay," fire hair, as she stuffed the rice into her tiny mouth. Elyse smiled and stroked her head. The other children asked for some, and she split the remaining rice between them.

A young boy came running into the village, shouting that he had spotted VC heading toward the village. Elyse jumped to her feet, dropping the bowl.

The old man turned to Elyse. "You must hide, there is no time for escape." He took Elyse inside a hut and moved aside some weaved mats hiding a trap door in the floor.

"Quickly, inside. Stay silent, do not come out until I tell you so."

Elyse climbed down the shaky ladder into the pit. She squeezed her eyes shut as she felt a moment's panic when the trap door was shut and the mats replaced. She steadied her breathing. Calming herself as she could see daylight through the cracks in the floorboards left uncovered by the mats. She heard voices of men when the VC entered the village. Coming closer and closer to the hut where she hid. Her panic rose again, and she covered her mouth with her hands. Sheer horror at her predicament rose as Elyse realized that she may have been tricked. There was a strong possibility the elder might turn her over to the VC to save his village, and Elyse cursed her own gullibility.

Soldiers stood directly above her now, arguing about weapons placed in the pit a week ago. The elder argued that other VC guerillas had removed the weapons a few days earlier, but the other man screamed at the elder, demanding to know who took his cache of weapons.

Elyse scooted her back to the wall of the pit, searching for the weapons as her eyes adjusted to the darkness of the pit. Biting her lip, she could see nothing but the beady red eyes that watched her from the far corner. *Rats.* The hair on her arms stood straight up, and she broke out in goosebumps as the rats advanced.

Her eyes swung back up to the floorboards as the argument intensified, and the VC guerilla repeatedly struck the elder, knocking him to the floor of the hut. The old woman screamed and cried as the soldier refused her entry to the hut to see to her husband and forced her out to the center of the village, ordering her and the other women to prepare food for his hungry men.

The elder laid on the floor above Elyse for a while, and she worried that he was seriously injured or dead. He stirred, and Elyse breathed a sigh of relief as she wiped at the tears that threatened to spill from her eyes while she kicked at an encroaching rat.

Eventually the sounds of the women's screams and children crying quieted as the VC left the village. After what seemed like an eternity, the mats were removed, and the trap door opened. Elyse climbed up and out of the pit and followed the frail elder outside. She stopped to thank him, looking into his frightened eyes.

"I'm so sorry he hurt you. Thank you for saving my life."

He nodded his head in response. "You must go now." Pointing east, he said, "Go that way. You will find American soldiers."

Thanking him, she left the village at a run.

She slipped through the jungle for a time. An hour or so away from the village, the sound of a burbling stream reached her ears. She gave a small giggle of delight as she found the small stream. Climbing down the shallow incline, she sat on the bank of the stream, soaking her feet, washing the blood and filth of the jungle off her soles, and massaging her arches. She ripped a strip of cloth from her dress to use as a washcloth on her face and neck. Then, she stripped off her dress and entered a shallow pool to rinse the grime from the rest of her body and wash her dress. The cooling water lifted her spirits. She had a momentary concern about bathing in her orange panties and bra, and then she laughed out loud. *It's like a bikini, and there is no one here to see me anyway.*

Elyse cupped the water to her lips and giggled as the water trickled down her bosom. Sighing, feeling a moment's regret that she would have to move on. She hoped to find Americans as the village elder said she would. Silently praying that she would find help.

Climbing back up the bank of the stream, she stood, wringing out her dress when she heard the snap of a branch. She froze, a million thoughts racing through her head. *Animal, human, friend, or foe?*

Elyse heard whispers. *Vietnamese, VC. Run.*

Dropping her dress in her panic, she stumbled through the thick undergrowth. *The sun. Where is the sun?* Elyse was turned around and could not get her sense of direction. *Just keep running.*

Elyse heard them as she stumbled onto an overgrown path. They were hot and fast on the trail behind her. They must have followed her from the village. Her heart raced, pounding in her chest as she ran through the jungle. She eventually came to a small clearing.

Where to hide? Think. Look for somewhere to hide. She backed up to the tree line, looking for somewhere—anywhere. Their chattering closed in behind her. *Oh God help me.*

Turning to run, she tripped and fell, partially catching herself in the shrubbery as she felt her bra catch on a branch just as someone grabbed her from behind.

CHAPTER 2

He had stood with stealthy silence to snatch her from behind. The man, an American, caught her and pulled her down into the ravine, hard, and on top of him. His eyes widened as she straddled his waist, her hands splayed out on his chest, and she opened her mouth to scream. To silence her, he rolled, flipping her on her back covering her mouth with his large hand. Pinning her arms over her head with his other hand, he disabled her easily. He stared down into shocked amethyst eyes.

Twenty or so Viet Cong poured into the clearing, searching for her trail amid the thick vegetation. Elyse sensed the other men who had come with her rescuer. Except for the man on top of her, they emptied their weapons into the enemy combatants.

Elyse squeezed her eyes shut and tried to still her racing heart at the sound of gunfire and the smell of gunpowder, amidst the cries of the VC at being ambushed by American troops.

Then silence descended. Elyse opened her eyes to stare into the face of the handsome man. A strong jaw line framed intense brown eyes with long dark lashes. The dark stubble on his camouflage painted face, and the full lips stunned her into momentary silence.

As he perused her face and hair, his slow wicked smile set something off in Elyse. She narrowed her eyes and, with a cry of rage at the forced intimacy, she bit down on his hand. Cursing, he loosened his hold on her, and she rolled and scrambled to get away from him.

She didn't get far. He caught her by the leg and dragged her back by the hips. She kicked at him, pushing off his chest to scramble away again. He grunted in pain as he grabbed her by the waist and flipped her onto her back again. They both noticed her bare breasts at the same time. His eyes widened, and he inhaled sharply, while she shrieked and covered herself. She scooted back on her bottom up against a tree, arms over her breasts, and breathing heavily. Searching for her bra or something to cover up with, she grabbed the fronds of a nearby fern and pulled them over to cover herself.

CAPTAIN ELIJAH CORRINGTON, US Marine Corps, Force Recon and his six-man team were on a reconnaissance mission watching the movements of the VC. He could not believe what literally fell into his ditch. Incredulous, he crouched down in front of her and whispered hoarsely to the woman peeking out from behind the ferns.

"Who are you?"

"Elyse Booker, I'm American," she replied.

He nearly choked at the vision of what remained uncovered by her arms and the ferns, her heaving chest, obvious distress, and terror at her state of undress made him soften his gaze. Cap, as he was called by his team, looked around and spotted her orange bra up above in the shrubbery where she had stood. No help there; it was practically shredded from the gunfire. He motioned for the man now standing above to hand it down to him. He then tossed it to Elyse.

Her cries of "No. Now what?" brought a smile to his face. He took off his rucksack, dug around for a minute, and handed her a green tank top.

He climbed out of the ravine to give her privacy and faced his team. Judging by the bewildered looks on their faces, they had just as many questions as he did. What was an American woman doing on her own in the jungle?

"Henson, get on the horn with headquarters and tell them what we found."

The Captain turned back to Elyse just in time to see his shirt coming down over her breasts. He groaned, wondering what the hell he was supposed to do now. *A woman who looks like that… She fills out my shirt pretty damn good.* He offered her his hand as he stared down into her mesmerizing eyes, and his breath caught in his throat. *Sweet Jesus, those eyes.* They reminded him of the darkest amethyst. She accepted his hand, and he lifted her out of the ravine.

"Hmph." he grunted. *Barely weighs a sack of potatoes.*

Elyse stood before him in silence as he looked her over. She was tiny. He noted the pink flush to her cheeks, the bare feet, and—

Sweet Jesus, orange panties.

Her amber-fire hair had slipped from its bun and flowed to curl around her breasts and sway with soft ringlets to her waist. He noted her small waist, smooth-muscled belly, curvy hips, and ass. *God, she's perfect in every way.* His perusal went back up to her more-than-generous breasts and to her beautiful face where he noted the narrowing of her eyes.

"Do I pass muster, Captain?"

Sassy as well. He narrowed his eyes back at her, looking down at her bare feet again.

"Where are your shoes? Clothes?"

The delicate shrug of her shoulders set a slight jiggle to her breasts, and he inhaled when he felt that familiar arousal and hardening in his groin. He abruptly turned to bark out orders to his men to get the kill count and destroy any enemy weapons.

Henson signaled to the Captain. "I've got some answers for you Cap. Her name is Elyse Booker. She's the daughter of the US Ambassador to South Vietnam. Her chopper went down fifteen clicks from here. They've been searching for this chick for two days."

"You're telling me this woman has been alone in the jungle for two days?"

"Yes, Sir," replied Henson. "We are to escort her back to Khe Sanh and stay with her. The Commandant will explain everything when we arrive."

Captain Corrington raised his eyebrows. "What the fuck is the ambassador's daughter doing in a combat zone?"

Henson shrugged.

"No *bird? We have to escort her through the deep jungle to Khe Sanh, another twenty clicks away? Why?"

"Sir, they don't want anyone to know where she is or give out her location to the VC. We can catch a bird once we get closer to base."

The Captain raised his eyebrows. "It's a hell of a lot harder to haul her through the fucking jungle than do a simple extraction with a chopper ride." Cursing under his breath he turned to look at his new charge. *Christ. She's fucking gorgeous.*

Captain Corrington strode over to her and introduced himself and each member of his team. "I'm Captain Elijah Corrington. This is Staff Sergeant John 'Sarge' Miller." A tall black man with a sparkle in his brown eyes stepped forward. "It's a pleasure to meet you."

Radio Operator, Lance Corporal Bill Henson, smiled and bowed to her. Medical Corpsman, Rick Marstow, "Doc," ever so discreetly looked her up and down. With a smile a mile wide, he winked at her. Lance Corporal Bobby Arnold, reached out to shake her hand and held her hand a moment longer than necessary. Lance Corporal Joseph "Mountain" Brown, smiled and winked. And Lance Corporal Andy Johnson, reached out to shake her hand.

"Men, this is Elyse Booker, daughter of US Ambassador Booker."

They all stood open-mouthed, still somewhat shocked at their find.

❧

SHE LOOKED from man to man, they towered over her slight five-foot frame.

She smiled at them. "You can all close your mouths now, you'll let the gnats in."

Mountain laughed. "It's not every day you find a red-headed runt in the jungle, Miss Booker,"

Elyse laughed. "Runt? It's not every day a girl's chopper crashes into the land of the giants." He grinned at her.

"Please, all of you, call me Elyse." They nodded their heads in agreement.

❧

ELYSE TOOK A CLOSER look at the Captain. Six-two, a mop of black, wavy hair trimmed short on the sides, fit and well-muscled, long legs. A handsome battle-hardened man, slightly arrogant with a wicked smile. A man used to giving orders and having them followed. She watched him from lowered lashes as he moved about the clearing, instructing the men as they counted and searched the bodies of the dead Viet Cong and prepared to leave. She sucked in her breath as she felt her color rising at her own thoughts at meeting such a man.

ELIJAH REVIEWED his maps to look for the best route forward. It looked like he'd have to lead his men and his new charge across rough terrain unsuitable for a woman, but she had come this far on her own. They'd make do. He heard the collective groan of his men as he turned to see Elyse crawling on the ground searching for something. He watched as she let out a delighted laugh as she found what she was looking for: bobby pins. She sat on her knees and twisted her hair into an upswept bun, inserting the pins as she went, breasts jiggling as she moved. He groaned and turned to his men. His warning glare to them spoke volumes, off limits, keep your eyes to yourselves. He turned back around to face her.

How am I going to get that distraction to Khe Sanh? Christ. We gotta find her some pants. Something to cover that sweet ass up or we're all dead.

CHAPTER 3

The men and Elyse moved through the jungle, using machetes to hack out a pathway as they went. The only thing they could find to cover her up was a pair of the Captain's boxer shorts, green like the shirt.

※

THE CAPTAIN WATCHED her as he followed behind her and the team, looking at his form-fitting boxers which rode low on her hips and enhanced the round curves of her bottom. She was still tantalizing, but at least she was somewhat covered.

He noticed the droop in her shoulders and her weak smile, indicating how exhausted she was. All the men were tired and hungry as well. With daylight fading fast, Elijah decided they needed to stop and rest for a few hours. They chose a small area hidden well within the foliage. The men each chose a seat resting against trees, roots, anything they could find that was semi-comfortable. Some tipped their helmets to cover their eyes for a snatch of sleep, while others sat talking as they pulled out their C rations to eat.

※

ELYSE STOOD in the middle of the group, unsure of what to do. She needed to go now. Turning to head into the jungle to seek a suitable private spot.

"Where do you think you are going?" asked Elijah.

"I need to use the powder room."

"You are never to move in any direction without assistance," he spat.

"We will find a spot for you to relieve yourself, but you will not be left alone."

"What? Oh hell no." she ground out. "There's no way I'm doing that."

HE WAS JUST as outraged that this little slip of a woman was not only defying him but doing it beautifully. Her eyes flashed as she blushed two more shades of pink.

"Miss Booker, either do as I say or hold it."

"You know I did perfectly fine on my own before I fell into your ditch."

"Yeah, perfectly fine with twenty VC chasing you down. Oh, yes, you were perfectly fine."

Elyse furrowed her brows and glared at him.

"Out here, even we don't go out there alone. We all have someone stand guard while we do our business." He tossed her his shovel. "Here you go, you've got to bury it."

Mortified, Elyse replied, "I'm okay. I don't have too, Oh My God. Am I seriously having this conversation with you?"

Elijah grinned. "Johnson, take Miss Booker into the jungle and find a spot for her, give her some privacy but do not leave her alone."

"Aye aye, Sir."

Johnson guided Elyse into the jungle, his own color ten shades redder than Elyse's. He turned his back on her while she went into the bushes. Elyse and Johnson returned a few minutes later. When they returned, Elyse noted that the men sat or laid in a circle, feet almost touching. One man was chosen to guard while the others slept.

Elijah patted the ground next to him, and Elyse grudgingly sat down. He offered her a C-ration that she promptly declined. She wasn't hungry and did not eat when upset anyway. He shrugged his shoulders and wolfed down his C-ration.

"Get some rest, Elyse," he said as he laid down. Within minutes, he was softly snoring.

She sat with her chin on her knees for a long time. *How can anyone sleep in this place? There are bugs everywhere.* Then, to drive the point home, a large black beetle crawled over one of the men's legs. Elyse jumped and almost shrieked in terror. *Sleep, impossible.*

ELIJAH WAS startled awake by Elyse's movements. She still sat chin on knees staring off into the night, watching for bugs and any other creepy crawly that might approach.

"You need to sleep."

"I can't. There are bugs everywhere."

Elijah grinned. *Typical woman.* "It's the jungle, there are lots of bugs out here. Are you a city girl?"

She nodded. "Yes."

"What are you doing here?"

"I live in Huế City for my job."

"How long have you been in Nam?"

"Almost twelve years."

He was shocked. "You haven't been back to the world for twelve years?"

"What do you mean, the world?"

"The United States, the real world."

"I've traveled back with my father for short visits a few times, but it's been a long while since I've been there."

"I can't fathom that."

"This is home to me. This is where I grew up. I live and work here. I understand the people and the culture. I know no other place."

"And the war?"

"I've been sheltered from it."

"Well, you're about to find out in a big way. Come lie down. I'll watch for bugs."

Elyse looked relieved and was soon curled into a little ball and out cold next to him.

When Elijah next woke, she was curled into his arms and they laid together as spoons. He could smell her hair and feel her soft body next to his. He moved to extract himself from her warmth, much to the amusement of the men.

Ten minutes later, the men were all up and ready to move, but Elyse still slept. Elijah knelt down to wake her. She was not waking up. He put his ear to her heart. It beat out a strong rhythm, but she was out cold, and they needed to leave soon.

He gently shook her to wake her. "Elyse, wake up."

She struggled to open her eyes.

"Good morning, sunshine," Elijah murmured.

Her eyes slowly opened as comprehension dawned on her.

"Do you always sleep so soundly?"

"Since birth," she replied. "A hard sleep for hours. Always scared the wits out of my parents." She still snuggled into the poncho he had covered her with during the night.

The lingering sleep fog made her docile as a kitten, and Elijah decided he liked the sleepy Elyse very much.

"Coffee. I wish I had a big cup of steaming hot coffee."

"We're already behind schedule, the most I can offer you now is some grape Kool-aid and a C-ration."

Elyse grimaced. "No, thank you."

Once he was assured that she was awake and functioning, he gave the order to "saddle up," and they left the area a full twenty minutes behind schedule.

By afternoon, they came to a small area hidden within the foliage, a perfect place for the men to rest and recuperate. The pace this morning had been grueling. The heat of the day was oppressive and made worse by the high humidity. Elijah told Elyse to sit down on the ground and rest, and Johnson offered to take her into the jungle. Once she returned to the hidden spot, the men were in various states of relaxation. Some dozed, and others were eating.

Elyse sat down by a tree, lost in contemplation, chin on knees, arms wrapped around her legs. She noticed her feet were dirty and disgusting. She sighed, wondered about her father, and how worried he must be. Did anyone tell him she was alive and well? She wondered where they were taking her. She almost felt sorry for herself but knew she would make the best of it.

Elijah sat down next to her and offered her a C-ration, which she politely declined.

"When's the last time you ate something?"

Elyse furrowed her brows into a frown. She had to think long and hard about that. *When was the last time I ate?*

"I gave most of the rice to the children in the village, so that doesn't count. I ate breakfast before I left the compound in Huế City. I found some berries to eat yesterday, and I had to fight a monkey for half a banana."

"Village? What village?" Elijah barked.

"The one I was in an hour or so before I met you."

"That VC village is where we were heading to do reconnaissance."

"They're not VC, Captain."

"How do you know that?"

"The elder told me so. They're just frightened farmers. They don't like VC or Americans."

"And I suppose you speak Vietnamese?"

"Fluently, yes. He was very kind to me. The elder gave me food and water and told me which direction to go to find Americans. He also hid me from the VC when they came through the village."

"Wait, what? Why the fuck didn't you tell me that before? Tell me everything."

"The VC came through the village, they beat the elder, forced the women to cook for them, and were looking for weapons they had left there. The elder did not want their weapons stored there. I could hear them." Her voice dropped to a horrified whisper as her eyes widen like saucers. "I could hear them, the women screaming and crying. I think... I think they were raped."

He nodded his understanding. "War is hell. We'll make arrangements to evacuate the village to keep them safe from the VC. So now tell me, did you eat?"

"No, as I said, I gave most of the rice to the children."

"What do you mean you fought a monkey?"

"I climbed a banana tree. The monkey didn't want to share."

"You climbed a tree, one of those?" He pointed up at a tall banana tree. "And you were fighting a monkey, up there?"

"It was just a little monkey," Elyse said.

Elijah shook his head in disbelief. "You still need to eat. The compound was three days ago. You need to eat now to keep up your strength."

"I don't want to eat now. I'm not hungry."

"Eat, now, and that's an order."

"Excuse me, I don't take orders."

"Eat this now, or I'll feed it to you myself."

She narrowed her eyes, glaring at him while cursing under her breath. Elyse took the opened can and peered inside. "That's disgusting. They make you eat this garbage?" She handed the can back to him.

"Eat it, Elyse."

"Fine." She hissed at him. Throwing him a dirty look, she started eating and almost gagged. She knew with no real food in her stomach for three days she may not keep it down. Her eyes shot daggers at him, and she turned her back on him.

ELIJAH WATCHED her as she ate. He couldn't blame her. The C-rations were garbage, but packed with protein and vitamins, enough to sustain the body.

"Turn around, Elyse, I want to see you eat the whole can."

He wouldn't put it past her to hide the food in the same manner a small child would hide her peas. Amethyst eyes flashed in anger. She half-heartedly stirred the ham and lima beans in the can and took small bites. She finished most of it and handed it back to Elijah. He looked inside the can.

Grinning, he said, "You didn't eat the lima beans."

"I never have—and never will—eat lima beans," she replied.

"Brat."

Elyse sputtered her outrage and turned away from him again. Elijah smirked and contemplated her back, particularly the kissable spot on her neck and the uplift of soft, amber-colored hair, an unusual color. Not carrot-top red or golden blonde but a mix of fire and light.

He rose and returned to his spot. *Ten more minutes. Enough time for a cat nap.* He pulled his helmet low over his eyes and soon he was asleep.

CHAPTER 4

Another grueling day behind them brought them closer to their target. Athlete that she was, Elyse struggled to keep up with the men's fast pace. When they came across a small, fast-moving stream, they crossed it single file. The first three men along with the Captain had entered the stream. The water appeared to be chest deep and fast moving.

Elyse contemplated the stream. She didn't want to get wet with night-fall fast approaching. *It's not that wide. I'm a ballerina, I can make it.*

Elyse backed up and took a running, graceful, leap straight over the heads of the men in the stream. All four looked up to see legs sailing over-head. Elyse landed on the far bank, and with a grin on her face, turned to look at the men in the stream. Shock and admiration shown on their faces. All except the Captain.

"Elyse, don't move, stay where you are."

Elyse backed up, turned, and walked into the nearby clearing and sat down on the grass. It felt cool and refreshing. She longed to rest her cheek on it.

Elijah saw red as he pushed his way past the men in the steam and climbed the embankment of the stream. Marching into the clearing, he could barely contain his anger as he strode over to her and hauled her to her feet. "You little fool. Don't you ever pull a stunt like that again." He shook her like a rag doll.

Elyse pulled away. "What is your problem? I did not want to get wet, so I jumped the stream. No big deal."

"It's not the jump," Elijah said. "It's the landing. The far bank could have been booby trapped. This clearing could have been booby trapped or worse. I told you not to move, and you disobeyed my orders and walked in here, anyway. You will start doing as you are told from this moment forward."

"I don't take orders, Captain," Elyse retorted.

Elijah grabbed her arm and pulled her back against him hard. He grabbed her by the back of her hair and forced her to look up into his eyes. "You will do as you are told without question. I know how to deal with spoiled brats."

"You wouldn't dare," Elyse spat back at him.

"Keep testing my patience, Elyse, and I'll show you what I dare."

THEY SEARCHED for and found another hide-site deep within the jungle to rest for the night. Elyse flounced over and sat down next to a tree, mumbling to herself about arrogant Marines and what they could do with their orders.

She smiled as Arnold and Mountain approached her and offered them a seat next to her.

"Where did you learn to jump like that? Mountain asked.

"I'm a dancer."

"Like a Go-Go dancer?"

Elyse laughed. "No, Ballet. I'm a ballerina. Though I will admit that I own a pair of white Go-Go boots."

"So, what's a powder room?" Arnold asked.

Elyse giggled. "I'll tell you what a powder room is, if you tell me what they mean when they say saddle up."

Mountain and Arnold laughed.

"Move out. It means we're leaving," Arnold replied.

"Is that all?" she said. "I kept looking around for horses to magically appear."

"Okay, now what's a powder room?" Arnold asked.

"I believe you call it the head," Elyse replied between giggles.

Arnold rolled his eyes.

"Why?" Mountain asked.

"Well-brought-up ladies do not say they're going to the head or even admit to bodily functions."

Arnold grunted. "I suppose they don't fart either?"

Trying to contain her mirth. "I can't believe I'm having this conversation with you, but of course they don't."

Mountain looked perplexed. "Really?"

"No, girls don't fart, they fluff," she replied.

⚜

ELIJAH SITTING across the way watched as Sarge sitting on the other side of Arnold quietly listening to their conversation choked and spit his mouthful of water out. Doc next to him shook in silent laughter as he pounded Sarge on the back. The corners of Elijah's mouth twitched, but he gave no other indication he heard them.

⚜

ELYSE GLANCED UP, eyeing the Captain as he rested against a tree. They caught each other's eye, and she shot him a cool, haughty look, and he pulled his helmet over his eyes in a dismissive manner. Mountain and Arnold, taking the hint from the Captain, took their leave, settling down in their own spots to catch some sleep. Exhaustion set in, and it wasn't long before Elyse was fast asleep.

⚜

ELYSE AWOKE A SHORT TIME LATER. Nightfall had already settled in.

Elijah's voice came low and insistent in her ear. "Don't move."

His hand was quick as lightning as he pulled a snake from the tree just above her head and flung it into the jungle. Elyse opened her mouth to shriek in terror, but he covered her mouth with his hand.

"Hush, brat, it's gone."

Even though she felt ridiculous, Elyse started shaking. "Bugs, big bugs and snakes. What else is in this nightmare jungle?"

"Are you cold?"

She nodded, and he put a long-sleeved shirt around her shoulders and laid his poncho on the ground for her. "Rest now. I'll watch for bugs and snakes."

<hr />

ELIJAH STARED off into the night as Elyse curled into the warmth of his body. *Nice little package, fits perfectly under my arm.* His thoughts took him to the stream crossing earlier. *Magnificent,* was the only way he could describe being on the underside of Elyse's jump. *Dangerous, but magnificent.* He had to reach her somehow and make her understand his orders were for her safety. This place was hell on Earth and no place for a stubborn, impetuous woman. Soon, with a nod to the man on guard duty, he settled in to sleep as well.

<hr />

ELYSE WOKE with the arm of the Captain around her waist, his hand resting on the curve of her hip. Her head laid on his chest. She made a sound that was more of a kitten's mew.

Elijah looked down into her face. "Good morning, brat."

Elyse's sleep-fogged brain couldn't comprehend his sarcasm, so she snuggled closer to his chest and sighed her contentment. Elyse's eyes flew open when she realized her head lay on his chest and her proximity to him. She sat up, her hands splayed on the ground, and she stared into his gorgeous brown eyes. *My breath.* Her hand flew up to cover her mouth.

"I think I need a toothbrush," she said.

<hr />

He was stunned into silence as his eyes roamed her face, her tousled hair, loosened from her bun as she had slept, fell in soft waves to curl around the curves of her breast and hips. The cleavage she unknowingly displayed, and that delightful tiny mole on the top of her left breast. Her eyes, *Purple? No, amethyst.* Porcelain skin and pink pouty lips. He had never seen a more beautiful woman, and he shook his head to clear his thoughts. *Focus man, focus.*

He leaned over and grabbed his rucksack. Opening a side pouch, he pulled out a spare toothbrush still wrapped in clear plastic and handed it to her.

"I guess I came prepared." He handed her his canteen. "It's Kool-aid."

"You brush your teeth with Kool-aid?" she asked incredulously.

He gave a wry grin. "Not just any Kool-aid, grape Kool-aid. Fresh water when we can find it can be nasty. This covers the taste of the iodine pills we use to sanitize the water."

He picked her bobby pins off his chest and the ground next to him and handed them to her. "You have ten minutes then we move out."

⚜

"Seven men were ready within ten minutes. You took twice as long." The Captain stated as she moved to pass him on the path.

"Girl. I had to brush my teeth, wash my face. Thank God Mountain had water. I had to fix my hair and eat another nasty C-ration. I thought I did pretty well."

He grunted, rolling his eyes in response.

⚜

When they came to another stream, the Captain and Sarge pulled out the map to get their bearings. Once assured of their direction, the team entered the stream to cross. Without warning the Captain lifted Elyse into his arms and stepped into the stream.

"I can cross on my own, Elijah. Is it alright if I call you that?"

He liked the sound of his name on her lips and he nodded his head.

"I'm hanging onto you till we cross, since I don't want a replay of

24

yesterday's antics." They were mid-stream now. "And we know you can't follow orders."

"Again, you forget yourself, I don't take orders," Elyse replied.

Nodding his head, he gave her a long cool look. "Is that so?" He dropped her right into the stream.

&

ELYSE INITIALLY CAME UP SPUTTERING, snarling, and ready for battle but, instead, she refused to give him the satisfaction. So, she gave him her back and finished the crossing, struggling up the embankment on the other side. She made it up with a helping hand from one of the team, all of whom struggled to squelch their laughter before turning back to glare at the Captain.

&

ELIJAH HAD JUST CLIMBED up the embankment himself and was teetering on the edge. He gave her a wolfish, appreciative smile as his gaze touched on the wet shirt clinging to her curves with her twin peaks enticingly pushing through the thin fabric.

&

ELYSE REALIZED the show she was giving him, and with a snarl and a side kick to the chest, she sent him sprawling spread eagle back into the stream. Ignoring the looks of the other men, she strode angrily away, trying desperately to pull the shirt away from the contours of her body.

&

A SOAKING wet Elijah climbed back up the embankment and stood glaring at Elyse. She turned to face him, and with a sweet smile, said, "Blackbelt."

He pointed his finger at her. "You… I'm going to haul you back and throw your sweet ass back into that ditch."

Elyse rolled her eyes and turned away but, not before the Captain saw the smug smile of satisfaction on her face.

Looking at the amused faces of his men, he glared at them. "What the fuck are you assholes laughing at?"

They shook their heads and stifled their grins. "Nothing, Sir," they responded as one.

The Captain followed the line of men as they carried on. A few more hours, and they could call for the chopper.

Elijah thought back to the way she looked at the stream. She was not your average woman. Other than not being able to wake up in the morning, she kept up with the men pretty well without complaints. And that leap over the stream and a black belt to boot. He rubbed his chest where her kick had landed and grinned. She had sass, had to give her that.

⚜

ELYSE SWATTED at the mosquitos as they descended upon her time and time again. Distracted by the ruthless pests she didn't see the large roots of the tree's until she tripped over them cutting her foot. Elijah's strong arms reached out to catch her. He caught the scent of light perfume as he pulled her to him.

"You're bleeding, let's take a break and have Doc take a look at your foot," Elijah said.

"I'm okay, it's not bleeding that bad," Elyse replied.

"We can't afford to leave a blood trail, and you need to wash that perfume off and put some bug juice on or they won't leave you alone."

Embarrassed by her clumsiness, Elyse nodded her understanding.

⚜

SHE SAT with Doc while she watched him administer to her wounds.

"You have a nice bedside manner," Elyse said.

Doc looked around the jungle and grinned. "No bed. Your foot should be fine. It won't interfere with your ballet dancing."

"How did you know I was ballet dancer?"

"I knew it the moment you leaped over our heads in the stream. My

26

wife, Julie, drags me kicking and screaming to the ballet at least once a year when I'm home from deployment."

Elyse grinned. "Now, now, it's not that bad."

"Na, it's not that bad, and I eventually enjoy the evening, but I enjoy watching my wife's face as she watches the performances the most," Doc replied.

"That's sweet, you must miss her very much." Elyse said.

"I do, and my two little boys as well." Doc replied.

Elyse eyed the Captain as he sat with Sarge reviewing maps.

"How about the Captain? Is he married as well?"

Doc glanced over at the Captain. "Cap? Hell no, he's a confirmed bachelor."

Elyse absorbed the information with a smile.

"I don't think my foot needs big bulky bandages."

Doc held up two band-aids. "Nope, just these."

Doc finished putting the band-aids on her foot and stood to leave. "You'll be dancing again soon."

"No, I won't, my ballet slippers were in my suitcase on the chopper. They're lost to me. No slippers until I get my trunk that was on the second chopper with all my other clothes and things," Elyse replied.

"Maybe your trunk will be at the base camp when we arrive," Doc said.

"I hope so. I must look ridiculous in the Captains boxers and shirt."

"No actually, you look pretty damn good." He turned and strode over to the Captain.

⚜

"SHE'S ALL SET, CAP," Doc stated.

Elijah glanced over at Elyse with a smirk on his face. "I bet you enjoyed that Doc?"

"Damn right."

⚜

27

By MID-AFTERNOON, Elijah pulled Sarge aside. He was almost positive they were now being followed by VC. That they only followed and did not attack spoke volumes. The Americans had something they wanted: Elyse. *What else could it be?* Sarge sent two men to double back and count how many followed. When they returned, they reported six VC following them.

ANNOYED that they couldn't engage the enemy without putting Elyse in danger, Elijah decided they would have to go deep into the jungle to keep her safe while making their way to meet the chopper. Elijah looked at Elyse, at her fair skin and hair that glowed like fire in the sunlight. Her appearance was like a beacon of light pointing out her exact location to the VC, and she would not like what he had to do. He pulled off his helmet and filled it with dirt, poured Kool-Aid from his canteen into the helmet to make mud, and motioned for Arnold to bring her forward. Elyse stopped in front of Elijah.

"Elyse, you're a girl."

"Yes, I know that." Elyse replied, with a mischievous grin.

He gave her an impatient look. "You are not going to like this one bit."

She pulled away. "What are you doing?"

"I need to camouflage your hair and skin."

"Why?" she asked.

"Must you question everything? We're all still in danger here," he replied. "If we need to hide, we must cover your hair and that fair skin, so you don't give our location away."

He started smearing the mud on her face and arms. He then went to put the now empty helmet on her head, but it fell off with the tremendous volume of her hair piled on top. He looked at the bun on her head. "That needs to come down."

She reached up and started pulling the pins from her hair. To him, it almost seemed to fall in slow motion as it swayed down around her waist.

He filled the helmet up again and made more mud. Before he could smear it in her hair, he saw the twinkle in her eye and that she was laughing at him. She reached into the helmet grabbed a handful of mud and smeared it in her hair herself.

"I was a tomboy for the first fourteen years of my life. I'm not afraid of mud," Elyse explained.

With a grin on his face, he asked, "So what happened?"

She smiled at him. "One day I looked in the mirror and saw curves."

"And man was doomed from that day forward," he quipped.

Elyse looked him in the eye, ever so lightly leaning in toward him. "And more so now."

He raised an eyebrow and put the helmet on her head. The mud ran down her face and he smeared it around her smooth cheek while he looked her up and down.

"Somewhere in those curves I swear I still see the tomboy."

She rolled her eyes and as she turned away. "Oh trust me, it's still there." Working the mud through her hair, she braided it.

Sarge ordered, "Saddle up."

They moved deeper into the jungle and eventually lost the VC following them.

⁂

WHEN THEY CAME across another water way. Elyse threw up her hands in disgust. "Are you serious? Another one? How do you ever get dry?"

Elijah smirked but kept moving.

This one was murky and not as deep as the last. More of a swamp, she assumed.

They crossed single file with Elijah ahead of her and the gentle giant they called Mountain behind her.

She was halfway across when she saw a creature swimming in an S movement toward her, the biggest snake she'd ever seen. She shrieked in terror and gave into the natural reaction to find higher ground away from the snake. She scrambled toward the nearest height.

⁂

MOUNTAIN, at six-five, was every bit the Iowa farm boy. Heavily muscled, blonde tousled hair, his mischievous blue eyes, widened as she scrambled to climb right up his body.

29

She stood on him, teetering on his shoulders.

"Hey, what are you doing runt?" Mountain questioned. She pointed at the snake and Mountain used the butt of his weapon to guide it away.

❧

"QUIET." Elijah snapped, turning around at her shriek. It was all he could do to not burst into laughter at the comical sight of Elyse climbing to stand on Mountain's shoulders.

"What in God's name are you doing now?"

"A snake, a big… big, big, big snake."

"You've got more trouble than snakes, Elyse. You're covered in leeches."

❧

"WHAT?" She looked down to where Elijah's gaze rested. She had no sooner inhaled to deliver an earth-shattering scream, when Elijah yanked her off Mountain's shoulders and covered her mouth with his hand.

"No screams, brat. We'll get the leeches off."

Elyse was in a panic. "Get them off. Get them off of me."

"Calm down, Elyse," he said, as he carried her over to the embankment.

They used mosquito repellent, or bug juice as they called it, to get the leeches off themselves and each other. Elyse sat on the ground as Elijah poured the bug juice over her legs. She grimaced, covering her eyes, unable to watch him pull the leeches off her skin.

"You need to check under your shirt."

Elyse's eyes widened, as she felt up under her shirt. "Oh, God, there's one under my left breast." Mortified, she held her shirt up to uncover the lower portion of her breast.

❧

ELIJAH WAS TRANSFIXED by the breathtaking sight of the bottom of her creamy white globe. He poured bug juice on the leech and was tormented by his knuckles brushing against her breast. He checked her back, and then whispered, "You need to go right over there behind those ferns and thoroughly check yourself down there.

※

WHILE SHE WAS GONE, Elijah checked himself and found a few leeches. He pulled the disgusting parasites off. The picture of Elyse's lower breast would forever be burned into his brain. He closed his eyes to help cool his lust.

Elijah looked up as Sarge approached. "Where's Elyse?" Sarge asked.

"In the bushes checking for more leeches."

Sarge grinned. "You're not helping her?"

"You trying to kill me, Sarge?"

Sarge chuckled. "I'm going to take Johnson and do a quick recon of the area."

Elijah nodded.

Elyse returned from the brush. "I'm okay. Nothing else. What hell is this? Snakes, leeches, bugs."

"Vietnam, Elyse. Vietnam."

"How do you do it day after day?"

"We just do."

"Thank you for helping me, Elijah."

"You're welcome, brat."

Annoyed now, she frowned at him "I'm not a brat."

He grinned at her. "Oh yes you are."

※

SARGE AND JOHNSON returned from the reconnaissance of the area, running low to the ground. Fingers to lips. Elyse's retort died on her lips as Elijah stiffened. Signaling Mountain over to her side, he hissed into her ear. "Stay absolutely silent, lie flat on the ground, don't move unless Mountain tells you too."

※

Sarge signaled the Captain over. Speaking in hushed tones. "Cap, NVA supply convoy, just over that ridge. About six convoy trucks and about one hundred soldiers."

Every bit the Marine, the Captain scoped the area. Swamp behind them, small ridge in front. To the left, deep jungle, and to the right a ravine. Perfect, exactly what he needed. He used hand signals to instruct Mountain to take Elyse into the ravine.

Elyse and Mountain crawled on the ground to the ravine. Sliding on their bellies they reached the bottom of the ravine to lie on their stomachs while Arnold, Henson, Johnson, and Doc partially laid in the ravine. Weapons ready, they watched and waited.

Elijah and Sarge crawled on their bellies to the top of the ridge to further recon the NVA, then silently made their way back down the hill to join Elyse and Mountain and the rest of the team in the ravine. Henson handed Elijah the radio as they made the call into headquarters. As the Captain relayed coordinates and listened to instructions from headquarters personnel, his gaze stopped on Elyse and he cursed under his breath. Signaling to Mountain to cover her mouth, he watched as a six-inch centipede crawled over her arm and off into the ravine.

⚜

Elyse's eyes were as wide as she watched the centipede crawl across her arm, and she suppressed a shudder of revulsion at Mountains insistent whisper in her ear.

"Don't move. Poisonous, if it bites you, you're dead."

She didn't move, her heart pounded in her chest. She wasn't sure in that moment if she was more frightened by the enemy, the centipede, or the hardened expressions on the faces of the Marines who surrounded her. That was the moment she realized they were protecting her, and tears sprang to her eyes. She blinked back the burn of tears and calmed herself. Elyse heard the Captain whispering fiercely on the radio.

"Need I remind you that I have a woman with me?" After a couple more minutes of quiet conversation he hung up the radio and whispered. "We have ten minutes to get Elyse the fuck out of here before all hell breaks loose."

The men nodded, and they moved out with cat-like stealth and speed pushing her through the deep jungle.

Ten minutes later, two F-4 Phantom fighter jets thundered through the sky overhead while Elijah and the team pushed her faster and faster through the jungle, and further away from the jets' target. A minute later, the ground shook below their feet as bombs fell and exploded in the jungle behind them with the repercussions knocking Elyse to the ground as the heat of fire warmed their skin. They kept pushing on, harder and faster, until finally, they stopped to rest. Elyse fell to her knees as Elijah and the team flung themselves to the ground around her. She sat on her knees and stared at them while they stared right back.

For the first time in four days she felt the enormity and horror of everything she had been through. The silent tears rolled down her face. She turned away from them, pulled her knees up close, wrapped her arms around her knees tucked her face in her arms and cried heart wrenching sobs.

⚜

THE TEAM and Elijah looked at each other, shaking their heads and shrugging their shoulders. Each man at a loss for words and what to do.

⚜

ELIJAH SIGNALED to his men for privacy and sat down next to her. Gathering her into his arms, he held her. He was surprised she had held out for so long and the tears hadn't come sooner. She clung to him and sobbed her misery. He stroked her hair, quietly speaking, while he calmed her tears.

Elijah rose and signaled to Henson to sit with her while he went to speak to Sarge.

Henson sat down by her. He gave her a shy smile. His dark brown wavy hair and black horned rimmed glasses framed intelligent brown eyes and a strong jaw line,

"You hungry? I've got some crackers and peanut butter," Henson asked.

33

She nodded her head, and he handed them to her. She quietly munched on the snack, a welcome reprieve from the C-rations.

"You gotta boyfriend somewhere?"

She shook her head. "How about you? A girlfriend or a wife somewhere?"

"Na, but there's this chick I've got my eye on back home. Angela, saw her at the Drive-In back home in Ohio."

"A chick? What's a chick?"

"A girl. Chicks are girls."

Elyse nodded her head. Her eyes widened. "The Drive-In, you've been to one?" Elyse asked. "I've seen them in the movies and on TV. I've always wanted to go to one."

Henson grinned. "You've never been? I'll take you sometime, you come to Ohio and we'll go. Maybe you'll sit in the back seat with me?"

"Wouldn't it be easier to watch a movie from the front seat?" Elyse asked.

Henson grinned again. "Probably."

Johnson sat down on the ground on the other side of her. They were soon joined by Mountain and Arnold. They regaled her with Drive-In theater stories and memories of home.

❧

THE SINGSONG LILT of her soft laughter as they flirted outrageously with her caught the attention of Elijah sitting with Doc, and Sarge. Watching the team with Elyse, Elijah shook his head.

"The princess is holding audience with a bunch of lovesick pups," Elijah stated.

Doc and Sarge chuckled.

"She's about their age," Sarge stated.

Elijah rolled his eyes. "She's off limits. We move out in ten minutes. I'm telling her five so we can roll out of here on time."

He rose from his seat on the ground and approached the group, and the team scattered at his barked orders to prepare to leave.

❧

"They all invited me to their hometowns so I could go to the Drive-In with them. They're going to buy me popcorn and soda, and I'll sit in the backseat with them," Elyse said.

"Do you have any idea of what goes on in the backseat?" Elijah asked.

"No."

"I figured as much," he replied. "You've got five minutes before we leave. Oh… and it's pop."

"No, it's soda."

"Pop."

She gave him a sideways flirtatious smile. "Compromise? Soda pop?"

His smile reached his eyes, and he nodded his head in approval.

He turned and strode over to face his team. His glare of disapproval told them they had crossed a line. In a hushed voice: "I'm only going to say this once. Your job right now is to see Elyse safely to base camp. It's obvious to me, if it isn't to you, that she's an innocent, a virgin. I don't mind you talking with her but keep it clean and respectful. I have to be able to trust you in her presence. Any one of you steps out of line again I will beat you to a pulp before I throw your ass into the brig and throw away the key. Is that understood?"

"Yes, Sir," they responded.

"And a thousand sandbags to fill once we get back to base camp ought to kill those backseat urges," Elijah stated. The men groaned at their future punishment.

Two hours later, after popping a can of purple smoke to show their exact location, they met the chopper at the agreed-upon coordinates right on schedule. Elyse was having none of it.

"Oh, hell no. I am NOT getting on one of those ever again." She turned and ran. Elijah ran after her, caught her, threw her over his shoulder, ran back to the chopper, and handed her in before jumping in himself.

Elijah sat with his back against the bulkhead with Elyse trapped between his thighs. Her eyes were closed, and she appeared to be praying. He understood her terror, having survived a crash or two himself, but he was weary, and in need of a shower, and real food.

They'd be at their destination within half an hour. *It's no easy task hauling a five-foot nothing, one hundred pounds of sass through the jungle. One hundred pounds of sass.* He laughed out loud. *Perfect.* He tipped his helmet to cover his eyes determined to get a cat nap in before landing.

He was jolted awake by the sound of gunfire as the gunner aimed and fired his M-60 into the jungle below. The pilot was taking evasive maneuvers to avoid enemy gunfire. One look into Elyse's face, and Elijah swept her into his arms and held her close to his chest.

A few minutes later, it was over, and they approached the base camp at Khe Sanh.

CHAPTER 5

Base Camp One, Khe Sanh

THE CHOPPER TOUCHED down on the makeshift landing pad and airfield. The men started disembarking the aircraft. One of them lifted Elyse out of the chopper, and Elijah jumped out after her. It started almost immediately, the hooting and hollering of red-blooded Marines who hadn't seen a fair-skinned, red-headed woman who looked like that in many, many, months.

EMBARRASSED AT THE ATTENTION, Elyse felt her cheeks burn and she had the instinct to cover herself but didn't. Head up and shoulders squared, she walked behind Elijah. In what was clearly an effort to block Elyse from the catcaller's view, the team fell into a protective circle around her. She was grateful for their protection.

They continued their walk until they stopped in front of a tent where an older, salt-and-pepper-haired man stood with his aides.

"Colonel Braxton, Miss Elyse Booker," Elijah said.

The men parted and Elyse stepped forward.

⁂

COLONEL BRAXTON EYES swept the tiny woman standing in front of him. Her familiar unusual eyes peered up at him through long dark lashes. She had dried mud on her face and fire red hair in a thick braid hanging down her back. He noted her dirty feet and military issued men's underwear as clothing. She had a body that wouldn't quit and a dazzling smile. She was a beautiful young woman, and he, and the men around him inhaled sharply, and he wondered what the hell was he thinking.

"Miss Booker, I'm pleased to meet you. I'm sure you're exhausted from your ordeal," Colonel Braxton stated. "Captain, I'd like to speak with you inside."

"Heinz," the Colonel bellowed. "Where the hell is Heinz?"

A young Marine stepped out from behind the colonel.

"Escort Miss Booker to the VIP tent."

"Aye aye, Sir," Heinz replied.

"And Captain," the Colonel said, "your men are to stand guard over Miss Booker."

⁂

ELIJAH TURNED and signaled the team to follow Heinz and Elyse. Elyse followed Heinz and looked back into Elijah's eyes. He still stood at attention but, winked at her questioning look, and she smiled. It was brilliant. He had never been the beneficiary of that smile before. *Christ.*

Elijah followed the Colonel and his aides into his office and stood at attention.

"At ease, you might as well have a seat Elijah." Colonel Braxton said. "This is going to take us awhile."

"Aye aye, Sir," replied the Captain as he took a seat.

"Headquarters has been notified of Miss Bookers safe arrival, and in turn, they will notify the Ambassador. Elijah, there's no other way but to come right out and say it. You've got friends in high places. These orders are coming directly from General Morgan. You, and one of your teams are assigned to the safety and protection of Miss Booker until further notice. I'll let you determine which of the five teams in your platoon to use."

Elijah came to his feet in protest "Sir."

"Sit down, Captain. Hear me out. You're a highly decorated Marine. You're honorable and well respected. Although you may disagree, you're the perfect man, along with any one of your teams, for the job."

"Sir, I respectfully disagree. I know nothing about women or how to care for them. Especially this one. I don't know what she needs, wants, or even what she eats. God knows she doesn't like C-rations."

"As cliché as it sounds, I've yet to meet a woman, including my own wife, who comes with * SOPs. You'll figure it out as you go," Colonel Braxton said.

Elijah sighed and ran his hands through his hair. "Now will you tell me why?"

"Before you get yourself all worked up. We don't expect this to last more than a few weeks at most. As you're aware, Miss Booker is the daughter of Ambassador Booker, but she's also the Godchild of General Morgan, the commander of United States Forces."

One of the aides let out a long whistle, as the Colonel continued.

Elijah stood to pace the room.

"From here on out, the safety and security of Miss Booker will be referred to as Operation Amethyst. You will report directly to General Morgan on any issues with Miss Booker. Her life is in danger. The North Vietnamese have expressed a great interest in her. They intend to capture and sell her to the highest bidder to help fund the war. They also planned to use her as bargaining tool against the Ambassador to disrupt any chances for the peace talks to succeed, or to strong-arm concessions from him."

"Then why bother with the peace talks?"

"From what we've been able to gather, it's some lower level North Vietnamese politicians and Generals, not necessarily their president."

"How do they even know of her?" Elijah barked.

"She's a world-renowned, beloved, prima ballerina, currently performing with the South Vietnamese Royal Ballet in Huế City. The

Vietnamese have a name for her, *dansseur que pleure*. The dancer who weeps."

Incredulous, Elijah asked, "A ballerina? A Prima ballerina?"

"Yes Captain, a full-fledged, twinkle toed, twirling ballerina."

"Why didn't they just put twinkle toes on a plane to Saigon? Or better yet, back to the world?" Elijah asked.

"We can't, she'd never arrive. South Vietnam is crawling with spies. They search for her now as we speak. If we would not have thwarted their plan's she would already be lost to us."

"What plans?"

"The original plan was to send you and your team to Huế City to pick her up and escort her through military channels to the embassy in Saigon. Navy Seals discovered a North Vietnamese fishing boat just off the coast of Huế City. Upon questioning the fishermen, they determined the boat was waiting to transport Elyse north. It appears they were ready and waiting to implement their plans to kidnap her. This has been confirmed by the CIA.

We couldn't wait. It was at their urging that Elyse was evacuated when she was. I shudder to think what would have happened if we would not have been able to get her on that bird to bring her out here. As it was, the Ambassador, a retired Marine, who is a good friend of mine, was unsure if she would even follow his orders and board that chopper. It was most unfortunate that her chopper was shot down. We lost a few good men but are blessed she survived and was rescued by you."

The Colonel smiled, "I've known the Ambassador for years but have never met Elyse before today, but I've heard her father's stories. You, and the whole damn Corps are in for a hell of a roller coaster ride."

Elijah gave him a wry grin. "Yeah, I already knew that one."

"It's your job, Captain, to keep her hidden from the locals and spies and keep her safe until she can be safely delivered to her father. I will tell you right now she is not going to be happy about any of this and to complicate matters, your orders are she is to be told nothing, not a word."

"That's not very fair to Elyse."

"It's not my place or yours to question General Morgan's orders or her father's decisions."

"Aye aye, Sir."

"I did notice her unusual attire."

"Yes, she was half naked when we found her."

The Colonel raised an eyebrow. "That had to be, the Colonel cleared his throat, interesting."

"Yes, Sir, it was beyond description," Elijah replied, with a wide smile.

"I was told she had a trunk on a second chopper. Did that arrive here Sir?"

"Not that I'm aware of. I think in the interim, while we locate her trunk, Captain, we need to find Miss Booker some pants. We've got some smaller men on base. Maybe someone's got an extra pair."

Colonel Braxton turned to his silent aides. "If you would give me a few minutes alone with Captain Corrington."

The aides stepped outside, and the Colonel turned to Elijah. "There's one more thing. Miss Booker is off limits to every man in the Vietnam Theatre, save you. I don't know why or their reasoning, but I was told to inform you."

Elijah's eyebrows shot straight up. "Is this a test? Sir?"

The Colonel grinned. "You're dismissed, Captain."

⁂

ELIJAH EXITED THE COMMAND POST. Running his hands through his thick hair, he stood for a moment and processed the information he had just learned about Elyse. He shook his head at the depth of danger she was in.

Off limits to every man but me… what the fuck does that mean?

Being a ballerina explained the perfectly formed leap over his head at the stream and the sass. Elijah had thought his responsibility for Elyse would end once they had reached the camp, but it was not to be. He had full control and responsibility for her safety, along with every action and move she took for as long as the brass deemed it necessary. He had the feeling there were going to be a lot of battles, but he was determined to win the war. He had no doubt he'd have her under his thumb in short order.

He strode toward the VIP tent and gave whom he considered his best team, their new orders. They'd take four-hour shifts of guard duty twenty-four hours a day. A cush gig, and a well-deserved reprieve from fighting the

41

VC. Elyse's protection was the team's main duty until further notice, like it or not. He dismissed all but Mountain to stand guard.

He stood outside the entrance and called for permission to enter. Inside, he found Elyse sitting on the floor soaking her feet in a large basin of water. She had already washed her face and hands. He noted a standard issue bunk with blankets and a pillow; a small desk with a battery-operated radio; writing materials; an overhead light with a pull string; and a small bureau with a comb and a pile of wash cloths, soap, and towels. Her tent was a small space, located at the far end of the camp well away from the raucous Marines.

"Are you comfortable?"

"Yes Captain, this is fine."

"Once you're settled, I'll scout the camp for the private shower. I know there's one here somewhere. You will be escorted to and from it. You are to go nowhere without an escort."

At the sight of Elyse's furrowed brows, he continued, "No arguments. You are never to be alone unless you are inside this tent. We will bring you your meals and, for now, you will avoid all contact with the Marines other than my men."

"Am I a prisoner?"

"Of course not."

"Then why the prisoner rules?"

"There's five thousand men out there and you're a big temptation."

" Me? How could I be a temptation?" Elyse asked.

"Where's my trunk?"

"We're not sure."

GLANCING down at his boxers she frowned. *At least they're comfortable.* "This is silly, in men's boxer's, I'm a temptation," Elyse replied.

"Just stay put." He turned and left the tent.

ELYSE PACED HER TENT, speaking aloud to herself. "Of all the nerve, I'm practically a prisoner. Stay put my foot."

She peeked out the door to see if there was a guard outside. There was. *Damn.* She scoured the tent for an alternate escape route and found a spot on the back side of the tent where the bottom lifted up. She'd have to bide her time. After so long in the jungle, Elyse was anxious to dance again, and first light would be best. She wished she had her ballet slippers. They were in her small suitcase on the chopper when it went down. The rest of her beautiful clothes were in her trunk, which had been hauled by another chopper. Who knew where that ended up? It would be difficult, but, manageable to dance without her slippers. Dawn couldn't come soon enough.

Elijah came about half an hour later to escort her to the shower, a one-stall, open-sky enclosure with a shuttered door so short that Elyse thought it would barely hide her body. She turned to Elijah. "You're kidding, right?"

"This is it, Elyse. You'll have to make do."

"We'll keep everyone away from this area when you shower. There's no hot water, so trust me, you'll make it quick anyway."

Elijah laughed as Elyse scowled at him. Elijah handed her a clean tank top and boxers. "Here you go, brat. You'll have to hand wash what you have daily. We'll see what we can do to find you some pants tomorrow."

"Thank you Elijah." She stepped into the shower, throwing her towel and clean clothes over the top rail. She peered out into the darkness, but Elijah had disappeared. She disrobed and pulled the string to turn the water on. She shrieked as the cold water hit her body.

⚜

ELIJAH WAS OUT THERE, observing without being observed. Her legs were gorgeous, slim, and well-muscled. The shutters covered just below her bottom to just above her breasts. When she reached up, he could see the top portion of her breasts. Her neck was long and slim, a perfect profile. This area was definitely off limits when Elyse showered. Elyse washed her hair first, and Elijah was amazed at how long it took to wash and rinse. He found himself jealous of the washcloth as she scrubbed her body. She was

43

breathtakingly beautiful. He was beginning to feel like a voyeur but couldn't take his eyes off her.

※

ELYSE FINISHED the shower and tried to wrap up her hair, grumbling to herself. "Itsy bitsy towels, for Pete's sake." She pulled on the clean clothes. She'd have to go without panties for now. With only one pair, they'd have to be washed daily. She tied a knot at the bottom of the shirt and pulled on the boxers. They settled on her hips. She pulled the towel off her hair to rub it dry and stepped out of the shower enclosure. She peered into the darkness looking for Elijah and called out his name.

※

ELIJAH STEPPED into the meager light, drinking in the sight of his shirt sticking to her still moist body. Elyse's shower time would be an exercise in willpower. He couldn't, wouldn't allow anyone else to escort her to and from. He was barely holding it together. Who knew what another man might do?

He escorted her back to her tent, passing many young Marines along the way.

A Marine greeted them as they passed him along the pathway, his eyes and wide smile showed his delight at seeing a woman.

"Evening, Miss, Sir."

"Good evening, private." They replied in unison.

"It's going to take them some time to get used to a woman on base," Elijah stated.

"Not to sound ungrateful for everything you've done but I need to get home and find out why it was so critical that I leave Hué City in such a rush, or is my father coming for me?"

"He won't be coming for you. My team and I will be escorting you to Saigon once all the logistics are worked out," Elijah replied.

"Logistics? What's so complicated about just putting me on a plane to Saigon? I don't need an escort, I'm perfectly capable of…"

"Yeah, yeah, of taking care of yourself. You won't be taking a plane.

You will do as you are told to do. You will be escorted to Saigon via military transportation whether you like it or not," Elijah said.

"Do as I'm told? I would have thought you would have figured out by now that I don't do as I'm told."

"The only thing I've figured out about you is that I should have thrown you back in that ditch."

When they arrived at her quarters, he opened the door for her and gestured with his hand for her to enter.

"Good night, Miss Booker."

"Captain." She glared at him and stepped into her quarters.

❦

ELYSE PICKED at her dinner on the tray left on her desk. She wasn't really hungry. She shoved it aside and got up off the bed. *Insufferable, arrogant, sexist, beautiful brown eyes, and that dagger tattoo on his forearm. So strong and… sexy.* She shivered and shook her head to clear her thoughts and sighed.

She still had clean water to wash out her clothes, so she washed and hung them to dry. She found a comb and worked for over an hour to untangle her hair. When finished, she stripped naked and climbed into the bunk. Tomorrow was another day, soon enough to explore the camp, she said her prayers and fell to sleep.

❦

ELIJAH LAY, restless, in his bunk. Thoughts of Elyse tormented his mind, from her fiery temper to her mesmerizing eyes. He remembered how she felt lying beneath him in the ditch, her softness against his chest. He'd never met a woman like her before. Maybe it was her sass and spirit all wrapped up in a body that didn't quit.

A few days more here in Khe Sanh, and once they had the all clear, they'd escort her to Saigon to deposit the tiny temptation on the steps of the embassy and into her father's care. He would be rather sorry to see the one hundred pounds of sass go. *Those lips, looked so kissable.*

CHAPTER 6

Elyse rose in the hour before dawn, quiet as a mouse. She dressed and grabbed the small radio after making sure the batteries worked. She figured some softly playing music shouldn't waken anyone. She peered out at the guard at the door. Good. He should stay put. She crept to the backside of the tent, lifted the bottom, shoved her radio out, and crawled out. *Freedom.*

The area between the tent and the perimeter of the camp was a decent size with enough room for her to dance. She could see artillery cannons of some kind in the distance. She scanned for guards and saw none, but she'd have to be careful.

Elyse turned the radio on low. An Armed Forces radio station played rock music for the troops. She listened to the beat of the song. It wasn't Tchaikovsky, but she'd manage. She stood and swayed to the music, feeling the rhythm in every pore of her body. For the next half hour, she twirled, pirouetted, leaped to her soul's content and, before the sky turned pink, she was back in her tent with a smile of contentment on her face.

Stay put. Elyse giggled. What Elijah didn't know wouldn't hurt him. Another hour's rest was in order, so she snuggled down in the blankets and fell back asleep.

When Elyse woke an hour later, the camp was in full gear, and the voices of a multitude of men carried through her tent. Elyse peeked out the door. The guard, Johnson, was at the far end of her tent with his back to the door. Elyse saw this as her opportunity to explore the camp. She snuck along the side of the tent until she rounded the corner. She found the powder room unopposed and continued to explore the camp. Eventually, she found the mess hall by following the aroma of freshly brewed coffee to the screened-in tent.

Curious, she opened the door and walked in. Looking around she noted the twenty or so long tables with benches, more tables where they served the troops their meals, and the kitchen in the far back where the hot meals were prepared. No one but an old cook and his staff were inside.

She introduced herself. "Hello, my name is Elyse."

The old man beamed at her, "You can call me Cookie."

"I smelled coffee."

"Yes, we have coffee."

He pointed to a large urn of the fresh brew. She smiled her gratitude, poured herself a cup, and sashayed out the door, running right into a group of Marines.

"Good morning boys," she said.

Most stood open mouthed at the beautiful woman standing in front of them. She asked one of them for a cigarette. He tapped one out of its package, handed it to her and lit it for her. She thanked him and stepped away. She heard them and smiled as she walked away.

"Do you see that?"

"What's a chick doing here?"

"I don't care what she's doing here, I'm in love."

"No one is going to believe us, someone pinch me."

"Pinch yourself, you fucking queer."

She walked over to a nearby hill overlooking a valley she had spotted earlier and sat down in a hidden spot. The sun was rising in a glorious mix of pinks, red, and orange. The sky was a baby blue dotted with soft fluffy clouds. The long field of green grass edged by bunkers and perimeter barbed-wire fencing overlooked the mossy, green, mist laden valley. A lazy river wound its way east toward the South China Sea, all in direct contrast to the stark, red clay of the barren base camp.

She smoked the cigarette and drank the strong, bitter brew. She admitted to herself it should be her last cigarette. Elyse didn't normally smoke, but she occasionally enjoyed one. After running into those men, she knew word would spread, and Elijah would hunt her down. She sighed knowing her break for freedom would be short-lived.

ELIJAH CALLED out to Elyse from her door with her breakfast tray. No answer. Still sleeping? He walked into the tent. No Elyse. He spun and rushed out the door.

"Where is she?"

"She was in there," Johnson stammered. "I heard her moving about earlier."

"Well she's gone now."

Elijah sent his men off in different directions with orders to find her. As he stalked the camp, he heard men talking about seeing a woman. "Big tits, red hair, smooth skin, drop dead gorgeous."

"Where?" Elijah demanded. "Where did you see her?"

"Over by the mess, Captain. Just a couple of minutes ago."

Elijah ran to the mess hall but didn't find her inside. He scanned the area around the hall and spotted her sitting on a hill, staring off into the distance—and smoking.

Elijah came up behind her, stepped in front of her and crouched down to eye level. He took her cigarette and ground it under the heel of his boot. She was startled and looked pensively at her cigarette under his boot. She opened her mouth to protest but stopped short at the look in his eyes.

"Were you not told to stay in your tent? When I tell you to do something, I expect you to obey me."

"Obey you? Are you serious? I wanted some coffee."

"It doesn't matter. You could have told the guard your needs, and he would have assisted you. Instead you disobeyed me by sneaking out. He hauled her to her feet and took her by the arm. "Let's go."

Elyse was a showstopper, and every Marine stood watching her as they walked back to the tent. Once they got back, she gave Johnson an apologetic look and stepped inside the tent. It was hot and oppressive. Elyse's mood slipped extensively. *Great. it's going to be miserable in here all day.*

Elijah stepped to the far end of the tent and pulled up the canvas. A delightful breeze came through the screen, and Elyse breathed a sigh of relief.

"You can only have this side open, if you open the other side, you'll have nothing but prying eyes watching your every move. But close this back side at night."

Elyse nodded her understanding.

"You are to stay put Elyse and I mean it. This is not the place to be reckless and you will be punished if you do this again."

Elyse raised a delicate eyebrow at the threat. "Punished? You're threatening me?"

"Yes, punished. You will find I'm a man of my word. I never ever threaten without being prepared to carry out the threat."

"I'm neither a Marine nor a child. How do you punish a woman?"

"I'll cross that bridge, if, and when, I come to it. Follow my orders, do as you are told to do and stay where I put you, and we'll get along just fine."

Outraged, she pointed at the door. "Out."

Sassy little firecracker. Elijah suppressed his base urge to throttle her right here and now. "You'd be wise to heed my warnings brat."

Elijah took his leave, barking at her new guard, Arnold, that she was not to leave unguarded. Meanwhile, he had to find Johnson. He found Johnson in the mess hall.

"Johnson."

Johnson looked up at Elijah as he sat on the bench across from him.

"Sir. I'm sorry, Sir. She got past me."

"I'm not going to say it's okay because it's not. Elyse is unusual. She's not going to stay where I put her." He smiled a wry grin remembering her anger at being told to stay put. "We just have to watch her and see to her needs."

"What do girls need, Cap? I've got three sisters, but I don't know."

"I don't know either, but you've got more experience than I do."

The man sitting a few seats down from them shook with laughter. In a loud voice, for all to hear, he said, "Did you hear that boys? The Captain here wants to know what girls need."

Another man called out in response. "*Boom boom. Girls need boom boom."

Once the raucous laughter died down in the hall, Elijah shook his head. "No, she doesn't need boom boom. Let's get out of here, we'll go over to supply. I need some help finding some fatigues to cover her up."

They walked into supply. A scruffy looking sergeant stood on the other side of counter. "What can I do for you Captain?"

"I need fatigues and a shirt."

"And a roll of duct tape," Johnson said.

"What's the duct tape for? Elijah asked.

"I don't know. She said she needed duct tape," Johnson replied.

"I only have a few pairs here. What size are you, Sir?" The Sargent said.

"Not for me, for a woman," Elijah replied.

"Hot Damn, so it's true. There's a woman here on base," the Sargent stated.

"Fatigues and shirt, Sargent," Elijah replied.

"How big, Sir?"

"Small, tiny. With his hands he showed him. Her hips are about this big. Her waist about so big, her... he stopped. Her... are. Just give me the smallest you've got."

Grumbling, the Sargent who had waited on each detail went to the back of the tent and soon returned.

Setting the clothes and duct tape on the counter. "This is the smallest I got, Captain."

Johnson grabbed the T-shirt and held it up. "Sir, this shirt is not going to work."

Elijah, becoming impatient with the task barked. "Why not? She's small."

"Sir, she's small, but she's got big.... I think girls might need room in the front or it's not going to cover anything the way you think it will.

Elijah raised an eyebrow. "Christ. Is that right, Sargent?"

The Sargent smirked and shrugged his shoulders. "Let me show you Sir." He held the shirt flattened against his chest with his chin holding the top and pulled the twin peaks out with his thumbs and forefingers. "See how it scoots up?"

"Na, that's not big enough, she's way bigger," said Elijah, as he grabbed the twin peaks from Johnson's hands and pulled them further out.

The guffaws from the doorway made both Johnson and Elijah drop the shirt like a hot potato. He looked up to see Lieutenant Colonel Wilson in the doorway and his retort died on his lips.

"Sir," Eli said.

"Carry on, Captain. I'll wait while you shop for Miss Booker." replied Lieutenant Colonel Wilson, a grin plastered on his face.

"Aye aye, Sir," said Elijah.

"Let me see those fatigues." Elijah held them up, cursing under his breath. "These will fall right off her hips. You're sure this is the smallest you've got?"

"Yes, Sir."

"Any small men on base that might have an extra pair of fatigues?"

The Sargent scratched his head. "I don't think anyone on base has more than one pair of fatigues. I just happened to have a few pairs here in supply."

"I'll just take these." replied Elijah.

"You may want to re-think that, Captain," the Lieutenant Colonel said.

"Why is that Sir?"

"You're walking a fine line here. Too big, and she's going to think, that you think, she's fat. Too small, and they'll be hidden away in some obscure drawer never to be seen again. It's a lose-lose scenario."

Elijah cursed under his breath again and ran his hands through his hair.

"Alright, I'm going to have to bring her up here to try this shit on."

"There ain't no dressing rooms here Captain. I mean, she can change right here. I don't mind," the Sargent said.

Elijah glared at him. "I think I'll wait."

With a nod to Johnson, he grabbed the duct tape and they walked out the door.

ELIJAH, standing with some of the officers, watched Elyse as she ran across the far field, Arnold following behind her. Her girlish laughter carrying in the wind as she danced around playing with a few of the camp dogs. Spotting him, she smiled, waved, and continued on her way back to her quarters. They all watched in admiration. It was hard not to.

"How the fuck are we supposed to control five thousand men with that fine ass on base?" Another Captain said.

Another officer, Captain Saxon, replied, "Ass? Did you see that rack?"

"Well you gotta admit she's a boost to morale just walking around the camp," Captain Jorgensen stated with a smile. "The brass must be out of their fucking minds to send her here."

"So how did you get such a cush gig, Elijah?" Captain Saxon asked.

"I don't know, but the brass were oddly insistent that I be the one to deliver her to her father in Saigon. We'll only be here a couple of days," Elijah replied. "We'll just have to control the troops with an iron fist. She's off limits, mind, body, and soul, and it starts with us."

"Isn't that Morelli's big scout dog with her?" Captain Saxon said.

"Holy shit, yeah. No one's been able to get within a few feet of him since Morelli was *KIA a month or so ago," Captain Jorgensen replied.

Captain Jorgensen asked, "Any truth to the rumor that she jumped over your head midstream, Corrington?"

Elijah grinned, nodding his head. "My team talks too much. And that fiery red hair should be taken as a warning to every man here: you play with fire and you will get burned."

CHAPTER 7

Late the next morning, Elyse was bored out of her mind, a dangerous position for her to be in since that was when she got into the most trouble. One of the dogs had followed her back to the tent and apparently decided he was here to stay. She was told the very large, German shepherd dog's name was "Dog." *Not a very creative name*, she mused. She asked the guard, Arnold, if she could sit outside and get some sun. He agreed, so she grabbed a blanket off her bunk and spread it at the far end of the open area between the tents.

It was a beautiful day, not too hot yet. Elyse lounged on her tummy on the blanket, feet in the air, and cigarette that she had bummed from Arnold in hand. She eyed the perimeter. Some kind of barbed wire fencing enclosed the base camp, an important stronghold and Marine Corps garrison outpost, which appeared to be about a mile long and half a mile wide with a long runway for the constant supply planes landing and taking off.

This part of the camp was less congested. Elyse assumed that's why they put her down here. Off in the distance was the jungle's tree line, and farther away, mountain ranges and hills where other small outposts also manned by the Marine corps were located. Elyse recalled it was infested with bugs and snakes, and she could not suppress a shudder. Dog had made himself at home on the blanket. She petted and talked to him as they sat enjoying the scenery.

Such a beautiful country. Sad it was so war torn. Thousands had died in this "War." Thousands more were homeless and starving. Throw into that mix the tens of thousands of American men who were serving their country fighting this war. It was a sad state of affairs. Elyse could not stand suffering of any kind and this tore at her soul.

She was so lost in thought she didn't hear Elijah come up to her. When she turned her head and laid it on her arms, all she saw were Elijah's boots. He plopped down on the blanket next to her and took her cigarette and chucked it. They sat in companionable silence for a bit, just soaking up the sun and scenery.

ELIJAH LIKED the way her hair glowed in the sun. He was tempted to remove the pins holding it in place so he could watch it tumble down.

"Why do you do that?" Elyse asked him.

"What?"

"You keep taking my cigarette."

"It's bad for you."

"I haven't had more than a puff off each one."

"Good."

"You're a little old fashioned, aren't you?"

He scowled at her. "I can take you around the camp now and show you where you can and cannot go."

Elyse was excited at the prospect of an adventure. Elijah helped her up, and they along with Dog walked toward the center of the large sprawling camp. It had many sparse looking temporary buildings, large tents, a huge ammunition storage area at the other end of the base camp. Along the way, he pointed out various points of interest, most of which were "off limits." The men's showers and sleeping quarters, sectioned off areas for different units, and pup tents as well as any cannons, tanks, or weapons of war were a no-go.

Then he pointed out where she could go. "The mess hall. Okay. Also, the recreation area where some of the men hang out at during their off times is okay, but always keep your guards close."

He stopped in front of a bustling area. "C-Med, our main medical facility. We have doctors and corpsmen to see to the needs of our wounded. They perform surgeries and get them stabilized before the *dust off choppers take them to the hospitals in the rear."

"Perhaps you'd allow me to help in some small way with the wounded?"

He gave her a small rueful smile. "It can be pretty gruesome in there."

"Even the most severely wounded men need someone to hold their hand and offer kinds words and comfort," she replied.

"We'll see. I'll check with the doctors."

"Captain Corrington."

Elijah turned around as he heard his name called.

They were approached by an older balding man. Short, a bit on the paunchy side with a calming demeanor.

"Father Mitchell," said Elijah. "Elyse, this is one of our chaplains, Father Mitchell. He can see to your spiritual needs if need be. Father, this is Miss Elyse Booker."

The priest looked her up and down. "Miss Booker, Colonel Braxton has filled me in as to the circumstances of your presence here. I will say a prayer thanking the Lord for your safe arrival and continued safety."

'Thank you, Father," she said.

"I conduct a small mass on Sunday's if you're interested."

"I'm hoping to be home by Sunday Father," Elyse said, "but thank you. I will keep it in mind."

They turned to leave, and Elyse stopped short. Not thirty feet away stood two men with their backs to her, stark naked, wearing nothing but their helmets and boots. In front of mirrors leaning against sandbags on top of a bunker, they shaved their lathered faces unaware of her presence. They must have seen her reflection in the mirrors as they both turned around in surprise.

Flustered, her hands flew up to cover her eyes as the men grabbed their helmets off their heads and covered their private areas.

Elijah swore under his breath. "Father, will you please see to that?"

The priest was as flustered as Elyse. "Of course, my son."

With no way to go but forward so Elijah guided her past the naked men.

They murmured their greetings. "Miss, Sir."

Elijah glanced down at their helmets, a smile tugging at his lips. "Men."

He glanced over to Elyse. Her eyes still covered by her hands which also partially covered the pinkest cheeks he'd ever seen. He moved her quickly away from them. From behind them, they heard the priest admonishing the men, and laughter as the whole exchange had been witnessed by more than a few of the troops.

"You can uncover your eyes now. I apologize, evidently not everyone was aware of your presence on base."

Her heightened color fading, she replied, "Yes, I assumed that."

They continued on with their tour. His biggest rule was for her to stay inside the perimeter of the camp. He pointed out the bunkers, trenches, and fox holes surrounded by sandbags. Any attack, he said, and she was to hit the bunkers.

All along the way, she noticed she was being observed by groups of Marines, some at rest, some working to fill sandbags, and some digging trenches. Still others were preparing to go out on patrol.

She waited while Elijah stopped to talk to another officer and made introductions.

"Elyse, this is Gunnery Sergeant Adolfo Cruz, also known as Gunny, second in command of my platoon."

Elyse shook the short, stocky, thirty-something, Puerto Rican man's hand as his dark eyes danced in delight.

"Bomboncita, I've heard a lot about you," he said.

"Little candy? And I've heard you're a smooth-talking *Lobo," she replied, with a sassy sweet smile.

Gunny's smile widened with pleasure when he realized she had understood his Spanish.

Elijah and Gunny's talk turned to military matters, and Elyse turned around and noticed the thirty or so men standing across the way from the path she stood on. Looking from man to man, they stared at her and she stared back waiting for someone to say something. They didn't, so she did.

"Surprise." she softly said.

Instantly enchanted, their faces broke into grins as their gazes dropped to her breasts.

With two fingers she pointed to her eyes. "Eyes... up here." They grinned again when she narrowed her eyes and pointed a chiding finger at them.

Elijah turned around. "That's the rest of my platoon, I'll introduce you to them after you've had something to eat," Elijah said.

Smiling back at them, she turned away when Elijah placed his hand on her back to guide her the few steps down the path and into the mess hall.

ELIJAH OPENED the door to the mess hall, figuring she might be hungry. For Elijah, it was going to take some getting used to having multiple pairs of eyes watching her every move. Elijah stared them down until they turned away. They got in the chow line and viewed what was offered to satisfy their hunger. She chose a cup of coffee and buttered toast and bacon for Dog.

"That's it? You'll blow away in the wind if you don't eat."

"I'll eat when I can identify what I'm eating," Elyse said.

They sat at a table at the far end of the mess hall. Elyse nibbled on her toast and sipped her coffee, while slipping the bacon under the table to Dog.

"Where are you from?" Elijah asked.

"My 'home' is with my father in the American embassy in Saigon, but right now, I live in the American compound in Huế City."

"What are you doing so far north of Saigon?" Elijah asked, knowing full well the answer.

"I'm the Prima ballerina with the South Vietnamese Royal ballet in Huế City."

"Where were you heading when your chopper was shot down?

"Home, my father called me home for some emergency. I'm not sure what's going on, but he was unusually insistent that I return."

Elijah nodded his understanding. *She has no clue what's going on.*

"Where am I now, Elijah?"

"Khe Sanh."

"Khe Sanh? That makes no sense. The chopper was supposed to take me south to Saigon, not west toward Khe Sanh."

"Perhaps the chopper pilots were," Elijah replied.

"I'm many things, Elijah, but ignorant is not one of them. I know my geography well."

"I'm sorry, I meant no offense," he said. She was smart. He'd have to be careful with his words.

They spoke of the base camp, its location, and purpose. Elijah was impressed with her questions and level of understanding regarding military requirements. They spoke of politics, both American and Vietnamese. Elyse explained that as an only child of the widowed ambassador, she was basically raised with men, friends of her father, politicians, and military brass alike. She'd had many discussions and arguments with them, and many considered her as a daughter.

Which, Elijah mused, was why she was where she was. The darling of powerful men who did not want her to fall into enemy hands.

OTHER THAN HER FATHER, Elyse had no other family to protect her. This on top of the obvious culture shock she would experience since she had lived in Vietnam since the age of ten. Top military and CIA had determined the current plan of action to get her home was the best path forward.

Elijah shook his head at their line of thinking. He understood that for all her wisdom, she was still an innocent and learning the ways of the world. Unscrupulous men of many countries would seek to use her to justify their own means. Elyse must be protected at all cost.

With those thoughts in mind, he rose from the table, helped her up, and escorted her to the exit. He smirked as she blew a kiss to Cookie, and they left the mess hall amid the men's raucous laughter at Cookie's heightened color.

Five thousand men in camp, and the only man that she pays any attention to is the old cook.

CHAPTER 8

Early afternoon, Elyse decided it was time for her own exploration. With a radio in hand, Dog at her side, and Henson trailing behind, she walked to the rec area. She was soon sitting on top of a bunker of sandbags laughing at the antics of the men. Music blaring, they tried to convince her to dance with them. She sweetly declined. She decided she wouldn't dance unless they all danced together. Hence, Elyse's line dancing was born. She taught them moves to go along with whatever songs came on the radio, and they danced the afternoon away. Elyse's laughter lifted the morale of the men, and that afternoon, she became their darling as well.

Elijah heard the music, the men's laughter, and Elyse's tinkling laugh as he entered the area. His jaw dropped at the sight of Elyse and at least twenty men dancing. The swing of her hips and breasts had him transfixed.

It's like bees to the honey, he thought. Every man there, those who danced, and those who observed, thoroughly enjoyed themselves. He spotted Henson and signaled him. It was time to go.

Elyse grabbed her radio, called to Dog, and with a wave to the men and a promise to return, she left the area to return to her tent.

She sat on the bunk thinking about the afternoon's dance session. She made a mental note that next time she would convince the shy guys to participate. They came in all shapes and sizes from the biggest men she had ever seen to the smallest. She wanted them all to feel included. She was developing a rapport with Elijah's team members as well. It was a lot of fun, and she was safe with them.

Dawn came and Elyse crawled out the back of the tent. She knew if anyone caught her, Elijah would not be happy, but she had to dance. Ballet could be intensely private. You could not always perform, you had to be free first, to let the music determine your moves and choreograph your dance movements. She was not ready to be seen, so she danced for herself, to celebrate life and the dawn of each day. She was back within an hour, happy and feeling deliciously wicked.

Late in the afternoon, Elyse sat with some of the men in the rec area talking. From her viewpoint, she could see the helipads. Three choppers were currently coming in for a landing. Elyse watched Marines disembarking from the aircrafts. She was squinting to see and shrieked with joy. *My slippers.* She was on her feet and running toward the choppers. Alarmed, the men ran after her.

Elijah stood with other officers up by the command post tent watching as Elyse ran by with Dog, on her way to the choppers, with ten men and Arnold in pursuit. *What the hell is she doing?*

He saw her run up to a Marine making his way from the helipad. Hanging around his neck by silky ribbons was a pair of pink ballet slippers. Surrounded by his comrades, he handed her the slippers. "I believe these belong to you."

Elijah arrived on site just in time to see her plant kisses all over the young Marine's face. The Marine blushed, while his comrades pounded him on the back. Laughing, Elijah shook hands with the Lieutenant of the newly arrived team. "There's a surprise welcome for you, Flint. Where did you find Elyse's things?"

"We were at the chopper crash site to retrieve the dead and found a few remnants of her suitcase."

❖

ELYSE HUGGED her slippers and whispered a prayer of thanks for their return. Out of the corner of her eye, she spotted something else. A piece of blue lace peeked out from beneath the shirt of one of the Marines. She walked over to him, looked him squarely in the eye, and held out her hand.

Elyse lifted her eyebrows and again held out her hand. The Marine sighed and gave it up, pulling a pair of panties out of the top of his shirt and placing them in her hand. She held out her hand again, and the Marine continued pulling panties out of his shirt: baby blue, white, yellow, pink, and purple. She held her hand out one more time. The Marine shook his head. He didn't have any more. She turned to look at his comrades. She raised her questioning eyebrows at them till the last man sighed, came forward, and dropped a pair of red panties into her hand.

Waving a chiding finger at them, she showed mercy, and gave them a brilliant smile, thanking them for returning her items to her.

❖

BY THIS TIME, Elijah's grin couldn't have gotten any bigger. Captain Flint cleared his throat and said that was all they found. Laughing, Elijah clapped him on the back, and they walked up to the main tent as Elyse ran ahead of them. The men watched as she sat down on a pile of sandbags, her panties at her side, and put her slippers on, tying the ribbons around her slim ankles and paying no heed to the men.

❖

ONCE THEY WERE ON, she stood en pointe, pirouetted, and headed back out to the now-empty helipad where she seemed to have no care as to who was watching her. She danced, totally immersed. She only felt her slippers and the movement of her body. She had missed this so much. Even her

61

early morning dancing did not compare with having her pointe shoes back. When she finished, the men who watched clapped, hooting and hollering their appreciation. Having forgotten they were there, she danced with a rare abandonment usually reserved for her private practice. Feeling her heightened color, she sat down, removed her slippers and ran back to her tent. Her joy knew no bounds at the return of her most prized possessions.

ELIJAH WATCHED HER JOY, her passion, and her lust for life. She was the most graceful, beautiful creature he had ever seen. It was a privilege to witness her dance. It was breathtaking, and he noticed a lump in his throat and a fast-developing hard-on. Elyse Booker was a fascinating woman. When he spotted her abandoned pile of panties, he excused himself, grinning while he walked over and picked up the pretty, little lacy things. He smiled and sauntered back to her tent. He stood outside, calling out to her for permission to enter.

"Come in, Elijah."

He cleared his throat and handed her the panties. "You left these behind."

ELYSE BLUSHED. It was a new experience to have all of these men handling her intimate apparel. She thanked him as he turned to take his leave. Smiling, she lovingly stroked the silk of the ribbons of her slippers as she hung them on a hook on the wall.

PAUSING AT THE DOORWAY, Elijah looked back at her hair coming loose from its bun, the drops of sweat on her chest from the dance, the curve of her breasts against "his" shirt, and her pink, slightly parted lips. He was going to need a cold shower.

By early evening Elyse was back down at the rec area. The men had set up a makeshift volleyball net and invited Elyse to join them. Though it was Elyse's first time playing the game, her jumping and leaping skills came in handy, and she excelled. With every jump and save, she laughed, and Dog jumped in and played as well.

The first time one of the player's hands brushed across her breast, Elyse chose to ignore it. The second time, the same man grabbed her by the waist. She worked to avoid the lovestruck Marine's hands. The third time was a caress across her bottom.

"Enough." With a snarl, she gave him a well-placed kick to the groin. Another to his chest sent him flying, and he landed on his back. All play had stopped. Elyse was furious.

"Touch me again, asshole, and I will cut your hands off." She would not allow them to disrespect her. Johnson was at her side in a heartbeat as the men stood in surprised, if not, embarrassed silence. She looked at them all, grabbed her things, and left.

She made Johnson swear the incident to silence. "Do not tell Elijah."

She had handled it and that was enough for now. It was a decision she would later regret.

Later that evening Elyse was still upset. The man's amorous attention was unexpected. Other than the crass comments about her body when they thought she couldn't hear them. They had always behaved as gentlemen. She would have to be more careful. Elijah was not to learn what happened. He'd beat the man within an inch of his life.

Elyse walked between some tents on her way back to her own tent. She had ditched Johnson. She heard someone call her name from the outside of a tent. Thinking it was Elijah, she walked over to where she thought he was standing. The same Marine stepped from the shadows.

"Elyse, I love you." he said. His voice thin and taut.

"Oh, shit." Elyse backed up, wary of the man.

"Why did you hurt me like that Elyse? You know I love you."

"Paul, that's your name, right? You don't even know me. I don't know you. I'm off limits to you and every man here."

He advanced on her. "I don't care, I know you love me too."

"I'm sorry Paul. I don't love you. You're just in a bad place at a bad time. I'm sure you have someone at home waiting for you," Elyse replied.

"You fucking bitch."

He lunged at her, his fist making contact with her cheek and knocking her to the ground as he jumped on her before she had a chance to clear her head.

She snarled in outrage when he ripped her shirt and pawed at her breasts. She boxed his ears just as she heard an ethereal growl as Dog jumped the man from behind, allowing her the chance to roll to her feet to her ready stance.

Afraid of what Dog could do the terrified man she called him off.

"Dog, come to me."

Dog came to her side and sat down. "Good boy."

Paul was angry now, back on his feet, his stance wide and threatening. A sneer marred his homely features, his hands formed tight fists. Dog growled deep in his throat and bared his teeth while moving to stand in front of her.

Paul ran off just as Sarge, Johnson, Mountain, Henson and Arnold rushed into the area between the tents.

"Christ, Elyse. Are you alright?" Henson asked.

"I'm fine, Dog stopped him."

Sarge barked orders, "Arnold go get Doc, Johnson find Cap, Mountain and Henson, you follow that asshole. I'll stay here until Cap and Doc get here then we'll find you."

⁂

ELIJAH STOOD outside the colonel's office giving instructions to Gunny for his other four patrol teams. They reviewed maps spread out on a large table on where the teams were to spend their time watching for VC and NVA movements. His man, Johnson, who was supposed to be guarding Elyse ran at full speed toward the group. "Sir, it's Elyse. You've got to come."

Elijah sprinted after Johnson. They came to where Elyse sat on the ground as Doc administered to her cheekbone.

"Ow." Elyse squinted in pain.

Elijah hunched down in front of her, took her chin, and gently turned her face to get a good look at the swelling bruise and scuff mark on her cheek. His anger barely controlled. "Who hit you?"

"Ow. ow. Paul, his name is Paul."

"Are you alright? Did he try anything else?" Seeing an obvious rip in her shirt and her cleavage exposed. Elijah knew what that meant, and he stood up in a rage, not even waiting for a reply.

Another man came up to Elijah. "We got him, Sir."

"Take care of her," Elijah said.

Doc nodded. "Aye aye, Sir."

Elyse jumped to her feet. Grabbing Elijah's arm. "No, you can't, the man's not right in the head. Elijah, please, Dog and I hurt him far worse than he hurt me."

⁕

HE TOUCHED her cheek with gentle stroke of his hand, his eyes showed his concern.

Looking over at Doc, his eyes hardened. "Keep her here."

Elijah strode quickly and with anger over to where the man was being held, followed by members of his team.

When he came into the rec area, he saw that Mountain and Henson held the amorous perpetrator by the arms. The short and stocky man with a shaven head stood angry and defiant with bloody bite marks on his forearms from Dog. They pushed him toward Elijah and backed away. The men that were there formed a circle around the two.

"I didn't touch her man," Paul said. "Whatever that slut said, she's lying."

Elijah gave the man a look of sheer disgust. Looking at Sarge, Elijah turned and walked away.

⁕

SARGE IN TURN nodded to Arnold.

"You hit a woman." Arnold roared at the man. his fist landing on his face with a solid thump. The man sailed to the ground on his back, his fists pounding the man again and again.

Elyse sat with Doc who had turned away to grab a bandage from his medical kit when she jumped to her feet and ran toward the fight. Doc was on his feet chasing after her, abandoning his medical bag where they had sat.

She penetrated the circle, thinking to stop the beating, but Sarge grabbed her by the waist, holding her back. "No, Elyse, we have to make an example of this guy."

Elyse watched in horror as punch after punch landed on the man's face until he was nearly unconscious.

Elijah scooped her up from behind and hauled her away, tucked under his arm. He set her down some distance away from the fight.

"Didn't I tell you to stay with Doc?" Elijah said.

"I can't believe you are allowing that beating," she stated.

"What beating?" Elijah replied.

"What do you mean what beating? The one I just witnessed."

That's not a beating, it's called barracks justice."

"Why were you alone?" he growled at her.

"Well, technically I wasn't alone. I had Dog."

"That wasn't what I meant, and you well know it."

"Well, I sort of ditched Johnson."

"You ditched him?"

"I've been ditching guards since I was twelve, this is nothing new to me."

Angry now, his brows furrowed together. "You can't do that here, brat. What happened here today is a prime example of why you need to behave."

"Behave?"

"Yes Elyse, behave," he ground out.

She became aware of him as he stood, commanding and powerful in front of her. Her heart raced when he reached out his hand to cup her chin as he lifted it until her eyes met his. Her skin tingled from his touch as she gazed up into his eyes.

"You're restricted to your quarters."

Incredulous, her mouth dropped open. "You're grounding me?"

"Yeah," he replied.

⁂

THE FIGHT OVER, Doc and Sarge observed from afar.

"Ten bucks says she catches him," Sarge said.

"No fucking way, but you're on," Doc replied. They grinned, shook hands and walked to where Doc had left his medical bag.

⁂

AN HOUR LATER, Elijah was livid when Johnson came clean about the incident earlier that day with the same man. "You withheld information from me? If you had told me sooner, the bruises on Elyse's face could have been avoided. Don't ever withhold anything regarding Elyse from me again. Get your shovel, Johnson. You've got a trench to dig."

A contrite Johnson nodded and left.

She's got them all wrapped around her pinky. It was time his entire team learned who gave the orders around here. Ten minutes later, other than Sarge, the team stood at attention. Elijah stood before them every bit the angry Captain. His hands on his slim hips, his stance wide as he glared at his team. His voice was cold and crisp. "It's come to my attention you've all been concealing something from me. And that is the fact that Elyse has been ditching you. I want your eyes to never leave her person, I want you sticking to her side like glue."

"Sir." Arnold replied, "She's so tiny we lose her in a crowd."

"Perhaps we should strap a whip flag to her ass, Arnold," Elijah replied sarcastically. "Why don't you start by looking for someone who looks like this?" Elijah made a gesture indicating a curvy woman. " "There's only one here. Can't miss her. Elyse is a master at escaping our protection. You must know she is looking for the first opportunity to take advantage of your inattentive behavior. Do not lose sight of her again.

"Six Marines. Six hardcore, big, bad ass Devil-dogs, and all of you, including Sarge, are being beaten, beaten by one hundred pounds of pure, unadulterated sass. She's got the six of you wrapped around her pinky. You are not to listen to her sweet words. You are to follow my orders. If something happens, I am to be notified right away. Now get your fucking shovels. I want a subterranean bunker built just outside of Elyse's door. Big enough to hold all of us and that tiny troublemaker. You're dismissed."

Now to deal with Elyse.

When he came to see her, she sat on a blanket outside the tent watching a glorious sunset with Sarge as her guard. With a nod, he sent Sarge on his way.

Elijah plopped down on the blanket next to her.

"I just heard about the earlier incident with the man who attacked you."

"Damn."

"You are never ever to withhold information from me or ask my men not to tell me when something happens."

"I thought I had handled it," she replied.

"That is not your call to make. If I had known about the first incident, the second would never have happened."

Elyse looked at her hands in her lap. "I'm sorry, I was wrong."

Elijah lifted her chin and looked into her eyes. "Promise me. Promise me that if anything ever happens again, you will come to me right away."

"I promise."

He caressed her cheekbone. Still tender, she winced.

"I don't ever want to see bruises on your face again," he said.

TWO DAYS LATER, Elyse was up early. On her way to the mess hall she spotted another one of Elijah's teams lined up barefoot for an inspection prior to leaving on a mission.

"What are they doing, Mountain?"

"Checking for jungle rot."

"What's jungle rot?"

"Trench foot or immersion rot. You have to keep your feet clean and dry in the jungle, or they can rot off."

Elyse grimaced and then smiled. She ran up and stood at attention at the far end of the line of Marines.

The last Marine in line looked down at her and smiled. "Morning, Elyse."

"Good morning, Percy."

"What are you doing?"

Elyse grinned. "Foot inspection, of course. Let's see if he notices."

The sergeant walked along studying each man's feet and looking for the telltale signs of jungle rot. He stopped, looking at the very last set of feet. She wiggled her pink polished toes at him.

Grinning, he said, "Good morning, Elyse."

"Good morning, Sergeant Jones. How did you know it was me?"

Looking up to see her brilliant smile, he said, "Cute little feet, and they know I'd deck the first Marine who wiggled his toes at me."

Elyse laughed. "Do I pass muster?"

"Needs closer review."

She clucked her tongue at him. "You're bad, Sarge. Go easy on them today."

"Never. Need to make sure all the ladies here return at the end of the mission to see your bright and shining smile."

"I'll be here waiting," she said, then she addressed the men. "Be safe out there, boys."

Then she ran back to Mountain's side. She smiled at him but couldn't hide the sadness in her eyes.

"Why do you torture yourself?" Mountain asked.

"I don't want them leaving to go fight without knowing someone is here thinking of them."

"Just don't forget Cap has forbidden you to be over here when they return."

"I know, and I guess I understand, but it's not about me. It's about them."

"It's too goddamn painful when someone doesn't come back."

"Now you sound like Elijah," Elyse said.

"He's right," Mountain replied.

"Come on, Mountain, I'll buy you a cup of coffee."

Mountain grinned. "That mud swill is free."

"That's good because I don't have any money anyway. Maybe it's time for a game of poker?"

"Poker? You play?"

Hooking her arm through his with a wicked grin, she said, "A little."

CHAPTER 9

Later that week, Elyse sat on her blanket with one of Henson's books in hand. Dog slept next to her. She heard weak cries almost like those of a baby outside her tent. She got up to investigate and saw a tiny bunny stuck in the barbed wire. Looking around for Mountain, she remembered his emergency run to the head. She delicately stepped through and over the treacherous fencing and pulled the tiny rabbit free of the wire. On her way back, she realized she was stuck and could not get back out.

Now I've done it. "Dog, you need to go get Elijah. I cannot move."

Dog was off at a trot, searching for Elijah.

ELIJAH SAT in the Colonel's office discussing the war and reviewing maps with the other officers.

"Corrington, isn't that Elyse's dog?"

Dog was jumping up and down outside the screen door trying to get his attention. His meeting over, Elijah stepped outside. "What is it, boy? Where's Elyse?"

Dog was barking now. He wanted Elijah to follow him. Elijah followed Dog all the way to where Elyse stood trapped. His voice was gruff with anger simmering just below the surface. "What are you doing, brat? What have I told you about going outside of the perimeter fencing?"

Elyse chose to argue the point. "Don't be ridiculous. I am not outside of the perimeter. I am 'in' the perimeter fencing."

"Don't play semantics with me. You need to stay inside the perimeter."

"The bunny was stuck and crying. Obviously, if I could have gotten in and out without you finding out, that would have been my preference."

"No surprises there," Elijah said. "You should have called for help. Where's Mountain?"

"In the powder room."

"Goddamn it."

"Be reasonable. He had to go. It's not like he could go right here."

"That barbed wire is razor sharp. If you had fallen, you could have been cut and bled out. The perimeter is mined too. You could have been blown to bits."

She went pale. "I'm not cut or blown up. I'm okay, just stuck."

Elijah lifted her out and set her on her feet. She set the bunny down and it hopped away. Dog looked after the fleeing bunny and whimpered.

"No Dog, it's just a baby. Leave it be."

"Go back to your quarters and stay there," Elijah said.

"What? You're going to punish me for this?"

"Yes, go back to your quarters now."

Mountain exited the head, and Elijah walked away shaking his head.

Again? Elyse glared at his retreating back.

❧

ELYSE WALKED toward her tent with Mountain trailing behind. Halfway there she saw the main gate open and Marines returning from patrol were walking in.

Outside the perimeter, indeed. I'll show you outside the perimeter. A lump caught in her throat. She'd had enough. *I'm going home. I'm leaving, just as I arrived in this godforsaken jungle.*

With that, Elyse dropped her blanket and book, peeled off Elijah's shirt and removed his boxers, stomping them into the ground.

"Whoa, Elyse what are you doing?" Mountain called to her as he ran to catch up. She turned and headed for the gate in only her patched-up orange bra and panties. She paid no attention to the cat calls and wolf whistles. *Whatever.* She paused at the gate, hands on hips, and glanced back to the men standing behind her with a wicked smile. Then she stepped outside of the perimeter. *I'm going home. To hell with you, Captain.*

ELIJAH WAS busy cleaning his weapon when he heard the cat calls and wolf whistles. He looked up and saw Mountain frantically waving at him.

"Elyse just walked out the gate," Mountain hollered.

"Are you fucking kidding me?" Elijah sprinted to the gate.

The Marines stood at the gate, watching her. Some had not seen her before and stared in surprise. Elijah stopped at the gate, hands on hips, watching her walk down the road. *Look at that, bold as brass.*

He was about to go after her when he heard someone calling his name. He turned to see one of his best friends. Captain Christian John, newly re-assigned to Khe Sanh, had just arrived on base with his company. They grabbed each other and pounded each other on the back. They turned and stared in appreciation after Elyse making her way down the road.

"A girl. That's a girl," Christian said. The shock apparent on his face.

"Yeah."

"Who is that, Elijah?"

"That, is one hundred pounds of sass."

Elijah never took his eyes off Elyse. "I have to go catch her."

Elijah took off at a slow jog with a grin on his face. *Never a dull moment.* "Elyse, where are you going?" he called out.

She turned and started walking backwards so she could face him. "Go away. I've had enough of your war. I'm going home."

Elijah was halfway to her by now. "How are you getting there?"

"I'm walking obviously."

Elijah picked up speed. She shrieked, turned, and began to run. Elijah turned up the speed, caught up to her, picked her up, and threw her over his shoulder despite her protests. Then he turned and headed back toward the gate. Elyse pounded on his back as the men watching from the gate laughed and cheered.

"You son of a bitch. Put me down." She howled when he reached up and smacked her on the bottom.

He had made it just inside the gate when he lost his balance, his feet went out from under him, and he landed flat on his back. Elyse landed on her knees, and her legs straddled his face. Their mutual shock as their eyes met was momentary. Elyse shrieked her outrage, and his eyes widened.

"Holy shit."

Elijah grabbed her by the bottom, sat up, and set her on his lap. Now her rage was directed at his hands on her bottom. She reached back to remove them, and he pinned her arms behind her. "Calm down, Elyse. Don't move."

With her breasts jiggling back and forth, he saw it coming seconds before it happened. *That duct tape isn't going to hold.*

Her bra split and she came spilling out in all her glory. Stunned, he let go of her arms. She snarled, covered herself with one arm, and delivered a stinging slap with her other one. As she scrambled up, her breasts pummeled his face, then she raced away. Elijah flopped back down, arms spread wide. *Sweet Jesus, did that really just happen?* He then rolled to his knees, shaking his head. Christian arrived at his side as Elijah stood up, hands on his knees, breathless.

"Beaten by muff and titties, my friend?" Christian asked, laughing.

Elijah grinned and breathed in deeply. "That… was… amazing." He shook his head and rubbed his still stinging face. "I've got to go. She'll be inconsolable after that. Meet you in half hour by the officer's area." Elijah took off at a trot, spotted her clothes, book, and blanket lying on the ground, and stopped to pick them up on the way to Elyse's tent.

❧

ELYSE SAT ON HER BUNK, face inflamed, her useless bra on the floor. *Oh my God, what just happened?*

❧

WHEN ELIJAH ARRIVED at her tent, he didn't bother calling for permission, he just walked right in. She was a fetching sight as she tried to cover herself with her hands and sheet.

"You should have come back to the tent when I told you to." He tossed her the blanket and scooped up the bra and her ballet slippers as well. He grabbed her other shirt and boxers on the clothesline drying.

"Next time maybe you'll listen to me. You're restricted to your quarters. The team will let me know of your needs." With that, he turned to walk out.

"Are you serious? You're grounding me, again?"

Elijah grinned ear to ear at her as he slipped through the door.

"You bastard," she shrieked. "You took my clothes."

SHE WOULDN'T BE GOING ANYWHERE like that. He had been tempted to take her panties right off her as well, but he well knew how that might end. He dumped her things on his bunk and headed over to the officer's area to meet Christian. When he sat down next to his buddy, the grin was still plastered on his face.

They talked for hours, and Elijah told Christian every little thing about the red-headed ballerina terrorizing the camp. The talk soon moved to some of Elyse's exploits in the jungle, and he had Christian in stitches with his description of Elyse sailing over his head with her now famous leap across the creek.

Elijah eventually had to go get some food for Elyse as he didn't want anyone else entering her tent. He went to the mess hall and grabbed a tray for Elyse. There was quite a bit of teasing from the men. Some had seen what happened and word had spread. Elyse would be mortified if she heard the comments.

When he took the tray to Elyse, he gave her his long-sleeved shirt to wear, and escorted her to the head and back. She didn't say a word to him. He knew she was stewing.

"I want to apologize for what happened today," Elijah said. "I never intended to humiliate you."

"I'm sure all of you got an eye full," she replied.

"If it makes you feel any better, you were mostly blocked from their view by my body."

"But you saw almost everything."

"What I saw, was beyond beautiful."

Not knowing how to respond to his compliment. "I want to go home, Elijah."

"We leave here the day after tomorrow."

"That's wonderful news." Elyse replied, with a smile.

He turned to leave.

"Elijah."

He turned back around.

"Once this over and I'm back in Saigon or Huế City. Will you, will you come to see me once in a while?"

He crooked his finger at her. "Come here."

She moved to stand in front of him.

He reached out to touch her smooth cheek, the bruises fading. He stroked it with his thumb in a sensual stroke to caress her full lips and back again. "Yeah, I'll come see you."

He pulled her into his arms, his lips descended onto hers. Slow, teasing, their mouths melded, tasting, flicking, tongues exploring.

He tore himself away from the sweetest kiss he'd ever had. "Christ Almighty, who taught you to kiss like that?"

"You're my first kiss."

"I have to stop." He turned to leave again, stopped, and turned back around. Looking her up and down. "My shirt?"

She raised a delicate eyebrow.

He gestured with his hand to give it up.

"Turn around."

He did, resisting the temptation to peek.

"Okay, you can turn around."

He turned back to see her wrapped in a sheet, shirt in hand. His gaze caressed her red hair as it flowed down one shoulder and curled around her breast. To her other shoulder, bare, soft and smooth. She felt the tingle of butterflies in her stomach and she shivered at the intensity in his eyes.

"You fully intend to continue to leave me in here half-naked, don't you?" she said.

He took the shirt from her outstretched hand. "Yeah."

"Sweet dreams, Captain."

"Miss Booker."

He returned to his own tent for some much-needed rest. He fell asleep thinking about the scent of a woman, that kiss, and her bra bursting open with Elyse spilling out.

CHAPTER 10

The golden hour just before sunset, Elyse walked the perimeter of the camp with radio in hand. Johnson, her guard, remained in step with her the entire way. She had packed her meager possessions and made ready to leave the next morning at Elijah's instructions.

Two and a half weeks in the jungle, this camp, and dealing with Marines was more than enough. She was anxious to return home to Saigon. Elyse eyed the guard post bunkers, enclosed with openings facing the jungle. Sandbags were packed on top and around the sides with eight feet between each bunker.

She smiled as an idea came to her, what an amazing place to dance, and she climbed to the top of the first one.

"Christ. Elyse, get down from up there," Johnson said just as a bullet pinged by his ear.

Elyse looked down at him, not realizing the danger she was in. "try to keep up Johnson." She spun through a few dance moves and leaped to the next bunker, breasts swaying, hips swinging. She leaped and danced to an amazing tune playing from her radio and she never felt so free. It was exhilarating.

ELIJAH SAT QUIETLY CHATTING with his team when a movement on the bunker line guarding the perimeter of the base caught his attention. He stood up along with the others.

"Do you see that, Cap?" Sarge said.

Elyse, how do women move like that? He stood frozen, watching her leap from bunker to bunker and dancing in between. He could hear her laughter, the music, the shoulder shimmy's, the shimmy of her breasts, the sensual swing and sway of her hips.

"Son of a bitch," Elijah said. For all her innocence Elyse was primal. Elijah was certain she had been sent by the devil to torment him in every way imaginable, and now she had just broadcast her whereabouts to the NVA by her movement on the bunkers.

Elijah took off running with a curse under his breath. He had to stop her. Judging her speed and timing and how long it would take her to reach it, Elijah climbed a bunker seconds before Elyse arrived. The moment she landed, he grabbed her around the waist, pulled her down flat on her back, and rolled off the bunker holding her tight until they landed on the ground on the backside of the bunker. He rolled from his back pinning her body under his to hold her still.

"Elijah," she breathed.

"You would test the patience of a saint. You just gave away your presence to the NVA. Are you aware there are snipers out there? You need to stay off the perimeter bunkers. Where's your guard?"

"Three bunkers behind," she replied.

Johnson arrived at that moment, out of breath and cursing. Hunkering down behind the bunker next to them. "Sniper Fire, Cap."

Elijah looked into her shocked face.

"You little fool you could have been killed."

"I'm sorry."

"I'm sorry doesn't cut it when I'm zipping you up in a body bag. This isn't the city. You're in the jungle surrounded by the NVA and VC. Men die out here every fucking day. Start listening, do as you are told, or you will die out here as well."

"Okay, okay," Elyse replied, frightened by his angry tone. Elijah sent her back to her tent with strict orders for Johnson to keep her there. Something was in the air tonight he could feel it.

The NVA's attack started close to dawn. It would have happened regardless of Elyse being in the camp or not. The NVA now had another motivation, other than protecting their access to the Ho Chi Minh Trail, to take the strategically located base camp.

ELIJAH WOKE with a start at the first whistle of incoming mortar shelling. Having slept partially clothed, he grabbed his shirt and weapon in the blink of an eye and was out the door. Racing around the side of his quarters followed by the team. Elijah, along with Doc, who had guarded her, burst into the darkness of her tent to find her out cold, deep in slumber.

"Elyse, wake up, come on wake up," Elijah yelled.

Elyse groaned, "No, go away."

"Come on, Elyse, wake up."

Reaching to pull her from her bunk, his hands made contact with smooth soft skin and the curves of her full breasts and he pulled back in surprise.

"You're naked. Where's your fucking clothes?"

"Well I don't know, somewhere," Elyse mumbled.

Doc yelled, "Here." Tossing her clothes to Elijah.

Elijah pulled her up into a sitting position. "Put these on."

She pulled the shirt on as instructed and he handed her the boxers.

"Come on Brat, wake up, move faster."

She had flopped back down on her bunk.

"Elyse, put these on, now."

"It's too hot."

"Now Elyse."

She pulled them on as Doc grabbed the blankets and sheets from her bunk as Elijah grabbed her by the waist and hauled her, slung under his arm, to the newly built underground bunker.

Soon, from the relative safety of the bunker, Doc laid a blanket on the dirt floor and Elijah laid her down and covered her with the sheet. She curled up into a little ball like a kitten as Dog laid down beside her with a whimper.

"I don't think she ever really woke up, Cap," Doc said.

"You're right. She's going to be in for a hell of a surprise come morning."

Leaving Mountain and Dog behind to guard Elyse, Elijah left the bunker with his team to assess the situation.

The fighting was fierce and bloody. The cries of "incoming" and the all too familiar thump, thump sound of artillery shells had them ducking and rolling for cover as the NVA pounded the base. Small arms fire, grenades and mortar shelling were returned by the Marines defending the base.

Feeling somewhat relieved that Elyse was for the moment safe, Elijah knew he'd have to wait until first light to assess if her location was safe enough.

Dawn came shortly after and with it a short break in the action followed by continuous pummeling on the American forces. Elijah and the team returned to the bunker. Elyse still slept.

Looking at his charge slumbering, he lowered himself to the ground leaning against the dirt wall. The team hunkering down as well.

"Has she woken up at all?" Elijah asked.

Mountain shook his head. "Not a peep out of her, Cap."

Shaking his head in disbelief. "She'd sleep through the atomic bomb. Get some rest men while you still can. Lights out," Elijah ordered. The men doused the light and closed their eyes as exhaustion overtook them. An hour later they woke. Quietly talking amongst themselves about the conditions outside of the bunker.

ELYSE WOKE up an hour later to the earth shuddering beneath her body and the men's voices.

"Oh my God, do you have to be so loud in the morning?"

She opened her eyes to the pitch blackness of the bunker. Feeling the warmth of Dog next to her she sat straight up. "What the hell?"

The light came on and Elyse stared in astonishment at the seven battle-weary men in front her.

Looking around at the darkness beyond the reach of their meager lamp.

"Where am I? What is all that racket outside? What is going on?" Her questions rolling off her lips not giving them a chance to respond.

"We're under attack, we're in the bunker," Elijah replied.

"How did I get here?"

"I carried you," Elijah said.

"Well, why didn't you wake me?" She asked.

They looked at her incredulous as a massive explosion, shook the earth to its very core.

❧

ELIJAH FLEW across the small room and covered her, face down in the dirt, with his body. Explosion after explosion shook the base. Dirt fell from the ceiling in a choking dust as the men let loose strings of colorful expletives.

Elijah still lay on top of her. *Soft on this side too.* His body betrayed him as he felt himself harden against her soft bottom.

"What the hell is that?" She asked.

"Main ammo dump just blew up," Sarge replied.

❧

ELYSE THOUGHT TO HERSELF. *That's not really what I was asking about, but okay.*

❧

ELIJAH QUICKLY PULLED himself up to a sitting position. Looking down at Elyse as she rolled back over. *Why does she have to be so soft?*

"We'll be in here for a long while," Elijah replied.

❧

ELYSE HUDDLED with Dog and a constant guard at her side. She was forbidden to leave the bunker alone. Food and water were brought to her when they could do so safely. Occasional lulls in the action during the early morning cover of thick fog allowed her to stretch her legs, use the powder room, and chat for a few minutes with battle fatigued Marines before she'd be escorted back to her subterranean bunker. Wrapped in blankets to keep out the chill of the dank, dark, cold earth. Elyse prayed for all the men out there fighting as she listened to the roar of machine gunfire, cannons, explosions, and the rumble of shaking earth. She covered her ears to block it all out. She was miserable but knew it was far worse for them.

<hr />

TWO WEEKS LATER, Elijah crouched down to enter the Command bunker. Nodding to the guards at the entryway. He walked into the underground command post. Stopping in front of Colonel Braxton, he stood at attention.

"Sir, you wished to see me."

"Elijah, yes, yes I did."

"How is Miss Booker holding up?"

"Surprisingly well, Sir."

"Let's go in here so we can speak in private, Captain."

Elijah followed him into the Colonel's private area within the bunker.

"There's been a change in plans. Are you aware of the Vietnamese custom to celebrate their New Year, their Tet?"

"Yes, Sir."

"There was supposed to be a cease fire during the Tet. Instead bases and cities across South Vietnam came under attack by the VC and NVA. That includes Hué City, Saigon, and the embassy. There's still fighting going on in Hué City and some of the bases. The Ambassador was seriously injured. We're damn lucky you didn't deliver Miss Booker to the embassy before this started. Even here, under siege, she's safer than anywhere, for now, that is. Get her out anyway you can if worse comes to worst, but do not allow her to fall into enemy hands."

"Aye aye, Sir."

"You're going to have to keep moving her to keep her safe. You can't take her to Saigon any longer. Her entire ballet troupe in Hué City were all slaughtered by the NVA in their search for her during this Tet offensive."

Elijah's eyes flew wide open. "Jesus Christ."

"She's not to know anything. I think we've both learned that if she knew how bad off her father was, nothing would prevent her from flying to his bedside. And that's what the enemy wants. You are to hide her wherever you can. There are hundreds of American bases in South Vietnam. Work with MACV headquarters to have them make accommodations for your party."

"Aye aye, Sir."

"Both General Morgan and I have the utmost confidence in you, Captain."

"Thank you, Sir. Will the Ambassador recover from his wounds Sir?"

"It's still too soon to tell."

"She'll be all alone in the world if he doesn't."

"I know. How is she spending her time now?" Colonel Braxton asked.

"Reading and kicking my team's ass in poker."

The Colonel grinned. "Bring her up here if there's a lull in the action. We could use some cheering up, and your expertise could be used as well."

"Aye aye, Sir."

"You're dismissed, Captain."

FOR TWO AND a half months this was how she lived. Working at the command post, bringing coffee, back rubs to tired shoulders, and a smile and kind words when despair set in. Sometimes Elijah took her to the C-med area to comfort the wounded men waiting for *"Dust off" choppers. More often than not, she sat in their own underground bunker and worried about her newfound friends. She knew many had died or were wounded.

Elyse looked around the hustling command post. Multiple men hovered in front of maps hung on the walls. Portable phones along with radio equipment sat on desks and makeshift tables made of empty crates, the air was thick with cigarette and cigar smoke. She added cream and sugar to a cup of coffee for the Colonel. Adding it to her tray, she took it over to him and she slid it across the small table in front of him.

"Thank you darlin'."

"You're welcome Colonel."

She delivered cups of the fresh hot brew to the other men in the command post, saving the best delivery for last. She leaned over Elijah, accidentally brushing her breast against his arm.

Elijah had been pouring over maps all day. Now his eyes were drawn to her slightly exposed cleavage as his arm tingled from her touch. His eyes rose to meet hers as he managed a small smile.

His exhaustion was apparent to her. Moving to stand behind him, she set the tray down and expertly massaged his aching shoulders. "You're tired Elijah, you need to rest."

He rubbed his eyes. "Are you ready to return to the bunker, brat?"

She knew full well how dire their circumstances had become. "We won't be back, will we?"

"No, it's time to evacuate you."

She nodded her head. Thinking of his kisses in rare moments of privacy, or this morning when he had slid his hands up her shirt cupping and kneading her breasts and leaving her wanting more. More of what, she wasn't sure. She wondered if she was being promiscuous in allowing his fondling and kisses, but she also knew it was so right to be held in his arms. She smiled at him now, just wanting to feel his reassuring arms around her again. She watched as Elijah nodded to Arnold to check the conditions outside.

❧

ELIJAH and the team stood outside the bunker where Elyse was huddled as nightfall descended on the base camp. Time after time, Elijah's plans to evacuate Elyse were thwarted, and his frustration grew by the hour. Things were not going well. They had one more chance after so many choppers were shot down to get her out of Khe Sanh. It was dangerous, but Elijah knew they had no choice but to try. They didn't know how much longer they could hold out before the base camp was overrun by the NVA.

A C-130 supply plane was heading in to drop supplies. They could make it—at a run. He went inside to talk to Elyse.

She glanced up at his entrance into the bunker. "Elijah, what's going on out there?"

"Listen to me: we are going to try to make a run for the supply plane," he said, pulling her into his arms.

"I'm not sure I understand you, Elijah."

"The plane will come in for a landing, but it won't stop for us. We will have to run right up to the back and into the belly of the plane before it takes off again."

Her mouth dropped open. "Are you insane?"

"We can do this, but you must do everything I say. When I say run, you run. If I say drop, you hit the ground. Do you understand me?"

"I'm scared."

"I know, brat, but you'll do just fine." Pulling her in for a sweet kiss, he grabbed her small bag. "Ready?"

She nodded, her stomach churning, she wrung her hands.

They lay down in the trench midway alongside the runway. The burning fires, thick smoke, gunfire, and explosions of mortar fire lit up the night sky all around them.

"Here it comes, Cap," Sarge shouted.

The C-130 cargo plane came in at a sharp angle, never stopping as a back ramp dropped and replacement troops pushed the cargo out the back door, down the rollers, and off the ramp on the back of the plane.

"Now," Elijah shouted. "Run."

ELYSE, Elijah, and his team, along with Dog chased after the plane, dodging debris and the carnage of war. Bullets pinged by their ears as Doc and Henson made it onboard, followed by Mountain, Johnson, Arnold, and Dog. Elijah, Elyse, and Sarge were almost there, but when they were just feet away, she tripped and fell. Scraping her knees as she landed, she rolled with Elijah and Sarge to a stop in a crumpled heap on the runway. She glanced up to see the rapidly accelerating plane leaving without them. Because of her they had missed it.

ELIJAH KNEW what his men would do moments before they did it. They were a team and didn't leave anyone behind. Running back down the ramp and off the plane, the team rolled to the ground and took cover. Then they all watched as the plane lifted off and was immediately hit by rocket fire, crashing and rolling in a huge fireball of twisting metal that shook the very earth where they lay on the runway. In shock, they watched as the aircraft continued its sickening roll and skidded to a stop at the far end of the runway.

Elyse heard screaming. She didn't realize it was coming from her own mouth until Elijah grabbed her by the shoulders and shouted at her over the din of battle. "It's all right, Elyse. Listen to me. Listen. I need you to be brave and strong. We're going back to the bunker. Now."

Elijah helped her to her feet, and they all made a run for it. He threw her to the ground when they spotted the shadows of NVA soldiers trying to overrun the perimeter fencing. The team laid on their stomachs firing their M-16's into the human wave of a ground attack by the encroaching enemy. Back on their feet at a run they all made it back to the bunker.

Once inside Elyse collapsed into Elijah's arms, sobbing in her relief.

"Are we going to die here, Elijah?"

"I can't promise you we won't but, live or die, we will be together. That's all that matters now. Be brave, brat. No more tears." He brushed the hair out of her eyes. "I've got to go. I'll be back."

As Elijah left, Elyse sat down on her make-shift bed on the ground and wiped the tears from her face as she curled into a blanket. She had wanted to cling to him, to beg him to stay inside, safe, with her. Instead, she held onto Dog as she prayed for the souls of the men lost tonight.

She was numb by the time Johnson came to sit by her side. He took hold of her hand and started singing a song. *"One hundred bottles of beer on the wall, one hundred bottles of beer."

Smiling through her tears, she sang along as the Earth continued to shake and quiver beneath them. They had made it down to eighty-nine bottles of beer, when Sarge stuck his head into the bunker and called Johnson outside.

"Someday, Elyse," Johnson said, "I'll buy you a beer."

Elyse smiled. "I've never tasted beer."

"Icy cold, you don't know what you're missing." Grinning, he left with Dog at his side.

ELIJAH KNEW they were in trouble. Food and water were limited, and ammo was running low. Trying to get supplies in was a nightmare, and they could no longer evacuate Elyse without putting more Marines—and Elyse—at risk. The destruction of the supply plane was horrifying in itself but, knowing they could have all been killed if not for Elyse filled him with a relief that horrified him even more. But there was no time to grieve for the men lost aboard the plane. First, he had to keep Elyse safe.

The choppers were fairing no better than the planes, and their scouts relayed that the NVA were now trying to tunnel under their base camp. The team stood in a half circle around him.

"Men, we have to discuss what to do with Elyse if we're overrun. She can't be left to suffer unspeakable horrors and torment at the hands of the NVA if she is captured."

"What the fuck does that mean?" Mountain asked, his anger evident on his face.

"As quickly and painlessly as possible, she will have to die," Cap replied.

Their cries of outrage and anger would forever be burned into his soul.

"You want us to go in there and kill that beautiful woman, a good friend?" Henson cried, as he grabbed the Captain by the collar.

"Stand down, Henson." Elijah shoved him back. "Do you think for one minute that I want to see the life fade from those beautiful eyes? But you must think of her right now, think man, all of you. She would suffer. Beatings, torture, rape by multitudes of men, and if she's lucky, eventually death. Or she ends up on the auction block, sold to the highest bidder. What kind of life would she have then? All that we know of Elyse. What kind of fucking life would she have?

"If we're overrun, and there's no hope. Last man standing, is that understood?"

Looking down at their feet in abject misery and with heavy hearts, they nodded in agreement.

"If we survive, she in never to be told any of this. Is that also understood?"

"Yes, Sir," they replied.

⚜

ELIJAH CURSED the day he brought her here. He cursed the top brass for making the decisions they made. She didn't belong here. This was so unfair to Elyse. She did not deserve to die in a place like this. He was tired. It was his turn to rest, so with a nod to Sarge, he went inside to be with her for a little while.

When Elijah walked inside the bunker, he heard her softly singing, "Twenty-nine bottles of beer on the wall, twenty-nine bottles of beer…" She looked as exhausted as he felt. They both needed a break and some rest.

⚜

SHE LOOKED up as he entered the bunker. The thick black stubble of beard on his face was covered in red clay dust and his eyes held a vacant, sad look.

"Sit down, Elijah." She helped him remove his flak jacket, setting it aside with his helmet and weapon.

Massaging his aching shoulders.

"Are you hungry?"

He grunted his response and watched as she prepared a C-ration for him to eat. He wolfed it down and drank a long drought of Kool-aid from the canteen she handed him. She straightened the sheets and blanket on the floor.

"Come lie down, you need to rest," she whispered.

"I'm filthy, I'll trash your little bed."

"Lie down, we're all filthy," she replied, and he moved to obey her command.

She grabbed a soft cloth and poured water from another canteen on it, dabbing the cloth on his face to wash off the dust. She leaned over and placed a soft fluttery kiss on his lips as he closed his eyes giving in to her touch and his own exhaustion.

Lying down next to him she fell asleep curled into the curve of his body. Held close, his arms wrapped around her holding her to his chest.

They woke to the sound of a massive explosion and the rumble of the bunker as it caved in around them. They could only feel, not see each other.

"Elijah, what happened? Are we trapped here underground?" Panic in her voice, she cried out, "We'll suffocate."

"It's okay, it's okay. We must have taken a direct hit to the bunker. Breath… just breath. Do you smell that? Fresh air is coming in from some-where." Without thinking he ran his hands over her body. "Are you injured?"

"No, just frightened."

"Come here." He pulled her into his arms and held her close to still her frantically beating heart. He knew they would be dug out but not by who.

If it was Americans, great. If it was NVA, he had a hand grenade. It would be better for Elyse to die here with him in his arms.

They didn't mean for it to happen, at least not yet. They were young, buried alive in the deep, dark earth, clinging to each other for hope and comfort. They did not know what the morning would bring or whether they would live to see it.

It started innocently enough with an electrifying kiss. His mouth moved to her neck, her ear lobes, and down to her breasts. Then he pulled her shirt off before he knew it. Elijah was aware she was a virgin. She tasted so good. Each kiss was sweet, and each touch was bliss.

He murmured into her ear as he suckled an ear lobe. "I wish I could see your eyes, and all of your beauty."

She shivered at the raw, sexual awakening of her body. "I need, I want, this ache inside."

Finding her lips with his again, his hands slid further down to roam her breasts and smooth belly, lower still to pull off her boxers and panties. To her backside to grip and squeeze her bottom then back around to stroke that secret place between her thighs. All the while she clung to him as his mouth never left hers.

He had her ready and wet. He entered her, feeling the barrier as he pushed.

"It will hurt but just for a minute," he told her, then he thrust in and she screamed into his mouth. He could feel the wet tears on her face as he kissed them away, giving her time to get used to the feel of him inside her. His lips never left hers as he moved within her. Eventually her legs wrapped around his hips as her hands on his shoulders slid down and around to grip his muscled back.

They only had this time and this place together. He brought her to the edge of ecstasy, and they reached it together as one. She screamed her pleasure into his mouth as he groaned into hers. He had never known such passion in a woman before. She excited him, thrilled him, and he knew he would want her again and again. They laid in each other's arms afterwards, slipping into the darkness of sleep as mortars exploded outside.

When Elijah woke to the sound of voices and shovels digging outside, he reached for the grenade. Then he heard a familiar voice. It was Sarge. *Thank God.*

He gently woke Elyse. "Wake up, brat, they're digging us out." He kissed her one last time.

Soon daylight shone through, and they were pulled from the bunker's wreckage. It was Dog who alerted them with his frantic digging to where within the bunker they were buried. Dog's cries and kisses at their rescue were a sweet reminder of the dog's loyalty. When Elyse looked into Elijah's eyes, they shared a secret, a moment in time. It would never be forgotten. He caressed her cheek, looking deep into her eyes he wondered how he could let her go when the time came. *I can't.*

It was over, finally. The destruction was complete. Nothing remained of the camp above ground, but the American flag still flapped in the wind and most of the five thousand battle scarred and exhausted Marines survived the seventy-seven-day siege to see the sunrise with no sign of the NVA in sight.

❧

AMID, the constant hum of the choppers evacuating the wounded, Elyse, Elijah, and the team walked out to an area close to the helipads and Elyse fell to her knees in shock. The bodies of many brave Marines lay lined up in body bags. Her grief ran deep, and she cried her despair at the loss of life. Elijah held her and let her cry into his shoulder. She had lived through death and destruction of war. Not many American women could say the same.

❧

ELYSE MOVED from wounded man to wounded man, offering a smile, comforting words, and holding their hands. She prayed with them and offered hope. Blood covered her hands as she knelt by a young black Marine who cried for his mother as his life blood seeped through his shirt. The Corpsman at his side shook his head in despair at her questioning look. She looked up to see Father Mitchell kneel on his other side and remained silent while she held the Marines hand as last rites were administered to the dying man. Once he was gone, a silent tear trickled down her face and Father Mitchell reached out to place a comforting hand on her shoulder. She gave him a weak smile as she covered his hand with her own.

"Elyse, it's time to go," Elijah said. Elyse looked up to see Elijah and the team standing above her. Their stricken faces shuttered their feelings as they watched the priest cover the young man's face.

She nodded her head and allowed Doc to help her up. Elijah handed her a bag with her ballet slippers and underthings inside.

"Where did you find it?" she asked.

"On the runway," Elijah replied.

She looked around the base camp at a loss for words. The team had stepped away to speak to a truck driver.

"Elyse, there is only one memory you might want to take away from this place. The rest is best left behind," Elijah said.

"It was beautiful," she said, with a small smile.

"It's hardly how I imagined in my dreams how my first time with you would be. You deserved champagne, rose petals, and a soft bed where I could look into your eyes, not a bunker in the dark," Elijah replied.

"You dream of me?"

"Yeah, I do."

He reached out his hand to stroke her cheek. Keenly aware of the eyes watching them, he let his hand drop to his side.

CHAPTER 11

Elyse leaned against the side rail of the troop transport truck as they left Khe Sanh base camp. Watching the scenery pass by, the truck made its way eastward down Route Nine. Massive bomb-craters, burned vegetation, and the remnants of charred tree's and rice paddies, dotted the war-torn countryside framed by dark lush mountain ranges to the north. They passed by village after village of tin ramshackle shacks the locals called home. She saw the children only once, for just a moment. Standing by the roadside just outside of their village. Half-naked, they waved and called out to the troops. Some brave children risking life and limb, ran up to the trucks in the convoy line whenever they slowed down, they bartered with the troops selling soda for the troops to quench their thirst.

SHE FOUND herself snatched from behind by Elijah and pulled to lie flat on bed of the truck.

"You can't be seen by the locals," Elijah said.

"Why not?" she asked.

"Just do as I say and stay down when we pass by locals."

"The whole country is locals. How could you possibly expect me not to be seen?"

He gave her a wry grin, "We're going to give it our best shot."

❧

ELIJAH SIGNALED for Elyse to sit on the bed of the truck and lean against the back of the truck cab. Sitting down, she glared up at him as he sat on his perch on the bench that ran the length of both sides of the truck. Sarge handed Elyse a piece of gum. She accepted it, unwrapped the treat, and chewed, all the while watching the white fluffy clouds in the sky pass by. The driver rotated between hitting the gas and slamming his brakes and she was tossed from one end of the truck bed to the other. Crawling back up, she grumbled the whole while.

"Stupid truck driver, I swallowed my gum," Elyse said.

"I'm going to put rocks in your pockets to keep you in place," joked Elijah.

"Your boxers don't have pockets, just this funny hole in the front."

Elijah grinned at her. "You have no idea what that's for do you?"

"No, should I?"

"Nope, you're good." He shook his head, she really did live a sheltered life.

The second time she was tossed about, she almost flew out the back of the truck. Only Mountain and Arnold's quick actions kept her inside. Elijah lowered himself down and sat on the bed of the truck behind her and pulled her into the safety of his arms. The bumpy ride had caused her hair to fall from its bun, so she pulled it in front of her and braided it. Elijah was fascinated, not only by how quickly she braided it but by the thickness and length of the braid.

"Why don't you leave it down?"

"It's hot and heavy."

She leaned back against him. Bumpy ride or not, she fell asleep in the comfort of his arms with Dog at their side.

❧

ELIJAH WAS ALWAYS amazed how she, not being a Marine, could fall asleep anywhere. It was a little bit of heaven and hell for Elijah to have her so close. He could smell her exotic scent, watch the pulse on her beautiful neck, and revel in an awesome view of her cleavage. She bounced at every bump of the truck, and he found himself tormented by the little package he held in his arms. He glanced up at his men, and their eyes all seemed transfixed on Elyse's cleavage. He grinned at them and they grinned right back.

❧

ELYSE HAD no idea where she was. This was a big base camp on the east coast of South Vietnam. The truck snaked its way through the congested, ramshackle town. Street venders with their carts mingled with the large troop transport trucks, jeeps, mopeds, and bicycles. The going was frustratingly slow. Elijah and Sarge stood facing forward leaning on the cab of the truck watching the traffic. Elyse sat on the bed of the truck and played a game of poker with the team with Mountain the clear winner. Laughing, she stood to stretch her aching muscles.

She leaned against the side rail of the truck, mesmerized by the South China Sea. The waves rolled in. The water so blue it faded into the sky on the horizon. White caps tinged each curling wave as they crashed ashore against the pristine white of the sand. It was beautiful, and it looked refreshing in the heat of the hot, sticky afternoon. She was hot, grimy, still covered in the red clay dust, and blood from Khe Sanh. She was over the rail and on the run before the team had a chance to blink.

❧

ELIJAH TURNED in time to see Elyse jump the rail. Stunned, they watched for a minute as she ran down the beach, stripping down to her bra and panties as she went, and leaving a trail of her clothes in the sand. Running into the sea, she dived in to come up to cleave the water with strong strokes as she swam further out in the surf.

Elijah pounded on the roof of the cab and instructed the driver to pull over and wait for them. They jumped down from the truck and made their way down to the beach. They stood silently watching her as Dog braved the surf and swam out to where she frolicked in the sea. She played with him for a few minutes, her laughter carrying in the wind mixed with the sound of crashing waves before she spied Elijah and his men standing on the shoreline.

⁂

SIGHING, she prepared herself to face his anger and swam in toward the beach. Walking in, she felt a twinge of guilt; they all looked hot and tired. She stopped at the edge of the water.

Looking contrite, she looked up at Elijah with her big, amethyst eyes. "I probably shouldn't have done that."

He handed her a dirty, but dry shirt and cocked his head toward the right. "Cover up, brat. You have a large audience."

⁂

HER EYES WIDENED, and she turned to see the one hundred or so men further down the shoreline watching her every move. *How did I not see them?* Pulling the shirt on, she cursed under her breath.

Elijah laughed at her. "You just made their day."

"That was not my intention," she said, rolling her eyes.

"Do you feel better now?"

"I feel like a girl again. You and the team should swim."

"And why is that?"

"You're all a little ripe," she said.

"Phew." Arnold exclaimed, after lifting his arm to smell his armpit.

"We need to get on base now," Elijah said.

"Says who?" Elyse asked.

"You're right," Elijah said, grinning at her. "Arnold, run up and get that driver from that sweltering truck. You've all got twenty minutes."

With a "Whoop. Whoop." the men dropped their gear and began stripping off their filthy shirts. Elyse watched with a smile on her face when they started unbuttoning their pants. They stopped and looked at Elyse.

97

"What? Seriously?" she said, but with a roll of her eyes and a wicked grin on her face, she turned her back until they were all in the water. Smiling, she pulled her shirt off, grabbed a bottle of shampoo from a pouch in Elijah's rucksack, and followed them back into the cleansing sea.

❧

TWENTY MINUTES later they were out, dressed, and walking up the embankment to where the truck was parked. Elijah scanned the area for locals and didn't see any. He hoped none had seen her jump from the truck. He signaled to Sarge to bring her forward. As he lifted Elyse up into the back of the truck, he admonished her, "We'll talk later about jumping out of moving trucks."

He narrowed his eyes as she gave him a sweet smile that was pure sass.

CHAPTER 12

Base Camp Two, Chu Lai, Early April

THEY PULLED into the base camp and the truck stopped to off-load its passengers. The men jumped down off the vehicle. Elijah lifted Elyse down from the truck to the customary wolf whistles and catcalls from the troops.

"Oh, for Pete's sake, Elijah, you'd think they've never seen a woman before."

"Not for a long while and not one that looks like you."

Elyse rolled her eyes and gave them a brilliant smile. They escorted her in their protective circle to the commanding officer's office.

Colonel Dixon, a medium height man with a balding head, who fancied himself a lady's man, welcomed Elyse to the camp.

"Miss Booker, would you care to have dinner with me tonight?" She caught Elijah's eye and just as Elijah was about to object to the invitation Elyse declined, claiming exhaustion.

"Perhaps another time, Miss Booker."

"Perhaps, Colonel Dixon."

Elijah escorted her to her tent. "Be very careful of Colonel Dixon.

"Don't worry, I steer clear of icky men like him. I've never dated before, but I recognize the men who give me the willies."

Elijah was shocked. "What? You? You've never been on a date?"

"No, I haven't. I've never had the time for it, and for the longest time my father wouldn't allow it anyway. You were my first kiss, and then I gave you my virginity."

Elijah smiled. "Why is that, why did you give me your virginity?"

She looked into his eyes. "I have no idea." She blushed and lowered her lashes. "It must have been the lack of oxygen."

Elijah laughed out loud at her quip. "Come on, brat. Let's get you inside and away from prying eyes."

THE VIP TENT was located toward the center of the sprawling base camp. Elijah posted four of his men around Elyse's quarters for additional protection. It was more of a screened-in wooden structure than a tent. Surrounded by sandbags, with wooden steps and a small porch. They hung blankets up to cover the windows for privacy for Elyse. It had the normal amenities for a VIP tent, and she was soon settled in.

"Stay inside, Elyse," Elijah said, "I'm going to scout around for the mess hall and head. I'll be back soon."

Elijah returned within half an hour. "This is a different kind of camp. You need to be on your guard at all times. It's bigger and has more troops than the last base camp."

He escorted her to the mess hall. You could have heard a pin drop the moment they walked in. Then a long slow whistle came from one of the tables. With Elijah sticking close to her, they stepped into the chow line.

The food was better than the prior camp, but something wasn't quite right. The cooks were paying more attention to Elyse's breasts than where they put the food on her tray. Elyse was spitting mad by the time they made it through the line. Elyse asked a cook a question about the chicken, but the cook mumbled something unintelligible, never taking his eyes off her breasts, and Elyse lost it.

"Excuse me, What's your name?"

"Private Smith, ma'am."

"Private Smith look me in the eye when you speak to me and keep your eyes off my chest. It's rude and disrespectful." Then she turned on the rest of the cooks. "That goes for all of you. The next time I come through this line your eyes had better be eye level. Understood?"

"Yes, ma'am."

"God. I miss Cookie." With that, she grabbed her tray and headed for an empty table.

⚜

ELIJAH STOOD THERE GRINNING. *Little spitfire.* With an extra added warning look to the cooks, he took his tray to the table and sat down next to Elyse with the grin still on his face.

"What?"

"You're not just a hundred pounds of sass. You throw some fire-crackers in there as well."

She smiled. "A hundred pounds? Where did you get a hundred pounds from? I'm ninety-eight pounds, and I've never hit a hundred pounds in my life."

Elijah grinned at her, shaking his head. "Fine, ninety-eight pounds of sass."

"Nice things come in small packages, Captain."

"Yeah, but so does C-4," he quipped.

More and more everyday Elijah found her spirit admirable.

They walked back to Elyse's quarters in companionable silence. It was a beautiful evening, and Elyse felt like she had steam to blow off. "Will you take me somewhere where I can dance?"

Elijah nodded in agreement. "For a short while at least."

She smiled. "You have my slippers in your backpack."

"Rucksack. It's called a rucksack."

"Backpack," she argued.

Narrowing his eyes at her. "Rucksack."

Laughing at him, she asked, "So, what do you call that green purse you carry in the jungle?"

Elijah looked at her perplexed. "Green purse? You mean my artillery bag?"

101

With a devilish sparkle in her eye, she whispered. "It looks like a green purse to me."

Nodding his head and pursing his lips, he noted the sparkle in her eye. "A backpack is a rucksack, soda is pop, Marines don't carry purses and we, have arrived at your hootch."

Sighing, she asked, "What…. is a hootch?"

He smirked. "A hut, your quarters."

Rolling her eyes, she said, "I completely forgot about my slippers."

"That, my sweets, is because you are arguing with me again."

"I'm not arguing with you. I'm merely explaining to you why I am right." she said with laughter.

They walked over to the officer's quarters. A little worried, she said. "Your quarters are little far away from mine."

"That's why you have four guards at your hooch until I can move closer."

He went inside and returned with her slippers and a radio. They walked to a sandy-grassy area nearby, and he lounged in the sun and watched her as she sat down to put her slippers on. After some warm-up stretches, she spun away, dancing slow and easy to a popular song. He was amazed at the strength in her legs as he watched her well-toned muscles flexing. He smiled, remembering how they felt wrapped around him.

Elijah heard voices behind him, and a group of Marines came over to watch as well. How could any man not watch her? He knew some of the men in the mess hall heard her go off on the cooks. Word would spread not to mess with Elyse. He didn't trust the colonel, though. He just may need to remind the man about who Elyse's father was, and that she was under the Marine Corps' protection. The stay here would be short-lived if the attitude about Elyse didn't improve.

After an hour or so, Elyse had tired, and came to sit with him in the grass. He watched her as she unwound the ribbons from her ankles and pulled off her slippers.

"Is it difficult to dance in the sand and grass?" Elijah asked.

"Yeah. I lost a lot of muscle-tone sitting in the bunker at Khe Sanh. It was a good thing I could at least do my floor exercises there. I find now that my muscles are a little more sore than usual, my stamina and balance are off a bit. Obviously, I'd prefer a smooth stage, but, given no choice, I can work with what I have available."

The sun was setting as he rose to his feet. Holding out his hand to her, he helped her to her feet, and they strolled back to her hootch.

·

ELYSE EXPLORED the base with Mountain and Arnold the next morning. The base was large with paved roads and quite a few permanent buildings, along with tents and barracks for the troops. It seemed everyone drove jeeps around the base. Elyse wanted to learn how to drive. With sweet talk and a brilliant smile, she convinced Arnold to be her teacher. More sweet talk to the requisition clerk and they borrowed a Jeep. The clerk at the motor pool pointed to the Jeep they could use. Elyse stood looking at the Jeep. It wasn't as nice as the Jeep it was parked next to. That one was clean and shiny and had a little flag attached. While Mountain's and Arnold's backs were turned and with a devious smile, Elyse took the flag off and put it on the older beat up Jeep.

With Mountain in the backseat, Elyse driving, and Arnold instructing her, they went up and down the back roads of the camp. When they realized she couldn't see over the steering wheel, they stopped while Mountain grabbed three sandbags from a bunker for her to sit on. Sitting on the edge of the sandbags her feet barely reached the pedals. It was rough going at first, but she mastered the stick and was soon whipping them around the camp. Laughing as she drove up over curbs and back down again. They found their way down to the beach and Elyse laughing, drove up and down the coastline, pluming the wild surf.

Heading back up a sand dune, they made their way back onto the base.

"Right side, Elyse, stay on right side," Arnold yelled, after a near miss with a troop transport truck.

She spotted Elijah and pulled up next to him. "Hey, baby, want a ride?"

·

"What in God's name are you up to now?"

"Arnold taught me how to drive." One look at Arnold and Mountain's ashen faces, and he felt sympathy for them. "You two, out."

They hopped out, Elijah jumped in, and Elyse took off. A look in the rearview showed Mountain kissing the ground. Arnold helped him up, leaning on each other they turned to stagger up the street.

"Okay, Elyse, let's return the Jeep to the motor-pool." It was the wildest ride Elijah had ever had. Pedestrians jumped out of the way as she sped through the camp, and other vehicles gave her a wide berth as she careened around corners. She pulled into the parking spot and shut the Jeep off.

"That was fun," Elyse said. Elijah was a little green around the gills.

Elijah was considering killing Arnold and Mountain. Vietnam was already a dangerous place; they didn't need Elyse behind the wheel to compound it. "Elyse, every word any man has ever said about women drivers is true about you. I think we'll keep you from behind the wheel for the time being. You need driver's education and a license before we let you loose on the world."

Elyse raised an eyebrow. "That was a really sexist comment."

Before he could reply, Elijah looked up to see two MPs with scowls on their faces standing in front of the Jeep.

Elyse slunk down in the driver's seat. "Damn."

Looking over at Elyse, Elijah growled, "What…. have you done?"

⚜

An hour later, Arnold, Mountain, and the rest of the team stood at attention in front of Elijah. He gave them a hard look and then began.

"You allowed Elyse to steal the general's Jeep? Are you numb-nuts out of your minds? You're fucking lucky the general was smitten by her smile and sugar-coated apology, or the three of you would have ended up behind bars."

He looked pointedly at Arnold and Mountain. "Has it ever occurred to the two of you, hell, any one of you, to tell her no? You just weaponized Elyse further by teaching her to drive. She already has plenty of weapons in her arsenal. Your job is not only to protect Elyse, but to keep her out of trouble as well. Next time she gets an idea in her head, I want the two of you to consider your own hides before you let her sweet talk you into her schemes."

"You're dismissed."

✤

ELYSE SIGHED. Ten more jeeps to go. How was she supposed to know shiny and clean with a flag meant it belonged to a general? Taking her bucket and sloshing the soapy water over the hood of the general's Jeep, she took the sponge and tried washing the dust off the windshield. Too short, she couldn't reach mid-window.

Climbing up on the front bumper and onto the hood of the Jeep and kneeling on all fours, she scrubbed the window. Sliding down off the hood, she asked Arnold for the hose to rinse the soapy water off. He handed it to her, and she turned around to see the twenty or so spectators. Trying to ignore them, she rinsed the Jeep off as she listened to their crass comments and whistles. If she had to listen to one more comment about her chest or bottom, she was going to scream.

Arnold handed her his long-sleeved shirt. "Here, this should help."

Smiling her thanks, she put the shirt on. Narrowing her eyes at the group of Marines, she said, "I'm not deaf. I heard every word you said. One more comment, and I'm going to let you have it."

✤

ELIJAH AND SARGE exited the small building with the clerk in time to see Elyse turn with the hose and aim the water straight into the face of a Marine who had wandered up to the group. She hosed the rest of the group down, and they moved back a respectable distance out of the reach of the hose. He didn't hear what the man said, though he could tell she was infuriated by it.

Okay, so maybe this wasn't such a good idea for a punishment, he mused. Elyse, water, and troops didn't mix well. Shaking his head, he strode over to her and took the hose from her hand. "Okay, Elyse, I can't have you hosing down Marines."

105

"You and your priapic Marines all need a cold shower. I have heard enough comments to last me a lifetime." Pointing her finger at Elijah, she said, "Well, let me tell you something. They're mine, my tits, and my ass."

Elijah's eyebrows shot straight up.

"I don't want to hear another word about them. Keep your eyes off of them and your comments to yourselves," she said, stomping off.

"Elyse," Elijah called out.

"What?" she yelled.

He pointed in the opposite direction. "Your quarters are that way."

Glowering at him, she stormed off in that direction.

He nodded to Arnold and Mountain to follow her.

She stomped back to stand in front of him, hands on hips. "Home, take me home. Now, I want to go home, now."

"You're quite the demanding little princess, aren't you? I can't take you home yet."

"What? Why not?"

"It's not safe."

"Safe? Are you serious? So, living through a siege with planes crashing in front of me and the NVA shooting at me, that's all safe? I am going home whether you take me or not. I am a big girl and I can take care of myself. I am going home." Elyse stomped off again, waving her arms and talking to herself. She stopped and turned around. "I will walk to Saigon if I have to. I'm going back to pack, and I am leaving. Just try to stop me."

Elijah watched as she turned around and walked away. "Son of a bitch. What the hell am I supposed to do with that?"

Sarge grinned. "Nothing, you're fucked. What's a priapic?"

Elijah grinned. "I believe, she just called all of us perpetual hard-on's."

Turning back to the men, Elijah gave the silent group a scathing glare before handing the hose to Sarge. "Elyse was right. They do need a cold shower. An hour or two should cool their libido and clean up their mouths in the presence of a lady."

⚜

ELIJAH NODDED to Mountain and Arnold standing guard as he knocked on Elyse's screened door and stepped inside. She straightened the ribbons on her slippers and slipped them into the small bag along with her panties. She smiled ruefully at the tiny number of belongings she now possessed.

"I wonder what happened to my trunk on that second chopper? Though I'm almost positive that even my pretty clothes wouldn't stop the comments or the staring. Hell, even if I wore a gunny sack it wouldn't make a difference. As long as they have any idea of what's underneath, their crude behavior is going to continue. I've never been exposed to this before Khe Sanh. My father's friends were like second fathers to me, and my male friends that I danced ballet with were never interested in me like that. They were just good friends. My guards at the compound, even the Marines who guarded the embassy were respectful. I have been sheltered all of my life. I don't know anything but what you have shown me, but these men said things, and they made me feel dirty and shame. I don't ever want to feel that way again. I won't allow it and I will start fighting back."

"The fault is mine. I should have never punished you out in the open. I won't make excuses for the men, or whatever they said to you, but they are being punished as we speak," Elijah said.

"Punished? How?"

"Let's just say standing at attention for a few hours in a cold shower should get the point across.

"Oh no. That's much too long."

"What did that last man say to you?"

"He called me 'Sugar tits.'" Noting the amusement in his eyes. "It's not funny."

"No, it's not. I'm sorry."

He PULLED her into his arms and kissed the tears off her face. He pulled the pins from her hair, and her locks fell to curl around her breasts and down her back to swing around her waist. His lips moved to her neck and her mouth.

With a growl deep in his throat, he hoisted her up and her legs wrapped around his back. He carried her to the bunk and laid her down. Moving to cover her body with his own, he continued his assault on her lips and slim throat.

Feeling torn, he had to stop, to remember her innocence. Though he had taken her virginity, he was unsure of his own intentions. Brushing the hair from her eyes, he gave her one last kiss and steeled his resolve. When he pulled away from her, she looked dejected. Walking to the door, he said, "You're restricted to your quarters."

Her confusion showed on her face, and he had to turn away.

"I mean it, Elyse. Stay put." With that, he walked out the door.

ELIJAH'S REJECTION of her cut deep. After a few tearful, sleepless nights she bided her time waiting for the perfect opportunity to escape. Just to be home, to sleep in her own bed, to see her father again, to hear his voice. She wondered why she hadn't heard a word from her father. She understood during the siege at Khe Sanh, but now? Something was wrong, she could feel it deep in the pit of her stomach. It spurred her on to leave this base and somehow make her way home. Brushing the ever-present tears from her eyes, she tied the ribbons around her slim ankles. With her confinement to quarters finally over, she was anxious to dance again, to feel free, to be free. Once outside with a nod to Henson and Johnson, she made her way to a deserted field on the far side of the base somewhat close to the main gate. Eyeing the bunker, she looked back at her guards with sadness in her eyes.

"You okay today, Elyse?" Johnson asked.

He doesn't want me. "No, I don't think I'll ever be okay again." With a nod to them she brushed the tears from her eyes and flipped on her radio. Feeling the music, she began to move.

"I don't like this, she's up to something, maybe I should go get Cap?" Johnson said to Henson.

"Yeah, they haven't been talking at all. If anything, Cap has been avoiding her, hasn't even checked in with us on how she's been doing during her confinement to quarters."

"He's been checking with Sarge," Johnson replied.

"Not sure what Sarge would say other than she won't eat and she's crying again," Henson said.

When Elyse jumped up on a perimeter bunker, Henson called to her. "Elyse, you're on a perimeter bunker. Get down."

Elyse turned, blew them a kiss, leaped to the next bunker, her hair flying behind her as she raced away.

"Fuck, go get Cap," Henson yelled. "I'll follow her."

Jumping down from the last bunker, Elyse raced toward the main gate. She ducked under the drop bar and ran down the street, away from the racket behind her. She knew they were all close behind her. Glancing back, she spotted the MPs, Henson, the rest of the Elijah's team and—God help her—Elijah.

She ran faster, leaping over carts in the street and avoiding a moped packed with a Vietnamese family, she ducked into a doorway to get her bearings. Half a block back they spread out to search for her. Looking ahead to her path, she took off again as someone shouted as they spotted her fire-red hair. She ran, she pushed on, narrowly avoiding a crash into pedestrians and bicyclists. She heard the screeching tires of a troop transport truck. She screamed, frozen in fear. Then she felt Elijah's breath on her neck as he pushed her, rolling them both out of the path of the truck.

She rolled to her feet and Elijah rolled to his. They circled each other as Elyse looked for an escape route. They were surrounded by Marines now, and she knew she was trapped so she turned back to him. Her chest heaved from exertion. Mud and debris from the street stuck her hair and road rash ran the length of her left arm.

"Let me leave, Elijah."

"I can't do that, brat."

"You're keeping me against my will."

"I'm following orders, including your father's. You're under our protection," Elijah replied.

"I don't care about your orders. I don't need protection. I want to go home. I am going home."

"That's a brave front for such a little girl."

"Don't patronize me, Captain. I can take care of myself."

"You wouldn't get a half a block from here without being raped or worse."

"Don't let my size fool you. I can defend myself."

"Really? Okay, brat, let's see what you've got."

"Show me yours first."

A snicker from the Marines set her resolve as they continued circling each other.

※

HE MOVED first and was surprised when she laid him out flat with a kick that swept his feet out from under him. He rolled to his feet with a newfound respect, she was far better than average at defending herself. Here he had thought the tiny piece of fluff was bluffing. He advanced on her and returned the favor. She rolled to her feet, and they continued their circling.

A crude comment about American Poontang from a Marine behind her earned him a kick in the face and sent him sailing to land on his back. Elyse turned back to Elijah with determination in her eyes.

※

ENOUGH OF THIS. He took her down again and, this time, he straddled her and held her arms in place over her head with his weight and strength. She struggled to escape, and he roared at her.

"Enough. Stand down, brat. Stop."

She stopped her struggles. They made eye contact, staring into each other's eyes, reading each other well. The sparks flew as neither could deny the attraction or their feelings. Her eyes filled, and she burst into tears.

He moved to his knees and pulled her close to his chest and she wrapped her arms around his neck.

"Shh, brat. I will take you home just as soon as I can, I promise, as soon as I can." He rose to his feet with her legs still wrapped around his back and he strode away from the group.

She whispered through her sobs so only he could hear. "I'm sorry, I'm sorry. I don't understand why you don't want me. I just want to go home and crawl into my bed."

He stopped, whispering hoarsely, "Is that what you think? That I don't want you? I want you more than you realize. I'm trying to do the right thing here, brat."

"We, you and me, we are the right thing."

He brushed the hair from her eyes. "Maybe so, but I can't touch you. What happened at Khe Sanh should not have happened. I knew better, but you're a temptation that I can't seem to resist."

She smiled and laid her head on his chest.

He took her back to her quarters. He knew the moment she fell into an exhausted sleep against his chest. He laid her in her bunk and ran his hand across her creamy soft cheek and fiery amber hair. She was beautiful, both inside and out.

Stepping outside her quarters, he addressed the team. "The locals saw her. We need to throw them off her scent or this base will be crawling with VC by nightfall. Find out if there is a hospital or field hospital close by. If so, find some off-duty nurses. I'm sure the six of you can sniff them out.

"Sarge, you and Doc supervise. I want those nurses in the same area, the same block, dressed the same as Elyse, acting the same way. Tell the locals it's a ritual celebration or whatever ridiculous story you have to tell them to get them to believe that what they just saw wasn't out of the normal for Americans here.

"If the nurses resist, let me know, and we'll get orders from the Commandant. Elyse must be protected, and this will provide cover for her escapade. I'll stay here with Elyse."

He went back inside her quarters.

＊

Sarge, Doc, Henson, Johnson, Mountain, and Arnold all looked at each other.

"Did he just order us to grab some nurses, put skivvies on them, and wrestle them in the street?" Mountain asked.

"You got a problem with that Mountain?" Sarge said.

Grinning, Mountain replied, "No, Sir."

"How many times do I have to tell you meatheads, don't call me sir, I work for a living," replied Sarge.

"All right, ladies, Move."

Four hours later Elijah heard Doc and Sarge return. Sliding out of the chair next to Elyse's bunk, he walked outside to see them laughing about their wild afternoon.

Spotting Elijah, Sarge stated, "Mission accomplished, Sir."

"Where's the rest of the team?"

"Last we saw of them they were pounding down a Shlitz beer with pretty nurses."

Grinning, Elijah replied, "Fraternizing with officers? They'd better not get caught. Any issues?"

"None whatsoever. A pretty fun group of ladies. They were more than willing to participate. All beautiful women. We even found a redhead. Locals were convinced it was all part of our May celebrations."

"Did the nurses question why?" Elijah asked.

"Just the head nurse on shift, and I explained it to her in private with as little detail about Elyse as possible. Elyse can expect to receive some female type items from Alice and the other nurses, and possibly a visit. No pants, though, since they're all tall women and nothing would fit our little black belt ballerina, but she'll see what she can scrape together and send it over."

Elijah nodded his approval. "Good job. Black belt ballerina. I would never in my wildest dreams equate the two together. She caught me by surprise, yeah. She said she trained in Karate, but I'd never seen her in action before today and I put it off to false bravado. I did not take her seriously, and that was my mistake."

Sarge smirked, his eyes held a hint of amusement. "You forgot about when she kicked you back into the stream."

Elijah raised an eyebrow, smiling, he rubbed his chest. "Yeah, I did forget about that one."

Sighing, he said, "I have to go write a report and explain this to the brass. She's still sleeping. Let me know when she's awake."

"Ah, and Sarge, leave Doc here, you'd better go rescue the team from themselves."

Grinning, Sarge replied, "Aye aye, Sir."

TWELVE HOURS LATER, Elyse opened her eyes. The sun was just peeking over the horizon. Realizing she had slept through the night, feeling rested after going so long without proper sleep.

She smiled to herself. Elijah did want her. He had called her a temptation he couldn't resist. She had seen the truth in his eyes and, for now, it was enough. Stretching her muscles, she noticed she still had her slippers on, debris in her hair, and felt the pain in her arm from the road rash. She must look a fright.

Pulling herself together she peeked out the door. Mountain and Arnold were just replacing Johnson and Henson as her guards.

Stepping outside, she greeted them. "Good morning."

"Elyse, you're finally awake," Arnold said.

"I need a shower," she said. "Is Elijah awake?"

"I'll go check. We're supposed to wake him when you got up anyway," Johnson replied.

When Elijah arrived, he walked her to the private shower he had found for her.

"Who taught you karate, brat?" he asked.

"My father. He's a Marine. What is it they say? Once a Marine, always a Marine?"

"Yes, that's true. What's your father's first name?"

"Arthur."

"Lieutenant Colonel Arthur Booker?"

"Yes, now Ambassador Booker."

He gave her a quizzical look. "What?" she asked.

"My father often speaks of your father. I never put two and two together."

"So, it's possible we've met before?"

"If we did, we were children."

⁂

ELIJAH STOOD outside of Elyse's quarters. They had just returned from Elyse's shower. Talking with the team about the heat of the day though it was late morning. Mountain glanced up and watched as nurses walked into the area.

113

"Cap, look, nurses."

Elijah looked up and saw about ten nurses advancing through the area. The determined looking group set their eyes on him and his team, and he felt the hair rise on the back of his neck. *Oh fuck.* Stopping in front of him. A sharp, good looking, middle-aged nurse stepped forward.

"Captain Corrington? I'm Major Boise."

"Yes Ma'am," Elijah replied.

"Captain, I've just come from Colonel Dixon's office. I've been informed that you have a young American woman held here."

"Yes Ma'am, we have a woman here for her protection."

⚓

ELYSE MOVED ABOUT HER HUT, straightening up as she went. Hearing a woman's voice, she stopped and went to the screen door. Looking out the door she noticed the ten or so women, obvious Army nurses, had encircled Elijah and the team. *What's going on?* With great trepidation she stepped through the doorway and out onto the small porch.

All eyes turned to her, and she felt her cheeks flush. She looked from face to face, noting the shock on the faces of the women. She became aware of how she must look to them standing there in Elijah's boxer shorts hanging from her curvy hips, bare belly exposed with Elijah's shirt tied just below her breasts. Suddenly, feeling very shy, and she self-consciously wrapped her arms around herself.

The nurses murmured as one. Major Boise turned to Elijah. The surprise evident on her face. "I want answers Captain. Answers as to why an obvious innocent was not housed with the women. And why a bunch of brutish Marines are holding a lovely young woman captive? And for God's sake, why doesn't the poor little thing have pants?"

Elijah inwardly groaned, and brusquely replied, "With all due respect, Major. We cannot house Elyse with the women unless you also want seven Marine's housed with them as well. Elyse is not a captive, I will explain some details, but not all, to you in private. And I can't find pants small enough to fit her, Ma'am."

Major Boise narrowed her eyes at the handsome Captain.

"Why didn't Colonel Dixon address your questions, Major?" Elijah asked.

"A weak man, he's terrified of me. He directed me to you for answers," she replied.

Elijah's eyebrows flew straight up as he stifled a grin.

⁂

ELYSE FOUND HER TONGUE, "Excuse me. Please don't talk about me while I'm standing right here."

All eyes turned to Elyse. Hands on her hips, "And I am not a poor little thing."

⁂

ELIJAH GRINNED, *That's my girl.*

"I see she has spunk," Major Boise said.

"Oh, you have no idea," Elijah replied.

"Well she obviously needs a little TLC. Give her over to us for a few hours and we'll see to her female needs. You and your hulking brutes can stand guard outside the barracks if you're worried about her safety."

Elijah looked to Elyse. "Is that okay with you? Do you want to go spend some time with the nurses?"

Curious now, Elyse asked, "To do what?"

"When's the last time you had a manicure, honey?" Another nurse asked.

Elyse looked at her fingernails. "Let's go," she replied.

⁂

THE NURSES SWEPT HER UP, and the laughing chattering group moved Elyse along toward the nurse's barracks. Elijah and Major Boise followed along deep in conversation. The team hung back as they also followed along.

"Scary, I don't think they were going to take no for an answer." Mountain said.

Sarge grinned, "I've never seen a more formidable looking group of ladies."

"What are they going to do to her?" Arnold asked.

"Primping and preening, girl stuff. Elyse needs this. She's been stuck with "brutish" Marines a long time," said Doc, as Johnson and Henson laughed at his quip.

"Did you see Cap's face when that Major first confronted him?" Henson said, with a hoot.

"Absolutely priceless," Johnson replied.

ELYSE SPENT the afternoon with the nurses. They clucked at her lack of shoes, and Elijah's boxers and shirt.

"Elyse, where's your clothes?" asked Major Boise.

"The Marines found my slippers and panties at the chopper crash site, everything else was gone. Somehow, they lost my big trunk. So, now I have no clothes, nothing, just two pairs of Elijah's boxers and two of his shirts," Elyse replied.

ONCE THE MAJOR left to see to her duties, Elyse's hair was trimmed, just an inch or so, and brushed till it shone with fire and sun. Then they ratted and teased her hair as they styled it into a fashionable hairdo with lots of hairspray and Dippity-Do gel. After a manicure and a pedicure, her nails were freshly polished with a pale pink color. They put make-up on her, despite her objections to the black eyeliner and heavy mascara. Someone opened a bottle of wine and they laughed, cups of wine in hand. The tipsy group danced up and down the barracks singing the lyrics to favorite songs.

THE NURSES WENT through their civilian clothes looking for something for her to wear.

She stood in front of them in her orange bra and panties, and they murmured at her curvaceous beauty.

"What is that on your bra?" Alice asked.

"Duct tape," Elyse replied.

"Duct tape? Why?" Ellen, a young blonde nurse asked.

"Well, the Marines sort of shot up my bra when they first found me in the jungle," Elyse replied.

They raised their eyebrows and gave her a questioning look.

"It's a long story."

"We're listening sweetheart," Jane replied.

"Well, I tripped, and it caught on a shrub and I ended up in the ditch on top of Elijah without it. Then the VC came into the clearing and my bra was a casualty riddled with bullet holes."

"Honey, what were you wearing after that?" A nurse named Maggie asked.

"Elijah's shirt and boxers," Elyse replied, as she blushed.

"I repaired my bra when we got to Khe Sanh with the duct tape."

Horrified, "Khe Sanh? You were at Khe Sanh?" Jane asked.

"Almost three months, during the siege." she whispered, as horrific memories filled her mind and her eyes filled with tears.

"We had some of the wounded here. The ballerina, you're the ballerina they spoke of. We all thought the men were hallucinating," Maggie, a carrot-top red-head stated.

"Yes, I'm the ballerina," Elyse replied through her tears. "Did they survive? The wounded?"

"Most of them. We patched them up and sent them to Taiwan to recover in the hospital there," Alice said.

"It was bad, so bad. They were so brave." Elyse cried, and the nurses cried right along with her.

"Why are you still with the Marines, Elyse?" Brie, a beautiful brunette, with deep brown eyes, asked.

"Home, I want to go home, but Elijah won't take me yet, and he won't tell me why," Elyse cried. "But Elijah takes care of me and he protects me."

"This Elijah, Captain Corrington, is he your boyfriend?" Brie asked.

"Boyfriend?" Elyse hemmed and hawed, wanting to protect Elijah. "I don't have a boyfriend," she replied.

Someone handed her a shirt to try on and Elyse put it on. Looking in a mirror at the revealing shirt, Elyse caught the looks of the nurses in the mirror. "This will kill the Marines," Elyse said.

Giggling, she pulled the shirt off. "I think I may need something a little more sedate."

"Honey, with that chest it's not going to matter too much. Anything you wear is going to kill them," Maggie replied, with a giggle.

You have a choice of giving them a sudden heart attack or a slow agonizing death," Brie said.

Elyse laughed, "Let's go with slow and agonizing, and how about some more of that wine."

ELIJAH and the team stood outside the nurse's barracks. Nurses came and went as the shifts changed. The team enjoyed themselves as they tried to engage the nurses from the previous day, but only received giggles as the nurses flashed flirtatious smiles at Elijah and the team.

ELIJAH LOOKED at his watch again. "What the hell could they possibly be doing in there for five hours?"

"I don't know, though I could hear they were singing a while ago." Mountain said.

"Girl stuff takes time. Hair, make-up, nails. All the customary female trappings," Sarge said with a smirk.

"Hey Cap, did you see that one chick, she was looking at you like you like she knew you," Johnson asked.

Elijah shrugged his shoulders, perplexed. "Never saw her before," he replied.

"We can expect Elyse to come out with her hair and make-up done. Maybe some new clothes. She'll be looking pretty and refreshed from her afternoon at the beauty parlor," Elijah said with a smile.

Elijah looked up as the door opened and Elyse, swaying, stood on the stoop with a few of the nurses. He did a double take, his mouth dropping wide open. Looking over at the nurses, who were also swaying as they stood beside Elyse.

"What the fuck did you do to her?" Elijah said to the nurses.

Elyse's once fashionably styled hair stuck straight out like a rat's nest from her head. The heavy eye make-up they had painstakingly applied had run with her tears and smeared around her eyes and face. She wore a red ruffled skirt that went mid-calf and white peasant blouse off one shoulder. She held a paper bag full of girl items in hand.

As she swayed back and forth, obviously intoxicated, Elyse giggled, "I had a wonderful time."

"You look like a raccoon, a drunk raccoon," Elijah laughed.

❧

"See, that's my Marine, the others are mine too, but I don't kiss them, just him." she said to the nurses with an exaggerated whisper.

"Did you know, Elijah, they have wine in there." She whispered with a hiccup.

Elijah grinned. "I see that. So, you had a wonderful time?"

More hiccups. "I had a wonderful time. And I learned a new word too. 'Horny.'" She giggled as she almost fell over. "At least the nurses explain what words mean, unlike Marines, who say many naughty words, but won't tell me what they mean," she whispered, with another hiccup.

Elijah's raised an eyebrow as he reached out to steady her and help her down the steps.

❧

The team stood back from them, watching, and they couldn't stop the grins that split their faces.

"Always, always, expect the unexpected with Elyse," Doc said.

"I'd sell my soul for a camera right now," Mountain replied, with a deep grin. He looked over to Sarge, Henson, Johnson and Arnold. They

119

couldn't hold it in, and their infectious laughter spread deep into rolling belly laughs.

"Drunk raccoon. Oh man, I am never, ever, going to let her live this one down," Arnold said, as he wiped the tears of laughter from his eyes.

※

"I SHOULD GO HOME TO BED," Elyse giggled. "Ooh, Elijah. There's a nurse in there. She said you look just like someone she knows. Her name is Brie. Do you know her?"

"No, no I don't," he replied, with a smile.

"Her man, he's in the Army, looks just like you but with blue eyes. She lost track of him and can't find him. His name is A-something, I don't remember now. I had a wonderful time."

"Yes, I see that. Let's get you to bed."

"Are you coming to bed with me?" Elyse asked.

"No, no, I'm not," Elijah said, with a grin and a shake of his head.

"Did you know Elijah, that I put the Ooooo- in your rah."

"Yes, you do," Elijah replied, amusement sparkled in his eyes and he laughed outright.

They started to walk toward her quarters.

"I want to dance." she veered off and started to spin and twirl.

"Nope, nope, no dancing. We're going back to your quarters," Elijah said. He picked her up, hoisted her over his shoulder and they headed back to Elyse's quarters with the hysterical team falling in behind them.

CHAPTER 13

An old Sherman tank was parked on the side of road of the base camp, maybe from WWII or Korean conflict. Elyse danced up to it, fascinated. She climbed up on top of the tank. Peeking inside, she couldn't see much so she climbed in to get a better look. She saw buttons, gadgets and knobs as well as a periscope. She raised and lowered it while peering through the lenses.

After pushing a succession of random buttons, she gasped when the tank roared to life. Terrified, Elyse tried to shut it off. Voices erupted outside the tank. She was trying to climb out when she stepped on a lever and broke it off. It fell on the floor jamming the foot petals down. The tank rolled forward.

"Damn…"

Despite her trying to shut it off, it kept moving forward. She was able to pull herself up to peer out the top to see Mountain and Arnold standing back where the tank had been parked with mouths hanging open.

"Help me, I can't shut it off," Elyse cried.

They ran after the tank and climbed up on top. They lowered themselves inside and all three of them tried to shut the tank off.

"Elyse, what buttons did you push?"

"I don't know. I didn't think it would start without a key. Don't you think it would need a key?" she replied.

They searched for a key. No luck. The men pushed random buttons trying to stop the tank, but the turret on top began to turn as the tank accelerated even faster. "Look for brakes or something," cried Mountain.

Outside of the tank, they could hear excited voices yelling, "Get out of the way."

They felt the tank go up and down as if it ran over something more than once.

"The periscope. Use the periscope to see where we're going," Arnold said.

Elyse pulled it up to view through the lenses. "Oh God. A fence and soldiers everywhere. Get out of the way." They crashed through the fence in a continuous forward motion.

"Pool, a pool. We're going into a swimming pool. Did you know they had a pool here? We should go swimming one of these days," Elyse said.

"Come on, Elyse, we have to get out," Mountain cried.

Arnold climbed out and Mountain pushed Elyse up to Arnold before climbing out himself. Just as the tank hit the pool and dropped in, they jumped from the side of the tank into the water. They swam to the far side of the pool from the now partially sunk tank with its treads still rotating. Climbing out, they looked back at the tank and looked at each other.

"He's going to kill us," Elyse said.

They turned around to find three MPs standing behind them.

"Damn."

All three of the MPs looked at Elyse and down at her breasts, smiling. Elyse followed their line of vision and shrieked. Her nipples beamed through the lace of her bra and shirt. Covering herself with her arms she glared at them.

ELYSE SAT with Mountain and Arnold in the brig.

"What a bummer, we are in deep shit," Mountain said. "Cap is not going to be happy."

"What do you think he's going to do to us?" Elyse asked.

"I don't know, firing squad," Arnold replied.

Elyse looked at him, horrified.

"I'm teasing you. *Khong Xau. Though guaranteed, we are going to get fucking smoked," Arnold replied.

"You guys speak in the oddest language I have ever heard. It's Marine Corps jargon, slang, cursing, all mixed up with Vietnamese. Do any of you just speak English?" Elyse said.

Arnold and Mountain gave her their boyish grins.

Elijah, Sarge, and the head MP walked into the room.

Elyse took one look at Elijah's face. She whispered to Arnold. "Maybe you're right about that firing squad."

"Ten-Hut." Sarge shouted.

Her guards stood at attention at the bars as Elyse stood in between them wringing her hands.

"I can explain," Elyse said.

⚜

ELIJAH WAS LIVID. He looked at the three of them, noting Elyse's wet hair and the large, long-sleeved shirt someone had given her that went almost to her knees.

"She's dangerous when she's wet," the head MP observed.

Elijah replied, "She's dangerous no matter what." He addressed them in a deadly calm voice. "A block and a half of destruction, a row of heads, two tents, three Jeeps, fences, and the fucking pool. Not to mention the tank. Are you insane? Whatever possessed the three of you to take a tank and drive it into the FUCKING POOL?"

"Elijah, I didn't mean to drive it into the pool. I tried to shut it off. They were helping me," Elyse said.

"You had no business turning it on or going anywhere near that tank. What will it take to get you to behave Elyse? You have been told a thousand times that military equipment is off limits. You are bound and determined to do as you please, and you will be punished for it."

Elyse glared at him knowing full well to keep her mouth shut.

"The tank will be removed, and the pool drained. The three of you will spend however long it takes to clean the grease and grime from the pool. You're restricted to your quarters until further notice."

The MP unlocked the door, and Elijah grabbed Elyse by the arm and pulled her out of the cell.

THE NEXT MORNING, they stood poolside. The tank had been removed and most of the water had been drained except for the deep end which still had a couple of feet of water in it. A coating of oil, grease, and grime covered the entire interior of the pool. Elijah handed Elyse a toothbrush and a bucket of soapy water.

"A toothbrush? Are you serious? This will take forever."

"Then I suggest you get your sweet ass into the pool and get busy."

Elyse glared at Elijah. "This is not fair."

"What's not fair, Elyse? You make a mess; you clean it up."

Arnold and Mountain were already hard at it. Elyse climbed down the ladder at the shallow end and started scrubbing a wall. She worked beside them, muttering under her breath, *who would have thought you could start a damn tank without a key.*

Music played from a radio not too far away. She shuffled her feet to the beat of the surfer song, singing the lyrics. Arnold and Mountain joined in, soon they were dancing right along with her, doing the Twist, the Swim, and the Watusi. When she tried to move, she slipped on the greasy pool bottom and landed on her bottom. She slid down toward the deep end, squealing with laughter as she spun about. She slid all the way as Arnold leaped to grab her arms, while Mountain held Arnolds feet. Continuing their slide down the slippery slope all three plopped down into the remaining water in the deep end.

Giggling, Elyse tried to crawl back up only to end up sliding down again.

Laughing hysterically, try as they might they could not get back up. They'd push each other up only so far just to slip and slide back down to plop back into the water.

WALKING BACK from surveying the damage Elijah heard their laughter. He had never heard Elyse laughing so hard before. He watched their antics for a few minutes. He had no doubt in his mind that the three mischief makers, hell, Elyse, and the whole team were the best of friends. In an odd way, he took comfort from the thought. They might get into trouble, but they would always protect her from those who would seek to do her harm.

Elyse glanced up to see Elijah standing at the edge of the pool, hands on his hips, scowl on his face, just as she slid back down. Mountain and Arnold attempted to stand up in the water, but Elyse's feet slid out from under her, and she went down again, taking them with her.

"Elyse, I'm going to tan your hide."

"You're going to have to get me out of here first."

Sarge walked over and stood looking at the threesome, shaking his head.

"Sarge, go find a rope." Elijah ordered. Returning a few minutes later, Sarge threw the rope down to them. Mountain and Arnold tied it around Elyse's waist, and Elijah and Sarge lifted her out. Then they worked on getting the other two out.

Eventually all three stood in front of Elijah, covered head to toe in a thin coat of motor oil and grease.

Elijah was exasperated.

"How, Elyse?"

"This is not our fault."

"Oh, I beg to differ. This entire fiasco is your fault."

"If you ever even breath on another tank again, you will not sit down for a month." In the end, maintenance had to use a powerful degreaser to clean the pool. Elyse, Mountain, and Arnold did two weeks of *KP duty instead.

CHAPTER 14

Elyse sat outside of the kitchen door taking a break from the heat of the kitchen with Mountain and Arnold. One week into her two weeks of KP, she enjoyed the work and took great satisfaction in seeing the smiling faces of the troops every day. Taking a sip of her soda she reflected on Charlie, the head cook. It had been a rough start from when she first arrived, but she got on famously with the cooks now. This morning, the head chef told her about the above average number of troops coming to eat at the mess hall she frequented. He told her they came to see her. She told him he was full of beans, that it was his fabulous cooking that brought them.

When she first started her KP, Elyse told Charlie she was a dangerous cook so she wouldn't be much help there, but she could organize, clean, and wash pots and pans pretty well. Charlie had decided that she would be an excellent server. So, she, along with Mountain and Arnold, who were doing double duty as her guards and their own KP punishment, served the troops their breakfast and lunches.

Holding the icy cold soda to her forehead, she was annoyed that her hair was curling into tight little tendrils around her face. Brushing the escaping tendrils back she smoothed her hair. The thick braid hung down her back.

Sighing, she stood up. "I suppose it's time to go back inside, boys."

Mountain and Arnold guzzled their sodas down, belching, they followed Elyse back into the massive kitchen. It was almost lunch time. Elyse tied a clean apron around her tiny waist. Looking down at her feet she smiled. Charlie had presented her with a pared down pair of men's shower flip flops to wear on her feet. It was a kind gesture, and she appreciated them considering the floors could be slippery and grimy by the end of the day.

She and Mountain stepped up to the serving line. The troops had started filtering into the mess hall. With a smile on her face she bantered with the men as they came through the line. They teased her, and she gave it right back at them. She heard it all: offers of marriage and dates, requests for her to stick her finger in their food to sweeten it up, and so many other questions. She laughed at how outrageous they were.

One man asked if she was on the menu. She pointed to a new sign on the wall that read, "Elyse is NOT on the menu."

One man asked her to marry him. She pointed to the gold band on his hand. "I'm not sure your wife would appreciate that too well."

"Ah come on, Elyse, you've heard of bigamy before."

"And I'm sure you've heard of a 'foot up your ass,'" she replied.

The men in line guffawed, and he grinned. Occasionally, she'd run into a man who couldn't take his eyes off her breasts. She'd snap her fingers in his face, and say, "Eyes, up here."

Elyse turned to grab a new pan of mashed potatoes from Arnold. When she turned back around, she was eye level with the waist of a man who had shuffled up the line. She started from there, but he just kept on going. He had to be six-nine. Finally meeting his amused eyes, she raised her eyebrows at the massive size of the Marine.

"What in God's name did your mother feed you to make you so big?"

Grinning at her, he replied, "Women. Teensy, weensy, women."

"Cheeky Marine. You're only getting mashed potatoes here."

The next Marine was nearly as big. He said, in a southern drawl, "Well aren't you just the cutest little thing. I think I'll just put you in my pocket."

Elyse grinned. "And what would you do with me in your pocket?"

"Why I'd just reach in every now and then and give you a little tickle."

Shaking her head and laughing, she said, "I bite. Consider yourself warned."

With a grin, he winked at her.

"You Marines are all impossible." she said in mock exasperation.

The next man was huge, with the widest shoulders she'd ever seen. He had tousled blond hair and the kindest blue eyes. Elyse glanced at the last name on his uniform: Olafson.

"Oh, good grief. A Viking."

He gave her a lopsided, endearing grin. "Viking, yeah," he said, his voice a deep rumble. "I'm about ready to go 'a Viking.'"

"You don't have a longboat or horns on your helmet."

"I can still capture me a slave girl."

Pointing her spoon at him, she said, "Behave, Viking, I'm already a captured slave girl."

Laughing at her, he said, "By who?"

"Why, the Marine Corps, of course."

He hooted with laughter.

The next man in line was small and thin. The man next to him explained to him that all he had to do was tell Elyse what he wanted to eat. A little befuddled, Elyse caught the eye of the second man with a questioning look. It was obvious to her the first man was slow-minded. Shaking her head, she wondered how such a man could be here in Vietnam.

Looking back at the man in front of her, she asked, "What's your name, sweetheart?"

"Jasper," he replied.

"Jasper, would you like some mashed potatoes?"

He nodded. "You're pretty."

"Why, thank you, Jasper. That's very kind of you."

ELIJAH WATCHED her from his place in line. She handled them all smoothly and kept the line moving, though not as fast as it should. He smiled and shook his head at how she laughed and bantered back and forth with the men. He was up next. Looking at him from beneath thick lashes, she spooned some mashed potatoes onto his tray.

"Well, speak of the devil," she said.

"Are you going to sweeten it up for me, Elyse?"

"Oh, I think you've had enough sugar for one day, Captain."

"You think it was enough, brat?"

"Maybe you're right." She put her finger in his mashed potatoes and gave them a swirl. Smiling, she stuck her finger in her mouth and licked.

Smiling while watching her, he nodded. "Okay, brat."

He sauntered over to a table at the far side of the hall to eat his lunch.

Sarge was up next, and she filled his tray as well. "I guess Cap should be careful what he asks for, huh, Elyse?"

Laughing, she said, "You got it, Sarge."

Laughing, the remaining team followed in line.

A Sargent stepped in front of Elyse. "Now that's what I like to see, a woman who knows her place."

Thinking he was joking, Elyse said, "And what place is that, Sargent?"

"Why, honey, there's three places a woman belongs: in the kitchen, on her back, or on her knees."

Elyse blinked. "Excuse me."

The men in line stopped talking, clearly waiting to hear Elyse's response.

"Yeah, a whore like you? Only thing you're good for is wrapping your pretty lips around…." Mountain reached across the table and grabbed the man by the scruff of his shirt.

"Let him go, Mountain," Elyse said. "You'll get in trouble. I'll take care of this myself."

Mountain released him and shoved him away as Elyse stepped around the serving table. Taking off her apron and throwing it to the floor, she slipped off her flip flops.

The Sargent laughed at Elyse, beckoning her closer. "What are you going to do about it, honey?"

Her first kick landed on his face, with another to the chest. Next was a knee to his balls, which had him doubled over, and her final kick sent him flying on his back and skidding across the floor of the mess hall. Following him, she knelt down, reached over, pulled his knife, and held it to his crotch.

"I pity you if you think there's no other value to a woman, Sargent. I pity you that you will never know the true love of a woman. I didn't understand everything you said, but I know it was sexual in nature. You're a nasty, small-minded, pathetic, little man and if you *ever* speak to me like that again, I will cut your balls off and shove them down your throat."

⁂

ELIJAH LOOKED up to see Elyse practically flying, her moves were so fast and smooth. She kicked a man and sent him skidding across the mess hall floor. The mess hall went silent in shock as Elijah flew across tables with Sarge and the team close behind.

He looked down at the man lying on the floor, who was bleeding from his broken nose and sweating profusely. Then he saw where she held the knife.

"Okay, Elyse," Elijah calmly stated. "You've made your point. Put the knife down."

Elyse stood and threw the knife to the floor. She took in all the astonished faces of the men in the full mess hall. Her eyes welled, and the tears rolled down her face.

"No, Elyse," Elijah whispered. "No, no, don't cry."

Wiping her tears with her hands, she turned and walked back into the kitchen, picking up her apron and flip flops along the way.

"Sarge, get that piece of trash out of the mess hall," Elijah ordered. Turning to Mountain, he asked, "What did he say to her?"

"He said a woman's place was in the kitchen, on her back, or her knees, and then he called her a whore and wanted—"

Elijah cringed at the man's crudity. "That's enough, Mountain, I get the picture." He followed her out into the kitchen. "Elyse?"

She stood at the sink, washing out a dirty pot. She turned to him. "I'm sorry, Elijah."

"No, I'm sorry I subjected you to the verbal abuse of animals."

"He's the only one. His venom caught me by surprise, and I was too quick to anger."

Elijah pulled her into his arms, and she sobbed against his chest.

He lifted her chin and kissed her lips.

Mountain and Arnold walked in, saw the kiss, turned their backs and prevented anyone else from entering the kitchen. "Are you ready to leave?"

"No, I need to finish the pots and pans first."

"Okay, brat. Don't stay too long. Keep Mountain and Arnold close."

On his way out he stopped to speak with the team. In full hearing of the men in the hall, he said, "I want you fully armed while guarding Elyse. Even though Elyse is a damn good black belt, I don't want to risk her being injured. Defend her. I don't care about the rank of the individual. I don't care what it takes. Protect her from anyone who attempts to physically or verbally abuse her."

❦

OUT IN THE MESS HALL, the men were stunned at what they had just witnessed. A slow whistle and a newfound respect set the tone. Talking amongst themselves, they concluded that you didn't mess with Elyse, she must be a virgin, and that their seven-man team would protect her at all costs. They wondered who she was and why she was on base.

❦

THE NEXT MORNING, Elyse was back at the mess hall serving breakfast with a smile on her face. Each man who came through her line complimented her and told her how they appreciated her smiles to start their day, laughing, she acknowledged them with a smile on her face. *smooth talking, cheeky Marines.*

❦

THE DESERTED MESS hall had cleared out, with the men off to their various duties. Elyse came out of the kitchen with a bucket of soapy water and a wash rag in hand, intent on washing off the tables she stopped to stand in front of the fan to cool her skin for a moment. A radio played a familiar tune as Elyse hummed along washing the tabletops. A song came on the radio, one of Elyse's favorite rhythm and blues tunes to dance too. Looking around, she thought, *No one's here. Why not?*

131

Kicking off her flip flops, she climbed on top of a table, eyes closed. She danced with sweet and slow abandon. Only opening her eyes to leap from table to table, she gyrated her hips, shimmied around benches, performed pirouettes and slow twirls, and swung her bottom back and forth. Her body felt the music, and she moved in rhythm to the sultry beat. When the song ended, and she turned around, she saw at least twelve Army Green Berets standing at the far side of the hall. They were fresh in from the jungle and looked dirty, tired, hungry and clearly surprised.

Damn. Elyse blushed a delicate shade of pink. "I'm so sorry. No one was meant to see that."

Their captain stepped forward. "That was perfectly fine with us."

"I'm not surprised." Elyse replied, smiling. "Are you hungry?"

"Yes."

"I'll tell Charlie and we'll get you some breakfast."

Elyse jumped down from the table and went into the kitchen. She found the cook and told him of the hungry soldiers, newly arrived from the jungle. Charlie went out to see how many men there were and to ask for a few minutes to make them some hot food. They whipped up some scrambled eggs, sausage, toast, and a fresh pot of coffee. Elyse and the cooks brought the food out, and the men jumped in line. Elyse and Mountain filled their trays with the fresh breakfast fare. Bantering back and forth with the men, they took their trays to the tables to eat. The last man in line was their captain.

A bewildered look in his eyes. "A fiery, dancing Venus. Why are you here?"

"Why am I here?" amused, Elyse replied. "KP, of course."

"KP? You're not a Marine."

Laughing, Elyse replied, "My secret is out. What gave it away?"

Looking her over, he grinned. "The whole tiny package. So, what did you do to get KP?"

She shrugged her shoulders. "I drove a tank into the swimming pool."

"You're joking."

"Well, not on purpose."

"You're wearing a Marine's shirt and boxers."

Laughing, she nodded. "Yes, I have no clothes."

"A woman with no clothes? Impossible."

"Well, I have lots of beautiful clothes in my trunk, which is lost somewhere in Vietnam."

"Your eyes are almost purple, like Amethysts."

"And yours are blue, Captain."

"You dance beautifully."

"That's not how I normally dance. You men are always sneaking up on me when I'm dancing. I was unaware of your presence."

"How do you normally dance?"

"Ballet, I'm a ballerina."

"A ballerina? Here in Chu Lai on a Marine Corps base doing KP? This just gets stranger and stranger. Why *are* you here?"

"Chu Lai? So that's where I am. I don't have the answer to that, Captain. Captain Corrington does, though. Let me know what you find out."

His eyes widened, excited now. "Captain Corrington? Which one?"

She gave him an odd look, "Elijah."

"Elijah, he's here? Where?"

"He's coming in the door right behind you."

❧

ELIJAH ENTERED the mess hall door with Dog at that very moment. He stopped to eye the ravenous soldiers eating their breakfast. Spotting the captain standing in front of Elyse, he strode toward them with a big smile on his handsome face. It had been too long since he had seen his brother.

"Brendan."

"Elijah."

Hugging him, Brendan asked, "What are you doing here, Elijah?"

"Special assignment." Reaching over, he tickled Elyse under the chin. "I see you've met her."

She narrowed her eyes at him and slapped his hand away.

The captain raised his eyebrows.

"Elyse, this is my brother, Brendan," Elijah said. "Brendan, this is Elyse Booker."

"Of course, Operation Amethyst." Brendan said.

Elijah caught his eye and shook his head. *Quiet bro… she knows nothing.*

133

"BROTHER?" Elyse looked at the name on his shirt. Corrington was spelled out clear as a bell. She wondered how she had missed it. "Yes, now I see it. You're both tall, dark, and annoyingly handsome." She smiled at them, and they grinned the same grin right back at her. "Breakfast, Captain?"

"Sure, why not," Elijah said.

She ladled some eggs along with sausage and toast onto his tray.

"What, no sugar today?"

Grinning at her, he said, "No, I'll pass. Though I may take you up on your offer later."

"Your eggs are getting cold, Captain. I suggest you eat them before you end up wearing them."

Brendan laughed. "A pepper pot, she's a tiny pepper pot."

Laughing together, the brothers sat to eat their meal. Elyse stood for a moment trying to remember what she was doing before their arrival. Dancing, she blushed again. What was she thinking? Dancing on the tables? Tables. She had to finish wiping down the tables.

Walking out into the dining area she found her bucket and wash rag and proceeded to wash down the tables. She hummed along to a tune on the radio, singing and swaying to the music as she moved from table to table.

ELIJAH AND BRENDAN spoke of family and the war. Brendan leaned over to watch Elyse, ignoring what Elijah was saying. Turning around, Elijah saw her, grinning at Brendan.

"If I wasn't in here, she'd be dancing," Elijah said.

"That's where we caught her when we came in, dancing on the tables."

"The little shit. She's forbidden to dance until her KP is over."

"Yeah, she said she drove a tank into the pool."

"Did she mention she took out a row of heads, some tents, jeeps, and a fence along the way?"

"Nope, she didn't mention that. It sounds just like some of our own adventures as kids. I seem to remember us driving some tractors through old man Hector's cornfield."

Elijah laughed. "Yeah, and Aunt Meg chasing us through the house with her wooden paddle when she found out. I still miss her, life's not the same without her."

Brendan pointed to Elyse. "That's a beautiful woman you've got there. How are you managing?"

"I've got a six-man team, a big dog, and round-the-clock protection for her."

Brendan chuckled. "That's not what I was asking. How are *you* managing? As in, keeping your hands to yourself?"

"It's complicated."

Brendan clamped his lips together to contain his laughter.

⚜

ELYSE FINISHED up with the tables and called to Dog to follow her back into the kitchen.

⚜

"DIMPLES." Brendan exclaimed.

"What?"

"She's got Venus dimples on her backside, one above each cheek."

Turning, they watched her make her way into the kitchen.

They looked at each other and grinned. "You've got to love dimples," Brendan said.

"You need a shower, dude," Elijah said. "You reek."

"Yeah, I've been stewing in my own stench so long I forgot how bad I smell. I'm off for the showers and a long nap. See you at lunch."

⚜

ELYSE WAS ready for lunch after a break to clean up. She brushed her hair and re-braided it in two French pigtails and then put on a clean tank top of Elijah's and tied it in a knot under her breasts. Exiting her quarters, she was followed by six fully armed members of the team and Dog. Looking at them oddly. "Guns and knives, boys? You know we're just going to serve lunch, right?"

"Cap's orders, Elyse."

"Where were you this morning?"

"Outside the mess hall."

"You know you're going overboard on this."

"Talk to Cap," Sarge responded.

"I intend to."

Elyse entered the deserted mess hall, shoving thoughts of Elijah's over-protective nature aside as she made her way into the kitchen to the welcoming greetings from the cooks on staff.

"Hello, boys," she said, tying a fresh apron around her waist. "Are we ready?"

"Almost, Elyse." Arranging bowls of fresh fruit and platters of cookies for the soon-to-arrive hungry men. She thought of the troops in the jungle and the awful C-rations they had to eat. It wasn't fair; those men needed to eat just as well. She knew Charlie worked hard to prepare and package hot meals to be delivered to the troops out on missions, but more often than not they ate the C-rations.

Carrying a hot pan of mashed potatoes out to the serving table, Mountain and Arnold walked on either side of her with Johnson and Henson taking up positions on both ends of the chow line. Sarge by the mess hall entrance and Doc by the kitchen entrance. Elyse was seething. This was completely unnecessary.

"I love you guys," she said, "but this is ridiculous." Elyse plastered a smile on her face and forgot her anger for a while. She bantered back and forth with the men and one private pointed out that she was, indeed, on the menu today. Looking over at the sign someone had crossed out "NOT." Giving them an exasperated look and pulling a marker from her apron pocket she corrected the sign.

Bending over to grab a utensil she had dropped every man in line peered over the table to either ogle her bottom or peek down her shirt depending on their point of view. Standing up she realized she had forgotten one necessary item she needed for serving men. Grabbing the piece of duct tape, she had left on the edge of the table she slapped it on her shirt and chest to hold her shirt next to her skin. She shook her head at them, and they grinned back at her.

"You're all impossible."

Elijah and his brother Brendan stepped in front of Elyse. Brendan watched with amused raised eyebrows as she unconsciously and angrily plopped huge, multiple, spoonsful of mashed potatoes onto his tray. She pointed her spoon at Elijah. "Why is the whole team here? And armed to the teeth to boot?"

"They're necessary for your safety."

"No, they're not."

"Don't argue with me, Elyse."

Plopping another large spoonful of mashed potatoes onto Brendan's tray, she said, "So what are you going to have them do? Shoot the next man who insults me?".

"Excuse me?" Elijah stepped out of line, strode around the serving table, and grabbed Elyse by the arm. He pulled her along through the kitchen toward the back door.

"Stop. Where are you taking me?"

"We're taking this outside."

"No, why are you so unreasonable?"

"I'm not."

"You are. I'm a big girl and I can take care of myself."

"Outside, now." He tried to pull her by the arm, but she pulled back again.

"I don't want to go outside."

"Either you turn around and walk out that door like the big girl you say you are, or I carry you out like a spoiled, petulant brat. Elyse." he growled.

"Fine." she gritted out.

⁂

BRENDAN WATCHED their interaction with an amused look on his face. The attraction was strong and obvious between the two, and the battle of wills told him she was going to give Elijah a run for his money. Grabbing his tray with an overflowing mountain of mashed potatoes, he stopped in front of Doc, watching them through the screened kitchen door.

Looking at Doc, he said, "Do they always argue like that?"

"Every day, Sir."

"It's good for him."

"All I can say, Sir, is that I've got nine thousand miles between me and my daily argument. Some days, I miss it, and some days, I'm grateful."

With a smile a mile wide. Brendan said, "Couldn't have said it better my-self."

Doc eyed Brendan's tray with a questioning look at the excessive amount of mashed potatoes on it.

Brendan laughed. "With every word she spoke I got another spoonful."

Doc grinned. "Enjoy your lunch, Sir."

"I DON'T NEED ADDITIONAL SECURITY," Elyse said.

"Don't argue with me, Elyse. You have no say in the matter."

"No say? Are you seriously saying that to me? Who do you think you are?"

"I am the man who takes your protection seriously. I won't allow another replay of yesterday's fiasco."

"I doubt anyone would be stupid enough to think they could speak to me like that again. Why do you think I held that knife to that man's crotch? Not only to get the message across to him, but to send a message to those watching that I don't mess around. I expect and demand respect and I can defend myself."

"That's not the point. Someday you're going to come across someone you can't beat. There's always going to be someone who is better. It happens to all of us. I don't want you injured or worse."

"The team will get tired."

"The team are Marines, they're just fine."

"So, we agree that we disagree on this?"

"Yes."

When he looked deep into her eyes, her anger vanished. "Don't do that. I'm supposed to be angry with you."

"No, you're not. You're supposed to understand that I want you safe."
He pulled her into his arms.

"Oh, so this is how you want your sugar?"

"You're sweet and sour, Elyse, and I can't decide which one drives me more insane." With that, he kissed her petal soft lips. When he remembered where he was, he set her from him. "Get back to work, brat. You've got KP to finish."

THE LINE at the serving table was empty. Elijah grabbed his lunch tray and sat down across from Brendan as Elyse went back into the kitchen. Brendan looked at Elijah and, with a chuckle, continued to eat his lunch.

"Women," Elijah muttered.

Five minutes later he heard her scream, and the sound of pots and pans clattering in the kitchen had Elijah flying back out of his seat.

Elyse came running out of the kitchen and Elijah caught her in his arms.

"What's wrong?"

"A bug."

"A bug? You're screaming because of a bug?"

"It was a huge, enormous, bug."

"Elyse, you're killing me. Unless the bugs are at least six feet tall, you are forbidden to scream over pests."

Elyse glared at him. "All the pests I know are at least six-foot-two."

He narrowed his eyes at her. "Arnold, you and Mountain go check for bugs so I can finish my lunch in peace."

"Aye, Sir," they said in unison.

Arnold and Mountain went into the kitchen with Elyse following behind while Elijah sat back down.

Brendan chuckled. "Looks like you've got your hands full."

"She kicks the ass of a man one day and the next she's screaming over bugs," Elijah replied.

Brendan grinned.

A huge racket erupted again from the kitchen with the sound of pots and pans hitting the floor along with more screams.

"Son of a bitch. What the fuck is going on in there?" Elijah slammed his fork down and was back on his feet heading toward the kitchen again. Elyse followed by Arnold and Mountain raced out of the kitchen with Arnold tackling Elyse to the floor.

"Don't run, Elyse." Mountain and Arnold yelled at her. "Did it bite you?"

"What the fuck are you three up to now?" Elijah asked.

Mountain glanced at Elyse. "Cap, that was no average bug. It was a scorpion."

Elijah dropped to his knees, scooped Elyse up, and flipped her over, looking for bite marks, running his hands over her arms and legs. "Were you bit, Elyse? Were you bit?"

"No. Why? Elijah, stop it." She slapped his hands away. "Put me down. I'm fine. I wasn't bit by the bug."

"Scorpions are poisonous and deadly."

Elyse was indignant. "Oh, so this one doesn't have to be six feet tall?"

"No, but please, no more screaming."

"That wasn't me this time." she snapped.

Elijah's eyebrows shot straight up and he glared at Arnold and Mountain.

Elyse groaned. *I just threw them under the bus.* "I mean, yes, yes, that was me. I'll try to stop screaming."

Elijah narrowed his eyes and looked the three of them over as they nodded their heads in agreement. "Elyse, I think I've had enough for one day. Let's go. Mountain and Arnold, you two can finish your work here."

Guiding her with his hand on the small of her back, he stopped back at the table to grab his tray, Brendan was laughing, pounding his fists on the table, tears running down his face. "Oh my God, Elijah. Is this what you go through?"

"Every fucking day, Brendan. Every fucking day."

Elyse glared at them, pointing her finger at Brendan. "You have made my shit list." Then she turned on Elijah. "And you, you ought to be grateful I'm here to bring some spark to your boring ass existence. The very least you can do is give me a gun so I can shoot the bugs less than six feet tall." With a toss of her pigtails, she stomped out the door.

With a grin on his face and a nod to the team to follow her, Elijah clapped Brendan on the back, dumped his tray, and headed out the door.

As Elijah walked her back to her quarters, Elyse said, "It's not a bad idea. Give me a gun."

"No, absolutely not."

"Don't be unreasonable, Elijah. Why can't I have a gun? I'm well-trained."

"We do not arm women. The subject is closed."

"You do understand that I own my own gun. I'm a sharpshooter and I'm pretty damn good."

"The subject is closed." He growled at her.

Elyse's mouth dropped open in outrage.

"Shut your mouth brat, you'll let the gnats in."

ELIJAH SAT with Brendan outside of Elijah's new quarters just across the pathway from Elyse's.

"Where are you heading next Elijah?" he asked

"Depends on the fighting. We're making our way south. It takes some coordination to make sure we're not moving her into a battle zone. The Tet Offensive threw a wrench into our plans. Now with Saigon and the embassy in shambles we can't take her there. Our options are limited. The bases in the rear are too big, and I worry more about our own forces. It's like a game of strategy."

"Yet she fights you?"

"Elyse has no idea what's going on. She thinks we're holding her captive."

"Why don't you tell her?"

"My orders are to keep it from her. I have no choice. How did you hear about Operation Amethyst?"

"Let's just say I was an adviser of sorts and leave it at that," Brendan replied.

Elijah raised an inquisitive brow.

Elyse sighed as she stepped outside her door. Spotting Elijah sitting across the way with Brendan, she was still stewing from his earlier comment about not arming women. She glared at Elijah. *Male chauvinist.*

Dismissing him from her mind and with a look to her guards, she walked off with Johnson and Henson scrambling after her. Catching up to her, the three headed off in the direction of the powder room. A few minutes later Elyse stopped outside the powder room door.

"Oh, for Pete's sake." *They put them up there just to get a rise out of me.* She ripped the poster of the naked woman off the door handed it to Johnson and went inside. A few minutes later, stepping back outside, she shut the door and there behind the door stood an ancient Montagnard man with a group of his men.

Dressed in loin cloths with long necklaces around their necks, they had wild hair and faces painted in terrifying designs. Their bow's in hand with packs of arrows on their backs, they were a fearsome lot. Startled, she screamed her terror as the old man smiled a toothless grin and reached for her. Johnson and Henson, standing not ten feet away, jumped into action as she took off at a run. Screaming Elijah's name, she ran with Johnson, Henson, and at least ten Montagnard men including the old man in hot pursuit.

Elijah chatted with Brendan while watching for Elyse's return. He sat straight up in his chair, the hair on the back of his neck rising at her first scream. "Elyse."

Both he and Brendan were out of their chairs and running toward the sound of her screams. The remaining team sitting not too far away from them outside of their own quarters followed suit. Her screams had stopped.

"Where is she?" Elijah screamed.

"There Elijah, follow the men running." said Brendan.

They followed the men pushing their way to the front of the pack.

ELYSE SAT on her knees on the ground. Johnson and Henson stood on either side of her with their backs touching each other. M-16's drawn and pointed at the Montagnard's who encircled them.

*

"MONTAGNARD'S. What the fuck are they doing here?" Elijah asked.

"Actually, they're with me," Brendan replied.

Elijah and Brendan stepped into the tense circle.

"Stand down men, they mean Elyse or you no harm," Brendan said.

Johnson and Henson looked to Elijah for confirmation, he nodded his head in agreement, and they lowered their weapons and moved to stand behind her.

The old chieftain spoke directing his comments to Brendan. Brendan acting as the interpreter nodded his head and turned to Elijah.

With a twinkle in his eye. "The Chieftain realizes this is unusual, but he is in search of a new bride since his old wife has passed, and he has chosen Elyse," Brendan said.

"What? Are you serious? He's got to be one hundred years old," Elyse cried, as she made to rise to her feet.

"Stay down and silent," Elijah hissed. He had heard of the Montagnard's, though he recognized them he was unfamiliar with their language, customs, or the place of women in their society. He looked at Elyse, her eyes, wide as saucers as she sat back on her knees.

As the chieftain spoke Brendan continued to translate to Elijah.

"He is willing to forego the usual customs of his people and instead of you paying him the bride price to take Elyse off your hands he will pay you."

Elijah raised an eyebrow then looked down at Elyse, her mouth had dropped open in shock.

"The chieftain offers you three goats and five chickens as her bride price."

The chieftain spoke more at great length.

"He said that even though she is puny and not at all sturdy, he still feels that her fire hair and her large breasts will more than make up for it." Brendan's amusement was evident as his eyes met Elijah's.

143

The chieftain spoke again.

"He just raised the bride price to an ox, four goats and six chickens including the rooster. Not a bad offer as bride prices go," said Brendan, clearly enjoying himself.

Elijah looked down at Elyse, the outrage clear on her face. Turning back to Brendan.

"Tempting," Elijah replied.

Turning to the chieftain he addressed him as Brendan interpreted his words. "Thank you for your generous offer but no. I have already marked the woman as my own."

"You're sure bro, I mean, come on, four goats."

Elijah narrowed his eyes at Brendan. "You're enjoying this way too much."

Brendan addressed the Chieftain, "He thanks you for your generous offer but no, the woman is highly prized and satisfies him for now. If she no longer pleases him, he will contact you to make arrangements. We highly value the relationship between our two peoples and do not want a woman to come between this partnership."

Clearly disappointed, the Chieftain nodded his understanding, turned, and left with his men.

Elijah offered his hand to help her up, and she slapped it away and got up on her own.

"So, you were tempted?" she snarled.

Elijah laughed out loud. "Be nice, I can always call him back."

"Oh, you are insufferable," she hissed. "I am not for sale."

She was taken aback at the flicker of sorrow in his eyes before he shuttered his feelings. Thinking to question him further she decided now was not the time. She moved past him and stopped in front of Brendan.

"And he clearly said five goats."

Brendan was surprised. "You understood what the Chieftain said?"

"Every word, Captain."

ELIJAH AND BRENDAN walked behind her watching the angry swing of her hips and when she entered her quarters and slammed the door shut, the echo carried far and wide as every man around hit the ground.

"Quit slamming that fucking door." Elijah roared after her as he and Brendan got up off the ground and sat back in their chairs. Looking at each other, they burst into laughter.

CHAPTER 15

The flagpole stood in the center of camp, its red, white, and blues flapping back and forth in the light wind. Just above the flag, Elyse's orange bra also flapped in the wind. She wondered how they managed to get it up there. It wasn't attached to the line that raised the flag at reveille and lowered the flag at retreat. Elyse narrowed her eyes. It was her only bra. *So much for hanging my clothesline outside.*

"What am I supposed to do with this, Arnold?" she asked.

"I have no idea, Elyse."

"Someone in this camp wants me bra-less."

"Everyone in this camp wants you bra-less," Mountain piped in, looking up at the flag pole.

Elyse gave him an irritated look.

"They greased the pole so you can't even climb it to get it down," Arnold said.

"Then there's nothing I can do, is there?" Elyse replied.

"Nope."

"I wonder how long before Cap spots it?" Arnold said.

"I'm not telling him." Mountain replied.

"If I get yelled at for tempting the troops, I'll tell him but, for now, I'll figure something out," Elyse replied.

A DAY LATER, a few minutes before reveille Elijah saw Elyse's bra flapping in the breeze. He looked over at Elyse and back up at the flagpole.

"Are you missing something?" he asked her.

She blushed a few shades of pink. "Um, yes, and it's up on the flag-pole."

"Why didn't you tell me?"

"What was I going to say? Obviously, someone stole it from my clothesline. I don't know how long it's been up there, but there it is."

Glancing at her breasts, he asked, "Why are you flat?"

"I figured something out."

"What did you do to yourself?"

The trumpeter blew his horn, Elijah stood at attention, and Elyse stood at his side with her hand over her heart. Afterwards, he took her by the arm and led her back to her quarters.

"Take it off," Elijah said.

"What?"

"Your shirt. Take it off."

"Elijah."

"Take it off."

"Fine." She pulled it off. She had duct taped her breasts flat.

"Why, Elyse? First you don't tell me about your bra on the flagpole, and then you do this to yourself."

"Elijah, I'm well-used to taping myself flat since that's what I do for ballet performances."

"You don't see too many chesty ballerinas, granted," Elijah replied.

"I use a special tape for performances. This tape is all that I could find here. I've been using it on my toes for months."

"Why?"

"It's excruciatingly painful to dance on your toes, Elijah. It's just what we do to manage the pain."

"How are you going to get that duct tape off of your skin?"

"I've tried. I can't."

"Why did you put it on to begin with?"

"Stubborn pride, I suppose."

147

"I didn't want whoever put my bra on the flag-pole to have the satisfaction of seeing me braless."

❦

ELIJAH NODDED HIS UNDERSTANDING. "Let's get this off, then we'll figure out something else."

He started pulling tape from her skin. Her skin was tender and raw by the time he finished. Elyse was relieved and Elijah was angry, not so much at Elyse but whoever had put her bra up the flagpole. It was disrespectful to the flag to begin with, and Elyse had suffered because of it. He'd deal with that when he was done here.

He left Elyse washing her tender skin with soap and water to remove the sticky tape residues. He went in search of the team and then a ladder. They were able to get it down eventually. Henson handed it to Cap. Elijah noted the patchwork duct tape holding the bra together. It also had to be rough on her delicate skin. He shook his head at her stubborn pride. She could have told him of her needs. He stuffed the bra inside his shirt and headed to the PX.

Once inside the PX he was directed to a small area with a few women's items. Lingerie, small vials of perfume, and trinkets. He looked around for more and was told that was all they had for women. Disappointed, he had hoped to find some clothes or shoes for Elyse. After paying for the items he had chosen for Elyse, he left the PX with a smile on his face.

❦

ELYSE FOUND the box on her bunk. Inside was an orange lace bra and matching panties.

Smiling, Elyse softly stroked the exquisite fabric. Elijah had excellent taste in women's underthings. She found the old bra at the bottom of the box and a bag of red licorice.

CHAPTER 16

It was the middle of the night when Elyse woke up starving. Peeking out from the blanket covering the door she saw that Sarge and Doc were guarding her. When their backs were turned, she opened the screen door gently and snuck off at a run toward the mess hall. The streets were dark. Spotting the patrol guards, she avoided them as she made her way across the base. Along the way, she remembered that she only had on Elijah's shirt and her panties.

Damn. I'm not going back to get dressed, I should be in and out of there in a heart-beat. She pulled the screen door open to the mess hall. It was dark inside as she tiptoed her way to the kitchen. After two weeks of doing KP here, she knew where everything was stored in the massive kitchen. While rummaging around in the fridge she found some fried chicken legs. With one in her mouth and one in her hand, she moved to the freezer chest. The big tub of chocolate ice cream was her goal. Finding the prize she sought, she reached into the bottom of the freezer. With her bottom adorned with red panties up in the air and her legs dangling, she grabbed a hold of the tub.

The lights flipped on. With a squeal, Elyse stood up fast, bumped her head on the freezer lid, and turned around. With a chicken leg hung from her mouth, the tub of ice cream cradled in her arms, and her other hand holding a chicken leg, she realized what she must look like.

Three MPs and Charlie stood staring at her. One of the MPs, after giving her a disapproving look, left immediately.

"Damn," Elyse mumbled.

With a glance to the MPs, Charlie, the head cook asked her, "Are you hungry, Elyse?"

"Starving."

He grabbed a bowl, took the ice cream from her and scooped a large portion into the bowl. He took her out to the dining area to eat. "Sit and eat, but you'd better make it fast. I'm sure Captain Corrington will be here shortly."

Damn. He's going to kill me.

❧

CHARLIE AND ELYSE chatted while she ate. He adored her. Her two weeks of KP had been the most enjoyable time of his deployment. She had given him a lot of ideas for streamlining the serving line, and his kitchen had run a lot smoother because of Elyse. If not for the MPs, he would not have sent for the Captain.

❧

THE MP WALKED UP to Sarge and Doc. "Are you missing something?"

They looked at each other and ran for Elyse's door. A quick look inside told them the obvious.

"Where is she now?" Sarge asked.

"The mess hall. She was hungry."

"Fuck." Sarge said, glancing at each Doc.

"Do we have to wake, the Captain?" Doc asked.

"Unfortunately, yes," the MP replied. "She needs to be released to an officer."

Sarge knocked on Elijah's door. "What is it?"

"Elyse snuck out of her quarters. The MPs have her at the mess hall."

"Son of a bitch." Elijah pulled his trousers on as Sarge entered. "Even you, Sarge? How did she get past you?"

"She's good, Cap, really good."

Elijah grinned. "I'm not surprised." Pulling his boots on, grabbing his shirt. "Okay, let's go collect our ninety-eight pounds of mischief."

Doc waited outside with the MP, and all four headed to the mess hall.

Elijah, Sarge, and Doc along with the MP entered the mess hall. The other two MPs stood just inside the door. Nodding at the MPs, Elijah's eyes adjusted to the low lights of the mess hall. Elyse sat across from Charlie, laughing and chatting with an empty bowl of ice cream and the bones of two chicken legs in front of her. Charlie got up when Elijah entered the hall. Elyse sat staring at her hands in her lap, she peeked up from lowered lashes to check Elijah's mood.

"You were hungry?" Elijah asked, his voice low and gruff.

"Yes." she replied.

"Why didn't you just ask?"

"The kitchen was closed. I didn't want anyone to get into trouble with me for raiding the fridge."

"So, you snuck past Sarge and Doc to roam the base in the middle of the night?"

"More or less."

"And you didn't think they would get into trouble for letting you sneak out?"

"It didn't occur to me. I never intended to get caught."

He nodded. "Okay, let's go. We'll talk when we get back to your quarters."

Elyse stood and walked around the long table. Elijah's eyes widened at her lack of boxers. She had on his shirt, which had shrunk and hung to just above her hips. She had on no bra and red panties.

"Like that? You left your quarters dressed like that? Are you out of your fucking mind?"

"What? I forgot the boxers. I'm mostly covered."

"Turn around," he growled at the men, and then he took his shirt off

151

and flung it at her. She slipped it on, and it hung mid-thigh, covering her panties. Grabbing her by the arm, he made his way to the door with his charge.

"Thank you, Charlie." Elyse called over her shoulder.

THE MEN LEFT STANDING there grinned. "God. She's hot."

ELIJAH TOOK Elyse inside her quarters and sat her down on a chair. Pacing back and forth in front of her, he ran his hands through his hair. "It's bad enough that you escape your guards, sneak out, and wander a base with over seventeen thousand Marines in the middle of the night, but to do so half-naked is by far the stupidest thing you have done to date. You are lucky you were caught by decent men. There are men out there who are not so decent. They would have left you raped with your throat slit."

"Elijah, I'm a black belt. I can defend myself."

"We've had this conversation before. Against some, maybe. There are hardcore men on this base. Men I know. Men who wouldn't even blink an eye at your self-defense and take you down."

"Elijah."

"Shut up and listen: if you ever do this again, you will not sit down for a month. Take this as your final warning, Elyse. You will regret it if you sneak out again. I don't care if you're hungry, thirsty, need to use the head, or whatever reason comes up in your brain. You go nowhere without your guards. Do you understand me? Do you understand me?"

Lifting her chin, Elyse ground out, "Yes."

"Elyse, I see defiance in your chin. Mark my words: this is your final warning. You're restricted to your quarters for the foreseeable future."

She glared at Elijah. "Fine."

CHAPTER 17

Elijah and Elyse strolled toward her quarters. He had taken her to the beach that day as a reward for behaving the past week. Producing an umbrella for shade and a large blanket, he had surprised her with a small picnic lunch with peanut butter and crackers, apples, bananas, bottles of soda, and a beer for him.

ELYSE SPREAD the blanket out while Elijah watched. Pulling the blanket back on her chosen side, she proceeded to dig two holes in the sand.

"What are doing?" Elijah said.

"Well, I'm making...." She stopped. "I'm making... um...." She blushed. "Titty holes."

Elijah raised an eyebrow. "Titty holes?"

"Well yeah, a girl has to be comfortable."

Elijah threw back his head and roared with laughter. "Only you, brat, only you."

"Don't be silly, lots of girls do it, haven't you ever taken a girl to the beach before?"

"No, you're my first," Elijah replied.

Elyse pushed the blanket back into place and settled herself on the blanket, placing her breasts in the holes.

"Good, I don't like to think of you with other girls."

Elijah sat back under the shade of the umbrella, looking at her skin and how she had rolled his boxers, so they were close to her magnificent ass. "You're going to burn that fair skin, brat."

"No, I won't. I have my Italian grandmother's skin. I tan very well, except my nose. It freckles."

Dog padded over and laid down on the blanket, gnawing on a large steak. Elijah looked at him oddly. "Where did you get the steak, boy?"

"He probably stole it off the grills further down. Serves them right after what they tried to pull the other day when I was down here with Johnson and Henson."

"What did the troops do this time."

"They put up a sign that said 'topless only beach.'"

Elijah grinned. "I take it you ignored it."

"Of course. They're relentless. They'd die if they saw my French bikini."

"You have a French Bikini?"

"Yeah, mostly strings, not much fabric, totally inappropriate. I bought it one day in total defiance of my father. I've never worn it."

"I'd like to see that."

"Find my trunk, Captain," Elyse said.

"Let's swim, I have an urgent need to cool down." Elijah replied.

After an hour or so, they packed up their belongings and headed back to her quarters.

They were almost there when Elyse heard an odd whistling noise overhead. She hadn't even blinked before she found herself being hauled like a sack of potatoes and rolled on her back into a trench with Elijah on top of her. The barrage of incoming missiles, gunfire, and return gunfire as the base was defended by the troops was deafening. Elyse covered her ears. Elijah prepped his ever-present weapon while peering out of the trench

"Stay down Elyse. Don't move."

Two more soldiers joined them in the trench. They were taking heavy fire. Elyse laid flat on the ground eyes squeezed shut. She opened her eyes just as one of the soldiers fell back with a bullet to the head. Elyse looked on in horror. When the second man fell, Elyse looked at Elijah, the only one defending their position from this trench. She grabbed an M-16 rifle and started returning fire on the enemy trying to get through the perimeter fencing. She was not going to allow them to take Elijah from her.

ELIJAH THOUGHT it was one of the men returning fire with such accuracy. He was more than a little shocked to look over and see it was Elyse. Right now, he had no choice. His rifle jammed and Elyse tossed him the M-16 that she had just reloaded. She grabbed the other soldier's rifle. The attack lasted a few more minutes, and then it was over. By Elyse's estimation she had killed five men. A Marine was well-trained to deal with death. Elyse was not. She covered her face with her hands and her whole body shook from the shock. Elijah gently pulled her into his arms. He remembered how he felt after his first kill.

"I hate this place, and I just want to go home." she cried.

"I know, I know." He kissed the top of her head, the pain for her showing on his face.

One of the men was dead, and the other gravely wounded. Elyse shoved aside her feelings about the firefight and tried to staunch the blood of the injured man while they waited for the medic to arrive. She whispered with the injured man and calmed his fears. When he passed away, she held him in her arms, speaking low into his ear, and eased his way into heaven.

Elijah watched her while squashing his own pain as she cried deep gut-wrenching sobs. When she quieted, he told her they would come for the two soldiers and take them home. He climbed from the trench and lifted her out. They were both covered in blood, dirt, and sweat.

Elijah found his team. All had survived the attack.

Some of the tents and buildings still stood. They found a private shower still standing for Elyse. Elijah stood guard as she showered and then took his turn while she waited. They returned to her tent. She didn't want him to leave her, so they lay on her bunk in each other's arms.

"Elijah?"

"Yeah?"

"I killed five men today. Am I going to hell?"

"You? Never. You eased that young Soldiers pain and suffering. You're an angel. Rest now, Elyse."

***

THEIR SECTION of the camp was pretty much in ruins. They would have to move her again. This time they were leaving by boat because they couldn't spare any choppers. Elijah made all the arrangements while waiting for Elyse to wake up. If she didn't wake soon, he'd have to carry her to meet the boat.

She woke up in his arms just before they got on the boat and snuggled into his chest. "Where are we, Elijah?"

"Almost to the boat. Then we'll meet another chopper at another location, then on to the next base camp."

"You know this is getting old, right? I don't understand why you don't just take me home to my father."

"We can't yet."

"Did you kidnap me?"

Elijah was stunned, "No, of course not."

Elyse looked into his eyes, feeling that he had told her the truth, she nodded her head.

***

THE SWIFT BOAT was moving fast upriver. While Elijah had gone inside the cabin to talk to the skipper, Elyse climbed to the top of the cabin. She wanted to feel the wind in her face as the boat raced up the river. They passed other patrol boats filled with Brown-water Navy men who patrolled the rivers and waterways of South Vietnam. In the distance, Vietnamese fishing boats overflowing with peasants, livestock, and fish floated downriver.

Elyse sat down, listening to the song on the radio, stretching out her legs and leaning back on her arms she lifted her face to the warmth of the sun, the wind, and the gentle cooling spray of the river. A chopper flew overhead with troops hanging out the doors to catch a glimpse of her. When they got buzzed by a second chopper Sarge called to Elyse.

"Elyse get down before the Captain or the locals see you up there."

Elyse breathed a sigh of resignation. Anything that might give her a moment's enjoyment was not to be allowed. "Fine."

She climbed down and leaned against the railing with Sarge as they watched the locals who lived in the hootches alongside the wide river going about their day.

"Look at that, Elyse," Sarge said, pointing out a young girl guiding her little round boat in the opposite direction on the far side of the river. "What kind of boat is that?"

"It's called a Thung Chai," Elyse offered. "It's a kind of bamboo basket the locals invented to avoid a boat tax by the French."

"How do you know so much about Nam, Elyse?"

"My father has been the ambassador through multiple administrations. I've lived here since I was ten."

"You've been in country for, what, eleven or twelve years now?"

"Almost twelve, Sarge. I don't remember what life was like in the United States. These people, Sarge, these people are beautiful. Their culture is beautiful and most, are just trying to live their lives stuck between a rock and a hard place. The VC or NVA come through, take their food, and sons to fight. They rape their daughters, hide their weapons in their villages. Then when the Americans come sweeping through, they find the weapons and burn the villages to the ground. No one wins in this war. Not the Americans or the locals because you don't know who to trust."

Sarge nodded, as she moved to sit leaning against the bulkhead. Elijah came out of the cabin and sat next to her. Elijah commented on the bruises along her upper arm, drawing the attention of the team who had lounged on the bench and floor of the boat.

"What are these bruises from?"

"Are you seriously asking me that? You're all guilty of bruising me."

"What?"

"You all need to take more care. I'm ninety-eight pounds and you're all big men. Every time I turn around, one of you throws me into a trench or a bunker, and I end up badly bruised and sore."

"I guess we'll all have to practice rolling you into a bunker without hurting you," Elijah replied.

Elyse rolled her eyes. "I don't want to be rolled period. I've already been flattened like a pancake by you."

His eyes dipped to her breasts. "We missed some parts."

She narrowed her eyes. "Don't even go there, Captain."

THEY PULLED up to a make-shift dock near the LZ.

"Cap, locals," Johnson said.

Elijah looked around, "Son of a bitch. Elyse, crawl, get inside the cabin. Sarge, take Mountain and Arnold, find out how many troops are up there, round up the locals, and clear a path through the village to the helipad so we can get through there without her being seen."

They walked up the pathway lined with troops, the villagers had been moved well away from the area before they passed through the small village and over to the landing zone where the Huey chopper waited for them. Elyse looked at Elijah, "Oh, hell no. Nope. No way. I've had e—"

A blast of wind turbulence from the chopper sent Elyse flying, her body rolling with each rotation of the blades. Elijah raced after her. He pulled her back to him. Racing back to the chopper he lifted her up to helping hands, and then he jumped on board.

He shook his head. "You literally blew away in the wind."

Elyse, exasperated, rolled her eyes. "That one doesn't count. It's not real wind."

CHAPTER 18

It was a longer flight to the next base. They had to change choppers because of a leaky fuel line to get to their southern destination. They were dropped off on a landing zone staging area lined with a few hundred troops at rest waiting to be airlifted north into battle.

The team stood in a tight circle with Elyse in the middle as they got their bearings. They talked amongst themselves about the plans for the next base while they waited for the arrival of the next chopper.

"Excuse me. Let me out," Elyse said.

Ignoring her, the team members continued their conversation.

"Will you big lugs, please move?"

"Do you hear a little squeak?" Arnold asked Mountain.

Mountain laughed. "Yeah, kind of like a teensy mouse."

"It sounds like a chipmunk," Henson said.

Playing along, Elijah added, "It's more like a gopher."

"Or a hamster," Johnson offered.

"No, a guinea pig," Doc said.

Sarge grinned. "Squirrel. definitely a squirrel."

They were all big men, towering a foot or more over her head. They all looked down at her as she crossed her arms and tapped her foot.

"Oh, Elyse, there you are," Elijah said. "Did you say something?"

"Very funny."

Grinning at her, Elijah said, "Okay, move out."

They walked down the road in their standard "protect" formation, with Elyse in the middle surrounded by the team. The troops surrounding them jumped to their feet and catcalled and whistled at Elyse as they jostled each other to get a glimpse of her as she walked by.

ELYSE ESCAPED the protective circle and stopped to chat with the men along the way to wish them luck in the upcoming battle. With Henson and Johnson at her side, she greeted the troops. Spotting an injured man with his head wrapped in bandages, she knelt down next to him.

Smiling, she asked, "Do you have a boo-boo?"

"Yes, ma'am."

She kissed his forehead. "There, that should make it better."

The Marine grinned from ear to ear. "I've got another one on my shoulder."

Laughing, Elyse said, "Don't push your luck, sweetheart." She moved on until she came to where Elijah and the rest of the team sat.

ELIJAH LEANED against his rucksack on the ground watching as Elyse made her way up the dirt road. Her lilting laugh bringing many a smile to the faces of the troops. He watched as she sat next to him and gave him a brilliant smile that lit her face up.

"You're an angel. You put a smile on their faces," Elijah said.

"It's got to be hard heading into battle. I can't even imagine what it must feel like."

Elijah handed Elyse his canteen. "Drink some Kool-Aid, brat."

"I can't. I already need to find the powder room and that will make it worse."

Elijah glanced toward the distant tree line. It was quite a way's away. *Damn. A woman complicates things.* "Really, Elyse?"

She rolled her eyes at him. "What else am I supposed to do?"

"Okay, relax, Mountain and Arnold, you two take Elyse to the tree line. You know the ropes. Give her privacy but do not leave her alone."

※

As Elyse straightened her clothes, she glanced up and looked straight into the eyes of a Viet Cong guerilla. She let loose a bloodcurdling scream. The VC guerilla, knife in hand, jumped at her just as Mountain and Arnold turned around. Mountain threw her to the ground as they unloaded their ammo into the man.

※

Pulling Elyse back as they retreated, they saw at least ten VC appear out of nowhere. They weren't firing their weapons which told them they wanted Elyse. Arnold and Mountain fired their weapons and killed at least three more. The remainder disappeared, but they continued firing into surrounding foliage.

"We gotta get Elyse out of here," Mountain cried.

"Crawl, Elyse. Stay behind us, low to the ground and crawl," Arnold said.

They were almost to the end of the tree line when six VC jumped out at Elyse.

Arnold killed two more. "Run, Elyse. Run."

※

Elijah stood watching the tree line on the other side of the meadow of tall grass blowing in the wind, anxiously waiting for the three to appear. They were taking too long. Dog, on a leash next to him, growled and whimpered his worry.

His blood ran cold at Elyse's scream and the erupting gunfire. Elijah and two hundred Marines went into instant battle mode and raced toward the tree line.

"Elyse." Elijah shouted. His heart raced and everything seemed to move in slow motion. He saw her running toward him with the VC in pursuit. He let Dog off leash, and the dog raced ahead with him and the remaining team close behind.

※

ONE OF THE VC tackled her from behind and another grabbed her feet and dragged her through the tall grass toward a *spider hole. She kicked him in the face and climbed back to her feet, fighting back. A kick to the groin, a throat punch, and a sidekick to his face sent the one man flying, but she was still being circled by three VC.

A second man jumped toward her, but Dog arrived and jumped the man, tearing at his throat with his sharp teeth. Elyse stood her ground in hand-to-hand combat with the remaining two. Mountain and Arnold were engaged in a full-on assault with the VC as they had backed up to the edge of the tree line. Arnold turned and screamed at Elyse to get down. She hit the ground as Arnold and Mountain emptied their weapons into the two remaining VC, and those still within the tree line.

On the run now, Arnold and Mountain scooped up Elyse, one on each side racing toward the troops, her feet no longer touching the ground. When the VC started shooting toward them, they threw Elyse to the ground again and hit the dirt themselves.

"Stay down, Elyse. Don't move," cried Arnold.

Huey Gunship choppers appeared out of nowhere and mowed down the tree line. The two hundred Marines were even with them on the ground returning fire on the VC. Mountain and Arnold were on top of Elyse protecting her with their own bodies while returning fire themselves. It went on and on for Elyse.

※

THE NOISE WAS DEAFENING to her, the smell of gunpowder, grease and the taste of fear mixed with the chaos of choppers coming and going. The wind, dust, and the screams of a full-on firefight as more and more VC crawled from their spider holes in the ground to engage the Marines.

Arnold and Mountain moved from on top of her, pulling her along as they crawled back toward the road further away from the gunfire as Elijah appeared at their side.

※

ELIJAH PULLED her into his arms. "Elyse, are you okay?"

She looked at Elijah stunned at what had just happened. She started to shake and couldn't speak. Terror still lit up her eyes.

Elijah had to get her out of the middle of this firefight. At a full run, he carried her back to the road and sat down with her still in his arms. "Come on, brat. Look at me. Are you okay? Are you injured?"

She opened her mouth, but no words came out. She burst into tears and her body shook with wracking sobs. When she finally found her voice, it was a whisper.

"Oh, God, Elijah, I was so scared. I was so scared."

"We've got you now. You're safe."

※

AN ARMY CHOPPER LANDED NEARBY. Elijah carried her to the chopper and set her inside. Dog jumped in and curled up next to Elyse to comfort her. Elijah and the team ran back to grab their gear. The chopper's gunner looked at Elyse who was focused on Dog's kisses. Then he turned to the crew chief and the pilots. With a sly look and a grin between them, the chopper lifted off .

※

ELYSE REALIZED they had taken off without Elijah and the team.

"No. What are you doing?" she shouted at the gunner. "Go back. Take me back."

The gunner made a signal indicating he couldn't hear her.

"Elijah." Elyse screamed.

※

ELIJAH TURNED in horror to look as the chopper took off with Elyse. He ran back toward the chopper and leaped to grab a hold of the skid. He missed it by inches and the chopper soon banked left and flew away. He threw his helmet to the ground, and the string of foul language that came out of his mouth was impressive.

Turning to Sarge, Elijah shouted, "Get me headquarters. We need to find out where that fucking chopper is heading. Did anyone get the tail code? Elyse is on that chopper alone, and she's probably terrified."

"She's got Dog with her, Cap," Sarge said.

It was a small comfort, but he'd take anything right now.

"Cap, the nose art on the front of the bird was a ghost," Henson said.

Elijah turned. "An Khe, Aiden is at An Khe," he stated as he watched the chopper off in the distance as it banked and headed southwest.

⚜

ELYSE WRAPPED her arms around Dog and buried her face in his fur. She trembled, remembering Elijah's words about unscrupulous men and what could happen to her.

The chopper landed at the Army base camp at An Khe. The pilots and gunners pulled off their helmets and exited the craft. After a few minutes their stolen prize jumped down from the chopper. Elyse glared at the crowd of soldiers that had gathered.

⚜

THE CROWD PARTED AND A TALL, handsome, dark-haired major with piercing blue eyes stood looking at Elyse.

⚜

TEARS IN HER EYES, her lower lip quivered. Steeling her resolve and trying not to show how truly frightened she was, Elyse acknowledged him.

"Major?"

"I'm Yarusso. Miss?"

"Booker." Her eyes narrowed. "By what right do you kidnap the daughter of the US ambassador from the Marine Corps? And I might add I am also the godchild of General Morgan. Take me back *now*."

❧

Major Yarusso said, "I can't send you back into the middle of a firefight."

❧

Elyse paled at his words. *Elijah*. Her fear for him showed on her face. "Then go get them," she demanded.

"Who?"

"Captain Corrington and his team."

"Your handler?"

Elyse gritted her teeth and replied, "No man handles me. I'm talking about my guards. I am not an animal to be 'handled.'"

A hint of amusement appeared in the captain's eyes. "Okay, Elyse, we'll sort this out. Are you hungry or thirsty?"

"Yes."

"Then, welcome to the Golf Course, let me offer you our hospitality."

"On two conditions, Major. One, Captain Corrington is made aware of my whereabouts so he can come for me. And two, no one touches me or harms me in any way. Don't let my size fool you. I can and will defend myself and I will hurt you. If not, know that he will hunt you down and gut you like a fish if I'm harmed."

"No one here will touch you. We'll notify headquarters of your 'accidental' kidnapping. A miscommunication."

Elyse gave him a sideways "you're bad" smile and nodded. "Then we have a deal?"

"Yes, we have a deal."

"Why did you call this place the Golf Course?" she asked.

"The CO had us cut the foliage back to ground level by hand. It's just a nickname that stuck."

Two hours later, after a hot meal and stimulating conversation. Elyse

165

was told the Marines' chopper had just landed. Elyse was on her feet, Dog at her side, running for the helipads.

Running into Elijah's arms, he engulfed her in his embrace. "Are you all right, brat?"

"I'm fine."

"Are you sure?"

"Yes, and you're okay? The firefight?"

"It's over. Your bladder averted an American bloodbath. There was a huge network of spider holes and an underground tunnel system right below us. They were preparing an ambush."

Elijah looked up and spotted Major Yarusso. Without a word, he threw down his helmet. dropped his rucksack and launched himself at the Major. Punches flew as they rolled in the dirt.

"Are you mad?" Elyse screamed. "Stop, Elijah. Stop."

Sarge held her from the fray as both men got back on their feet and circled each other like wrestlers. They jumped at each other until Major Yarusso started laughing. Elijah tousled the Major's hair while he pounded Elijah's back. Sarge let go of Elyse. She was confused. *What just happened?*

"Elyse, this is my brother, Aiden."

"Brother?"

"What is wrong with you?" she demanded, pointing her finger at Elijah. "You scared the wits out of me. You could have warned me." Then she pointed her finger at Major Yarusso. "And you. You knew the whole time I was here who my guard was, and you didn't tell me you knew him or that you were brothers. How? You have different last names."

"Half-brothers, Elyse," Aiden replied.

"Our mother was a widow with a one-year-old when my parents met and married," Elijah said.

"Haven't the two of you ever heard of a handshake or a hug? Instead you wallop each other and roll in the dirt. Men." They grinned at her like little boys.

"That's one tiny pepper pot you've got there, Elijah."

"Oh, you have no idea, Aiden."

"She said you'd gut me like a fish if I touched her."

"She said that?" Elijah laughed. "She's right."

Elyse stated, "I am not speaking to either one of you for the rest of the night."

"Come on, brat, calm your temper." he said, stroking her cheek.

"Fine." Then she smiled her brilliant smile at them, and the major was momentarily speechless.

"You're a lucky bastard, Elijah."

"Hmm, not sure." Elijah grinned. "I haven't decided if she's an angel, a she-devil, or a pleasantly shaped mixture of both."

Elyse rolled her eyes. "Whatever."

"I expect you'll stay the night?" Aiden asked.

"Do you have a VIP tent?"

"Yes."

"Okay, we'll stay, but I don't trust you Army bastards. I'm assigning the whole team to guard Elyse overnight."

Aiden laughed. "Good idea or you might find her snatched away again."

❦

ELYSE WENT over to the team and gave Arnold, Mountain, and the other's hugs. Clucking over them like a mother hen. "You're alright? No injuries? They assured her they were fine. Thank you, boys. Thank you so much."

They teased her about her "air running."

Elyse laughed. "Now I know what it's like not only to be a foot taller but to be flattened like a pancake. Between the two of you, that was a full four hundred pounds on top of me. Thank God I had an air pocket."

"Any time you're under me is okay with me, Elyse," Mountain quipped.

She slugged him in the arm. "Smart ass. What would your sweet little girlfriend waiting at home have to say about that?"

Mountain grinned. "Becky's five-eleven, an Amazon, and she'd roast my innards."

Elyse smiled. "Well, there you go." She went over and whispered to Elijah. "Powder room?"

"Aiden, where's the powder room?"

Aiden raised his eyebrows and grinned.

167

"The head." Laughing Elijah corrected himself. "Where's the head?"

***

As they strolled down the path leading to the head Elyse slipped her hand into his. They stopped in front of the head and looked at each other horrified.

"Oh, hell no," Elyse said. It was pretty much wide open with seating for six. "This is just great. Five of my friends and I can all go at the same time with everyone watching."

Elijah chuckled. "Don't worry. We'll fix it."

"Sooner rather than later, Elijah."

He sent a private walking by to haul ass and go get Major Yarusso, and to have him bring four to five blankets, a hammer, and some nails.

Once they had the privacy issue resolved, Aiden pulled a blanket back and signaled to Elyse she could enter the head. "Oh no. It's not quite ready yet."

"First you have to check for bugs, spiders, rats, snakes, Marines, and now, the Army."

Grinning, he complied, "All clear."

"Thank you, Major."

"We're all on the same shit list?" he asked.

"Pretty much," she replied.

***

Elijah and Aiden stepped away to give her privacy. Shaking his head, Aiden said: "She's all woman, isn't she? It never would have occurred to me until now that there would be privacy issues."

Elijah grinned. "Reconnoitering for Elyse is normally the first thing I do when we arrive at a camp. I find the head, the showers, the mess hall, and a somewhat private place for her to dance. Her needs are basic she asks for nothing beyond that. It's her rebellious nature and mischievous streak that has me pulling my hair out."

Elyse stepped out of the powder room. "Do you have a shower here?"

Elijah and Aiden looked at each other. "Oh, fuck," Aiden said.

ELIJAH AND AIDEN talked late into the night. Elyse, fresh from her shower, was exhausted and had fallen asleep leaning against Elijah's arm while he looked down at her.

"Where's the VIP tent?" Elijah asked.

"Four tents down," Aiden replied.

"I'll be back in ten minutes," Elijah said.

He carried her to bed, tucked her in, and made sure she had adequate protection. Then he returned to Aiden's quarters. "She's had a rough few days."

"What's the story, Elijah? Why is the Ambassador's daughter under the protection of the Marine Corps?"

He told Aiden the whole story.

"And last I heard the bid was two million," Elijah explained.

Aiden let out a long slow whistle. "That's quite a chunk of change for a virgin."

"Except she's no longer a virgin. If she's captured and they figure that out, they'll kill her in a horrific manner or worse, pass her around before they sell her off as damaged goods."

"So, was taking her virginity a mistake, Elijah?"

He shook his head. *No. Never.* "I made two big mistakes today," Elijah said aloud. "The first was trying to transfer choppers in a battle zone. We were told it was a safe LZ. Second, putting her on a chopper without the team being on board first. Neither will ever happen again. On whose authority she was kidnapped by the Army?"

"No one's. The CO is on R&R, Lieutenant Colonel Jones was KIA a couple of days ago, and I didn't authorize her kidnapping. I'm putting this on the chopper crew. They'll be dealt with, though I must say I'm happy to see you and to meet Elyse."

"I just have to be more careful on how and when I move her. Protecting Elyse is a full-time job. She fights me every step of the way. Elyse Booker is an uncommon woman, but it doesn't help to have the whole Vietnam theater drooling after her."

"Who could blame them," Aiden asked.

"I don't think Elyse appreciates being under the protection of the Marine Corps or myself."

"That's where you're wrong, Elijah. You should have seen her when she got off the chopper with tears in her eyes and her lower lip quivering. She was terrified being apart from you. Then I watched as she drew on her courage. I've never seen a woman do that before. Then I saw her fiery temper." He grinned. "And that's when I got an earful. Trust me, she values your protection."

Elijah rubbed his eyes. "I'm off to bed. It's been a grueling day for me as well."

ELYSE WAS up at sunrise with a smile for Mountain and Johnson. "I assume they have somewhere to dance here?" she asked them.

Mountain nodded with a smile. With her radio blasting, she danced with passion, letting the rhythm and harmony move her feet as she leaped from bunker to bunker.

AIDEN LEANED against a sandbag wall watching her. She was beautiful and a pleasure to watch. Elijah joined him.

"Elijah, if they've ever seen her dance expect that bid to hit two million. They'll be getting desperate to capture her."

"Two million bucks can buy a lot of bullets," Elijah replied.

"You'd better watch your back."

Elijah decided they would spend a few more days with Aiden.

ELYSE, Mountain, and Johnson left her quarters heading toward the mess hall. They passed many soldiers hard at work seeing to the needs of the camp. Some relaxed with cases of beer and games of chance. Elyse spotted one such group and stopped to chat. They offered her a seat at the table as Mountain provided her the five dollars in scrip she needed to be dealt in and the game started. She played them out and when finished stood up from the table tucking forty-five dollars into her bra. "Thank you, boys. Must have been beginner's luck."

They looked at her with skepticism as she walked away, and she heard one soldier comment, "Boys, I think we just got played."

Elyse spotted an enclosed powder room, and asked Johnson for his lighter, which she used to light her way inside. She locked the door and before she had a chance to turn around, the lighter sputtered out.

❧

STEPPING AWAY from outside the structure, Mountain and Johnson laughed about Elyse fleecing the soldiers. One of the soldiers wandered over and stood chatting with them.

"Where's Elyse?" the man asked.

Nodding toward the structure, Mountain said, "In the head."

The soldier's eyes widened. "Dude, that's not the head. That's the 'whack-shack."

Mountain and Johnson looked at each other.

"Son of a bitch," Mountain said.

Johnson went straight over and shouted to her, "Elyse, come out of there."

"Johnson, your lighter doesn't work. I can't see a damned thing in here."

With a sigh of relief, Johnson said, "Good, just come out."

"The door won't open. It's stuck."

"What do you mean it's stuck?"

"I can't unlock the door and I can't see how to open it. Damned lighter."

"Elyse, back up and off to the side. We'll break the door in."

No matter how many times they rammed it with their shoulders the door wouldn't budge. An audience of soldiers formed around the whack-shack. They tried a few different ideas to get her out.

"Someone find Cap," Johnson shouted.

"He's going to fucking kill us," Mountain stated.

❧

ELIJAH AND AIDEN sat in the mess hall tent enjoying a cup of coffee when he glanced at his watch. "I wonder where Elyse is at? She should have been here twenty minutes ago."

At that moment, Mountain appeared out of nowhere. "About that, Captain," he began, looking sheepish.

"What now?" Elijah asked, knowing from experience it couldn't be good.

"Sir, we have a situation."

Elijah raised his eyebrows. "And?"

"Elyse is trapped, Sir."

Concerned, he barked. "Trapped? Where?"

"Sir, Elyse is trapped in the whack-shack."

Aiden and Elijah looked at each other, horrified.

"The whack-shack? What the fuck is she doing in the whack-shack?" Elijah said.

"She thought it was the powder room, Sir," Mountain scrambled to explain. "She's in the dark. Johnson's lighter stopped working so she can't see anything."

"Jesus Christ."

They were out the door at a run.

❧

ELYSE STOOD inside the pitch-black shack. "Damned lighter."

"Elyse, are you all right?" Elijah called from outside.

"Of course. It's just dark in here."

"We'll get you out." Aiden ordered a private to go get a couple of crowbars.

"If I could get this lighter to work, then I could see what I'm doing."

"No." Elijah shouted. "No. Just wait."

❧

SHE TRIED AGAIN. Sparks turned into a consistent flame at last. Elyse held it up, "I got the lighter to work." Holding it above her head she looked around. "There's no hole in the bench to tinkle. Oh, there's a pull-chain."

"Aww, Christ," Aiden muttered.

She pulled the chain, and the light came on. Elyse looked around and saw poster after poster on the walls of women—naked women. Off to the side were a stack of magazines. She opened one of the magazines and her eyes widened.

Is that what I look like down there? Puzzled, she let the magazine dangle to her side. *A private shack? Posters? Magazines? What do they do in here?* Realization dawned on her.

"ELIJAH... GET... ME... OUT OF HERE."

The side wall of the structure dropped.

Elyse stood, fighting to keep a straight face.

"Um, I have a pretty good idea," she said. Looking at the obviously embarrassed men standing in front of her, "But you know, I really don't want to know." She bit her lip to stifle a giggle and stepped out. Barely able to contain herself, she handed Elijah the girly magazine and lighter and walked through the group of onlookers in silence. Once past them she burst into laughter.

"Wicked. She's wicked," Aiden said, with a grin on his face.

Elijah chuckled, handed Aiden the magazine, and followed after her.

❧

AIDEN OPENED the magazine and grinned in appreciation. He realized he hadn't seen this issue yet and closed the magazine.

❧

LATER THAT EVENING, just after supper. Elyse walked with Mountain, Arnold, Johnson, and Henson toward the powder room. Curious, she stopped to watch four soldiers playing some sort of game with dice.

"What are you playing?" Elyse asked. The soldiers stopped their play to turn and look at her.

"Craps, wanna play?" said a soldier named Potts.

173

"You'll have to teach me," Elyse replied.

"Okay sweetheart but we can't get caught, the CO doesn't like it when we play craps," Potts replied.

Another solder named Isaacs said, "Fuck, he ain't even here. He's on R & R."

"He'd confiscate our dice again, if he knew," Potts said, patting the ground next to him. "Come on darling, sit right here and I'll teach you a real man's game of chance."

BEFORE LONG ELYSE, sitting on her knees on the ground, had amassed a sizable amount of scrip on the ground in front of her. She rolled the dice again. "Seven, yes."

Potts rolled his eyes. "Again? Are you fucking kidding me?"

Elyse looked at him, gave him a beautiful smile. "Just lucky, I guess," she stated, as she collected her winnings.

They were all so engrossed in the game they didn't hear Elijah, Aiden, Doc, and Sarge come up behind them.

"Ten-Hut."

The men jumped to their feet and Elyse, wide eyed, *they'll get in trouble*, stuffed the evidence in her bra. Standing up, she turned around to see Elijah and Aiden standing in front of her. The team lined up to her right and the four soldiers to her left. *Damn, this is not good.*

AIDEN EYED THE GROUP. "While it's good to see Marines and Soldiers playing nice. I believe, Colonel Orgas has forbidden the playing of craps on this base." He walked back and forth in front of his men. "Now the Marines may not be aware of this rule, but you men certainly are." He stopped in front of the last man standing in line and held out his hand. "Potts, dice?"

"No, Sir."

ELIJAH, hands on his hips, went down to stand in front of Henson, the last man in line on the other end.

"Henson, dice?"

"No, Sir."

ELIJAH AND AIDEN each went through their own men asking the same question until they got to the center of the line. Looking at each other, they turned to look at Elyse.

ELYSE LOOKED up at them and gave them a half grimace, half smile. *Damn.* She groaned as Elijah held out his hand and gave her a give them up hand gesture. Elyse cleared her throat and gave Elijah and Aiden a half-hearted smile, her cheeks pinkened while she reached into her bra. Pulling out wad of cash, she placed it in his hand. Feeling around her breast, she pulled out some bobby pins and placed them in his hand. She kept digging. A penny, a switch blade. There was nothing left on that side. She cleared her throat again.

"Umm, other side, I guess."

Elijah lifted an eyebrow. Going to the other side, she pulled out another smaller wad of cash, a tiny Hot Wheel's car, two small cookies in a piece of cloth, then one die, and finally, the other die was placed into his hand.

"Anything else in there, Elyse?" Elijah asked.

"Just me," she replied. Elijah looked in amused silence at the pile of items in his hand.

"No pockets. I have to put my stuff somewhere," she explained. He held up the red Camaro and gave her a questioning look.

"I found it yesterday by a bunker, I was going to turn it in."

He held up a cookie.

"A snack for later," Elyse said, as she blushed another shade of pink.

Holding up the penny. "And this?" he asked.

"I found that at Khe Sanh, it's my lucky penny."

"And… this?" He pulled out the switchblade and pushed the button. It opened into a six-inch blade.

"I, um, won that in a poker game."

"I see."

"All of this has to be incredibly uncomfortable."

"Well, if you know anything about girl parts, you would know we squish in. I'm fine," Elyse replied.

The corners of Elijah's mouth twitched. "Mountain, do you have an empty pocket?"

Mountain checked the pockets of his fatigues. "Yes, Sir."

"It's officially Elyse's pocket for her things."

"Aye aye, Sir," Mountain replied.

Elijah handed everything to Mountain. "Except these." He handed the dice to Aiden and the penny back to Elyse, "And this… I'm confiscating." He held up the switchblade.

"Hey." Elyse protested. "Why?"

"I told you before, we don't arm women."

Elyse glared at Elijah. "You didn't arm me, I armed myself."

"Don't argue with me, Elyse."

"I'm not arguing with you."

Elijah rolled his eyes. "Sarge, you and Doc take Elyse back to her quarters."

Elyse's delicate brow furrowed into a frown. "Fine, that's just fine. I am going back to my quarters to burn my bra, in protest."

Elijah had to bite back his grin, "How are you going to carry your penny?"

"I will think of something," Elyse hissed. She moved past him and walked away with Sarge and Doc at her side.

❧

ELIJAH TURNED BACK to face Aiden with the grin still on his face.

"Cookies," Elijah said, with a shake of his head.

Aiden laughed. "Why the hell would she burn her bra?"

"Women libbers back in the world are burning their bra's in protest of male chauvinism," Elijah replied.

His eyes dancing in merriment. "Damn. And I'm missing it," Aiden said.

Aiden and Elijah turned back to the men standing in front of them.

"Now, let's chat about teaching the Ambassador's daughter how to play Craps," Aiden said.

THE NEXT MORNING ELIJAH, Elyse, Aiden, and the team stood next to the airfield waiting for the chopper to bring them to the next base camp.

Elyse gave Aiden a hug goodbye. "Feeling a bit hungry. Got any cookies?" Aiden asked, with a grin on his handsome face.

Elyse scowled at him. "No, just crumbs," she replied sarcastically, as she gave him an impish grin.

"You're one of a kind Elyse, don't ever change."

Elyse gave him a dazzling smile. "I will always be just me."

Aiden turned to Elijah, and they clapped each other on the back.

"Be safe little brother, take care of your tiny pepper pot," Aiden said.

"Keep your head low, bro."

The chopper landed and the team and Dog headed over to the helipad.

"How often do you get to Chu Lai?" Elijah asked.

"Once in a while, why?" Aiden replied.

"You need to go check it out," Elijah said.

"Again, why?"

"Dark brown hair, chocolate eyes. Quite beautiful, I believe Brie is her name."

"Brie? How do you know about Brie? I've been searching for her all over this God-forsaken country." Aiden replied, as a big smile split his face. Aiden clapped Elijah on the back, turned and walked away with a jaunty spring in his step.

ELIJAH TURNED to Elyse who stood with open mouth.

"Oh my God. Brie, it's Aiden she lost. And they've been searching for each other. That's so sweet," Elyse said.

Elijah's eyes warmly touched her face.

"I didn't realize you were a matchmaker, Elijah."

Elijah narrowed his eyes at her though the warmth still shone through. "Marines are not matchmakers," he replied.

"Sure, you're not."

He moved his hand to signal she should move to the chopper.

"No, I don't want to. I hate choppers."

"They're life-savers to us. Come on, I'll take care of you." He held out his hand to her and, sighing, she placed her hand in his.

CHAPTER 19

Base Camp Three, Tan Son Nhat, Early June

TAN SON NHAT was a big base with mixed military branches. Elyse's quarters were one room right next door to Elijah's quarters within the long one-story L-shaped building assigned to Marine Corps officers. It contained a bed, dresser, desk with a chair, as well as a sink with hot and cold running water and a surprise window air-conditioning unit.

Elijah settled her into her quarters with orders to rest while he scouted the camp. The showers were right outside of the officer's quarters. He could not find a secluded shower as in previous camps. This was going to be an issue. The showers were built with multiple stalls and the walls only went waist high. All Elyse had to do was look out her screen door and she would see men in the shower. Elyse attempting to shower in one of those stalls was a nonstarter. The screen door on her quarters was another issue. The area was not meant for a woman's privacy but there was nothing else available.

After discussing solutions with Sarge, Elijah sent him and Mountain in search of some wood and supplies. Sarge returned a short time later with wood panels, a box of nails, and a few hammers.

They nailed a wood panel to the inside of Elyse's screen door and installed a hook and eye as a lock. Then they addressed the showers. Choosing an end stall, they enclosed the entire stall in wood panels but left an open area at the top when they ran short of panels. They would still need three to four team members along with Dog to protect against peeping toms when Elyse showered. Other personnel of the camp would just have to understand and adjust.

Elijah was nailing in the last end piece of wood when he heard someone call his name. "Corrington, I'll be damned."

Elijah turned around and saw an old friend from officer training school. "Smith, how the hell are you?"

"I thought you were in Khe Sanh, Corrington?"

They exchanged handshakes and claps on the back.

"What are you doing here? And what are you doing to the showers?"

"I'm on a special assignment."

Elyse chose that moment to open her door and step outside. All activity had stopped and every man in the area watched her every movement. "Holy shit. Do you see that, Corrington? Where in the hell did that sweet meat come from?"

Elijah smiled his wicked smile and continued nailing the wood up to the stall.

"What did you say you were doing to the showers, Corrington?"

"I'm installing privacy panels for her."

"Whoa. She's with you?" Smith asked, astonished.

"Yes, she is," Elijah replied.

"Who is she?"

"Her name is Elyse, and she's under the protection of the Marine Corps. She's off limits, Smith," Elijah replied.

"That's a crying shame, Corrington. I'd love to see if there's fire in the bush."

"That's enough, Smith. Elyse is to be treated with courtesy and respect."

Smith snorted, "I know how to treat the ladies, Corrington."

Elijah called Elyse over to him when she returned. "Elyse, this is a friend of mine. First Lieutenant Robert Smith, this is Elyse Booker."

"Lieutenant, it's very nice to meet you." She held her hand out.

"Miss Booker." First Lieutenant Smith took her hand, turned it, and kissed her wrist while resting his gaze on her cleavage. Elyse raised her eyebrows and looked into Elijah's eyes while trying to pull her hand back to a safe zone. She caught First Lieutenant Smith's continued gaze on her breasts and her eyes narrowed.

Elijah clapped Smith on the back to divert his attention from Elyse. She was able to pull her hand back but not before Elijah noted she had made a fist with it. She was going to pop Smith if he didn't intervene.

"Elyse, don't you have unpacking to finish?" Elijah said.

"Yes, yes, I do." She gave them a brilliant smile. "Gentlemen."

She made a hasty retreat to the safety of her quarters with Mountain close on her heels.

❧

ONCE SHE WAS inside Elijah turned to Smith. "I told you she's off limits. You're damn lucky she didn't kick your ass."

"Whoa, Corrington, I was just enjoying the eye candy. What do you mean kick my ass? That tiny little sweet meat?"

"That tiny little sweet meat has taken down men bigger than you," Elijah retorted. "Watch your step with her. Neither Elyse nor I have patience for ogling. Also note that she has a guard twenty-four-seven. I'm sure you'll pass the word. It's great to see you, Bob."

"Yeah, Elijah, let's go into Saigon some night and tie one on, have some fun with the ladies."

"Yeah, sure, some night," Elijah replied. He shook his head as he took his leave. He wasn't sure how well this base was going to work out. He was going to have to post two guards to Elyse. He didn't trust the officers any more than the grunts. He knocked on Elyse's door as he spoke with Mountain. "I'll stay with Elyse for a while. Find Sarge and tell him to assign two men at a time to guard Elyse."

"Aye aye, Sir."

Elyse gave him permission to enter. "Your friend almost found himself flat on his back."

"I'm sorry, Elyse. I've spoken to him about his behavior but be careful around him."

LEESA WRIGHT

"Oh, I will. Just so you know, I won't hesitate to flatten any man, officer or not."

Elijah laughed. "I wouldn't expect anything less of you, brat."

"Elijah, will you please take me somewhere to dance later?"

"I'll take you this evening after dinner. For now, let's get you some chow."

"Chow? Elyse asked.

"Food," Elijah replied.

"Sounds good to me. I'm starving." Elyse laughed. "I don't know why I'm suddenly so hungry all the time."

They found the mess hall, and every man in there turned to look at Elyse as she entered. Those with their backs to the door were either nudged by their friends or noticed the expressions of their friends and turned around to see what had caught everyone's attention.

Elyse gave them a brilliant smile. "Good afternoon, boys."

Elijah rolled his eyes as they entered the chow line. The cooks were friendly and bantered back and forth with Elyse. She eyed the food offered and commented to Elijah that the men in the thick of things deserved the same quality of food. She chose a double helping of mashed potatoes with gravy. Elijah raised his eyebrows and smiled at her. "So, you like mashed potatoes?"

"I love them."

"Are you going to eat anything else?"

"No, I don't think so. This is plenty for me."

"You should try the liver and onions."

Elyse made a gagging noise. "I never have and never will eat liver and onions."

"Or lima beans," Elijah quipped.

ELYSE SMILED. She had forgotten about her first experience with C-rations. "I love chicken, fish, and a big juicy steak, medium rare. I also love most fruits and vegetables and sweets. I'd kill for anything chocolate or red licorice."

182

Elijah grinned as they sat down at an empty table. He shook his head. "I'm still going to have to put rocks in your pockets."

Elyse laughed. "I'll have to sew pockets on first. Do they have needles and thread here? I need to mend a couple of my shirts—and yours too."

Elijah smiled at her. "That's right. You said you made your own clothes."

"Yes, I do. With the right tools and material, I can make anything."

"I'll see what I can find for you. I know none of this easy on you."

❧

LATER IN THE evening after dinner was finished, with Elyse on his arm, they strolled the base. When a Jeep drove by, they locked eyes.

"No." Elijah said with a laugh.

She smiled at him. When they walked by an EM club, they locked eyes again.

"Absolutely not," he said. "I need you to stay out of trouble here, Elyse. No ditching your guards at this base. I have never in my life found someone who gets into as much trouble as you do."

Elyse laughed. "My father used to say 'trouble' was my middle name."

Elijah laughed. "What is your middle name?"

"Michelle, after my mother."

"Elyse Michelle. It has a nice ring to it."

"Thank you. What's yours?"

"Mikal, after my Irish grandfather."

"It's funny that we have similar names."

"That it is."

"How long have you been in the Marines?"

"Almost four years, so right out of college."

"I've been in since January," Elyse quipped.

Elijah smiled at her. "I follow many members of my family and am proud to serve my country."

"It's got to be hard, Elijah. A war like this, protesters at home. It's an unpopular war, and these are not easy times."

"I know, but I love my job."

"Now here I am, keeping you from doing what you love, though I'm not at all sure why you would love crawling through the jungle." She gave a delicate shudder. "Bugs, snakes, and God knows what else. I've read there's even leopard's and tigers out there as well."

"It's the jungle, lots of creatures call it home. And I have heard the stories of man-eaters that have attacked villages and dragged off locals for their supper. Always be on your guard."

Once their tour was complete, they returned to Elyse's quarters for her ballet slippers. They had found the perfect spot for her dancing not too far from her quarters. Elyse looked down at her slippers. No longer pink, they were stained red from the clay soil at Khe Sanh and were long past their normal use date. She did not know how long she could keep them together. Her sadness showed on her face.

"What's the matter?"

"My pointe shoes are nearly spent."

"Pointe shoes?"

"Yes, that's the real name for this type of shoe. Ballet slippers are a layman's term."

"How long have you been a ballerina?"

"I have studied ballet since I was eight when my father was the US Ambassador to Germany, but it's been about eighteen months as the Prima ballerina, the lead role in a ballet company. I was a professional ballet dancer for two years before I earned the role of Prima. I know as much about being a Marine as you know about being a ballerina. The two are complete opposites," she said.

His voice was a deep, husky whisper, "Ah, but opposites attract, Elyse."

She shivered as ripples of desire coursed through her body. "Yes, they do."

THEY HAD ARRIVED at her new dancing spot. Elijah lounged on the grass. His long legs stretched out in front of him while she went through her warm-up routine. When she was ready, she turned the radio on and struck a pose, waiting for a song on the radio to determine her moves.

The music began, and she started her workout. Elijah never realized a woman could leap and jump so far into the air. Her spins were amazing, if not dizzying. Her hands, the way she held her hands. So gentle, almost fragile looking. He knew their strength and their softness when she would slip her hand into his when they were alone. He yearned for the day he could feel her hands on his body again, touching, exploring. He inhaled at his train of thoughts and where they led.

Eventually she gained an audience. It happened everywhere she danced. Some had seen her in the mess hall. Some didn't even know she was on the base. She ignored them all and moved to the music.

The moment was perfection. She felt something land on her head and crawl through her hair. A creepy-crawly dread filled her as looked up to see black things flying above her. She reached up to brush at her hair and her hand came in contact with something. When it squeaked, she shrieked in terror. *What in the hell is in my hair?* She turned and ran, still screaming her terror as she tried to get whatever was in her hair out.

Elijah chased her down, tackling her to the ground. "Hold still, Elyse." He pulled it out of her hair and rolled off of her to his knees.

She sat up, still shaking, she looked at him in horror. "What was that?"

"You're okay, it's gone, it was a bat." Elijah said.

She inhaled. "A bat?" Shaking in revulsion. "I think I'm done for the night," she said, adding in some colorful expletives.

Regarding her with amusement, Elijah said, "You're developing quite the potty mouth."

"Me? Have any of you heard yourselves? Every other word is the F-word. I'm going to put a swear jar on the table in front of me in the mess hall. I'll make a fortune," Elyse retorted.

Elijah threw back his head and laughed a deep, rich, warm laugh.

"You'd better start by throwing in a few bucks yourself," Elijah replied, with a grin.

He helped her to her feet, and they walked back to their quarters in silence. The night was warm, sultry and humid.

"Not too many stars in the sky," Elyse mused. "I wonder why?"

Elijah looked up into the sky and cursed to himself.

He deposited Elyse in her quarters with a soft kiss on her lips. He sat on the steps outside of his own quarters, thinking about the woman who slept next door. He was finding it harder and harder to be the Marine in her presence when he wanted so desperately to just be the man. He wondered if he had to tell her—or even if he should tell her. She could not see the stars because of the lights of the city. They were five miles outside of Saigon. Elyse was five miles from home, and he could not take her there.

She would be devastated if she found out. There was no one there. The residence portion of the American embassy was partially destroyed in the TET offensive. He supposed there might still be embassy staff in the business part of the embassy, but he didn't know for sure. Her father was not there. He had temporary quarters while he recovered from his injuries on the hospital ship out in the South China Sea.

He couldn't risk Elyse getting her panties in a bunch and sneaking off to Saigon, thinking she could go home. The city was teeming with VC and spies. They could still lose her to capture. These were his orders from the brass. The same brass who didn't have to listen to her cry. It broke his heart to hear her beg to go home. This was a dangerous base camp to be at, but he had no choice.

He had to keep her away from the front gate with the camp name proudly displayed. Elyse would know from that sign where she was. He had to keep her away from the locals who came and went from the front of the base, and perhaps spied for the VC, and keep the men of the base away from her. It seemed like a monumental task guarding ninety-eight pounds of sass.

CHAPTER 20

Elyse awoke at dawn. After doing most of her warm-ups inside, she opened the door with her slippers and radio in hand. Arnold and Mountain stood outside.

"Good morning," she said, as she sat on the steps next to them and put her slippers on. Once they were on, she danced in the street. It was quiet with no prying eyes yet, and there was enough room to jump, pirouette, and perform more intricate moves.

The haunting sound of the music started, she arched her back, stretched a well-muscled leg forward, and moved her arms as if she were a graceful butterfly. Moving to the sweet music, her pirouettes were perfection as she twirled and jumped her Grand Jete's and Grand Adage's. From her intricate steps as she moved en pointe with delicate beauty, she fluttered and floated leaving the officers who filtered out of their quarters to watch her from the porch breathless.

Who knew women could move that way, her body told a story of exquisite allure and left them wanting more?

Elijah heard the music playing and padded barefoot to the door and out onto the porch. He watched her, entranced, as the music and her body melded to become one. Tears streamed down her cheeks, and it reminded him of something. What was it the Vietnamese called her? *Danseuse qui pleure*. The dancer who weeps. He knew this was where she belonged: dancing, with or without an audience. It was the music and the movement of her body as he watched both joy and sorrow play across her face. It was pure and raw, and it was the moment his heart loved her, though it had yet to register in his brain.

The song ended and Elyse locked eyes with Elijah, her eyes were for him and him alone. She said so much without saying a word. She smiled, gathered her radio, and went inside.

She needed a shower. She poked her head out the door to Arnold. "Will you please ask Elijah if I can shower now?"

ARNOLD NODDED and went over to Elijah. "Elyse would like to shower, Cap."

Elijah nodded. "Tell her to get her things." He returned to his quarters to dress.

THEY EACH TOOK UP A POSITION—ELIJAH, Arnold, Mountain, and even Dog—on each side of the shower stall, their job was to prevent peeping toms and give Elyse the privacy she needed to shower. She stepped into the shower enclosure and moved about setting up her things. Elijah stood close to the front of the stall, his back to the door.

She whispered his name. "Elijah, Elijah…."

He heard the panic in her voice. She had backed up and pushed the door open as she now stood outside of the stall. He looked down at her. "What the hell?"

"Elijah, snake, snake."

She stood clad only in her panties, clutching a towel to her bosom. Elijah looked inside the enclosure to see a large, long yellow snake wrapped around the shower head. Realizing it was non-poisonous, he breathed a sigh of relief. He stepped in, grabbed the hissing snake below its head and pulled the offending creature off the showerhead. He looked around for any other creatures and stepped outside of the stall.

"It's okay now."

Her face had lost all color. "This place is a living hell."

He grinned. "You'd better finish your shower. You have an audience."

Elyse looked around, realized her state of undress, turned about ten shades of pink, shrieked her embarrassment, and dove into the shower enclosure. With colorful language while she showered, she cursed Vietnam, bats, bugs, spiders, snakes, leeches, scorpions, and Marines in general.

"Once I'm no longer a captive, I swear I'm running away to a deserted island with only women allowed. No bugs, spiders, bats, snakes, leeches, scorpions, or rats allowed either. Damned Marines would probably storm the island. Then we'd all be screwed—literally. Bastards."

Elijah was holding his belly he was laughing so hard at Elyse's rant. Arnold and Mountain laughed as well.

"It sure sounds like the Corps made Elyse's shit list," Mountain said.

"Oh, I think the Corps made Elyse's shit list a long time ago," Elijah laughed.

Elyse came out of the shower glaring at Elijah. "Why didn't you tell me I was practically naked?"

Elijah wiped his eyes. "I'm pretty sure I was focused on dealing with that snake."

She scowled at him.

"Are you hungry, Elyse?"

"Starving."

"Finish getting ready and I'll take you to the mess hall."

"Fine. Give me ten minutes."

Mid-afternoon, Elyse had recovered from her early morning rant. She put her slippers on, and with Johnson and Henson in tow, she found a deserted road bordering a grassy area within the camp. The music played as she moved in slow and easy rhythm. Feeling the music, she danced with eyes closed as if no one was there. She didn't see the Jeep stop or the four men who jumped out of it. Air Force pilots, one and all. They watched her as she danced, their gazes lingering on every part of her. They circled her as she danced to a slow romantic song.

One spoke up. "You are too beautiful to dance to a song like this alone."

Elyse opened her eyes and smiled, making eye contact with her guards, who were now on their feet.

"Go get Cap," Henson told Johnson. "There may be trouble."

One of the pilots pulled Elyse into his arms for a waltz. "Hello, gorgeous, who are you?" he asked, twirling her into the arms of the next man.

Each man waltzed with her and plied her with questions.

"What's your name?" one asked.

"Why is a ballerina on base in Vietnam?" asked another.

She merely smiled at them.

She looked around the pilot dancing with her and saw Elijah approaching with Henson and Johnson. She made eye contact with him and gave him the "What are you waiting for" look while the pilots continued to twirl her between them.

"Elyse." Elijah held out his hand to her, and she took it. He moved her out of the circle of pilots and pulled her behind him. "Gentlemen, Elyse is off limits."

THE PILOTS LOOKED as if someone had just taken their candy away. They sized up Elijah, Henson, and Johnson, and noted the other four members of the team who stood a few feet back from them. None of them noticed the other Jeep that had pulled up.

"Ten-Hut." shouted the general's aide.

All the men stood at attention. Four-Star General Malcolm Morgan exited the Jeep with two of his aides.

"UNCLE SAPO." Elyse squealed in delight and flew into his arms.

He engulfed her in a bear hug. "Elyse, how are you? You look well."

He looked down at her attire and ballet slippers. "I hear you've been dancing all over my base and Vietnam."

"I didn't know you were here, or I would have come to see you," Elyse replied.

"It's okay, child. I'm a busy man." He set Elyse from him. "So, what have we here?" He eyed the Marines and Airmen. He walked along their ranks as if inspecting troops. He stopped in front of Elijah.

"Captain Corrington, I assume?"

"Sir. Yes, Sir."

"You and your team are doing a bang-up job taking care of our Elyse."

"Thank you, Sir."

"Any issues?"

"Other than she's stubborn and impetuous? No, Sir."

"That's our Elyse, keep your eye on her, Captain."

"Sir. Yes, Sir."

He moved on to one of the Airmen. "Identify yourself, Captain."

"Captain John Anderson, Sir."

"What's your part in this mix?"

"Sir, we spotted a ballerina dancing in the street and stopped to admire her dancing."

"Admired her dancing, huh? More likely you spotted a beautiful woman and stopped to admire her."

"Yes, Sir."

He moved back to the center where Elyse stood. "Elyse, I'd like you and Captain Corrington to join me for dinner this evening."

Elyse looked down at her clothes. "I'm honored, Uncle Sapo, but I'm afraid I'm a pauper now. My clothing trunk is missing."

"Don't you worry about that," he said, with a look at one of his aides, who nodded his understanding.

"Elyse, Captain Corrington, we'll see you at 20:00. I'll send a Jeep for you."

"As you were, men. And, Captain Anderson, I suggest you and your fellow pilots move along."

He turned, climbed into his Jeep with his aides and drove away. Once in the Jeep he directed his aides to find the top bachelor of equal rank to

191

Captain Corrington from each branch of the military on base and invite them to dinner as well. He wanted to see if Captain Corrington held Elyse's attention.

THE PILOTS MUMBLED their goodbyes and made a hasty retreat. Elijah turned to Elyse. "You call a four-star general Uncle Sapo? Isn't that Portuguese for frog?"

Elyse giggled. "I have since I could talk. He's my Godfather, Elijah."

He shook his head.

"What time is it?"

Looking at his watch. "Almost 16:00."

She gave him a look of pure exasperation.

"Four o'clock," he said.

Elyse squealed. "I'll never be ready in time." With that she took off at a run toward her quarters, leaving Elijah and the team in the rear.

Elijah rolled his eyes. "How could four hours not be enough time?" he asked Mountain, who shrugged his shoulders in reply. They followed after her at a trot.

Elyse needed another shower, and this time she made Elijah check for creepy crawlers and snakes before she went into the shower.

Two hours later, a package had arrived. Elyse opened the package and found a beautiful black cocktail dress. It was low cut and would show ample cleavage as well as plenty of leg, all of which had Elyse biting her lip. He had even supplied her with matching black pumps, a purse, and black silky underthings. Other than the nearly indecent cut of the décolletage, it was sized perfectly for her.

Someone on the general's staff knew women very well, Elyse mused.

Elyse put the finishing touches on her hair as she stood in her new bra, panties, and pumps. She didn't have any eye make-up or perfume, but she found a tube of soft, pink lipstick inside the little, black purse. She pinched her cheeks and applied the lipstick to her lips. This would have to do. She stepped into her dress and found she could not zipper it on her own.

Damn. She needed help. She opened her door and found Elijah standing there ready to knock.

"Oh, Elijah, you're here. Please zip me up." She turned and gave him her back. He zipped her up, and she turned to face him. "I don't know about this dress," she said. "It's almost indecent."

"Elyse you are stunning.".

She smiled at him. "So, do I pass muster?"

He grinned again. "Yes, you pass muster. I'll be fighting off every man on base. Are you ready? The Jeep should be here any moment."

"Yes, I think so."

"You look amazing in your uniform as well."

"Thank you, Elyse."

The Jeep pulled up. He offered her his arm, and they exited her quarters to wolf whistles and catcalls. Elyse rolled her eyes and curtsied as Elijah handed her into the Jeep.

They pulled up outside the general's quarters, and Elijah jumped out and ran around the other side to help her out.

Elyse looked at him. "Elijah, there is no ladylike way to exit without exposing everything."

Elijah offered her a wolfish smile and lifted her out of the Jeep. As she straightened her dress, smoothing it into place, Elyse heard her name called. She turned to see a friend from Khe Sanh, one of the first Marines she had taught to dance. With a squeal of delight, she ran across the street to give him a hug. With a promise to meet up with him again at the rec area, she proceeded to walk back to where Elijah stood.

WITH HIS ARMS crossed against his chest leaning against the general's Jeep watching her. His grin couldn't be contained. *She struts when she walks. It must be the high heels.*

She gave more than one-man heart palpitations and a sore neck as she walked kitty corner across the street.

She stopped mid-street, leaning her hand against the hood of a Jeep with four Marines inside that had stopped in the street to let her pass. Balancing herself, taking her shoe off, she shook a small rock out of her shoe. Looking up at the men in the jeep. "You don't mind if I use you for a minute, do you?"

"Baby, you can use me for as long as you want," replied a Marine who stood in the back of the Jeep.

With a chiding look, she mouthed, "Bad." She put her shoe back on, and with a smile, she blew them a kiss and was on her way.

One couldn't say for sure who had the better view, those from behind who watched the swing of her bottom and gorgeous legs or those in the front who saw the jiggle and sway of her breasts and hips.

She passed by a troop transport truck filled with Marines. They leaned over the side looking down at her as she passed by them. Someone called out her name, and she looked up to see their grinning faces. She gave them a gorgeous smile and continued down the street. Her beautiful smile and smoky amethyst eyes found and focused on Elijah.

ELIJAH WATCHED all the men around her bumping into each other and practically falling over themselves watching her. He shook his head. *Bees to honey. The brass had to be insane dropping a creature like Elyse onto a military base.*

She stopped in front of him. He smiled his wolfish smile at her. "Are you ready now, brat?"

"Yes, I'm ready." He offered her his arm and thought to himself, *It's a good thing I'm not a jealous man.* As soon as they entered the general's quarters, Elijah immediately knew the man's plan and was amused by the general's game. Suitors of equal rank were seated at the dinner table, all here to vie for Elyse's attention.

DINNER WAS FABULOUS, the conversation enlightening and engaging, Elyse laughed, and subtlety flirted with each man. She guessed her Uncle Sapo's plan the moment she arrived. He didn't fool her. She'd enjoy the evening regardless. She already knew who had her attention and her heart, Elijah.

Elijah spoke with the general while Elyse danced with one officer after another. It was at the general's orders that they were on this base. He wanted to check up on Elyse and talk to the Captain.

"How much does Elyse know?"

"She knows nothing, Sir."

"I'll leave it up to you to inform her when you think the time is right."

"Yes, Sir."

"Does she know where she is right now?"

"No, Sir. I've restricted her from the front of the base. She would be very, very angry if she finds out where she is."

"Yes, I'm sure she would," replied the general. "I know we've put you in a difficult spot, Captain, but we believe you will see to her best interests. She's a spirited woman. She needs a strong man who matches her spirit. We think that man is you, Corrington."

"Thank you, Sir." *Ah… that explains why she's not off limits to me.*

"She wants to talk to me after dinner. I'm positive the talk will include a plea to return home and questions about her father. I'm still trying to formulate what my response will be without angering her," the general said.

"Not to be unsympathetic, Sir, but good luck with that." Elijah replied, with a wry grin.

General Morgan laughed outright. "You're going to go far Captain."

During the dancing in the small drawing room after dinner, each man was honored to hold a beautiful woman in his arms as he spun her around the room. Elijah was, by far, the best dancer. Elyse relaxed in his arms, enjoying the dance.

"We haven't been this close since Khe Sanh," she whispered into his ear.

He grinned at her. "Yes, except then you had your legs wrapped around my back, and I had my hands on your…."

"Elijah, shh. Someone might hear you."

"You started it, brat."

She smiled at him. "Are you ever going to make love to me again?"

He smiled his wicked grin. "Yes."

"I thought perhaps you had lost interest."

"Never, would I ever lose interest in you." He twirled her away and back to him again. Then the music ended, and he had to give her up to another man.

Next she danced with a young army Captain, Gunnersen. She asked about his hometown, and he responded, "Owatonna, a small town in Minnesota. Not at all big or as glamorous as Saigon."

She laughed. "Saigon, have you ever been there?"

"Yes ma'am, at least twice a week."

"Twice a week? That's quite a distance to go twice a week."

"No ma'am, it's less than five miles from here."

Elyse stopped. "Where are we?"

"Tan Son Nhat, right outside of Saigon, ma'am."

Elyse's blood ran cold. *I'm almost home.* "Excuse me, Captain Gunnersen."

⚜

ELYSE TURNED and looked at Elijah.

He knew right then and there she knew where she was. The hurt and accusation on her face said it all.

"Why, Elijah? Why would you not take me home? Five miles. I'm five miles from home." She ran from the room.

Sighing, Elijah said, "Excuse me, General."

"Good luck, Captain," the General replied.

Elijah went out after her.

The General stood at the window watching Captain Corrington out in the street. *Oh, to be young again.* Turning from the window to his aides, he said, "Get me the Ambassador on the line."

He needed to fill Elyse's father in on his suspicions. His gut instinct told him Elyse and young Captain Corrington were in love. It would be up to Booker now on how he wanted to proceed.

CHAPTER 21

Night had fallen, and the base was dark except for the security lights and the occasional flare light. Elijah looked up and down the street looking for a sign of which way she may have gone. She was nowhere in sight. He headed back toward his quarters. He had to employ his team to start searching for Elyse. He cursed himself for not being straightforward with Elyse from the beginning, but he knew he couldn't have done so without the general's blessing. He had it now, but it was far too late. Elyse was furious with him. He didn't blame her. He would have felt the same way.

ELYSE WAS NO FURTHER AWAY than across the street from the general's quarters. She had run inside the officer's club to hide from Elijah. She peeked out the door to watch him look up and down the street and then walk off toward their quarters. She breathed a sigh of relief. Her emotions in a jumbled mess, she turned around to see where she was.

"Damn. A bar." She smiled at the twenty or so officers sitting at tables throughout the small club.

They stared, dumbstruck, at the beautiful woman standing at the end of the bar. The short black dress with a low-cut décolletage, red hair up in an attractive style with soft tendrils escaping. Her shoes in hand.

"What is this place?" Elyse asked.

"This is the officer's club, ma'am," replied the bartender.

"Not the EM club?" she asked.

"No ma'am."

"Oh, thank God. That's off limits."

An Air Force Captain stepped forward. "May I buy you a drink, Miss?"

"Booker, but please call me, Elyse."

"Elyse, a drink?"

Elyse was hesitant. "I should leave. I'm not sure I should be in here. I'm obviously not an officer."

"Nonsense, you're more than welcome to be in here."

"He's searching for me."

"Who is searching for you?"

Elyse thought of Elijah and his betrayal. "Never mind. Yes, I'll take that drink, Captain. Something strong, please."

"Whiskey? Tequila?"

"Tequila is fine. I've never drank anything stronger than wine before, but what the hell."

The captain smiled. "Then tequila it is. Bartender, one tequila for the beautiful lady."

Elyse eyed the officers in the club sitting at the ten or so tables. A Juke box in the far corner played music. Wood paneling lined the walls and the wooden bar glowed with a high polish shine.

It might be best if she kept them all at arm's length and within her sights. She hopped up on the bar and sat facing them.

They grinned at the unconventional young woman. Gorgeous legs and generous cleavage, shoes on the bar. She was the stuff dreams were made of. The bartender handed her the shot, a salt-shaker and a small bowl of quartered limes.

"Okay, gentlemen, explain what I do with this lime and salt-shaker?"

One explained. "Lick your hand, shake some salt on your hand, lick it off, drink the shot straight down, and then suck on the lime."

"Okay, here goes." She licked the salt, took a deep breath, and drank her very first shot. She sucked the lime immediately afterward. The tequila burned all the way down. "Lord have mercy." Elyse gasped.

They hollered, laughed, and clapped at her accomplishment.

As they chatted and laughed, Elyse told them she had just come from dinner with General Morgan, her godfather. That sobered them up a bit. Not a man there would dare to touch her inappropriately. But her easy smile and friendly nature soon had them relaxed, and she tried another shot of tequila.

"Gentlemen, this is not getting any easier," she said with a laugh. She told them she was a prima ballerina with the Royal Ballet in Huế City, that she made it through a chopper crash, survived two days in the jungle before being rescued by Captain Corrington and the team, and lived through the siege at Khe Sanh. She told them she just found out she was only five miles from home, the American embassy, her father was the ambassador and Elijah would not take her home.

They listened as Elyse ordered another shot, even though she was more than just tipsy. She laughed and giggled and did not notice the man who slipped out the door.

❧

HE WENT in search of Captain Corrington and found him by the main gate. Elijah was just getting ready to leave the base to see if Elyse had tried walking to Saigon.

"Captain Corrington?"

"Yes."

"Captain, we have something we believe may belong to you."

"What do you have of mine?"

"About yea high, drop-dead gorgeous, and quite tipsy."

"Elyse?"

"Yes."

Relief showed on Elijah's face. "Tipsy? Where the hell is she?"

"In the officer's club."

❧

199

ELIJAH WALKED into the club just as the bartender handed Elyse her third shot. When she spotted him, she shouted across the room.

"Elijah. See, I told you," she said to the men at the bar, "he always finds me. You're just in time, Elijah. A toast." She stood up barefoot on the bar. "A toast to my year of firsts. To my first kiss, my first love, my first drink, my first time driving a Jeep, my first chopper crash, my first dog—I think I drove a tank into a swimming pool in there somewhere—and my first killing of a man. Five of them. My first Marine dying in my arms.... Oh.... I lost my virginity." With that, she slammed her shot, teetered a bit, and passed out into Elijah's arms. He slung her over his shoulder and turned to the officers.

"How many did she drink?"

"Counting that last one, three."

Elijah grinned and shook his head. "She doesn't normally drink."

"We see that."

"Please don't judge her harshly. She will be mortified if she remembers any of this."

"Rest easy, Captain. She's a delightful woman. We hope things work out for her."

Elijah thanked them and headed out the door. He climbed into the waiting Jeep and settled Elyse on his lap. "Take us to our quarters, Sarge."

Sarge looked at Elyse. "Is she okay?"

"Our little runaway here is drunk and passed out on three shots of what smells like tequila." Elijah grinned. She was not going to feel good tomorrow.

Sarge laughed. "Three shots? That's it?"

"Yup, three shots."

Laughing, Sarge pulled away from the curb and drove down the street.

THE PATRONS at the officer's club spent the rest of their evening toasting Elyse's shoes, which she had abandoned on the bar. "Boys, if you ever had any doubt in your mind, those sexy black shoes represent everything we're fighting for."

"To hot, red-headed women."

"To: Elyse."

ELIJAH CARRIED her into her quarters and laid her on the bed. He pulled the pins from her hair, unzipped her dress, and stripped it off her body. When he flipped her back over, she sat up on her own, unhooked her bra, flung it on the floor, and flopped back down on the bed.

Elijah was surprised, he had never really seen her topless other than for a few seconds in the ditch when he first met her and when her bra burst open. It was too bad she was so drunk. He shook his head. Her toast in the club to her year of firsts was both touching and sad.

Elyse groaned. Elijah covered her with a sheet, found a basin, and sat down in a chair. It took about five minutes for her to vomit up the tequila. He held her hair and offered words of comfort. When she finished, he covered her back up. He knew she would sleep now, so he cleaned up the mess and quietly left. With a word to Henson and Johnson to wake him if she needed anything, he went to bed.

ELYSE WOKE with a groan and a massive hangover. Covering her head with her pillow, she groaned again. She was dying. She just knew it. *What happened?* She didn't remember much past that second shot of tequila. *Evil stuff. Never again. How did I get here? Where are my clothes? Oh my God.*

ELIJAH KNOCKED ON HER DOOR. He heard a muffled sound and walked into her quarters. "Good morning, sunshine."

A muffled curse was all he could make out.

He smiled. "Tequila is a strong liquor for your first drink, Elyse."

More muffled cursing with his name entwined in there.

Elijah smiled. "Here, take these aspirin and drink this water."

She poked her head out from under the pillow and scowled at him. "Tequila is evil." She accepted the aspirin, swallowed the pills, and laid back down, pillow planted over her head. Groaning again, she whined, "This is awful."

Elijah laughed. "Rest. You'll feel better soon."

Two hours later, Elyse was up and moving about. Still feeling a bit green, she craved a shower. As she showered, she moaned. With no memories past that second shot of tequila, she still didn't know what happened last night or how she got back to her quarters. Elijah hadn't told her, but she assumed he had something to do with it. Evil stuff, tequila.

CHAPTER 22

By late afternoon, Elyse needed something to eat. With Dog and her guards in tow she headed over to the mess hall. Coffee. She needed coffee, strong and black. She needed to think about Saigon and how she was going to get there. If Elijah refused to take her home, she'd do it on her own. But how? He would just find her and bring her back anyway. Was it worth the inevitable punishment? She didn't know, but the whole situation made no sense to her. Why didn't her father come to see her? If he was in the embassy, he would have been here already to take her home. The fact that he hadn't come for her told her he wasn't home. But why? What the hell was going on? Elijah was hiding something from her, and she wanted to know what it was.

She was tired and had no brainpower. She needed to dance, to clear her head, to think. She had brought her slippers and radio with her. The mess hall was deserted as she sat on the bench and put her slippers on. She was trying to think of where she might find a more deserted area on this side of the base, but her thoughts were all muddled. She did see bunkers along the perimeter of the camp on the way over. Bunker dancing sounded perfect to her. She was going to give Arnold and Mountain a run for their money today, and if she was lucky, she'd ditch them. With a wicked grin she left the mess hall.

She stood outside for a moment to get her bearings. *There. The start of the bunkers.* She turned to Arnold and Mountain. "It's a good thing you two are Marines."

"Why?" Arnold asked.

"You're going to need some stamina today." With a smile and a running leap to the top of a bunker, she switched her radio on. A Rolling Stones tune played, and with a pirouette she was gone.

Leaping between bunkers, the sound of her music and laughter trailing behind her. She danced up to an airfield. She spotted a bunker at the far end of the runway. The planes would take off and land right overhead. She made her way over there and landed on a bunker just as a Marine jet was coming in for a landing.

An F-4 fighter jet taxied to the runway, gunned its engines. It was exhilarating, the thrill of having a fighter jet racing straight toward her as she danced toward the jet only to have it lift off and go screaming over-head. Elyse reveled in the excitement as the next fighter jet took off.

Arnold and Mountain weren't so happy. They had almost caught up with her. With a giggle and a catch me if you can look, she leaped back up on the bunker. Once she was about six bunkers ahead of them, she jumped off and disappeared down a street. Ditch successful.

By dusk, Elyse sat on the very top of the watchtower just to the right of the main gate. She didn't know how long she sat there. She couldn't leave the base knowing Saigon and how dangerous it was at night. Elyse sat for a long time, just looking at the road home, and she struggled to understand Elijah and why he wouldn't take her home.

❦

MOUNTAIN CALLED TO ELIJAH: "There. There she is, Sir. Up on the top of the watchtower."

Elijah looked to the watchtower by the main gate. Relief at seeing her safe commingled with his anger and worry. He sent the team back to their quarters and walked up to the base of the watchtower. She looked over at him when he arrived at the top. Scooting over, she patted the spot next to her.

With a small, sad smile, she said, "I was wondering how long it would take you to find me." When Elijah sat down next to her, she began to speak. "I've been coming to this watchtower a few times a year since I was fourteen. I feel rather foolish that I didn't recognize this base from ground level. Look here." She scooted over to show him markings etched into the wood planks on top of the tower. "The first time I came here I marked it with my pocketknife. I always made sure I had my knife with me whenever I came out here." Lovingly touching the marks, she continued. "I was just here in December when I was home for Christmas."

"Funny, I was here on this base in December as well," Elijah replied.

Her expression turned wistful. "I don't have my knife this time and you confiscated the one I won." Smiling, Elijah pulled his knife from its sheath and handed it to her. Taking the knife from his hand, she then worked on etching her mark into the wood. She handed him back his knife and then watched as he etched a mark in the wood just below her line of marks.

"To mark my first visit," Elijah stated.

He sheathed his knife, and Elyse scooted closer to him. She pointed out various points of interest: the lights of the city and the mountain ranges. Scooting around, she pointed out the airfield behind them. "My favorite viewpoint. I'd watch the planes take off and land for hours some days."

They watched in silence as a military plane came in for a landing, coasting to a stop and taxiing over to its unloading zone.

"The fighter jets are always the best."

"Climbing up here is dangerous," he said.

"It's exhilarating."

"You're fearless and you scare me. You could have been shot."

"And you're over-protective, just like my father."

"Do you dance up here?"

"No, I never have. This was always a place for calm reflection for me. I feel close to home now."

"Elyse, this is a hostile combat zone now. I know you want to go home but you can't. It's too dangerous. I can't tell you why yet, but you must trust me."

With fresh tears running down her face, she said, "I do. That's why I didn't leave. I'm sitting here looking out over the city and the road home, and I can't leave because I have to believe in you."

Elijah engulfed her in his arms, kissed her face, and dried her tears.

They sat stargazing for a few more hours, watching the occasional plane take off or land while Elijah pointed out the various constellations and how to navigate by the stars.

"I wish I would have known this when I was alone in the jungle. I would have traveled more by night."

"I can't even begin to fathom you alone in the jungle, Brat."

"I've spent a good portion of my life alone while my father traveled for business. Granted I had my nanny, but no family. I was not frightened to be alone in the jungle. I was more terrified of the bugs and nightlife."

"It's time to go," he said, pulling her in for a kiss. His kiss sent shivers of desire through her as his mouth devoured her softness. She returned the kiss leaving him aching and burning with fire. Breathless, they parted.

Nodding her head, she expertly scooted over and began the climb down with Elijah close behind.

Once on the ground, he said, "You know I have to have this fenced in now? We can't have VC or anyone from outside the base climbing up the tower."

"I know, I expected it would be my last time up there."

"I'm sorry."

"I know." Looking down the road home, she said, "Damn, I could have at least grabbed some clothes from my closet."

Elijah smiled. "I'll see what I can do."

⁂

ELIJAH, Mountain, and Arnold went into Saigon the next day. Their objective was to see what they could find of Elyse's shoes, clothes, and sewing materials. He had the general's aide call ahead to allow them access to the embassy. They presented themselves at the gate and were escorted to the residence and Elyse's room.

He looked around the large feminine room. The closet was gone, a gaping hole in the wall in its place covered with a tarp. No help there.

Elijah stood for a moment at the foot of Elyse's bed and looked around the room. The best way he could describe the room was a bohemian hippie mix. Totally a reflection of Elyse's carefree style. An easel stood in the corner. A palette with globs of paint lay on a small table next to the easel, well used paintbrushes in a glass jar. A half-finished portrait with multitudes of yellow and pink wildflowers in grassy green meadow rested on the easel. *She paints?*

A purple area shag rug graced the white tiled floor. A large fluffy, inviting bed with purple fringed pillows with white mosquito netting draped the bed. A well-loved stuffed gray-and-white striped kitty lay on the pillow. He pictured Elyse lying in the center of the large bed, naked, as her arms reached for him. He shook his head at his mind's wanderings.

With her closet gone, her list of items she wanted was useless. His gaze wandered the room unsure of what she needed. He grabbed the kitty from the bed and moved about the room looking for items she might want. He looked up on the wall at the Remington 700 rifle with its scope displayed there. *Holy shit, she wasn't kidding.* He stopped at a small dresser. On top sat two items, a small music box and a snow globe. He lifted the lid of the music box and a tiny ballerina started doing tiny pirouettes to a tinny-sounding tune. The snow globe had a ballerina and glitter inside. He twisted the key on the bottom of it, and the theme song from *Romeo and Juliet* played its tinkling melody. He also found a sewing box, a small vial of French perfume, a hairbrush, two pairs of ballet slippers, and a filmy pink ballet skirt hanging on a hook. He stuffed everything into a rucksack and left the embassy.

ELYSE WAS SITTING on the steps chatting with Sarge and Doc when two of the Air Force captains from the other night at the Officer's Club pulled up in the Jeep. They hopped out of the Jeep, making much fanfare about returning her black shoes to her. Elyse blushed; she didn't even recall leaving her shoes behind. Evil tequila. They chatted for a while, and as they were leaving, Elijah, Arnold, and Mountain pulled up in a Jeep.

Elijah walked over and spoke with the two pilots.

"She did what?" He turned and looked at Elyse. Whatever they said to him made him furious.

"Damn."

They talked for a few more minutes, and then the pilots took their leave. Elyse nervously watched them, trying to decide if she should flee now or wait.

Elijah watched them pull away and then turned to look at Elyse. He stood with his hands on his hips. "Elyse, were you at the airfield the yesterday?"

Elyse blushed and stammered, "Um, yes. In a way, I guess so."

"More specifically, were you bunker dancing on perimeter bunkers at the end of the runway?"

"Well?" Elijah prompted.

"Yes. I was."

"Were you playing Chicken with fighter jets?"

"I wouldn't call it that."

"Do you know how dangerous that was? No more. The airfield is off limits. Get inside."

"What. Why?"

"Get inside now."

He handed her the rucksack, with a glare at Elijah, she grabbed her shoes, the rucksack and went inside, slammed and locked the door.

"Ten hut." He directed his ire at Arnold and Mountain. "What have I told you two about keeping her out of trouble? You let her dance on the runway playing chicken with fighter jets?"

"Elijah, it is not their fault." Elyse had come back through the door.

"Elyse, go back inside."

"No. I won't, I'm to blame. They cannot keep up when I'm bunker dancing. I chose to dance on the runway. If you're going to punish anyone, it should be me—not them."

"Trust me, Elyse, you will be punished."

Elyse blanched, but chose to argue the point. "You cannot punish them for something I did when they hadn't even caught up to me yet."

"Oh, yes I can."

They stood toe to toe on either side of the door.

"Enough, Elyse. Go back inside. And if you slam that door again, I swear I will break it down and you won't have a door."

"You go to hell. I'm not one of your Marines to be ordered about."

"Now, Elyse."

"No."

"Elyse," he ground out. "Get your sweet ass inside. Now."

"Make me," she screamed at him.

Challenge accepted. He threw her over his shoulder, strode through the door, and dumped her on her bed. He straddled her, holding her hands down above her head. "If you value your hide, you will stay here," he growled. "Do you understand me?"

"Yes, now get off me." Elyse was spitting mad now.

Elijah got up and moved to leave. "I mean it."

Elyse's response was to throw a glass from her nightstand. It hit the doorjamb just as he exited the room.

ELIJAH STOPPED and looked down at the shattered glass on the floor at his feet.

Okay, now she's asking for it.

He called out to Sarge to dismiss the men. He'd deal with them later. He turned back to Elyse and shut and locked the door behind him. Elyse scrambled from the bed. She put a chair between them as he advanced on her. The menacing look in his eyes told her she had pushed him too far.

"Calm down," she said. "It was just one little glass."

He batted the chair out of his way as if it was a tinker toy. He grabbed her, held her arms behind her back with one hand, and lifted her chin so she was forced to look up into his eyes.

"Don't you ever throw something at me again," he growled at her. "You're a brat. A wild, willful, spoiled brat."

"No, I'm not," she whispered back. "I just want you to be fair to them."

He kissed her, his lips, angry and punishing, then softening, teasing. Releasing her arms, he pulled her against him, and her arms slid around his neck. He left a trail of kisses down her neck and breasts as he pulled her shirt off and unhooked her bra. His lips never left her body as he pulled his own clothes off. He lifted her up, and she wrapped her legs around his back. They fell to the bed together, only stopped their lovemaking to rid her of her remaining clothes.

He murmured in her ear. "Open your eyes. I want to see them." She opened her eyes to look into his heavily lidded, passion-filled eyes.

Brat though Elyse was, he still needed her, wanted her. She tasted sweet, and he couldn't get enough of her.

He buried himself in her, and when he moved, she met him thrust for thrust. She screamed her need into his mouth and when it burst forth, he sought his own release. Groaning his pleasure, he nuzzled her neck, the soft hollow of her throat and kissed her lips. He felt like a school-boy it had happened so fast. He could only blame it on their building pressure to be together again. He kissed her lips, biting and nibbling.

"This time we take it slow. I want to know every inch of you."

"Show me. Show me more," she whispered.

MUCH LATER, Elijah whispered. "By the way, there's something here you never opened up." He handed her the rucksack.

She unzipped the rucksack and pulled out her stuffed kitty. "Binky. You found Binky," she said, bursting into tears. He held her again as she cried, holding her Binky. She cried for a lost home and life that she could not return to.

"I left Binky behind many years ago," she whispered.

"I know, but I thought it might give you some comfort now," Elijah replied.

She pulled out her music box and globe and stroked the two items.

"The music box was from my mother for my third birthday. She must have known I would be a ballerina someday. She died soon after.

"How did your mother die Elyse?"

"A horrible car accident."

He gave her an odd look. "Mine too."

Sadness played across her face. "I'm sorry for your loss."

"It was a long time ago. I'm sorry for your loss as well. Enough of the sadness, tell me about the globe," he said.

"The globe was from my father after my first performance of *Romeo and Juliet*, my favorite ballet." Tears ran down her face. "How did you know to bring these to me? All three of these are my most treasured belongings. Thank you so much."

"I don't know, something just told me they were important." Elijah pushed her back down, kissing the tears off her face and showering her lips with soft kisses. "No more tears, brat. No more tears," he whispered. Looking into her eyes, he said, "You're so beautiful, and you drive me so crazy, brat." He kissed her again. "I honestly do not know what to do with you."

That she defied him in defense of the team endeared her to him more than he would admit.

Elyse smiled. "More of this would be nice."

He pulled his fatigues on, grabbing his boots and shirt, he dressed.

"You caused a huge distraction at the airfield. The tower's air traffic controllers and the pilots have precision instruments they need to focus on. If they had missed the take-off, you would have been killed. That on top of dancing on perimeter bunkers."

Elyse grimaced. *Damn.*

"Tomorrow, you start a new punishment. Drill Instructor style."

She frowned as he leaned in and placed a soft kiss on her love swollen lips.

"You're restricted to your quarters."

SHE WENT to throw a pillow at him as he walked toward the door. He waved a chiding finger at her as he walked out the door pulling it shut behind him. She punched the pillow instead then pulled it closer to her. A smile played across her face as memories of the afternoon's lovemaking played back in her mind.

EARLY THE NEXT MORNING, the sun barely up, Elyse and Elijah stood next to a barren, rock filled area the size of a football field.

"If you ever go near any airfield or dance on the perimeter bunkers again, I want you to remember this moment and this punishment because you will be punished by something similar."

"Do you see the size of this field?"

Warily, she replied, "Yes."

He handed her a five-gallon bucket. "I want you to pick up every rock, big or small, on this field and dump them over there." He pointed to an area across the field from a few lawn chairs.

"To what purpose?"

"Don't question me, Elyse, get busy. Now," he barked.

She jumped at the angry tone of his voice. "Okay, okay." *Don't piss off the Marine.*

❦

MID-MORNING, Elijah watched her as she worked. She had started at the far end of the field and was about a quarter of the way down from where she started. He could tell she was angry by the set of her shoulders. Her grumbling occasionally drifting in the wind told him she still had not learned her lesson.

Doc and Sarge sat down in the chairs on either side of him. They brought the supplies he had requested of them earlier.

"She's filling the bucket too full, she can barely lift it," Sarge said. They watched as she struggled to lift the bucket and haul it to where she dumped it in the growing pile of rocks.

"Yeah, she's trying to rush to get it done. She'll figure it out and pace herself, eventually," Elijah replied.

"Take her out some water and food Doc. Give her this long-sleeved shirt and hat to cover her skin. Make sure she's okay. Let her have fifteen minutes for a break then get her back out on that field. I'll be back by then."

❦

ELYSE LOOKED up as Doc approached her.

"Come on Elyse, it's time for a break," Doc said.

She looked over to where Elijah had sat. "Is it okay with him?" She nodded toward Elijah's retreating back.

"Yeah, it's okay," Doc replied.

Doc took her over to sit in the shade and watched as she drank some water and ate a snack of peanut butter and crackers. He escorted her to the powder room and back again.

With sympathy in his eyes, he whispered. "Don't fill the bucket so full, keep the shirt and hat on."

She nodded her understanding and went back out to where she had left off in the field.

MID-AFTERNOON, she still worked to clear the field. Elijah watched her as she worked. He looked up when Sarge approached him and sat down.

"How's she doing?"

"She's slowing down, at least she's not filling the bucket so full anymore," Elijah replied.

"You trying to break her?" Sarge said.

"No, that's the furthest thing from my mind, but I want her to learn her lesson."

"You don't think she has yet?"

"No, no, I don't think so. Do you see the stubborn set of her shoulders? I've watched just about every negative emotion play across those tiny shoulders and her face. Anger, rage, fear, disgust to name a few. I'll know when she's reached the one emotion I want to see."

"Which one is that?" Sarge asked.

"Acceptance," he replied. "Acceptance of my authority and the rules. Rules that are for her safety and the safety of everyone on this base."

"Take her out some water, have Doc check her out again."

"Sarge, what's the one thing that you can think of that women don't like?" Elijah asked.

"Other than abusive drunks for husbands and the like, I'd say they don't like to be dirty."

In a quiet voice, Elijah replied, "Damn, I was afraid you were going to say that."

He looked over to Elyse. He could see the sweat stains down her back, and on the front of her shirt just below her breasts. Her hair was soaking wet, and she was covered in dust and grime.

"I fucking hate this," Elijah said, shaking his head.

"You're not going to let her shower, are you?" Sarge asked.

"No, no, I'm not," Elijah whispered.

***

ELYSE WORKED through the early evening, stopping only when they brought her food and water. The sun was setting now. The mosquitos and gnats were ruthless with their attacks as she swatted them away. Almost finished now, she only wanted a shower and to sleep. After dumping the last bucketful in the large pile, she dropped the bucket in front of Elijah. She couldn't hide her exhaustion, or the stubborn tilt of her chin.

"You're finished?" Elijah asked.

"Obviously."

"Ok, Elyse."

He walked her back to her quarters. Opening the door to her quarters, he waved her inside.

"Goodnight Elyse." He pulled the door shut.

"Hey, hey, wait a minute. I need a shower," Elyse called out.

Elyse stood in shock looking at the now closed door. *Are you serious? No Shower?*

She called out to him through the door. "You're a jerk, Elijah."

Fine.

She turned around and noticed the missing items. Her ballet slippers were gone and her one set of clean clothes, gone. Stepping over to the small sink she turned the water on, nothing.

He shut the water off as well. Ass.

She called out to no one in particular. "Two can play this game."

Pulling off her filthy clothes, she left them where they lay on floor. She shuddered at her own stench and climbed into her bunk.

***

ELIJAH SAT shirtless on the edge of his bunk. Pulling his boot off, he let it drop to the floor with a thump. He pulled off the other boot and then his fatigues. Neatly folding them, he set them aside. Lying back in his bunk, muscular arms folded behind his head. He could hear her moving about through the thin sheet rock of the wall. He heard her call out that two could play the game, and his gleaming white teeth formed a wide smile. *Stubborn brat.*

It was torture for him, knowing she slept on the other side of the wall. He touched the wall.

All I'd have to do is punch a hole big enough to pull her through. Make love to her and fall asleep with her in my arms.

Idiot. Today's lesson would be lost.

Steeling his resolve, he rolled over. His back to the wall, he drifted off to sleep.

He woke her with a gallon of water sloshed in her face.

"Get up."

She sat straight up. "Oh my God. Are you insane?"

"Up, now."

He soon had her dressed in her filthy clothes and back standing next to the field just as the sun peeked over the horizon. He handed her the bucket and pointed to the field. She looked at him befuddled and then she looked out over the field. *The rocks, they're back.* Looking over to where her rock pile was yesterday, nothing there.

"You're a jerk," she said.

"Get busy," Elijah replied.

"Who put them back there?" she angrily asked.

"You're not the only one being punished for your dancing on the runway."

Mountain and Arnold. "You can't do that to them. It's not their fault."

"I can do whatever I want. You need to learn that whatever you do, they are punished as well. Now get busy."

BY THE END of the day she was exhausted and hurting, but her stubbornness and anger had not dissipated.

Day three arrived, and she stood next to the field. All the rocks were again back in place.

"Something a little different today, Elyse. I noticed the rocks are getting sunburnt. Today, you flip them over, Elijah said.

"Let me guess, tomorrow I flip them back?" she replied, sarcastically.

"If need be. This can go on and on until you understand and accept the rules. Off limits, means off limits. You're a smart woman, I shouldn't have to state the obvious to you."

She stared straight ahead, not responding. Walking out to the field she started flipping the rocks over. She made it until mid-morning when her stubbornness slipped away, and she became angry again. Standing up she threw the rocks. Screaming her outrage, and anger, she threw rock after rock. She screamed her despair, and hatred for Elijah. She cursed the war that had taken the lives of so many. She cursed her father for leaving her here, for not coming for her. Spent, she fell to her knees crying.

That's when he saw it. Acceptance. *That's my girl.* He walked out to her, and sat, cradling her in his arms as she cried.

"I really don't hate you," Elyse sniffled.

"I know. Come on, let's get you a shower and a nap."

CHAPTER 23

The next morning Elyse was up early. She took a quick walk with Arnold, Mountain, and Dog to the mess hall for some strong coffee and a bite to eat. Arnold and Mountain cleared a path through the crowded walkways, stiff arming more than a few to make way for Elyse. More than one man turned to snarl a nasty retort just to spot Elyse and watch in silence as she walked between her strong protectors.

MOST OF THE men had left the hall as she sat reading the paper with her slippers and radio at her side.

"Why is it every single newspaper I have tried to read since we left Khe Sanh has half of the article's cut out?" She held it up to show them, peeking through a hole. "It looks like swiss cheese."

Mountain and Arnold glanced at each other and shrugged their shoulders.

"No idea," Arnold replied.

WHAT ELYSE DIDN'T KNOW IS that the staff in the mess hall went to great lengths at Elijah's orders to keep information regarding the Tet offensive and her father's injuries and recovery from her. They examined every newspaper and magazine, removing articles before they were placed out on the tables.

SHE LOVED the quiet time before the hall filled again with men. As Marines and Soldiers alike straggled in, more than a few stopped to chat with Elyse. Her easy laugh and friendly chatter soothed many a man homesick to just talk with a "round eyed" American woman. She found out where the rec area was from there, and later she went to check it out with Mountain and Arnold.

A few men were already there. She found her friend from Khe Sanh and sat with a few men with guitars and harmonicas playing along to tunes on the radio. She soon had them dancing and singing, forgetting the war and the circumstances that brought them all there.

An announcer spoke on the radio. An Armed Forces station, They played music requests and dedications specifically for the troops. "This song is dedicated to—and you're not going to believe this, boys—the beautiful ballerina seen dancing on base." The announcer laughed. "What drugs is this guy on?"

Elyse stared at the radio in shock. With a glance at Arnold and Mountain, she said, "Damn."

"Hey, he's talking about you," Arnold said.

THERE WAS NO DENYING IT. Plenty of men had seen her dancing already. With that, she rolled her eyes as the dedications came rolling in one after another throughout the morning. She continued dancing with the boys. Many were new recruits fresh out of boot camp, not yet assigned to their teams. This was the place where the platoon sergeants and leaders often came to choose their new recruits, known as "FNG's," or "fucking new guys."

In jest, a few of the sergeants offered to put her in their platoons. She laughed, put a Marines helmet on, and saluted. "Private Booker ready for duty." She tried on an ammo belt and a rucksack, and Arnold held her arm to steady her. "Now I look like a Marine."

With the ammo belt separating her breasts and bare belly, they grinned at her.

Sergeant Monroe stated, "Nope, no Marine has ever looked like that. What's your qualifications?"

"Let's see," she began, "I spent four days in the jungle, lots of bugs and snakes there. Two and a half months during the siege at Khe Sanh, I've killed five VC, and I'm a sharpshooter."

"Geez, you've got more experience than these clowns here. It's too bad you're a woman," Sergeant Monroe replied.

Elyse rolled her eyes. "Mark my words, boys: the day will come when a woman can be a Marine or Soldier, even a fighter pilot, and fight if she wants to."

They laughed at her, and she scowled at them. When Arnold made the mistake of letting go of her arm and she fell backwards from the weight of the hundred-pound rucksack. Still laughing, they pulled her back to her feet.

Elyse was ready to dance. She sat on sandbag wall and put her slippers on. With a "Ready?" to Arnold and Mountain, she spun away. Arnold and Mountain jogged behind her as she danced up the street heading toward the grassy area at the end. She had realized with a camp this size there was no chance for dancing in private, so she'd make the best of it.

Elyse stood on a corner, hands on hips, tapping her foot, waiting for traffic to pass. The only problem was they all seemed to drive excruciatingly slow when passing her.

A jeep stopped in front of her. The driver signaled with his hand for her to pass. Amusement shone in her eyes and she gave him an impish grin. She pirouetted across the street, stopping at the curb to curtsey, nodding her head in thanks to the astonished driver and his passengers.

At the next intersection she stopped. "Oh, for Pete's sake." she muttered to herself. *I'll never get to dance at this pace. I need to go where the traffic can't stop me.* She looked up and the roofs of the buildings called to her. They weren't that high and were quite long. An idea popped into her head. She jumped up on some barrels next to a building with a trellis-like frame and climbed to the top.

"Aww, come on Elyse. Stop." Arnold and Mountain called out. They stowed their weapons on their shoulders and started climbing up after her. They followed her across the main structure beam, stepping behind her.

Since it was more of a wide balance beam, Elyse felt a few gymnastics moves were in order. She performed a handstand into perfect splits, did a few back flips and cartwheels, and then continued dancing. As Elyse listened to the catcalls and wolf whistles from the street down below, the roof gave way beneath her. As she fell through, she realized it was a more of a temporary building tent structure and not at all sturdy.

She dangled from the now bent main beam before dropping down and landing on her bottom with an oomph. Elyse jumped up and watched as Arnold and Mountain slid down the beam and dropped to the ground. When they were all down, they realized they were back in the mess hall. They turned around and came face to face with four big MPs who stood with arms crossed and scowls on their faces.

Damn.

And that was when the entire structure caved in.

"WHERE'S ELYSE?" Elijah realized that she, along with Arnold and Mountain, had been gone for over an hour. He sent Sarge and Johnson to track them down. They returned a short time later.

"Um, Cap, the MPs have them," Sarge said.

Elijah and Sarge stood in front of the mess hall as engineers worked to right the tent.

"How? How in God's name did Elyse manage this one? I am going to chain her up and throw away the key."

ELYSE, Arnold, and Mountain sat in the brig at the MP headquarters.

Elyse sighed. "Well, at least I wasn't on the perimeter bunkers or the runway."

"I don't think that's going to matter. We're in deep shit," Mountain replied.

Worried now, she asked, "We shouldn't have to flip rocks again, will we?"

"I don't know, my legs are still bruised and sore from carrying rocks in my pockets when we had to clear the field," Arnold replied. "But, I'm a Marine. I've been smoked by Cap and Sarge more times than I can count, even before we found you in the jungle. That on top of a really sadistic Drill Instructor when I was in basic training. We can deal with punishments for infractions. We're more worried about you."

"I'm so sorry. I didn't mean to drag you into trouble again," Elyse said with concern.

"No worries, Runt," Mountain said.

⁕

THE DOOR OPENED AND ELIJAH, Sarge, and the head MP walked into the room. "Ten-Hut". Sarge shouted.

Arnold and Mountain stood at attention and Elyse stood in the middle of the two. She nervously slipped her hands into theirs.

The MP read the charges against them: "Destruction of United States military property, disorderly conduct." The list went on and on.

Elyse was grateful for the bars between them. The look on Elijah's face as the charges were read told her how furious he was. He looked like he wanted to throttle her.

"I can explain," Elyse said.

Elijah thanked the MP and the MP left. Then in a voice just short of bellowing, Elijah said, "I'm of a mind to leave the three of you in here to rot. At least then I'd know you'd stay out of trouble." He directed his anger at Elyse then. "What the hell were you thinking? Dancing on the roof? Handstands and back flips on the fucking roof, Elyse? Are you out of your fucking mind? You're lucky you weren't killed when you fell through. I'm of a mind to kill you myself just to end this bullshit."

Elijah then directed his ire at Arnold and Mountain. "And the two of you, I can see how she has you both wrapped around her pinky. Why are the two of you unable to stop ninety-eight pounds of mischief? Why can

221

you not keep her and yourselves out of trouble? The three of you together are a dangerous mix. You brought an entire mess hall down. An entire mess hall. I can't even. You're all restricted to your quarters. Elyse, give me your slippers."

"Elijah," she protested.

"Give me your slippers, now." He ground out.

She handed them over.

"And your radio."

She glared at him, narrowed her eyes, and cursed his name under her breath.

"What did you say?"

"Nothing."

"I'm warning you, Elyse. Give me the radio."

She handed it over as well.

"Since the three of you can't seem to stay out of trouble, the three of you can dig some trenches and fill some sandbags. That should make up for the time and effort a lot of people have to waste to right the mess hall and get it going again. After that you're all assigned to KP for a week."

Arnold and Mountain groaned.

"You two, will also have the additional punishment of shit burning duty."

"Elyse, I will discuss your additional punishment in private."

Elyse paled. She was not sure what that meant. "I'd rather clean the powder room, thank you."

Mountain and Arnold looked at her like she was crazy.

"I don't care what you would rather do. You have no say in the matter," Elijah replied. "You're lucky I've convinced them to drop the charges against the three of you."

"It's a good thing they didn't talk to the MP's at Chu Lai," Elyse stated matter-of-factly.

If looks could kill, Elyse would have been struck dead by Elijah's glare. "Let's go. And I don't want to hear another word out of your mouth."

THE MPS RELEASED THEM, and they walked out of the building right across the street from the mess hall. Elyse had the good grace to be embarrassed at the mess hall's destruction. *Who would have thought the roof couldn't hold a ninety-eight-pounder?* She sighed. *This is not going to be a good week.*

They pulled up to their quarters in the Jeep. With a scramble and leap, Elyse flew out of the Jeep and ran up the stairs. Then she slammed her door and locked it. She was not letting Elijah in here. She pushed all the furniture in front of the door to keep him out and sat on the bed to wait.

❦

ELIJAH CHUCKLED. He was a patient man, and she'd eventually have to use the head. He'd let her sit and worry about her punishment for a while.

After moving her furniture out of the way, she peeked her head out of the door. Johnson and Henson were on guard duty.

"Where's Elijah?"

They grinned at her. "He's not here right now."

"Oh, good. Take me to the powder room, please, and someone give me a cigarette. My nerves are shot."

Johnson handed her a cigarette, and they escorted her to the powder room and back.

She climbed the steps, opened the door, and went inside. She pushed the furniture back in front of the door, turned around, and realized Elijah sat there in the chair.

"Damn."

"Hiding Elyse?"

She turned back to the door trying to pull furniture out of her way to get out. He was on her in a heartbeat. Pulling her into his arms, he looked her in the eye.

"I will never understand in a thousand years how you manage to get yourself into so much trouble. Why do you take such risks? You're a daredevil. You have no fear for your own safety. You're no longer allowed to dance. Not on the inner bunkers, not outside of here, nowhere. You can't be trusted, and you don't seem to care about who you drag into trouble with you. It's the only thing you really care about. You're done."

"No, you can't forbid me from dancing."

"I can and I did. It's the only way to reach you. I'll give you fifteen minutes to think about this, and then you'll join Mountain and Arnold digging a trench."

"Please, please don't do this."

"You brought this on yourself," he said, and he walked out the door.

HER QUARTERS WERE at the end of the building with an air-conditioning unit on the side. She quietly pulled the unit out. Peeking out the window, she saw that the coast was clear. She climbed out and landed on the grass. She crept to the back of the building as she heard Elijah and some of the team talking out front.

SHE ONLY HAD a few more minutes before discovery, so she made a beeline for the front of the base. She had been smart enough to grab a bag with her things and her stash of scrip. She made it out the front gate, and once outside, she approached a young Vietnamese woman and offered some scrip to buy her Ao-dai, a Vietnamese long dress with pants and her hat. When the woman agreed, she convinced some other women to stand and block any view of them exchanging clothes. Once dressed, with her new bamboo hat, Elyse felt better knowing her red hair was covered and she would be less likely to be caught by Elijah. With a handbasket to hide her bag, Elyse started walking toward Saigon.

WHEN ELYSE's fifteen minutes were up, Johnson and Henson knocked on Elyse's door. No answer.

"Knock louder," Elijah called from the bottom of the stairs.

Still no answer. Elijah came to the top of the stairs, and with one kick, he broke it down. One glance at the open window in her room told him she was gone. With a grim look on his face, he came back outside.

"Get Sarge and the team. All of them. It appears Elyse is up to mischief again."

They searched the base. Elijah knew beyond the shadow of doubt that this time she had left the base. He cursed and ran his hands through his thick hair.

"Damn it." *She's bound and determined to do as she pleases. When I catch her, she won't be able to sit down for a month.* Sarge, Doc, and Elijah in a jeep followed by the team in another Jeep, and they left the base in search of ninety-eight pounds of mischief.

With her head down, Elyse watched them drive by, she kept walking following other Vietnamese on the road to Saigon. It was a long walk, but it gave her a chance to come up with a plan. The first place they would look would be the embassy. She had friends in the city. Perhaps they were still there. The first person who came to mind was her old ballet teacher. She adored her. There was also her spiritual adviser, and she had some old ballet friends too.

If Elijah contacted her father, he'd give them the location of all of them. Elyse admitted to herself she hadn't thought this all the way through, but she justified it in her mind. *He won't allow me to dance, but I can't accept that. I'm tired of being under his thumb. I'll figure something out.*

Then she remembered Tuan, the old gardener. Perfect. He lived close to the embassy in a home she considered safe. Hopefully, he still lived in the same place.

CHAPTER 24

Standing in the pouring rain, water droplets ran in rivers down the hood of his poncho and on to his face, Elijah wiped the rain from the stubble of his beard and rubbed his brow. He was beside himself. Six days. Elyse had been missing for six days. After going to the embassy and having a long conversation with the ambassador over the phone, he had the names and addresses of anyone Elyse would have known in the city. But still no Elyse. Even with some additional Marines to help with the search, they still had not found her. They knocked on doors, spoke with trusted local shopkeepers, chased down various red-headed women, nurses and such just to discover they were not the tiny temptation they sought.

Elijah knew the NVA did not have her, or they would have heard by now that she was captured. He was worried sick. That such a tiny slip of a woman could cause so much trouble was beyond him. When he had spoken with her father, he received a lot of advice on how to deal with her.

She had given the ambassador a lot of grief during her teen years in her unrelenting quest for independence. He resolved it by keeping her busy with various hobbies. Elijah had no idea she was an accomplished pianist, or that she played guitar, along with her ballet. Her most fulfilling activity was working at the orphanage close to the old embassy. It sounded to Elijah that she had been raised isolated and sheltered. His mind drifted back to a conversation he had with one of the Marines who guarded the embassy.

"She'd come down and play poker with us. Always had her nanny with her. As soon as that nanny dozed off, Elyse would be gone, climbing the wall to escape the compound. Those fucking no-good private guards she had never could keep up with her. A good kid, but kind of lonely, especially when the ambassador was gone. She'd come down here and dance in the gardens once in a while."

"She's a beautiful dancer," Elijah replied.

"Yeah, we were happy for her when she got that gig up in Huế City. We kind of hoped she had some freedom up there, even with her guards."

Elijah shook his head to clear the memory. Overwhelming sadness for her gripped him. *Why was she kept so isolated, protected?* Elijah had learned a lot about his little runaway mischief-maker, but he was starting to worry that the city seemed to have simply swallowed Elyse up. *Where was she?*

⚜

ELYSE STOOD on the corner looking at the embassy. The old gardener had died, she had nowhere else to go. As she waited for her chance, she realized they still had the same guard schedule. She knew how to get in and out without being caught by the guards. A portion of the embassy had been destroyed, with holes here and there blown in the side of the new six story building. Construction crews appeared to be making repairs on the building. There were signs of strife all over the city. *What happened here?*

Elyse climbed the wall and scooted across the grounds to climb the oh-so-familiar trellis to gain access to the second floor of the residential portion of the embassy.

Home. I'm home. She wandered the residence wishing her father was here, but she knew he wasn't. She walked into her bedroom and finally understood Elijah's seemingly random items he had brought back for her. Horrified, her closet was gone. What remained was a gaping hole in the wall now covered by a plastic tarp. Her clothes were gone. *All of my evening gowns, cocktail dresses, Oh God. My pink satin dress. My red shoes. Gone. My adorable outfits. All gone.* She did a quick calculation of what items were in her missing trunk. *Okay, okay, if they find my trunk, I'll still have some nice clothes. Oh My God. What happened here? I'm going to be sick.*

She figured she'd be able to stay here undetected. Six days later, she only had to hide once. This morning. She had to hang by her fingertips outside the gaping hole in the wall to avoid detection.

It was Elijah. Why he came back to the embassy, she had no idea. He only stayed a few minutes, and then he was gone. Relieved, she climbed back inside. It didn't surprise her that he still searched for her.

The fact that she was finally away from Elijah both elated her and filled her with deep sadness. She missed him, and she was only just now coming to grips with the depth of her feelings for him.

She was in love. She missed his kisses and his touch and the way he buried his face in her hair. But she hated the camps, the rules and restrictions, the lack of privacy, always feeling like she was on display. Yet her feelings were being overruled by her love of dance, to feel free. The thrill of jumps, and pirouettes. The way the music flowed through her body when she moved.

Elyse filled the bathtub thankful she had running water. A long soak was in order before bed. She sat in the bathtub shaving her legs and giggled out loud at a memory from just two weeks ago. Elijah had caught her shaving her legs with his Ka-bar knife. He had been annoyed, exclaiming that she had desecrated his knife. He went in search of his razor for her to use. He returned a short time later grumbling that Sarge had told him it would ruin his razer. He used his knife and finished the job of shaving her legs. Kissing her freshly shaven legs to check their smoothness, his words echoed in her mind.

"Next you'll have me painting your toe-nails."

"What's wrong with that? It's kind of sexy," she had replied.

He had smiled that slow wolfish grin she loved so much as he crawled up over her body to kiss her lips.

"You're not done yet," she laughed, as she raised an arm.

Looking at her armpit, he had snorted, "What? That? It's peach fuzz."

"It's shrubbery, pretty please," she had begged.

He lathered soap on her armpit.

"Quit squirming." Exasperated, Elijah said, as she rolled away laughing, for the fourth time.

"It tickles."

"Now hold still," Elijah said, as she bit her lip to keep from laughing and rolling away.

She had somehow survived while he welded his blade to complete the task, a grin on his face the whole time.

ELYSE CLOSED her eyes as the memory faded. *How will I survive without his touch?*

She found a fresh nightie from a drawer under her bed. Pulling open a second drawer, she found some old sheer ballet skirts and matching tops. *This is it, all I have now.*

Elyse lay in her bed listening to the pouring rain, Binky in her arms and thought again of Elijah. She wondered if she was forsaking the love for a man for the love of dance, and she cried, deep heart-wrenching sobs.

She decided that tomorrow she would return to Elijah. She got up to pack her bag. *Damn. Still no clothes or shoes.* Just some toiletries and what little she had found in her drawers. She climbed back into bed her mind made up. In control of her own life, feeling better than she had in months, she fell asleep thinking of his soft kisses.

ELIJAH STOOD at the end of the bed. She was so tiny in the large bed as he drank in the sight of her while she slept. Who would ever have thought such a tiny troublemaker would invade his every thought? He'd never really had time for women before. That ninety-eight pounds of sass had so deeply affected him was beyond his comprehension. He was thankful he'd found her. No longer angry, he'd had a lot of time for reflection. He stripped off his clothes and climbed into bed with her. He held her close as she snuggled into him and murmured his name. He slept the first good night's sleep he'd had in a very long time.

When Elyse woke in the morning, it was a full minute before comprehension set in. She opened one eye and stared at the broad expanse of his bare chest before lifting her gaze to his face.

He smiled at her. "Good morning, brat."

It wasn't a dream. He was really there. "Elijah," she whispered.

He kissed her long and slow, his velvet kisses plundered her mouth and her need for him grew in the pit of her belly. He then moved to cover her body with his own. He left soft kisses on her lips, leaving a trail from her neck back to her lips. She eagerly returned kiss for kiss. He pulled her nightie over her head, kissing every inch of her aching body. She cried when he entered her.

"What's the matter, brat?"

"I cannot give you up, Elijah."

"You don't have to."

She laid in his arms afterwards, replete and happy. She was well aware he would punish her for running away, but she didn't care.

His voice husky and smooth, "Don't ever run away from me again."

"I won't," she whispered.

"We have to talk about this."

"I know. I was wrong. I already packed last night and planned on coming back today."

"You were?"

"Home is wherever you are."

He kissed her, and they cuddled up together. He inhaled her hair and her scent. Her skin was as smooth as silk. He noticed it had grown more tanned and freckled since he'd first met her. He slid his hand down the length of her body, over her curvy hip, across her tiny waist, up her side, and over her breast and belly. She had the body of a goddess. He rolled her on her back, kissing the new sun-kissed freckles on her nose, her eyelids. Her lips parted. He couldn't get enough of her. She was an aphrodisiac, and every time he loved her, he wanted to love her again. He couldn't help himself.

"We need to return."

"I know. I'm ready, but how did you know I was here?"

"Binky."

"Binky?" She looked at her stuffed kitty.

"I had stopped here again to see if you had been here. You put Binky back on the bed, so I knew you were here. I sent the team back to the base, and I waited till nightfall."

"Sneaky Marine. I'm glad you found me."

"Me too, brat."

"Are you going to punish me?"

"You still have to do your KP, and trench and sandbags for the mess hall fiasco."

"And my dancing?"

"We'll talk about that later."

Her shoulders drooped a little, but she nodded her understanding. "I need to look at one more thing while I'm here."

"What is it?"

"Follow me."

He followed her into the drawing room. It was a large room with one wall of bookshelves filled with the classics. A comfortable sitting area graced a barely used fireplace with two brown leather chairs and a small matching couch.

Elijah eyed the books on the shelves. "Have you read these?"

"Every single one," Elyse replied, as she eased into one of the chairs.

"And this, this is my favorite chair. The perfect place for an afternoon nap.

Elyse stood and walked over to a baby grand piano that sat off to the side, covered in dust.

Elyse blew the dust off the piano key lid and sat down.

"This is my fourth treasured item. My father bought me this for my sixteenth birthday. I was afraid to come in here before. I knew I would just want to play, and I didn't want to alert the guards." She started to play the theme from *Romeo and Juliet*. Elijah watched her for a few moments and then sat down next to her on the piano bench. He picked right up where she was, matching note for note, upper and lower keyboard. They smiled at each other as they played.

When the song was over, she looked into his eyes. "You're very good."

"So are you, brat."

"My mother insisted I play, and after she passed away, my father made me continue my lessons. It was not something a grieving boy of eight wanted to do. Afterwards, I've always been grateful for his persistence."

"I think you have many hidden layers you haven't told me about." Elyse said.

"So do you. We need to leave, Elyse."

She stroked the piano keys and shut the lid. Elijah stood to stroll the room, pausing at a mantel filled with photographs. A tiny cherub with riotous red curls and her thumb in her mouth on the lap of a beautiful redheaded woman gave him pause. Her mother, he knew. Elijah had vague memories of her with his own mother.

More memories tugged at his subconscious, there was something familiar about the tiny tot as well. He walked past more photographs of Elyse at different ages. He stopped to view a beautiful, large, framed photograph of Elyse in a ballet costume. She appeared to float mid-air. All the photos spoke of a life filled with dance at a very young age.

They walked to the door, and she paused at the doorway to look back.

"Elyse, you'll see all of this again someday."

Fighting back the tears, she nodded.

They went back to her room to collect her things. The bed was freshly made by Elyse, Binky lounged in his place on her pillow. Elijah nodded toward the stuffed animal. She smiled, "Binky needs to stay here."

They walked to the doorway, and Elyse took one last look at the room, and her gaze stopped at the hole in the wall. Her brows furrowed in a deep frown as she pulled the door shut in resignation. *My clothes.*

"Please tell me you found at least one pair of pants or shoes," Elijah said.

"Nope," Elyse replied with a grin.

When they got outside Elijah climbed on a motorcycle. "Jump on."

"Whose bike?"

"I borrowed it from a friend."

"Aren't you worried about locals seeing me?"

"No, there's quite a few American women in Saigon. They think you all look the same."

"Seriously? And here I kept myself hidden and dressed as a Vietnamese woman when I ventured out."

Elijah laughed. "At least you followed one order." He put on a pair of sunglasses. "Let's go."

※

It was a thrilling motorcycle ride—another first for Elyse. She wrapped her arms around his waist and leaned into him. Once out of the city, she pulled up his shirt and hers and pressed her bare breasts into his back.

Christ, she drives me wild. Elijah liked the feel of her bare breasts against his back. It almost felt normal, as if he were back home in California with Elyse on his bike as they raced down the coastal highway. He could picture every detail.

When they made it back to base, Elijah drove over to the officer's quarters and parked the bike in front of her quarters. She got off the bike and started to walk up the steps to her place.

"Ah, no, Elyse." He grinned and pointed to the next room over. "No side windows."

"Ah, I get it." She went up the steps of the next room over. The things she had left behind were in her new quarters. She settled herself in and wondered if she was out of her mind. She was still restricted to her quarters and still had to dig trenches and do KP, but she was close to Elijah, and right now it was enough.

※

Early morning found Elijah sitting in a lawn chair just outside his quarters with a few other officers. Elyse began her KP duties over at the mess hall. The radio sitting on the ground beside him played popular tunes.

The disc jockey's boisterous voice eventually came on. "Well, boys, we've got about two hundred more dedications today for Elyse. Heard tell that she's a tiny redhead with buku tracts of land if you get my drift. Elyse, wherever you are, this song is for you. Boys, keep sending those dedications in, and we'll make sure we play them for her."

Stunned, Elijah looked at the radio and back at his fellow officers. "How long has this been going on?" he asked them.

"Holy shit, Elijah, we thought you knew. About two weeks or so. She's getting hundreds of dedications every day," Bob said.

Elijah ran his hands through his hair. "If they've given out her location, she's in grave danger."

He headed over to see if he could talk to the general, but he was off base, so Elijah set up a meeting for when he returned in a couple days. An idea came to him. If they used every Armed Services radio station within South Vietnam to play dedications and give false sightings, it would confuse the enemy as to which part of the country she was actually located in. He then had a quick meeting with some of General Morgan's aides and felt more confident that Elyse's safety was covered for the time being.

CHAPTER 25

Elijah had a surprise for Elyse. Something he had been thinking about for a while. Elyse had never been on a date. He wanted to take her on one. It was a bit risky, but Saigon was full of American women, most being nurses and correspondents. He knew a quiet little restaurant that served amazing steaks. Elyse would need new clothes, so he headed into Saigon. With help from the shopkeeper he found a violet-colored dress that would highlight her beautiful eyes. As the woman wrapped the dress he smiled. He couldn't wait to see her in it. At the last minute, he remembered shoes, and they found a pair of slip-on sandals. Elijah informed the team that once he left with Elyse, they were all free and were issued liberty passes for the evening.

Elijah found her lounging on a bunker, a book in hand.

"Elyse?"

She looked up and smiled her beautiful smile.

"I have a surprise for you," he said, handing her the package.

She opened the package. "Elijah, it's lovely."

"Tonight, brat, if you're willing, we are going on a date."

"Really? I thought you said Saigon wasn't safe?"

"The one thing I noticed when I searched for you was that there are many, many, American women in Saigon. You'll blend in just fine. You've got until 15:30 to get ready."

She gave him that adorable annoyed look.

"Seven thirty."

"What time is it now?"

"Three-thirty."

She looked horrified and jumped to her feet.

"Four hours, Elyse. Plenty of time."

"That's hardly any time at all," she shrieked, and then took off back to her room at a run.

He shook his head. "Women."

As Elyse showered, she could hardly contain her excitement. A date, her very first. And her date for the evening was the most handsome, frustrating, annoying, beautiful man she had ever met. She dressed with care. The dress was lovely, violet-colored, short, with sassy fringe on the bottom, skinny straps, and a low-cut neckline to show off her cleavage. She left her amber fire hair down for Elijah. With her new black sandals and her little purse, her outfit was complete.

ELIJAH KNOCKED on Elyse's door and waited. He had dressed in civilian clothes and was looking forward to the evening with Elyse. She opened the door, and they both stared at each other. At the same time, they said, "You look amazing."

With a laugh, Elijah asked, "Are you ready, brat?"

"Yes, I am." They left her quarters amid wolf whistles and catcalls from the officers in the area. He helped her into the Jeep, and Elijah and Elyse headed into Saigon for their first date.

The restaurant was delightful, one of a few that served American fare. He ordered for both of them: steak, medium rare, with a side of broccoli, a baked potato loaded with butter and sour cream, fresh bread, and butter. They topped it off with a bottle of red wine.

Elyse smiled. "Perfect, Captain."

"I recalled you said you loved a good steak," he replied.

They talked of life back in the world during their childhoods, though

Elyse admitted she had no memories of her childhood before Vietnam and could only go off of her father's hearsay.

Elijah raised an eyebrow. "No memories at all?"

"None, whatsoever. My earliest memory is the day we arrived in Saigon. I don't even remember living in Germany for two years. Though I do speak German and somehow retained my early ballet training," she replied.

They spoke of their families. Elijah had his father and brothers, but Elyse was alone in the world except for her father.

The evening was quite enjoyable, and the laughter and wine flowed freely. Elijah's lips were the most kissable Elyse had ever seen. Elijah looked up to see her gaze had turned sultry.

"We'll never finish dinner if you keep looking at me like that."

Elyse blushed. "I want to kiss you, Captain Corrington."

"The feeling is mutual, Miss Booker."

They finished their dinner and Elijah paid the bill and they left the restaurant.

⁂

As they strolled hand in hand, he studied her parted kissable lips, her smooth skin, and the way her dress molded to her breasts. He was mesmerized by the sassy fringe that swished back and forth with each swing of her curvy hips. The talk of Vietnam, and he knew why.

They turned a corner and entered an area teaming with night life. Many military personnel were out enjoying the warm, sultry, summer night amid bright lights and loud music. The bars and restaurants overflowed with men, a few American women, and Vietnamese locals. Elyse was a beautiful woman, she had more than her fair share of outright ogling and stares.

"Corrington." someone called out.

Elijah waved at some fellow officers he hadn't seen for a while and they stopped to chat. He introduced them to Elyse, and they practically drooled over her. Elyse was gracious and friendly and kept her temper in check, and soon they were on their way again.

Elijah cursed under his breath. He knew many people and each one of them appeared to be in Saigon tonight. But Elyse was gorgeous and delightful, and he tried to forget his worries. He spotted the bar he was looking for and escorted her inside. A drink and some dancing were in order, and he was determined for Elyse to enjoy her first date.

"I think we should avoid tequila, brat."

She giggled. "I think you're right. I'll just have some sparkling water with lemon."

They found a table close to the dance floor. Once their drinks arrived, he took her over to the jukebox and together they picked out some songs. He led her out to the floor, and they danced to a favorite rhythm and blues tune.

Elijah loved the way she fit in his arms. He spun her about, pulled her into him and back out again. He curled his arms around her waist as they moved to the seductive rhythm of the song. Both of them were excellent dancers, and they danced the evening away in each other's arms.

❧

LEAVING THE BAR, they strolled the street hand in hand. Elijah ran into more buddies, and he introduced Elyse to them. She chatted with the men for a bit and then stopped still when she saw her name on a billboard across the street. "Elyse" was performing tonight.

Elijah still chatted with his buddies as she wandered toward the bar, her curiosity getting the best of her. She had made it to the door of the establishment.

❧

ELIJAH LOOKED AROUND and spotted her and where she was heading into.

"Elyse, no."

All eyes on the street turned to her.

❧

SHE POINTED TO THE BILLBOARD, shrugged her shoulders, and went inside.

It was crowded with men, but Elyse paid no heed to them. She pushed her way toward the stage. A Vietnamese woman wearing a red wig and ballet slippers and not much else performed a dance on the stage. On the floor in front her, beer bottles, men were handing her money. Elyse, wide-eyed, stood with her mouth gaping open. *What is she doing?*

Elijah came up behind Elyse and put his hand over her eyes. "You don't need to see this, brat."

Once he was away from the stage, he lifted her and flipped her up over his shoulder and made tracks to get her outside.

Elyse howled for him to put her down. "Elijah, that woman is pretending to be me. What is she doing?"

"Captain Corrington?"

Elijah turned around to find Major Jamison, his superior officer, standing on the sidewalk with other officers from his company.

"Sir." Elijah saluted.

※

ALL THE MAJOR could see was a luscious shaped woman's bottom in purple panties barely covered by violet fringe slung over his Captain's shoulder and his Captain saluting.

He saluted back. "I assume *that* is Miss Booker?"

"Yes, Sir."

"How's that special assignment going, Elijah?"

"Fine, Sir."

Major Jamison, struggling to contain his mirth, nodded slowly. "I see that."

※

"ELIJAH, I am falling out up here and my bottom is exposed. Put me down."

Elijah cleared his throat and set Elyse down.

She slugged Elijah in the arm. "I am not a sack of potatoes to be slung over your shoulder at any whim." Clearly annoyed. "What is wrong with you? You do not introduce me to someone bottom first."

ELIJAH GRINNED as Major Jamison looked Elyse over, shocked at the tiny beauty as she straightened her clothing.

"Major Jamison, this is Elyse Booker."

"Explain yourself, Captain," the Major said.

Elyse was still miffed, her fiery temper rising with every passing moment. Before Elijah could respond, she addressed the major, wagging her pointed finger at him. "Oh, no, no, you are just going to have to wait your turn. Elijah, that woman, that woman was pretending to be me, and she was naked. What is going on?"

"Elyse, that was a strip club. She was entertaining the men."

Now Elyse was even more outraged. "That's entertainment? Now all of Vietnam believes I'm a stripper?

Elijah grinned. "Elyse, no one believes that's really you. It's all fantasy."

"I do not understand."

"I know, and that's okay."

"Why did you take her in there?" the major demanded.

"Don't be ridiculous. He didn't take me in there. I was curious as to why my name was on a billboard and went in on my own."

"Now maybe you'll listen to me, Elyse," Elijah said. "There's a seedy side of life you have no idea exists and it is dangerous. Maybe it's time to leave."

At her crestfallen face, he said, "Okay, let's get one beer, and then we'll go. Major, would you care to join us?" They did and the one beer turned into a few.

ELYSE LAUGHED, enjoying herself once more. The men's dry humor had her in stitches, and it was apparent to her how well-respected Elijah was by his superiors.

"Why did I not meet you at Khe Sanh?" Elyse asked Major Jamison.

"Sniper fire. I was wounded a day or so before you arrived and was recovering in the hospital at DaNang during the siege." he replied.

"You're okay now?"

He smiled, "Yes, I'm good."

Elyse excused herself to use the powder room. When she returned, four prostitutes had converged on the table, laughing and talking with the men. Elijah was trying to unwrap one woman's arms from his neck. He spied Elyse's raised eyebrows and set the woman from him, steering her to another man. When the woman tried returning to him, Elyse hissed a warning in Vietnamese to the women and they all left the table.

Amused, Elijah asked her what she said to make them retreat.

Elyse smiled at Elijah. "You don't fool me, Captain. You're just as fluent in Vietnamese as I am. You know exactly what I said."

"So, what did she say to them, Elijah?" Major Jamison asked.

Elijah grinned. "I believe she threatened to break her arms off and shove them up, never mind."

Elyse sat down next to Elijah, sniffing the air and his collar. Wrinkling her nose, she leaned in closer.

"You smell like a whore."

Elijah laughed at her.

Elyse looked at Elijah and whispered, "I don't share."

"Neither do I," Elijah replied with an easy grin.

It was time to go, they said their goodbyes left the bar. They walked hand in hand to the Jeep. Elijah started the five-mile trip back to base with Elyse curled up at his side.

Elyse sighed. "Thank you, Elijah. It was a lovely evening, though I enjoyed our quiet time together the most."

"Oh, we're not done yet, brat."

"Really, Captain? What else did you have in mind?"

He gave her a wicked grin.

"Oh really? Is that part of every 'first date?'"

Elijah laughed. "In every man's dream."

"Tell me, Captain, would the end of a first date start with something like this?" She nuzzled his neck and nibbled his ear lobe, lightly flicking with her tongue down his jawline.

"Sweet Jesus, Elyse."

With a wicked smile, she slid her panties off and hung them on the rearview mirror. Looking at the panties he inhaled sharply. She pulled the top of her dress off of her shoulders and pushed it along with her bra mid-waist. Then she pressed his hand to her breast, capturing his lips, she nibbled, flicked and teased his neck all while he was trying to keep his eyes on the road.

"Ah, damn, you're wicked."

She climbed on his lap, grinding against him and kissing him, as the Jeep careened back and forth across the center line. He captured a nipple in his mouth and swerved to avoid an on-coming Jeep. She arched her back against his onslaught of kisses, moaning with pleasure.

"Christ. We're almost to the base. I don't know if I should slow down or speed up."

"Speed up. I want you inside of me."

The lights of the base and guard shack came into view.

"Behave. We can't go through the gate like this."

Elyse climbed off his lap, pulled her clothing into place, and demurely sat back in her seat with a smug smile on her face.

Stopping at the gate, the guard eyed the purple panties hanging from the rearview mirror. Glancing over at Elyse, he gave Elijah a knowing grin. "Have a good night, Captain."

Spotting the panties, he inwardly groaned. "You too, private." Elijah replied gruffly. He pulled away and raced down the street.

Elyse scooted back close to him. "Hurry," she purred into his ear.

"Brat. You are going to pay dearly for every… sweet… tormenting mile you just put me through.

"I can't wait," she whispered in his ear.

He pulled up in front of her quarters, stopping with a screech of tires. He lifted her out of the Jeep and carried her up the steps two at a time.

SARGE AND DOC arrived to stand guard for their morning duty. They had returned early from Saigon the night before. Both were married men they had no need beyond a few hours of liberty and a few beers to stay in Saigon. They glanced at the Captain's odd parking job.

"It's still running," Sarge said, laughing.

"Do you think he was in a hurry?" Doc asked with a laugh as he pointed at the purple panties hanging from the rearview mirror.

"What do you think?" Grinning, Sarge shut the Jeep off and pulled the panties from the mirror.

"Lucky bastard."

"Let's go get some coffee. We're not going to be needed for a while. By the way, I believe you owe me ten bucks."

Recalling their bet, Doc pulled ten bucks from his pocket and slapped it into Sarges hand.

A KNOCK on the door well past noon roused Elijah from slumber. Moving quietly so he wouldn't wake Elyse, he answered the door to see Sarge. "Sorry to disturb you, Sir. You left the jeep running. I shut it off and pulled these from the rearview mirror." He handed him Elyse's purple panties.

With a sparkle of amusement in his eyes, Elijah nodded. "Thank you, Sarge. How's the team?"

"Still drunk."

Elijah laughed. "You and Doc might as well get some rest. I plan to spend the day with Elyse."

"Thank you, Sir."

Elijah shut the door and glanced at the panties in his hands and memories of the night before returned. After their wild drive home, she was more than willing to show him how much she wanted him. He had been taking it slowly with her, but last night's passion told him it was time to teach her more.

Smiling in anticipation, he headed back to the bed and stripped off his fatigues. Climbing back into bed, he gathered a sleepy Elyse into his arms.

"Mmm," she groaned, "please wake me up like this every morning."

He nibbled her neck and earlobes. "My pleasure." He rolled onto his back so she could straddle him.

"This seems familiar, like in-the-jungle familiar."

Smiling, he pulled her in for a kiss. He taught her how to ride him, as she arched her back. "Oh my God. Why did I not know about this last night? I so would have done this."

Laughing softly, Elijah replied, "It's probably a good thing you didn't. We would have been killed in an accident."

Rolling again so she was under him once more, he kissed his way down stopping first at that tiny mole on her breast. Then to each area of soft delight he'd kiss, suckle, and blew down her smooth stomach to her belly button. With each kiss he moved lower and lower watching her eyes for her reaction until he reached his goal.

"What are you doing? You can't do that."

"Oh, yes I can. Let me show you."

SHE LAY IN HIS ARMS, her body pink and glowing from his lovemaking. She wondered if she should tell him how much she loved him. She sensed that he wasn't ready yet.

Soon, she told herself, *soon*.

CHAPTER 26

It was raining again, it rained daily during monsoon season. Normally Elyse loved the rain, but today she was tired of being stuck inside and restricted by Elijah and the Marine Corps. She missed her freedom. She missed Hué City where she could walk in the rain with no worries. While she loved the team and was close to all of them, she hated their constant presence. Do this. Don't do that. Cap doesn't want you doing that.

She hated being told what to do, when to sleep, what to eat, where to go. She just wanted to walk in the rain and feel the raindrops on her face and pretend none of this existed.

She walked out her door to see Johnson and Mountain in their rain garb. Barefoot dancing in the rain was the perfect way to lift her spirits and clear her head. She twirled and swirled, dancing with girlish abandonment. She sang, jumped in puddles, and opened her mouth to catch raindrops with her tongue, and with one last twirl through a large puddle, she continued on into the mess hall with her smiling guards.

She stopped short when new eyes turned to her. Soaking wet, cold, and self-conscious, she covered herself with her arms. Eyeing the new face, she blushed and made her way to a table to sit. She started to shiver from the cold and her teeth rattled as she rubbed her arms to warm herself.

The man stood and went to the kitchen entrance. "Get me a towel and a blanket, on the double."

A cook handed him a blanket they kept on hand for Elyse, and the man sat down next to her, wrapping her in the blanket and grabbing her tiny feet to rub them between his large hands.

"Your wee feet are like ice."

Elyse was stunned by the bold familiarity of the man and tried to pull her feet back, but she was way too cold. The big, muscular man with carrot-top red hair and laughing green eyes, he ignored her discomfort and continued to rub her feet.

"Imagine my surprise when I looked outside and saw a wee, woodland fairy dancing in the rain. The trouble with Vietnam is it's hot and humid but the ground is cold and dank. In the rain, wee barefoot fairies can end up chilled to the bone."

An M-16 muzzle ever so slowly slid its way between his hands and her feet, and the man released her feet and held his hands up.

"Hands off the Woodland fairy, Mac," came Elijah's deadly voice.

The man sighed, brushing aside the rifle as he grabbed her foot again and continue to rub it.

"Just ignore him darling and he'll go away. What was I saying? Oh, yes, a dancing woodland fairy sheds her wings, turns into a fine woman, and enters this very mess hall. Now how does a fine Irishman like myself explain to a non-believer like Corrington that fairies do exist, and I just found me one?"

Elyse smiled at that.

"That over-exaggerated Irish brogue isn't fooling anyone, Mac," Elijah replied.

Mac looked at Elyse. She raised her eyebrows and shook her head.

"I'm cut to the quick. My own newfound woodland fairy doesn't believe my Irish brogue."

Elijah shook his head and again inserted the gun muzzle between Mac's hands and her feet.

"Persistent bastard, isn't he?" Mac asked her.

"Elyse Booker meet my college roommate and best friend growing up, Major Seamus McLoughlin, Mac." Elijah said.

Mac went to grab her foot and his hand was tapped by the gun again.

"You touch what's mine, Mac."

Leaning toward her, the man said, "Say it isn't so, wee fairy."

*"*Mo Ghra fior Fein,*" Elyse replied in Gaelic.

Mac pressed a hand to his heart. "Och. My wee fairy speaks my own true tongue."

Elijah rolled his eyes. "Do you even have a clue what she said, Mac?"

"No. Do you?"

Elijah smiled. "How did you find me here, anyway?"

Mac laughed. "I ran into Brendan on R&R. He told me you were here. I was heading this way and thought I'd stop by and see for myself."

Sitting down across from Mac, Elijah responded, "See what?"

"Why the wee fairy, of course."

Matt, the cook, came over and handed Elyse a stack of towels and a cup of hot chocolate.

"Thank you, you're an angel, Matt," Elyse said.

She rubbed her hair with a towel while her hot chocolate cooled a bit.

"How is Brendan?" Elijah asked Mac.

"He's alive, like us." Mac reached out to grab a tiny foot again, and Elyse slapped his hands away and scooted back. Turning toward Elijah, she crossed her legs and sat Indian style as she faced Elijah across the table. "I'm warm now, thank you."

Mac reached over and lifted one of her fire-colored wet curls to feel its silky-smooth texture between his thumb and forefinger and grinned at her when she pulled it back. Her blanket slipped, and he reached to pull it back up.

She slapped his hand away again. "Mac, pretend there's an imaginary line between us. This is my side—and that's yours. Keep *your* hands on *your* side of the line."

Mac grinned at her. "Och. A fiery temper to match the wild, red hair."

Elyse narrowed her eyes at him. "Cross that line once more, Irishman, and I'll show you a real fiery temper."

※

ELYSE LOOKED OVER AT ELIJAH, and he looked down to hide his grin. *You gotta hold your own with Mac, Elyse.*

247

SHE GLARED at him and took a sip of her hot chocolate and almost spit it out when she felt a long caress along her back to rest on her hip. With a snarl of outrage, she gave Mac a sharp elbow to the ribs, and the length of her arm across his belly hard enough to knock him backwards off the bench. He hit the floor with an oomph. With his legs bent, feet still up on the bench, and flat on his back, his mouth flew open in surprise.

Elyse jumped from her seat and turned on Elijah. "Some protector you are."

"I figured you'd be better off putting him in place yourself. With Mac, it has more meaning coming from you." He glanced at her perky breasts and the gum-drop high beams presented to him. "Uh, your blanket, brat."

Looking down at herself, she wrapped the blanket around her shoulders. "Ooh, you're all animals." With that, she turned to leave, but she was blocked in by their table, the Marines at the table behind them, and Mac still on the floor. "Fine." She stomped right over him, right up over his chest. Then she remembered she forgot her hot chocolate. Stomping back over his chest, she grabbed her cup and left the hall in a huff with her guards.

Mac roared with laughter. "Did you see that?" Hooting and hollering, he pulled himself up and sat back up on the bench still shaking with amusement. "The wee fairy just knocked me on my ass and stomped all over my chest."

Elijah grinned. "Welcome to Elyse's shit list. Didn't Brendan tell you not to mess with her?"

"He did, but I didn't believe him. Redheads—gotta love 'em."

"Takes one to know one. What's up, Mac? I know you're not here just to check out Elyse."

"You're right. Can we speak in private? I was sent with some private messages for you we didn't want to go out over the wire."

"Elyse?"

Sobering, Mac nodded.

Elijah sighed. "Let's go to my quarters."

"Perfect." Mac reached into his rucksack and pulled out a bottle of

Irish whiskey. With a nod and a few words to Sarge to take charge of Elyse for the evening, Elijah followed Mac out of the mess hall.

Elijah grabbed two glasses and set them down on the small table in front of Mac. His friend opened the new bottle of whiskey, sniffed the strong aroma, and poured a thumb-full into each glass. Elijah sat down in the other chair, swirled the liquid in his glass, and drank it down. He sloshed it around his tongue in appreciation.

"That's mighty fine whiskey, Mac."

"Only the best."

"How many *ARVN on this base?" Mac asked.

"As of right now, none. Why?"

"Keep it that way. We found out that an ARVN general is on the take, a spy for North Vietnam. What we don't know is which one. He's searching for Elyse using his own spies from within the ranks. The reward money offered for her capture has risen significantly along with her 'sale price.' She's at two and a half million U.S. dollars as of yesterday."

"Christ. Another layer of danger. That alone will add more limitations on the bases I can move her to if I also have to check for ARVN forces as well." Running his hands through his hair, Elijah poured them both another shot of whiskey. "So, they're on to our shell game."

"Yes, they know she's being moved from base to base. By the way, using the Armed Forces radio stations to confuse the enemy with false sightings was pure genius."

"There's got to be somewhere we can hide her back in the world?" Elijah ventured.

"We both know there isn't, or that's where she'd be right now. She's safer here in 'Nam than anywhere," Mac replied.

"There are some who would argue the point, including myself," Elijah said.

"They still do."

"Do you know whose bidding on her?" Elijah asked.

"We have a pretty good idea on some of them. One is an Arab prince. If he buys her, she'll disappear into some harem never to be seen again. She'd also be a bargaining chip to be used as leverage against the ambassador and the Paris Peace Accord, if they ever get it set up. Your wee fairy is at the center of subterfuge and the fight against communism. She must be kept hidden and protected."

Elijah shook his head as he absorbed the new information. "And she doesn't have a clue."

"ELIJAH, you said she was yours. If you fail, are you prepared to do the right thing for Elyse to prevent her capture?"

Elijah poured a full glass of whiskey and downed it. "I was prepared at Khe Sanh, but now?" He shook his head. "More than anything I want to see her live a full and productive life away from here."

"Elijah, if worse comes to worst, your orders are to end her life."

"You can't order me to do that."

"It's not coming from me, my friend. It's coming from the Pentagon and the State Department. Her father is unaware of that order. Also, in case you're unaware, General Morgan is to be replaced as the Commander of United States Forces. The ambassador still has a lot of sway in Washington, but there are a few short-sighted men within the top brass who feel that Elyse should not be our concern."

"We no longer have that layer of protection we had with General Morgan, but we'll have to see how it plays out with his replacement. So, there's that too."

"Do you have any good news, Mac?"

"No, just a big bottle of Irish whiskey to ease the pain, my friend."

"How long have you been CIA, Mac?"

Mac smiled. "I can neither confirm nor deny. I can see the attraction between the two of you, you know. She's a beautiful woman. I came here expecting to meet just a woman. I never expected to meet a woman with fire like that. You can kind of understand why they want her so badly."

Elijah smiled as he swirled his whiskey. "She's an exceptional woman. I've never met anyone before with such a thirst for knowledge. She's far too inquisitive for her own good. A perfect storm of sweet and sour with sass and naivety all neatly wrapped up in the prettiest tits and sweetest ass I've ever seen. Don't tell her I said that."

They both grinned, gave a silent toast, and clinked their glasses together.

※

ELYSE WALKED into the mess hall before most of the camp was up. Spread eagle on one table snoring quite loudly was Mac. On another table lay Elijah. Both reeked of whiskey and had the normal tent at their crotch. Elyse giggled, averted her eyes, and fanned the air to clear the smell. *Good grief, they must be drunk as skunks.*

She grabbed a cup of coffee and sat down by Elijah with a days' old swiss cheese newspaper. Sighing, *stupid missing articles.* Scanning the headlines, she read about protests, the war, articles about politics, and local news. She turned to the comics—she always read them first—then the horoscopes. She avoided the obituaries and went for the crossword puzzle. Pencil in hand, she worked to complete the puzzle. She looked up to see Elijah's red eyes watching her.

She flashed him a smile. "Good morning."

He grunted in response and reached out to brush the hair from her eyes. "My wild Irish rose," he whispered.

Elyse giggled. "I think I heard enough renditions of that song last night."

Elijah smiled. "Yeah, we were pretty wasted."

※

LOOKING AROUND, he realized he was in the mess hall lying on top of a table. Wondering how he got there, he groaned again, and covered his face with hands. Sitting up, he climbed off the table and made his way outside. When he returned, he saw that she had placed a cup of strong black coffee, a glass of water, and two aspirin from the cook's supply on the table for him.

Elijah smiled his appreciation and downed the aspirin and water. Mac snorted and rolled over, almost falling off his table. Catching himself, he sat up and gave them a bleary-eyed look before heading outside and returning a few minutes later. Elyse had placed a cup of Matt's strong black coffee on the table for him as well, and he went over and grabbed some cream, sugar packets, and a spoon. Pouring five packets of sugar and a couple packets of dried creamer into his cup, he stirred the mixture and sipped it with a sigh of pleasure.

Elyse grinned. "Have a little coffee with your cream and sugar, Mac."

He smiled. "Blonde and sweet, it's the only way I can stomach the swill they pretend to call coffee here."

Someone opened the door, and Dog padded inside to come lay at Elyse's feet. She warmed her cold toes in his fur coat.

Looking under the table, Mac commented, "Do you think you could have found a bigger dog?"

"He's the one who adopted me," Elyse replied.

Elijah smiled at the memory of Dog following her across the field at Khe Sanh. "He's a good dog and a strong protector. Hates the VC too."

"He's not alone there," Mac said.

Elyse scanned the newspaper again and grew excited. "Look, a picture of my father and an ARVN general shaking hands. I've met him before."

Elijah glanced at Mac.

"Let's see that picture, wee fairy," Mac said, and she handed him the newspaper.

"Where and when did you meet him?" Elijah asked.

"Why, just last year before Christmas when my father came up to see my performance of the *Nutcracker*. I met the general afterwards. Then we had a lovely dinner at a local restaurant. My father and I flew home to Saigon to celebrate Christmas the next day, the general followed a few days later. He's quite a vain man, and very arrogant. I really didn't care for him."

"Have you ever met any other ARVN generals, Elyse?" asked Mac.

"No, just him."

Elijah nodded. "I suppose you've met plenty of South Vietnamese dignitaries?"

"I've met many people through my father: dignitaries, politicians, brass, other American ambassadors and their families, presidents. You name them, and I've probably met them over the years."

"What about other foreign nationals?"

"Many, I've been hostess for many parties at the embassy. We just had a lovely Christmas party at the embassy last December, with many of the guests invited by the general and my father, of course. Why do you ask?"

"Just curious," he said in a low, pained voice.

She narrowed her eyes at Elijah. "You don't fool me, Captain. What are you not telling me?"

❧

ELIJAH GRABBED the newspaper and moved away from the table with Mac. He ripped the picture out of the newspaper.

Whispering to Mac. "Are you thinking what I'm thinking?"

"Yeah, they used that lovely Christmas party at the embassy as their way to showcase Elyse and start the bidding."

"The timing is right on point."

"We have to notify the ambassador and find that guest list."

An explosion resounded outside, and the earth shook beneath them. Elyse found herself on the floor with Elijah on top of her. The firebase artillery pounded in response as Elyse looked up to see the rest of the team enter the mess hall looking for her. As one, they all exited the mess hall to take refuge in an underground bunker. The sound of battle, running feet, cursing men, and explosions brought back vivid memories of the siege at Khe Sanh, and Elyse squeezed her eyes shut and covered her ears to block out the sound and the memories. Elijah held her tight and calmed her fears.

❧

AFTER AN HOUR OR SO, the bombardment ended. Elijah sent Sarge and Mountain to assess the situation and to see if it was all clear. They returned shortly declaring it was all clear. The attack by the VC on the western side of the base was thwarted with no loss of life, but many were injured. As they climbed out of the bunker, Elijah said, "They're probing our defenses here."

Elijah looked over to Elyse and worried that they knew she was here. Mac's relay of orders from the night before played back in his mind. He rubbed at his eyes as his headache returned. If the worst came to pass, he knew he'd die right alongside of her.

Chasing the morbid thoughts from his mind, he stroked her cheek and asked her if she was injured. She shook her head.

"Johnson, Henson, take Elyse back to her quarters and stay inside with her. The rest of you are to stand guard outside her quarters. If we have another attack, I want all of you there to protect her."

"Aye aye, Sir," Sarge replied.

"I need to make some calls, Elijah, time is of the greatest importance," Mac said.

Nodding, Elijah walked with Mac over to the MACV command post.

⚜

AT THE TEAM's poker game later that night, Elyse smiled as she lay her cards on the table.

"I believe my royal flush beats your four of a kind, Mac." She scooped the pile of winnings in front of her. Sarge, Doc, and Mountain threw their cards on the mess hall table in disgust.

"I'm out," grumbled Elijah.

"Me too," said Mac.

Mac narrowed his eyes at Elyse. "My wee, woodland fairy, is a card sharp."

Elyse smiled her brilliant smile at him. "I'm not a card sharp. I'm just very good, which, my dear Mac, makes me a card shark. There's a difference."

"Och, now I'm broke. How am I going to get home?"

Elyse rolled her eyes and gave him ten dollars in scrip. "Due and payable in full next time I see you Mac. Besides, you don't fool me. All you need to do is hop on any chopper in Vietnam, and you're back to your base without paying a dime."

Elijah laughed. "I warned you not to play with her, Mac. I've watched many a man walks away with empty pockets after playing with Elyse."

Mac turned to Elyse. "Why is that, wee fairy?"

"What was your first thought when you sat down and saw that I was playing with the team? I'll answer that for you. Your first thought was:

'Why, isn't she the cutest little thing, playing poker with the big boys?' That's where you made your first mistake. Most men can't put aside their egos. Instead of seeing an adversary, they see a mere woman, and because they can't get past, um, physical attributes, they make the mistake of thinking women are brainless and can easily be beat. I win because I'm not taken seriously, and because I've been playing for a very long time. I'm very, very good."

Mac's eyebrows rose as he turned to Elijah. "I just got dressed down, didn't I?"

Elijah grinned. "You had it coming, Mac."

Mac shook his head and grinned. "Some men don't care and will only ever see you as a cutie playing with the boys."

"I know. They're just jerks, but I'll still walk away with their money," Elyse replied.

MAC WAS LEAVING in the early morning. Elyse said her goodbyes and gave Mac a hug.

"Be safe, Mac."

"You, too, wee fairy."

Elijah escorted her out of the mess hall and to her quarters.

"Go on Elijah, go back and spend some time with Mac."

"You're sure."

"Of course. I'll still be here tomorrow. Mac won't. You can still come see me if you get lonesome in the middle of the night."

He kissed her lips. "Good night, brat."

"Good night, Elijah."

EARLY MORNING, after Mac had left on the first chopper out. Thinking about the attack the previous day, Elijah decided it was time to move Elyse. Calling Sarge and the team over to where he stood, he explained most of what Mac had told him. They needed to be on guard for South Vietnam's ARVN forces, Elyse was not to be seen by them.

HENSON AND ARNOLD stood guard waiting for Elyse in the powder room behind one of the buildings close to the helipads. Elijah, and the rest of the team waited for them over by the chopper.

Elyse exited the powder room, still spooked by the thought of Montagnard's standing behind the door she peeked around the door. Satisfied, she shut the door and crossed to where Henson and Arnold stood.

"READY? CAP IS WAITING," Arnold said. Elyse grimaced at the thought of another chopper ride.

"I've got some new books for you to read," Henson said. Elyse smiled, Henson, the quiet, somewhat shy bookworm, plied her with books, whenever and wherever he could find them. They shared a great love of adventure and fantasy brought by books, and he was opening up to her more and more every day.

Three Chinook transport choppers flew overhead drowning out Elyse's response as her hair flew in circles around her head and she fought to keep her footing. They landed close to them and the back door of the choppers dropped down and ARVN troops started disembarking the aircrafts.

Elyse gasped in shock as Henson and Arnold threw her to the ground covering her small frame with their own.

"What are you doing?" Elyse cried.

"Stay down and quiet," Henson ordered.

Henson and Arnold looked around, seeing no way out of the predicament they were stuck in. The ARVN forces wandered around the Chinooks. Another chopper landed nearby, and six new Marines disembarked and stood in confusion. Watching the new arrivals, *FNG's*. Henson got an idea, he glanced over at Elyse sizing her up,

"Keep her here, sit on her if you have too," he said to Arnold, as he dashed out to the helipad. He ran up to a Marine, newly arrived in Vietnam, and demanded his seabag. Terrified, the freckle-faced red-headed kid, in his neat clean fatigues and shiny new boots, did as he was told and handed over his seabag and watched in horror as Henson dumped every-thing out of the bag at his feet and dashed off.

Henson slipped into the tall grass where Arnold and Elyse lay in hiding. Pulling her along they crawled to the side of the building. Some of the ARVN troops wandered their way and sat on some sandbags piled up along the front of the building.

Henson opened the seabag. "Get in," he demanded.

"What? Are you serious? I am not getting into a duffel bag," Elyse replied quite indignantly.

"It's called a seabag, not a duffel bag. Now get in the fucking bag Elyse, your life depends on it."

Elyse raised both brows in shock at Henson's curt tone. Frightened, she moved to comply. She wiggled into the bag and they pulled it up and over her head. The very top of her head still showed. Wild red curls blew in the wind as they tucked them inside the bag. Henson hefted the bag up over his shoulder.

"How does it look?" he asked.

"I can see the outline of her legs and that she's curled up in there. I'm going to have to follow close behind you to block anyone's view," Arnold replied.

Henson looked up to see Mountain and Johnson trotting toward them. They eyed the ARVN soldiers as they scanned the area with questioning eyes looking for Elyse.

Mountain and Johnson's eyes widen in surprise when they realized where they had her hidden, and they nodded their head toward the other side of the airfield.

"Cap sent us to find you. The chopper is waiting," Johnson said. They grinned at each other and took off at a trot with Henson and his precious cargo in the lead. Mountain snatched a green towel off the neck of a red-headed kid as he ran by and tossed it over the top of the seabag to hide her hair.

ELIJAH, Sarge and Doc stood by the chopper waiting for Elyse and the rest of the team to arrive. Elijah looked at his watch and sighed. *Ten minutes behind schedule, again*. He had watched as the ARVN landed. Formulating a plan of action in his head, he watched the ARVN soldiers wandering nearby.

He looked to Sarge. "Sarge, go track them down. Circle around the airfield and take Elyse to the southern edge of the camp and we'll fly over and pick you up there."

"No need Cap, here they come," Sarge said.

He looked over and saw his team heading his way at a trot. Looking for Elyse, the concern showed on his face as he kept a wary eye on the ARVN soldiers.

Henson stopped in front of the Captain and Sarge, with Dog on a leash. Elijah's eyes flickered with recognition as a stray strand of red curls got caught up in the turbo wind of the chopper and flew straight up above Henson's head. Mountain captured the wayward curl and innocently tucked it inside the bag.

Looking Henson in the eye, Elijah leaned to the left to see what was on his back. Spotting the green seabag and meeting their telling eyes with amazement, he nodded toward the chopper and the team grabbed their rucksacks off the ground at Sarge and Doc's feet. They boarded the chopper, gently handing in the seabag.

THEY OPENED the bag and had her out as the chopper lifted off the ground. As the chopper flew overhead close to the ground, Henson tossed the bag and towel out the doorway. The seabag landed on the ground at the poor red-headed kid's feet with a thump and the confused kid looked up to see his towel floating down toward him.

ELYSE GAVE them all an accusatory glare, she was more than just mad.

"Did you have to run and shake me all over the place? I'm going to be sick." She covered her mouth and gagged as vomit rose up her throat.

"Whoa." they all cried out. Elijah and Doc moved her to hang her head out the chopper door as she was violently ill. The door gunner watched from his perch. Fighting back the bile that rose in his own throat, he closed his eyes.

They sat her back up when she was finished. Looking at the ashen faces of the men around her, embarrassment flooded her pale cheeks. "Sorry."

CHAPTER 27

Base Camp Four, Duc Pho: Mid-July

THIS BASE CAMP was different from the others. Elijah was excited when they landed. The same as when they landed at the other bases, the team had to form a tight protective circle around Elyse as the base personnel catcalled and whistled at her during the long walk from the helipad to the Commandants office.

Elijah gave the Commandant a big smile, and it was returned with a smile a mile wide.

The man gave Elijah a hug. "Boy, I'm glad you're safe."

"Colonel Corrington meet Miss Elyse Booker."

Elyse stepped from behind Elijah and murmured her greetings. The man had Elijah's eyes, and she looked over at Elijah with a questioning gaze. "Elyse, Colonel Corrington is my father."

"Elyse, you're a rare and true gem and beautiful as ever. I know your father well," the colonel said. Elyse returned his smile. He was somewhat familiar to her, but she didn't recall from where. "My aide will escort you to your quarters to freshen up. I'll send Elijah along shortly."

TOGETHER, Colonel and Captain Corrington entered the office. "I'd like some answers, son. Are you telling me that poor girl is running around Vietnam in boxers and no shoes on her feet? Where are her clothes?"

"Elyse's trunk never caught up with her. I have no clue where it ended up. This was the best we could do. Some of the men and I made a trip into Saigon to the embassy, but her closet was destroyed and her clothes gone. I assume blown out with the blast. I found a few mementos but no clothes."

"Son, I know Ambassador Booker well. He would not be pleased if he knew Elyse's situation."

"Sir, Elyse does have some underthings, ballet outfits, and her slippers."

"She has her slippers, eh? I saw her dance once up in Huế City. Had dinner with her father afterwards. Beautiful girl, breathtaking dancer. We'll make her as comfortable as possible. You're dismissed."

ELYSE WOKE WELL BEFORE DAWN. She debated on whether to sneak out for a session of dawn dancing. She grabbed the transistor radio from the dresser and her trusty slippers and crawled out from the back of the tent. She ran to the closest open area, well away from prying eyes and, with the radio on low and her slippers on her feet, she danced to greet the dawn.

ELIJAH PACED HIS TENT, his thoughts on the war and the temptation sleeping next door. He had been awakened by another nightmare. He had dreamed he was wrapping her in a body bag. He noticed a slight quiver in his hand as he ran his hands through his hair. He was fortunate to have a private tent this time, so he was alone with his thoughts. He stared out into the darkness, troubled by the bad dream. He stopped short. Was that music he heard? His curiosity was piqued. Marines did not play music in the middle of the night. He left his tent and followed the low sound of the music. He rounded the corner of his tent and came across Elyse dancing.

Such grace and beauty, and such disobedience. His nightmare and all of its horror came rushing back into his mind. What the hell was she doing out here alone? Elijah growled deep in his throat. The sky was just turning pink. *Anything and anyone could be out here.*

Little fool. She would have to be punished and just the way he had warned her about before. He walked up on her, and she did not see him until it was too late. She started running, but he caught her and swung her up over his shoulder. He carried her kicking and screaming to her tent with a curt order to Henson to leave the area. He sat on her bunk, fully intending to spank her. What stopped him he couldn't say for sure. Elyse scrambled from his lap with tears running down her face and calling him every name in the book.

"Knock it off, Elyse, or I'll wash your mouth out with soap as well. You deliberately disobeyed me. You knew that if I caught you this could happen. You were warned. This is on you. Even after what you were told with your actions sneaking out at Chu Lai you still did this. You are to stay in this tent. You are to go nowhere but the head with your guard for the next two days. If you disobey me again, I will not stop. Do I make myself clear?"

She had never seen him so angry before. She nodded.

He strode out of the tent, furious with Elyse. Punishing her was the last thing in the world he wanted to do. He wanted to make love to her, but disobedience would not be tolerated in the middle of a combat zone. It could end up getting them both killed or worse.

He bellowed for the guard. "How the hell did she get out, Henson?"

"There's no way she came out this door, Cap. I was sitting right here, and there is no way she could have slipped by me."

"Then how? From now on there will two guards on duty at all times. If one of you doesn't stop her, the other one will."

Elyse heard Elijah dressing down Henson and felt a rush of guilt at his denial. She knew she would have deserved it if he had continued and actually spanked her. She had been getting away with it for so long, she had forgotten his threats to her backside if she disobeyed him. However, that didn't mean she would forgive his high-handedness. Literally, in all her twenty-one years, she had never been spanked, and it wasn't happening now. Lesson learned she would never ever sneak out again.

CHAPTER 28

Later that day Elijah was still angry that she took his kisses so sweetly but was still defiant in following orders. *Women.* He went to talk to his father. He told him of Elyse's early morning escapade.

"Elijah, I remember Elyse as a child. She's always been high-spirited. I'll leave it up to you to best deal with her. She needs to follow orders. Just keep in mind the last thing you want to do is break her spirit. I have faith you will find a way to work it out."

HE SPOTTED her just outside of the mess hall over by the head, alone. "What are you doing out of your tent?" Grabbing her by the arm, he demanded, "Where is your guard?"

"Henson is in the powder room. I'm waiting for him."

"This is not the way it's supposed to work, Elyse."

"Maybe so, but he's sick. Don't be such a jerk."

"Watch your mouth."

She yanked her arm back. "You're hurting me, but I guess you enjoy that, don't you? Just stay away from me."

"Elyse," he growled out.

"What are you going to do about it, smack me in the mouth?"

"I do not abuse women."

"Really? Really?"

"You need to behave."

"I am not a child. You have no right."

"Elyse, I have every right to keep you in line."

"Keep me in line? In your dreams. I'm not one of your Marines. I will never, ever be kept in line. I am not yours to abuse or use and, you, Captain, can just go fuck yourself."

Henson chose at that moment to exit the head. "Henson, escort Miss Booker back to her quarters, and I will deal with you later."

Elyse glared at him, turned, and walked away.

SO MUCH FOR working it out with Elyse. All he ended up doing was getting into a shouting match with the tiny she-devil every time he saw her, and she didn't back down. And so, it was for the next three days. Every time they saw each other, they ended up in a battle.

The second day, Elyse exited the powder room. Mountain and Arnold stood off to the side waiting for her. Laughing and reminiscing on some of their adventures they walked toward Elyse's tent.

Elijah and Sarge came out of the mess hall. Spotting each other they gave each other a wide berth as they circled each other to stand on opposite sides of the mess hall entrance.

"Now what are you up to?"

"It's none of your business."

"Everything you do is my business."

"I don't know who you think you are, Elijah, but the fact is that not everything I do is your business. You seem to enjoy publicly humiliating me. Fine. I'll shout it to the camp. I had to pee."

"Are you sure you're not using the head as an excuse to get out of your quarters?"

"Wow. Last I remember, you told me I'm not a prisoner."

"You're not a prisoner. You're being punished."

"Punished for what? Wanting half an hour of privacy to be able to pretend this nightmare I'm in doesn't exist?"

"You know the rules, Elyse, you can't have free rein of the base in the dark running around half naked."

"Half naked? I'm wearing what I danced in at dawn right now, these are not my clothes. If you don't like what I'm wearing I suggest you find my trunk, in fact, you know what? You're right, I don't like what I'm wearing either."

In the blink of an eye, Elyse stripped off Elijah's shirt and threw it to the ground. "Here's your briefs as well. There, take your 'clothes' back. I don't want you or your clothes touching me ever again."

Elijah nearly choked. *God, she was beautiful.* "Okay, Elyse," he said, pointing to her orange bra. "I believe I bought that as well."

"You are just going to have to wait for it back," Elyse ground out between clenched teeth.

"Mountain, give Miss Booker your shirt."

Mountain took off his shirt and handed it to Elyse. Defiantly raising her chin, she put the long-sleeved shirt on, buttoning it all the way up. It reached to her knees. Reaching in with her arms inside, she unhooked the bra and let it drop to the ground. She flipped it up to Elijah with her foot, and it landed on his arm.

"Elyse," he hissed.

"Be careful what you wish for, Captain."

"You're out of line. That was not necessary out here."

"You're the one making this public, Captain. You're such a coward you can't even fight with me in private. You have to make sure our fighting is seen and heard by all." She turned to walk away. "Oh, wait. Silly me," she said. Pulling her arms inside the overly large shirt. "These are yours as well."

She slid her panties off and with a little wiggle they dropped to the ground. She walked away leaving them where they fell. Elijah picked up the panties, roared in rage, and slammed his fist through the mess hall door. "I need a fucking drink."

ELYSE WALKED into her tent and laid down on her bunk. She hadn't eaten for a couple of days. She was too upset. Her trays were piling up, ignored. Lying in her bunk, she wondered how long this was going to go on. She didn't have the energy for eating, fighting, or anything but sleep. Exhausted, she fell into a deep hard sleep.

THE THIRD DAY they both happened to be in the mess hall at the same time.

"What are you doing out of your tent?" Elijah said.

"What do you mean?" Elyse asked.

"You're restricted to your quarters."

"Bullshit, you only said two days."

"I remember saying three."

"You said two days. Otherwise Johnson would not have brought me here to the mess hall."

"What is it with you, Elijah? All you do is criticize my every move. Am I taking up precious Marine space, or is just the fact that I'm in the same camp as you? I'll help you out here, I'll go home."

"We've already been through that, brat."

"That's right. We have, and I did just fine without you. I'm a big girl, and I can take care of myself. I don't need you or the Marine Corps."

"Okay, Elyse. You're such a big girl, you can start from this moment forward killing your own bugs. I'll just forbid everyone in this camp from helping you."

Elyse's eyes teared up and her lower lip quivered.

"God. You're such an ass, Elijah."

"Really? If I'm an ass, then you're a cunt."

That was it. The straw that broke the camel's back.

"Cunt? I'll show you a cunt."

With the devil in her eye and vengeance on her mind, she grabbed the first thing available, and that happened to be a glass soda bottle that she aimed right for his head. Elijah saw the look in her eye and knew he had made a serious mistake. He grabbed a tray to block the projectiles as bottles, glasses, trays, and whatever else she could find flew along with more than a few choice words. Eyes wide, he, along with every man in the mess hall made a hasty retreat out the door. They all stood outside looking at each other.

"That chick just went all out ballistic," a Marine named Gomez said.

"Geez, Cap," Henson commented. "You gotta know better than to call a woman that."

"Man, she is pissed," Sarge said.

"That's one hot-temper," Mountain replied.

"Sir, you've been real nasty to her for three days," Arnold said. "I've watched her cry every time you've attacked her, so I really don't blame her, Sir."

Elijah raised his eyebrows at Arnold's sharp tone. "You forget your place, Lance Corporal."

"I apologize, Sir, but she's a good friend, and she's hurting."

Lieutenant Colonel Mike Porter strolled on over to Elijah. "Got a red-headed wife myself, Elijah. Been scorched by her temper more than once. Call a woman a name like that and you can damn well expect she will go all out redhead on you. Might find yourself hanging from the rafters by your balls if you don't watch your mouth by disrespecting a woman." He winked and walked away.

Elijah nodded his understanding. *Yeah, big mistake.*

They all sat down to wait out Elyse's anger.

⬧

ELYSE WAS FURIOUS. How dare he speak to her that way? She had to admit that she, herself, had called him more than one nasty name over the past three days, but she knew what that word meant, and it was the lowest of the low.

Fine, call me what you want.

Elyse was tired and just wanted it to end. She found a broom and dustpan and began to clean up the glass and wipe down the tables and benches, rearranging as she went. She didn't want anyone else hurt because of her temper tantrum. Once finished, she squared her shoulders and walked out the door past Elijah and the men sitting outside.

"It's all yours, gentlemen." She went back to her tent, determined to stay there for the rest of the day.

⚜

THEY ALL WENT INSIDE EXPECTING the worst. Instead they found it neat and tidy.

"She rearranged the mess hall again, didn't she?" Doc said.

"Yeah, she does that a lot. Can't tell you how many times she's had us help her rearrange her quarters." Mountain replied.

Elijah stood with hands on his hips, shaking his head. With a glance at the door, he knew what he had to do. He left the hall.

Sarge shook his head. "Poor bastard."

Doc grinned. "He'll learn."

Elijah stood outside of Elyse's tent after dismissing Johnson. With a great amount of trepidation, he walked in. She lay on her belly, feet in the air, book in hand, and wearing a nightie. The surprise was the glasses on her face. He stopped and stared. If that wasn't the hottest thing he'd ever seen, he didn't know what was. He scooped her up in his arms and kissed her with an urgent need. "God, Elyse, you drive me crazy."

⚜

HE CONTINUED to ply her with kisses. She never had a chance, weary from the fighting. His kisses were intoxicating. She couldn't think straight. She knew she was in the wrong, and she supposed he had every right to be angry with her for sneaking out, but she found herself just wanting him to hold her and love her.

⚜

ELIJAH DID NOT WANT to fight anymore. He had never met anyone like Elyse before. She was a firestorm, a flame he would return to again and again. He burned with every touch, every kiss. She brought out the best and the worst in him.

After loving her he lay with his face in her hair breathing in her scent.

269

He wished they could be anywhere but here. He thought of the motorcycle ride back to base from Saigon. It had felt so natural. More and more he thought of living back in the world with Elyse at his side.

She stirred, and he looked down at her. She still wore her glasses.

"I didn't know you wore glasses, brat."

She smiled. "Only when I read. I brought them back from the embassy." She moved to take them off. "Leave them. They're hot."

She smiled and wrapped her arms around his neck. "How are eyeglasses hot?"

"It's kind of that librarian look, all prim and proper. You just know that you want what's underneath because it's so hot and sexy."

She shook her head. "Men are insane."

"And women drive them so."

He kissed her, then. It wasn't fair for a woman to have so many attributes. Legs, bottom, big breasts, eyes to lose yourself in, pink parted lips. Where to start?

That exquisite mole on her breast had always fascinated him. Their lovemaking was slow and sweet as a soft song played on the radio, and when they got wild and broke the bunk, they laughed till they cried. Eventually they slept.

WHEN ELYSE WOKE on the floor surrounded by pieces of the broken bunk, her memories of the night before had her blushing. She wondered what else she didn't know.

"You're blushing, brat."

"Elijah, teach me. Teach me how to love you like you loved me."

He pulled her up from his chest to look into her eyes. "It may be too soon for that."

"Show me, Elijah."

Ten minutes later, Elijah knew he had created a wicked, wicked creature.

ELIJAH LAY on his back and Elyse on her stomach, their legs entwined. She traced the dagger tattoo on his forearm with her fingernail.

"I don't like fighting with you. It hurts me too much," Elyse said.

"I don't like it, either, but the best part is the make-up sex."

Smiling, she whispered, "You are bad, Elijah."

"No, bad is dropping your panties. That's bad—wicked bad."

She blushed. "I suppose I should not have done that."

Elijah smiled. "At the time I was livid, but now when I think about it, it was hot. You don't fight fair."

"I'm sorry. I'm new to this fighting stuff."

"I'm sorry, too, brat."

LATER THEY ENTERED the mess hall together to the stares of the men who wondered if they should go for cover now or wait. Elyse gave them a brilliant smile, and they relaxed. The war within the war was over at last. They still wondered who won: the Captain with his relentless attacks or Elyse with her retribution meant to drive a man to drink.

CHAPTER 29

Elyse rolled over, intent on sleeping for a while longer. She heard a rooster crowing off in the distance, and she buried her head under the pillow to block the sound of the annoying racket. She was cold. Her sneaky Marine had stolen her sheet during the night again. She stole it back and snuggled into his back for warmth.

Elijah rolled over. "Brat. You stole my sheet."

Elyse groaned. "No, you stole it first."

"I'm cold, and why won't that chicken shut up?"

"What chicken?"

"I heard a chicken-rooster crowing."

He brushed the hair from her eyes. "No chickens here, brat." He nuzzled her neck and breasts, and she wrapped her arms around his neck.

"I know I heard a chicken," she insisted. Kissing his mouth, she slid her leg up the length of his long leg, hip, and up to his back.

"You are a wicked, wicked creature, and you know I love it when you do that."

Much later, Elijah raised his head from Elyse's delectable lips. He thought he heard the crowing of a rooster. Nah.

AN HOUR or so later Elyse stepped from her tent with a blanket and books in her arms. She was supposed to meet Elijah at the mess hall. With Arnold and Mountain in step with her, her nose buried in a book she made her way to the mess hall.

Elyse glanced up and stopped. A large rooster stood in the pathway. Elyse took another hesitant step, and the rooster flew at her. With a screech of sheer terror, she flung all that she was carrying and took off running. The rooster chased her all the way to the mess hall. She slid into the screen door of the mess hall, yanked it open and ran inside. She pulled the newly repaired door shut and stood there breathing heavily.

Mountain and Arnold ran up to the door practically falling over each other they were laughing so hard.

"That is not funny." she said, glaring at them.

They could not stop laughing at her.

"Fine, keep laughing. I am not speaking to either one of you today."

Elyse looked around for Elijah, but he wasn't here yet. She poured herself a cup of coffee. She'd wait to eat until Elijah arrived. She sat down at a table to read the paper. Mountain and Arnold came inside. Still laughing, they sat at another table with the rest of the team.

Elijah walked into the mess hall, grabbed a cup of coffee for himself, and sat across from Elyse. Noting her heaving chest, he asked, "What happened?"

"Why don't you go ask the laughing morons over there."

☙

ELIJAH LOOKED over at the team. "Okay, I will do that."

He went over to talk to his men, and Mountain couldn't contain himself as he retold the story in an animated, exaggerated manner. The resulting boom of laughter along with Arnold's comments that he had never seen anything so fucking funny in his life had her seething. But she ignored them and continued reading her paper.

Elijah came back over to the table, trying to contain the grin on his face. Elyse looked over at him as he sat next her. "I told you I heard a chicken or rooster or whatever."

"I'm sure it's gone by now."

"I hope so."

They eventually got their breakfast, and when they finished, Elijah had to leave.

"Behave today, brat." he said as he stroked her cheek.

Elyse leaned into his hand and smiled. "I'll try, but no promises."

She peeked out the mess hall door. The coast was clear; not a rooster in sight. She still refused to speak to Mountain and Arnold as they followed her back to the tent.

ELYSE LAY on the ground alongside two snipers, Marley and Russo, two of best sharpshooters in the company. Johnson and Henson looked on as she examined the weapon. Looking through the scope, she scanned the tree line. She liked the feel of the weapon, and she knew the scopes were the best available.

She didn't hear Elijah come up behind her as he hauled her to her feet.

"What are you doing over here?"

"What? You never said I couldn't come over here."

"Why aren't you doing something girlie?"

"Wow… just wow." She pulled the sidearm she had strapped to her waist and emptied the gun into the target practice cans lined up on the sandbags. She hit them all.

"Something girlie? That was an incredibly rude and sexist remark. My father trained me so I could defend myself. He insisted that I train in gun safety, so I became an excellent marksman and sharpshooter. Living in a war-torn country he felt a good offense would be my best defense, which was why I am also a black belt.

"What you don't seem to realize is that it is possible for a woman to be many different things. Don't ever make the mistake of discounting my abilities just because I'm a woman." She pulled the clip, handed him the weapon and her gun holster, and walked away.

ELIJAH LOOKED at the handgun and holster, the cans she had just shot down, and the angry swing of her hips as she walked away. He let out a long, slow whistle. He looked at Marley and Russo and at Elyse's retreating back. He thought of the number of VC she had killed. Yeah, he deserved that dressing down.

SHE WAS HALFWAY BACK to her tent when the rooster jumped out at her again. With another shriek of terror, she was off running. This time it was Johnson and Henson running after her laughing.

ELIJAH HEARD her shrieking from where he stood. A slow smile lit his face. That fucking rooster was after Elyse again. If he'd known that's all he needed to keep her in line, he would have bought a whole flock.

FOR THE NEXT WEEK, every time Elyse stepped outside of her tent at some point the rooster would ambush her and chase her through the camp. Except today. Today it had three hens for company. Elyse's shrieks of terror as four fowl chased her through the camp had most of the prankster Marines howling with laughter. Her wild entrance into the mess hall was compounded by the three hens following her inside. Elyse jumped on top of a table and eyed them as they pecked at the floor beneath it.

"Where the hell are these chickens coming from? Someone is playing games at my expense."

Sarge followed her inside and shooed the chickens out of the mess hall. "Elyse, if you don't run, they won't chase you."

"Yes, they will. They're Satan's chickens and that rooster is Satan himself."

"It's the same with the troops, if you don't show them how much their pranks get to you, they'll stop."

"They hung fake spiders in the powder room last week, and they were shooting pea's with straws down my cleavage the week before that" she sniffled.

"I know," Sarge replied. "Don't let them see you sweat."

❧

ELYSE PEEKED out the mess hall door. Seeing all was clear, she stepped outside the mess hall and took a few steps. The rooster jumped out from behind a barrel. Elyse was cornered and had never climbed a tree so fast in her life.

Elijah stood with his mouth hanging open, which turned into a grin, then outright laughter along with the ten or so Marines he had been talking with.

"That thing terrifies me, and you are laughing."

Elijah wiped at his eyes and looked up into the tree at her. "I'm sorry, brat. I never thought I'd see the day you'd be treed by a rooster."

"What is wrong with you? Are you a Marine or not? Help me."

Elijah scooped up the rooster to wring its neck.

"For the love of God. No. Please no."

"You said it terrified you."

"I want it gone, not dead."

Grinning, he handed the rooster to Mountain. "Find an outgoing chopper and get rid of these fucking chickens. Come down, brat."

Elyse dropped down from the tree. Wary, she hid behind Elijah still eyeing the rooster in Mountain's arms. Mountain coaxed her over to pet the rooster. She warily approached, and the rooster clucked as she began to stroke his feathers.

"You ought to be grateful," she said to the rooster. "I just saved you from having your neck rung."

"Elyse, go get a piece of bread," said Mountain.

She ran inside the mess hall and came out with the bread. Breaking off pieces, she fed them to the rooster.

"See, he's cool. He won't chase you again," said Mountain.

"You would know Mountain, I forgot you were a farm boy."

Elijah watched the exchange. He was proud of Elyse. She had faced her fear and overcome it. Now maybe the camp would have some peace

CHAPTER 30

Mid-morning, one week later, Elyse walked to the mess hall. Her queasy stomach needed something. There were a few men in the hall when she entered. She looked at what was left over from the morning's breakfast. The quality of the food and what was offered made her stomach turn. How can they eat this garbage? No fresh fruit or veggies. Just greasy swill. Ugh.

While she loved Cookie and was happy he had been transferred down from Khe Sanh, but he was an awful cook. Her mind traveled back to the day when Elijah had taken her by the hand and bade her cover her eyes as they entered the mess hall. Uncovering her eyes to find her old friend Cookie standing in front of her had brought her to tears. She hugged the old cook who blustered at her as he hid his own tears.

Cookie came out of the kitchen. "Morning, Elyse, I have some nice melons and apples for you."

"For me?"

"Yes, they came in with the supplies yesterday."

"Why didn't you put them out for breakfast?"

"They're not for the troops. They're just for you."

"What?"

"They send special food up for you."

Shocked, she asked. "Are you telling me they don't offer this to everyone else?"

"No, they don't."

"Show me what you have for me?"

He took her back to the kitchen and discovered his stash of fresh melons, vegetables, and big baskets of apples. Elyse was outraged. "Are you telling me that these men who are dying for our country aren't entitled to decent food?"

"I'm just following orders," he replied.

"Bullshit. Cookie, cut up those melons and whatever you have set aside for me and put them out at lunch time."

"I can't, Elyse."

"If they can't eat what I eat, I won't eat a bite and it will all go to waste. Give me those apples."

Handing baskets of apples to Mountain and Arnold to carry, she untied her shirt and filled it with apples. "I'll be back."

Elyse walked the camp handing out apples to the troops. She chatted with each man and left them with a smile on their face, eating the first piece of fresh fruit they had had in a while.

⚜

COOKIE SOUGHT out the Captain and explained the situation as well as her threat not to eat if he didn't comply.

Elijah smiled. There was no doubt in his mind that she would carry out those threats. "Give her what she wants," he said.

His little fighter, always seeking fairness in an unfair world. He found her a few minutes later with her shirt still full of apples. She offered him one. He eyed her cleavage, which was a little more exposed from the weight of the apples and was disappointed she wasn't offering the fruit he really wanted. Yet seeing her smiling again made him accept the apple anyway.

She looked fetching this morning. Tendrils of hair framing her face, her exposed cleavage, her smooth, muscled belly. His briefs riding low on her curvy hips, and her shining eyes. He groaned. He'd love to take her right here and now.

"Your eyes betray your thoughts, Captain."

He grinned at her and took a bite of the apple. She reached over, pulled his hand to her, and took a bite of the apple, while never breaking eye contact, then she sashayed away. He watched the swing of her hips and remembered the feel of them in his hands. He shook his head to clear his thoughts. All around him the men were eating their apples with smiles on their faces.

CHAPTER 31

Elyse vomited for the second time this week. It had been happening off and on for the past month or so. She had considered approaching Doc for help but had brushed it aside, thinking it was just the heat or stress. Tired, hungry, and aching with tender breasts, she was befuddled at what was wrong. She needed something to settle her stomach, so she headed to the mess hall. A few of the team sat drinking their coffee when she entered the hall with Arnold.

Standing in the serving line with Arnold, she looked in horror at the breakfast provided. She watched as the cook placed a piece of toast on her tray and ladled a thick, white, gloppy substance with chunks of chipped beef over her toast. Nausea rose up her throat as her stomach turned.

"What... is that?" she asked Arnold in a horrified whisper.

"SOS, shit on a shingle," he replied. "It's not too bad."

Elyse groaned when the aroma hit her nostrils and her hand flew up to cover her mouth. She ran outside to be sick in the grass behind some tents. She felt lightheaded, and when the ground and darkness rushed up to meet her, she collapsed. Doc was there at her side when she came to. The team stood off in the distance watching with worried expressions on their handsome faces.

"Lie still. Just breathe. Elyse, is it possible that you're pregnant?" Doc asked.

Comprehension hit her like a brick. She was pregnant.

"A baby? Oh God, what am I going to do?" She hadn't been paying any attention to the obvious signs. Her heart pounded in her chest as her mind raced.

"When was the last time you had your period?"

Blushing, she realized she hadn't had her period since just a few weeks before the first time they made love in the bunker in Khe Sanh. It never occurred to her that she would get pregnant. Yes, she had been a virgin, but she knew where babies came from. She looked at Doc, stunned. "Khe Sanh. Oh, God. Please don't tell him."

"I won't, Elyse, but he deserves to know."

Doc and Arnold escorted her back to her tent. Doc squeezed her hand as he left.

"It's going to be okay. Go and lie down and rest for a while."

Her thoughts were going a hundred miles per hour. She wondered how to tell Elijah or even if she should tell him. She had some time before she would start to show. Maybe she would be in Saigon by then. Her father would know what to do. She missed him. He would definitely know how to help her. Elyse sat down and wrote her father a letter, pouring her heart out about everything. She told him she was pregnant and that she was in love.

She gave the letter to the Johnson to have it sent to wherever her father was. She was physically and emotionally exhausted, so she slept another hard sleep. She woke well past noon the next day. Elijah sat by her bunk. He had stopped in to check on her, he worried when this happened because she was completely vulnerable.

"Hi." she murmured.

"Hi, how are you feeling?"

"I feel okay. How long did I sleep?"

"About sixteen hours."

"Hold me, please."

Elijah climbed into the bunk with her and held her. Kissing her brow and her lips, he held her for a very long time.

He cajoled her into getting dressed and walking down to the mess tent.

He had to get her to eat. He told her she was going to blow away in the wind again if she didn't eat.

She gave him an easy smile and turned to look at the fare provided. Liver and onions again. Fruit and salad were added, but her stomach still rolled. One battle at a time. She saw Cookie and smiled. After giving Cookie a big hug, they took their dinner to the table to eat.

Elijah shook his head at Elyse's obvious affection for Cookie.

"Eat, Elyse, we need to fatten you up."

"Oh, trust me, that will happen sooner than you realize."

He gave her a quizzical look, and she just smiled.

CHAPTER 32

The sky was fading fast with the last brilliant colors of blue, red, pink, and orange fading into dusk. It was a peaceful night. The crickets sang their song and the night creatures responded in kind. A sky full of stars was just beginning to shine through. It was a night for lovers and dancers. Elijah and Elyse finally came to an agreement on when and where she could dance. He understood her need for privacy and her drive for perfection. He was generally the one who guarded her when she danced at dusk.

He lounged on the blanket close to her tent, with Dog and his ever-present weapon at his side. She danced in her red-clay stained ballet slippers that crisscrossed up to her ankles. He loved to watch her move. The well-defined muscles in her legs, her long neck and the way she held her head. Her graceful arms, and even the way she held her hands. The leaps were amazing, even when she fell, she'd get back up and do it again and again until she mastered the move. He could see how complicated it was to move her body the way she did. The dancing on her tippy toes fascinated him, it made her look taller when she danced.

It soothed his soul to watch her. The music on the radio changed, and she moved to the beat of the new song, Elijah was amazed she could change her style to meld with the music. He was falling for his tiny ballerina deeper and deeper every day.

He caught something running toward Elyse out of the corner of his eye. *WHAT the hell is that?*

"Elyse," he screamed at her. She heard him and stopped mid-pirouette. Running full boar at her was a large leopard. Elyse screamed. Elijah sprinted toward her just as the leopard leaped. It was stopped short by Dog, who attacked the big cat from the rear. A vicious fight between Dog and leopard ensued. Dog did not win the battle.

"Elyse, run, run." Elijah urged.

She was frozen in terror and dared not move. Elijah dropped to one knee with his weapon in hand. The leopard turned and leaped at Elyse to make the kill; Elijah's shot rang out at the same time Elyse screamed. Amidst the chaos, Marines began pouring out of their tents to see what was going on.

"Elyse." Elijah ran over to pull the dead leopard off her. "Elyse," he said again, but she was limp in his arms.

Doc appeared at his side. Checking her over, he said, "No sign of injury, Cap. I think she must have fainted."

Elijah held her to his chest, trying to slow his frantic heartbeat. Slowly she came around and her memory of the attack returned to her. "Dog? Oh, Dog." Elyse tried to crawl to where Dog lay.

"Let me be with him," she cried.

"Shh. No, baby no," Elijah said lifting her into his arms. "It's okay." He looked down at Dog who was bleeding out fast. "Don't let him suffer." His men nodded. "And I want to know how that animal made it inside the perimeter. I want every inch searched and repaired."

He turned and carried Elyse up the embankment toward the tents. They heard the shot as the team put Dog out of his misery. She sobbed into Elijah's shoulder.

He stayed with her and held her till the tears subsided and she fell asleep. It was a close call. If she had been alone, the incident could have ended in tragedy. *She's going to have to dance during the day from now on. Maybe I should find her a puppy.* Eventually his mind cleared of his worries and he slept.

They woke up at the same time and faced each other. He kissed her but went no further. He escorted her to the shower. She still had grass and twigs in her hair, and he helped her pick them out. A shower, clean clothes, and food would make them both feel better. Afterwards, Elijah had some matters to see to, so he left Elyse at her tent.

Up by the colonel's office lay the carcass of the animal. It was a huge, well-muscled cat. A crowd had gathered to look at the beast. It was a one shot to the heart kill. They pounded Elijah on the back and complimented his skill with the rifle. He was amazed he had made the shot. He still couldn't get Elyse's screams or his own terror out of his head. He shuddered to think what could have happened if he had missed the shot.

❧

ELYSE ASKED to see the leopard. She stood looking over the animal. It was beautiful, and she felt overwhelming sadness at its death. She thought of Dog and his last heroic act. She had to find out where they buried him. With tears running down her face, she turned to walk back to her tent and bumped into a Marine new to the camp.

"Well aren't you the sweetest piece of ass I've seen in a long time."

Elyse blinked. "Excuse me?"

"Oh, yeah. I heard about you, honey. You're Corrington's whore. How about you give me some of that?"

Elyse backed up, and a pivot kick followed by a sidekick to his face sent him rolling down the pathway.

She fled down the path, running past the man's now-inert form lying by the mess hall. Then she stopped, her breathing ragged, tears running down her face. She fell to her knees.

Is that what they all think of me? Maybe they're right, I am pregnant and unmarried. Oh God.

❧

ELIJAH WAS JUST COMING out of the mess hall with Sarge when he saw the Marine rolling down the hill.

"What the hell?" Then he saw Elyse. "Elyse, did he touch you?"

"No one touched me."

Obviously upset, she couldn't look him in the eye.

"Elyse, look at me. What happened?"

285

"He, he called me your whore, then asked for some of what I'm giving you."

Elijah's expression turned hard, and he ran over to where the man was just getting up.

"No." she shouted, running after him.

Elijah grabbed the man by the scruff of his shirt and pulled his fist back to deliver a blow.

"No, he didn't touch me. Elijah, Stop."

He dropped his fist but still held onto the man by his shirt. He shook him hard. His voice cold and deadly. "You son of a bitch. Elyse is no man's whore. She is the only thing saving your scrawny ass. If you ever make another comment like that to her again, I will pound your face into the ground, and I will not stop until you are dead. Do you understand me?"

"Yes, Sir." terrified, the man named Smith, replied.

Elijah shoved him away. "Get out of my sight." He turned to Elyse and brushed the tears off her cheek.

"Elijah, do they think I'm your whore?"

"No, but I suspect they know there's something going on between us."

She looked up into his eyes and held his gaze. "Do you think there's something going on between us, Captain?"

"Every time you scream in pleasure." Chuckling, he reached over and tickled her under the chin.

She slapped his hand away. "Cheeky Marine."

Elyse walked over to the mess hall, as was her habit when not restricted to her tent. She usually had her coffee and something simple to eat, while she read the old newspapers.

Unbeknownst to Elyse until Mountain told her about it, most of the men who broke their fast when Elyse was present had a running bet going. Inevitably a new arrival, young and old alike, would still try to hit on Elyse. Most considered Elyse a challenge. The bet was timed on how long it would take for Elyse to send the new arrival packing. Since the new arrivals egged on by their new buddies didn't know Elyse and her capabilities, they were often blind to the game.

This morning one particular man saw Elyse sitting quietly in the far corner reading the paper. He sauntered over to Elyse and sat down across from her.

"Hello, beautiful."

Elyse looked up. *Oh God, here we go again.* Most of the time Elyse was amused and sent them packing right away. From the get-go, this one grated on her nerves, but she had to be patient.

Elijah had heard about this mess hall game and had to see for himself. He watched from outside of the screen door. He spotted Mountain, watching from the kitchen, and noted the hidden stopwatch in the hands of one of the privates. Another private acted as a makeshift bookie. And then, of course, there was the amorous young man across the table from Elyse, oblivious to what was about to go down.

"I'd really like to get to know you, baby. I think you should meet me behind the bunkers tonight."

The young man grabbed Elyse's hand and started stroking her fingers. She raised her eyebrows at the man's audacity.

"Let go of my hand," she replied.

"Come on, baby. You're beautiful. We'll have a good time."

Elyse smiled. "Really? And you think you are man enough to handle me? I tell you what, if you value your future generations, you'll let go of my hand."

"Come on, baby. You know you want it."

Elyse pulled her hand back from his and delivered a stinging slap, while giving him a kick under the table between his legs, knocking him backwards off the bench.

Elijah was not surprised. She really could protect herself. Nevertheless, Elijah strode inside and over to the young man, grabbed him by the scruff of his shirt, and slammed him up against the wall. "I believe you owe Elyse an apology."

He stammered an "I'm sorry," and Elijah threw him out the mess hall door. Then he went back in and sat across from Elyse.

Openly amused, Elyse said, "I'm surprised you waited outside for so long."

"I wanted to see how you handled the situation."

"They're usually not so crude and insistent."

"I'm sorry, Elyse."

"Why are you sorry?" she asked.

"Men can be pigs."

"They certainly can," Elyse replied, "but right now it's four thousand against one, and I'm winning."

Elijah raised an eyebrow. "How so?"

"See over there? They're counting up their booty and looking for the winner."

"E. Booker, I believe, won the pot. Wait here."

Elyse pulled a piece of paper from her bra, walked over, turned in her ticket, and walked back counting her winnings: a whopping five hundred-fifty-three dollars in scrip. She sat back down across from Elijah. He sat, along with the rest of the men in the hall with his mouth open.

"Close your mouth Elijah, you'll let the gnats in." She smirked. "I had Mountain buy tickets for me every day since this started, so I knew the time to beat. I just had to keep that disgusting man hanging on long enough to get the longest time. They won't be playing this or any other games with me again."

Elijah blinked. "Did you just fleece an entire base camp?"

"Yes, I did," she replied, with a mischievous grin.

Elijah grinned. "You are shrewd and cunning."

"Thank you."

CHAPTER 33

Elijah could hear her tinkling laughter as he walked into the rec area. He had a surprise for Elyse, with his arms behind his back, he called her over to him.

"Close your eyes and open your arms, brat."

She did as he asked, and he placed a warm, cuddly puppy in her arms. She opened her eyes and squealed in delight. He was a black-and-white chihuahua with splotches of brown, less than a year old.

"His name is Soup."

"Soup?"

"Arnold said that was the name on his cage. I suspect the correct translation on the cage was probably "dog to make soup."

"Oh." she mouthed. "That is terrible. Poor little puppy. Soup, indeed."

"I know he's nowhere near the size of Dog, but I have come to realize that size sometimes does not matter. That, and Arnold couldn't leave him behind."

"Thank you. He's perfect just the way he is. It's sweet, and so thoughtful of you."

Soup lay hidden in the shade of the tower, and Elyse sat up on top of the watchtower. It was the perfect spot to watch the goings-on in the camp.

Choppers flew overhead and buzzed the towers as the gunners and troops waved at her when they passed by. Elyse waved back and watched as they landed over on the helipads. Troops with supplies exited the aircrafts as other troops ran up to help unload. Elyse turned to see a platoon coming up the road. They walked single file on both sides of the road. They looked hot, tired, and happy to see the camp entrance. They hadn't spotted her as she crawled to the edge of the tower. She looked down watching them as they entered the gate of the camp.

Elyse turned in time to see a large spider as it creeped its way toward her. Trying not to panic she searched for a way to escape the advancing monster. She looked over to the other watchtower on the other side of the gate and at the thick foot-wide wooden center beam that ran between the two towers. Checking it for strength and sturdiness, she crawled out onto the beam to the center. She spotted Elijah walking toward the gate searching for her.

"Damn." She laid down flat on the beam. She could tell he was not too happy because this time she had ditched him. She probably shouldn't have but she was desperate for any little bit of freedom and privacy she could find.

If she could get over to the other tower and climb down from that side, she could avoid Elijah and get back to her quarters. Forgetting about the Marines entering the gate below, she started to crawl but stopped short when she saw another huge spider heading toward her from the other direction. She tried to back up but there were more spiders approaching from her rear. She must have disturbed a nest. Baby spiders swarmed the beam. Eyes wide, she flicked spiders away from her.

Oh God... oh God... oh God.

A loud crack of the beam resounded as it began to split, and the returning Marines hit the ground below, obviously thinking it was ground fire. They saw nothing out of the ordinary, though, and stood up talking amongst themselves wondering what they just heard.

"Damn." Elyse stopped. Worried now about the strength of the beam, but being chased by spiders, she had to go forward. Another crack and the beam split in the middle, leaving Elyse dangling, desperately hanging on.

ELIJAH WALKED toward the main gate. Spotting a familiar form he walked up behind him.

"Hey, Collin."

The Marine turned in surprise. "Elijah."

Standing right below a dangling Elyse, they pounded each other on the back and embraced as brothers long separated do.

"What are you doing here?"

"We've been temporarily reassigned here."

"That's great. Does Father know?"

"Yes."

"What are you doing here?" Collin asked.

"I'm on a special assignment. She's...." They heard another crack, and they both looked up.

"I take it that's your special assignment?" Collin said.

"Jesus. Elyse."

ELYSE TRIED to scoot herself up the beam closer to the second watchtower. The biggest spider crawled onto her arm followed by some smaller relatives. Trying to shake them off, she loosened her hold on the beam, lost her grip and, with a scream, she fell. Collin caught her in his arms.

"Jesus Christ. There're women falling from the sky," he exclaimed.

Elyse was in shock. Not only because someone had just caught her but... *Oh my God, There're spiders in my hair.* Another loud crack sounded from above, and they looked up as the second tower started to lean inwards toward the gate. Eyes wide, they all dove for cover as it fell with Marines jumping out of the tower. It fell into the first tower, and with a domino effect, the first tower started its lean with more Marines jumping out as it all came crashing to the ground.

Sitting up, Elyse ran her hands through her hair. Shaking her head, she shuddered as spiders fell on her shoulder. Screaming, she jumped to her feet and did a heebie-jeebies dance.

Elijah sat up, looked at the towers, the dust clouds, and the Marines around them coming to their feet. Furious, he whipped around to glare at Elyse.

"How?"

"Screw the towers. There are spiders in my hair," she screamed at him.

Coming to his feet, he helped her brush the spiders out of her hair.

He growled at her. "What the hell were you doing up there?"

"I can explain."

He roared. "I'm tired of your explanations."

"Don't bellow at me Marine. I was just sitting on top of the tower, and I got chased by spiders out onto the beam."

"Spiders, you got chased by spiders?"

"The towers are infested," she replied.

"You do more damage to base camps than the VC and NVA combined."

Insulted, Elyse replied, "I do not."

He brushed another spider off her breast. Her eyes widened, and she slapped his hand away and whispered, "Stop. Everyone's watching."

"Go to your quarters and stay there."

"That's always your answer, isn't it?"

"Elyse, go to your quarters now."

The defiant tilt of her chin as she narrowed her eyes at him thinking to defy him. Taking her by the chin, he growled at her. "Little big girls need to know when to stand down, or they run the risk of having sore bottoms."

Her eyes widened at his threat, and she glanced down toward the man still sitting on the ground watching them.

"Fine."

She turned to the man sitting on the ground watching them. "Thank you."

She left the area walking briskly toward her quarters with the team and Soup right behind her.

COLLIN CAME to his feet with a grin on his face as they watched her walk away.

Elijah narrowed his eyes and glared. "She-Devil."

They turned to survey the damage. Collin said, "There's no way that tiny pepper pot brought those down."

"I know. There had to be something wrong with their construction to begin with, which I seriously doubt. More likely, they've been tampered with."

"Hmm, there's another reason they would fall, Elijah."

Elijah glanced at him and then down at the ground. "Son of a bitch, the VC? Tunneling right beneath us?"

"And the ground below the towers became unstable?" Collin nodded his head. "Let's find out."

With a crew of Marines and some men they called tunnel rats whose expertise was underground tunnel systems, they cleared the tower debris and found a massive tunnel system with barracks, a small hospital, and a cache of weapons right below the base. The prior inhabitants had made a hasty exit, and the Marines found a treasure trove of VC information left behind.

Elijah's father, Colonel Corrington, came to inspect the entrance to the tunnels. "Assholes were hiding right below us. Thank God Elyse brought the towers down."

"Elyse and a spider infestation," Elijah replied. At the colonel's raised eyebrows, Elijah explained.

"She said spiders chased her out onto the beam."

The colonel grinned, then shuddered in revulsion. "If it had been me. I would have taken a flamethrower and burned them to the ground."

Knowing their father's own aversion to spiders, Collin and Elijah grinned.

"I need to go deal with Elyse," Elijah said. "Not only did she ditch me, she brought down the towers, and she could have been killed or injured."

Colonel Corrington said, "Keep in mind, Elijah, that this is the second time she's inadvertently discovered tunnel systems. Go easy on her."

"She has a habit of showing us where our vulnerabilities are the greatest."

"It sounds like Elyse marches to the beat of a different drummer,"

Collin said.

Elijah growled. "Elyse doesn't march. She pirouettes through life like a tiny tornado."

WELL PAST DARK, Elyse stood in her pink panties with a soapy washcloth in hand. She scrubbed her face and neck to wash off the dust of the day.

"Elyse."

She turned with a squeal. "Marine, why are you always sneaking up on me?"

Trying to open her eyes without getting soap in them, she leaned over to rinse her face. Grabbing her towel, she turned to face him as she dried her wet skin.

Elijah stood in the doorway. He was covered in dirt and his sweat-soaked black hair had curled. His brow and bare muscled chest we're shiny with sweat. With a five o'clock shadow of beard stubble on his face he was all man.

Elyse inhaled at the sight of him, feeling her desire rising. Grabbing the soapy washcloth, she walked to where he stood in front of the door. Putting his hands on her shoulders he wiped the soap bubbles from her neck. Pulling her close, he kissed her lips. She washed his chest with the cloth. Placing a kiss on the soapy spot she had just washed, she continued washing his chest and neck and stood on her toes to place kisses on his chin.

"I'm pretty filthy, brat."

"I don't care. I'm sorry about today."

"You could have been killed."

"I wasn't."

"You got lucky, again."

"Not so lucky. I lost my radio."

He pointed to her table, to the radio and his shirt he had placed next to it. "I pulled it out of the rubble."

She smiled a small smile. "Thank you, Elijah."

"As it turned out, you did us a favor. We found a VC tunnel system under the base. Your ninety-eight pounds of sass would not have brought those towers down if the ground beneath wasn't compromised by the tunnels."

"Seriously?"

"It doesn't excuse you ditching me or being on top of the watchtower to begin with."

"I need privacy, Elijah."

"You get all the privacy you need inside this tent."

"It's not the same."

"We've been over this before, brat. Ditch the team or me again, and you'll find your sweet ass chained to your bed."

Elyse's mouth dropped open. "You wouldn't dare."

"I've told you before. Keep testing my patience, and I'll show you what I dare."

Elyse narrowed her eyes and with soapy washcloth in hand, she shoved it in his face and swished it around. Then she pushed with both arms on his chest and sent him flying out her door to land on his ass in the dirt outside.

"Bitch." Elijah roared in frustration. He sat, trying to get the stinging soap out of his eyes. Someone appeared at his side and handed him a towel. He wiped his eyes and looked up to see Collin, fresh from the showers, standing over him, chuckling.

"What did you do?"

Elijah shot daggers with his eyes toward her door. "I threatened to chain her to her bed."

Collin's eyebrows shot straight up. Elyse's door opened, and she flung his shirt she had found lying on her table out at him and she shut the door. Rising to his feet, he glared at her door and called out to her. "Elyse, you're restricted to your quarters for the next three days."

"Go to hell, Captain."

"No, you go to hell."

"Fine, I will, but I'm dragging your pathetic ass kicking and screaming with me."

Collin grimaced. "Ouch. You're just digging a deeper hole for yourself. Come on."

With a nod, Elijah followed Collin over to the other side of his quarters next door.

⬥

ELIJAH HIT THE SHOWERS, and when finished, he sat down in a lawn chair outside his quarters. Collin tossed him a cold beer. Nodding his appreciation, Elijah opened the can and downed the cold brew. Leaning back in his chair, he said, "Ahh, sometimes if I close my eyes, I can pretend I'm back in the world, sitting on my front porch."

"And who's sitting next to you, Elijah?"

Grinning, Elijah said, "Against my better judgement, that shrew next door who just threatened to drag my pathetic ass to hell."

Collin grinned and raised his beer in a toast. "To women."

Elijah grinned and raised his beer.

⬥

DAY FIVE ARRIVED, and off of restriction, Elyse still had not spoken to a single soul in the camp. The mood of the camp was dark and down.

Elijah and Collin sat just outside the command post.

"Leave it to Elyse to give thousands of men the cold shoulder all at once," Elijah muttered.

"Give her time, Elijah."

Soup lay curled in Elijah's lap. "What say you, Soup? Times up, I think. Okay, boy, you know what I want. Go get them."

Soup took off at a trot. A short time later, he returned with a pair of pink panties in his mouth. He dropped them in Elijah's lap.

"Now what did I say? We've had this discussion before. I wanted the orange ones, go get the orange ones, boy."

Soup trotted off again and soon the dog was running back through the camp with orange panties in his mouth and Elyse in hot pursuit.

"You little pervert. Give those back."

Soup ran and jumped into Elijah's lap, dropping the panties into Elijah's hand.

"Good boy."

Collin covered his face and howled with laughter. Elyse caught up to find Soup sitting comfortably in Elijah's lap. She stopped short in front of Elijah and Collin. She looked at the two men so similar in looks.

"Elyse, this is my brother, Captain Collin Corrington. Collin, this is Elyse Booker."

*"Ta beaut'e me coupe le soufflé," Collin stated in perfect French.

*"Tu es aussi aveugle qu'une chauve-souris," Elyse replied.

Elijah was stunned. "You speak French?" Then he remembered one night when she had murmured something in French in her sleep.

"Fluently, Monsieur, along with Vietnamese in a few dialects, a smattering of Gaelic, German. I'm working on my Spanish, and of course, English."

"I'm not surprised. What else can you do?" asked Elijah.

"I have many interests. My father kept me busy to keep me out of trouble."

Elijah arched an eyebrow.

Elyse blushed.

"I don't think it's possible to keep you out of trouble, brat."

Elyse narrowed her eyes at Elijah, looked at Soup, and then wagged her finger at the little dog.

"You are a traitor and a panty thief."

She turned to Elijah. "You taught him that, didn't you?"

Elijah gave her a wolfish grin.

She snatched the panties from his hands and turned to Collin. "It's a pleasure to meet you."

"Likewise, Elyse."

Then she was gone.

"That went better than I expected," Elijah stated.

"She's lovely, Elijah. Absolutely breathtaking. You're going to have your hands full with that one, and I pity the man—meaning you Elijah—who thinks he can put her under his thumb. If you want to tame her, learn to work with her. Instead of giving orders, try asking for what you want. Women like that are few and far between."

"You know this from one meeting?" Elijah asked.

"You forget I have Belinda. Trust me, little brother. I know exactly what you're going through."

Elyse counted four splinters from the towers in her right hand. Angry and red, they were infected and painful. She had tried to get them out to no avail. She had kept a bandage wrapped around her hand, and whenever Doc approached her asking to see her hand, she hid it behind her. Time and time again, she rebuffed his offers to help.

"No, I'm fine Doc, it's just a few splinters. They'll work their way out on their own."

Mountain, Arnold, and Doc sat in the mess hall watching out the screened-in windows for Elyse.

"There she is. Right on time," Mountain said.

Doc grinned. "Are you ready? Let's do this."

They came out of the mess hall and stood in the path. Elyse stopped ten feet away. She eyed them as they approached her. Johnson and Henson circled behind her. She noticed Doc was holding his medical bag.

"Oh no. No, no, no."

"Just let me look at it, Elyse," Doc said.

"No, it's fine. Really, it's fine."

"Don't be such a baby. Let me look at your hand."

"No."

"Okay, then we do this the hard way."

Their circle tightened now. There was no escape. They took her gently down and held her to the ground against her protests.

"Just let me do it myself," she cried, but they wouldn't listen.

Elijah, Collin, and Sarge came around the corner to find the team holding Elyse down on the ground.

"What the fuck are you doing?" Elijah asked.

Doc grinned and held up his tweezers. "Two down and two to go."

Elijah crouched down to survey Doc's handiwork. Then he looked at Elyse and the team members holding her down.

"Big baby. You should have let Doc look at it a week ago."

Elyse narrowed her eyes at Elijah but refused to acknowledge him.

"Got 'em. Okay, you can let her go," Doc said.

Grinning, Henson said, "On three boys. One, two, three."

They let her loose and rolled to their feet. Elyse sat up, wiped the tears from her face, and looked at her hand.

"Oh, it doesn't hurt anymore."

Elijah rolled his eyes and helped her to her feet. Elyse eyed the team as they stood looking at her. Feeling a bit sheepish, she said, "Thanks, Doc."

Doc grinned. "How about a poker game, Elyse?"

"You're on."

Inside the mess hall, she allowed Doc to put some salve and band-aids on her hand.

"Keep the bandages on for a day or so to keep the dirt out."

Elijah shuffled the deck while Collin eyed Elyse. "You play poker?"

"A little." she replied with an impish grin.

TWO HOURS LATER, Elijah and the team rolled their eyes and hid their grins as Collin eyed his twenty dollars lying on the table in front of Elyse.

"How long did you say you've been playing poker?" Collin said.

"Since I was ten, though my father only ever allowed me to play with poker chips," Elyse replied.

"I thought you said you only play a little?"

"I do play a little and win big." With a wink, she took a sip of her hot chocolate.

He narrowed his eyes at her. "You should meet my wife, Belinda."

"You're married? Where is your wife?"

"Taiwan, she's a nurse at the military hospital there."

"I'd love to meet her."

"Someday you will. You remind me of her."

"Oh, so she has spark?"

Collin grinned. "Yes, she has spark. Too much some days."

"You must miss her very much."

"I do, but at least she is closer than most men's wives. I'm going to go see her next month."

"I hope you have a lovely visit."

Collin grinned. "Trust me, I will."

CHAPTER 34

Elijah was not sure he'd survive Elyse. Sitting down across from her at the table, he said, "Elyse, you need to be careful how you dance in front of the men."

"What do you mean?"

"You're already a temptation. Most women don't look like you."

Elyse scoffed. "Don't be ridiculous, I look like all women. You do realize I dance ballet? What are you saying? That my ballet is provoking the men? I'm not even sure how to respond. I choose to dance at dawn because of men and my need for privacy. It's not my fault I am here, but here I am. I'm sorry that you and this entire base camp are 'tempted' by me. I'm sorry that my body displeases you, but I will dance however I want, whenever I want, and you cannot control that. I do not understand why you would want me to feel shame."

"Elyse," Elijah growled. *She's killing me.* "Don't twist my words. I am not displeased with your body or your dancing, nor am I trying to shame you. I'm just saying watch when and how you dance and who your audience is."

Indignant, she pulled herself up to stand tall at her full five feet. "Twist your words? Let me tell you something: I am the youngest Prima Ballerina in the world. Do you know what that means? That means I am the best at what I do, and I do it for the most prestigious ballet company in this country. I have sacrificed, I have starved, I have worked my muscles to the point where they felt like jelly. I have fallen and gotten back up to try again. I have given everything to be the best against many odds, including my size, and it's been one of many challenges, and I have met it all head on.

"Don't you dare try to hold me responsible because your Marines are hot and bothered every time I pirouette. Control your men, Captain. I cannot even walk through this camp without getting groped and pinched some days. None of this is my fault. You control every aspect of my life. You are not controlling this too. I dance for myself, for me, and me alone.

"Try to understand, Elijah. I do not have the luxury of dancing to Stravinsky or Tchaikovsky here. There is no Khachaturian. They don't play music from ballet composers on the radio. I dance to your music. I take the choreographed steps from beautiful ballets like *Swan Lake* and *The Firebird* and move to the music of the Rolling Stones. It is all I have. But you must understand I'm doing the very best I can in a place where I am all alone and where I do not belong."

"You are not alone here, brat," Elijah said.

"Yes, I am. I am alone here just like I have been alone most of my life. You have family, friends, and the Corps. I have no one but my father and he's always working. I spent most of my life alone with paid nannies and guards. I grew up alone and lonely. Everyone was paid to be with me just like now. You're paid, the team is paid. I have no family or friends anymore. All I have is my father, and I don't know where he is, and my dance."

"I'm sorry."

"I don't want your pity, Elijah. I want you to understand."

"I do understand. Do you honestly think I want you here? In this place? In the middle of a war? That I don't wish we had met during another time, another place. I may be earning a paycheck, but you are all I think about.

"What you said is not fair to me or the team. Grow up, Elyse. You're not the only one here who feels alone or wants to go home. I get it about the music and the dance. Just tone it down a bit."

"Grow up? Just what do you think I've done these past months? Do you believe I haven't been affected by all of this as much as those lean and mean Marines out there? I have nightmares just like you do. The only difference between me and everyone else here is that I cry. I have never cried so much in my life as I have since the day my chopper crashed."

With that she crossed the mess hall, scooted out the door, and slammed it shut. Elijah cringed at the door slamming while fighting the instinct to hit the deck. He walked to the door and watched her walk away.

Shit, she's coming back.

She had turned around and came back to stand outside of the door.

"Just so you know, Captain, I've trained in many forms of dance, and I am more than capable of making you and each and every man on this base suffer in ways you've never dreamed of."

She turned and walked away.

Elijah scowled. That twenty feet of heavy-duty chain sounded better and better every day.

OF ALL THE NERVE. Elyse brushed the angry tears from her eyes as she climbed on top of a bunker. Sitting there in the middle of the camp, her silent tears flowed. She looked up as Johnson sat down next to her.

"Hi."

"Hi, Andy. I'm not sure if I'm very good company right now."

"I know, but I figured you needed a friend right about now."

She smiled a sad smile. "I'm sorry if you heard that. I didn't mean it the way it came out."

"You've got friends here. The whole team considers you a friend."

"Even though I'm a girl and not a Marine?"

He laughed. "Yeah, even though you're a girl. You're a special girl. Not in a girlfriend type way, but you're still special. And we're all in this shit show together.

"You need to cut Cap some slack. He's a great officer. Always been right there with us, unlike some officers who send the grunts out to do the dirty work while they stay safe back at base camp. He's worried. Some of the guys here are getting antsy with a woman on base."

"Oh, so seeing me reminds them of what they can't have?"

"Yeah, something like that."

"Why don't you just go build a whack-shack like the Army did?"

Johnson blushed and Elyse blushed as well.

"I did see inside of it," she explained. "I'm naïve, but I figured that one out pretty quickly."

"Maybe I'll mention it to Cap," Johnson said.

"Hey, did you know there are women in the Marine Corps?" Johnson asked her.

"Not out here there aren't."

"Of course not. They're at some of the bases in the rear."

"They fight?"

"Hell no. They're secretaries for the generals and stuff like that. There's civilian women back there too. They work at the service clubs. Donut Dollies, they play bingo and other games. Keeps the boys happy just to talk to a round eye."

"Round eye?"

"Yeah, American women like you. Helps with homesickness."

She lay her head on his shoulder. "Thank you, Andy. I feel better now."

He put his arm around her. "You're going to be okay. You've got Cap, you've got the team, and me. You'll get through this."

"I'm in love with him, Andy."

"I know. I think we all know."

"But he doesn't."

"Then you should tell him."

"I'm not sure he's ready to hear it. I'm tired of fighting with him, but he's so… frustrating."

"I think, but I don't know for sure since I've never been in love, that when men and women are just learning about each other and how to be together, it takes time."

"There's more, I'm going to have a baby."

He looked at her in shock. "What are you going to do? Does Cap know?"

"I lie in my bed at night wondering what to do, and no, he doesn't know."

"You've got to tell him everything," Johnson said.

"I know, I just don't know how. I'm scared. What if he doesn't want me then? I've heard they force women into homes for unwed mothers, then force them to give up their babies for adoption."

"Yeah back in the world they do that, but you're safe from that here. And I'm sure Cap would not allow that to happen to you or his baby."

She gave him a small smile and wiped the tears from her face.

"Got some pictures from home yesterday. Want to see them?" Johnson asked.

She squealed in delight as he pulled the pictures from his shirt pocket.

ELIJAH WATCHED THEM FROM AFAR. For the first time in his life he felt jealousy. Not jealousy of another man near Elyse—he had no worries about Johnson or any other man—but jealous that it wasn't him sitting there comforting her. He had handled it badly. He had never meant to criticize her ballet or give the impression he was blaming her. He was trying to warn her to be on her guard. He walked over and stopped front and center before her. He nodded to Johnson to leave. Johnson squeezed Elyse's hand, jumped down from the bunker and walked away.

Elyse turned to look at him, and a single tear ran down her cheek as she crawled to the edge of the bunker. When they came face to face, he reached out and brushed the tear from her cheek as she closed her eyes to the feel of his touch.

"I sometimes fumble words and end up saying things I don't mean. Or they just come out the wrong way. You're a beautiful ballerina. Your ballet dancing is above reproach. None of this is your fault, and I'm sorry it came out the way it did."

"I'm sorry too." She leaned her forehead onto his. "I know I'm not alone. I have you, and that means more to me than anything. None of this other stuff matters as long as I'm with you. I burn for you, Elijah."

Inhaling, Elijah almost forgot where they were. "Come on, brat. Let's take this somewhere private."

THE NEXT DAY Elyse sat on a bunker between Henson and Johnson. A few Marines walked by carrying enough wood and supplies to build a whack-shack. Elyse and Johnson, catching each other's eye, grinned.

CHAPTER 35

It was a full-time job guarding Elyse Booker. War raged on. Troops came and went on patrol. The artillery was fired in response to requests for back up support. Men lived and died every day.

Elyse floated around the camp, her laughter infectious, providing moral support to the men. Throughout the day, she could be found peeling potatoes with Cookie, dancing at the rec area, giving council to many a man after a Dear John letter, working with a few Marines to teach them how to read. She brought camp morale up to an all-time high, and they loved her for it.

She didn't get into too much trouble these days. Today, however, was different. It was hot and humid, Elyse still had not told Elijah about the baby. She was feeling miserable from the heat. Some men worked on the perimeter of the camp adding additional barbed wire. There was an opening in the fencing where they went through bringing their supplies back and forth and straight down from them was a small lake. *A swim? Why not? It looks so inviting, go for it.*

She ran down the hill, through the perimeter and waded out into the lake. She swam while Mountain and Arnold stood on the shoreline trying to convince her to get out of the water.

Up on the hill, Elijah sat in his chair, binoculars in hand, scanning the perimeter. His eyes roamed to the men working the perimeter, to the small lake, further on, wait… what…? Back to the lake.

He bolted out of his chair. "Are you fucking kidding me?"

Elyse was outside of the perimeter swimming in the lake.

Elijah raced down the hill. He was going to kill her.

Meanwhile, Elyse took pity on her guards and exited the lake. She wrapped herself in her blanket and looked up to see Elijah charging down the hill. He did not look happy. Elyse had but a moment to rethink her impetuous actions, and he was upon her.

He picked her up, threw her over his shoulder, and carried her up the hill to the camp. He was yelling at his men and yelling at her all the way up.

Elyse wiggled from his grasp and took off at a run. Evading capture time and time again, she only enraged him more. She ran into the mess hall, and he followed her in, cornering her.

A few men sat drinking their coffee, their cups frozen in mid-air as they watched.

Elijah turned to the men and barked. "Get out. Cookie, take your crew and get out."

Cookie tried to protest.

"Get out now." Elijah repeated. They took their leave, shooting a look of sympathy at Elyse.

Elijah stood there looking at Elyse. She was soaking wet, having lost her blanket somewhere. Her shirt stuck to her curves, leaving little to the imagination. He pulled his belt off as he advanced on her slow and cat-like. She put tables between them.

"I have told you a thousand times to never leave the perimeter and there you are, outside of the perimeter, swimming. What were you thinking, Elyse? Or did you think at all? Do you ever stop to think there may be consequences for your actions?"

Elyse saw the belt come off. "What are you doing? I had my guards with me, it's not like it was closed off. It was open. Stay away from me."

After more cat and mouse games he had her cornered, she looked down at the belt in his hands and then up into his eyes with fear in her own.

"You would hurt me?" she whispered.

He looked down at the belt in his hand, and with barely contained fury and a foul curse flung it against the wall. "Enough, you do not realize the risks you take and how you endanger us all."

"You son of a bitch. How could I possibly endanger you?"

"You want to know why? Okay Elyse, I'll tell you why. The CIA found out that you're 'for sale.' North Vietnam has a price on your head. The decision was made to move you out to Khe Sanh for your protection before we moved you south to Saigon. While we were under siege at Khe Sanh, the Tet offensive happened where every major city and most bases were attacked by the NVA and the VC.

"One of their objectives was to find you. The embassy in Saigon and the American compound in Huế City were left in shambles. Your father was seriously injured. Pentagon brass and Washington Politicians, including your father made decisions on your behalf.

"We've been leap frogging from base to base all in an effort to hide you and make your presence and whereabouts unknown. If the VC or NVA knew you were here, we will be attacked. Now I may have to be move you again, the locals probably saw you in the lake, saw you, just like everyone else here, parading around half naked in wet clothes. You're acting like a fucking whore."

Elyse sucked in her breath as her heart broke into a thousand pieces. Then she began to speak, her voice soft and low. "My father? Is he alive?"

"Yes, he's alive."

Elyse breathed a sigh of relief. "Why? Why would you not tell me he was hurt? I could have gone to be with him."

"That is why I didn't. It would have placed you where they wanted you to be."

"What do you mean by 'for sale?'"

"North Vietnam government means to capture and sell you to the highest bidder. Last I heard the bid was at almost three million dollars. We got you out of Huế City just in time, or you would have ended up chained to a rich man's bed somewhere in the world or dead in the TET offensive."

A sob stuck in her throat. "Okay, okay. So, you and the military brass chose to keep me in the dark, to make decisions about me. Without informing me. You take away my opinion and my voice. You tell me nothing. Do you think me stupid? You could have told me."

"I was not permitted to tell you anything until General Morgan gave me permission to do so when I saw fit."

"Like this Elijah? You tell me like this? Did it ever once occur to you that I may have worked with you for my own safety?" she asked.

"You uprooted me from my home, my life, my career. My chopper crashed, leaving me with nothing but what I had on my back. I have asked you for nothing other than to go home, and yet you have taken everything from me. Everything, Elijah. You took everything," she whispered.

His voice raw with emotion. "I took nothing from you but what you freely gave me. I did not do this to you. You blame me for decisions I had nothing to do with, nor was I asked for my opinion. I'm following orders, orders to protect you. I have no choice."

"Choice? You've told me I have no choice, that I must obey… and yet you withheld the reason why. I am not a Marine. Is property of the United States Marine Corps stamped on my bottom? No, I am a woman. I have lived through a siege, killed VC, and had men die in my arms. I have seen things no woman should ever see. I do not belong here."

"I know you don't belong here. No one believes you belong here," Elijah shouted.

"And then… Then after all of that, you call me a whore. I can show you a whore. I can choose ten or all of the men on this base as my lovers. No one would deny me. That is a whore. I gave myself to you because I'm… because I'm in love with you. But maybe, just maybe, a whore is your true opinion of me.

"So, fine, Captain, you want to call me a whore you go right ahead. But remember this: "I… am… not… your… whore." With tears rolling down her face she turned with head held high and walked out the door.

Elijah had gone pale at her words. *She loves me.* His heart raced in pure elation, *and I just destroyed her,* then his heart sank in despair and anguish to settle in the pit of his stomach.

He ran his hands through his hair and walked out the door to face the men who looked at him in silence. "I did not mean to call her a whore," he said.

Colonel Corrington spoke, "Captain, I'd like to see you in my office."

Elijah followed his father inside his tent.

"Ten-Hut, Captain. What the hell is going on? I just got a phone call from Ambassador Booker. It appears he received a letter from Elyse. He wants the name of the man who deflowered his daughter. I'm going to assume after what I just heard that man is you. How the hell am I going to explain that the man is not only one of my Captains, but my son, and it happened on my watch?"

"Sir, it did not happen on your watch."

"Where the hell did it happen?"

"Khe Sanh, Sir."

"In the middle of a siege?" The colonel roared.

"We were trapped in a bunker. We did not expect to survive the night. It just happened, Sir."

"Are you still sleeping with her?"

"Yes, Sir."

"You're very taken with this slip of a girl."

"Yes, Sir."

"Do you love her?"

After a pregnant pause, he said, "Very much, Sir."

"At ease, Elijah. I'm speaking as your father now. I have no doubt that you will do the right thing. Elyse is a high-spirited girl. I don't want to see her spirit broken. You may have already done that. I suggest you go make peace with her. Figure out what you want in life and whether you want Elyse to be part of it. If not, prepare yourself, another man can be found to protect her. You're dismissed."

Elijah swallowed hard, as a knot formed in the pit of his stomach. "Aye aye, Sir."

Elijah flung himself into a lawn chair. He stared at his feet. Everything Elyse said was true. They, including himself, had taken away her voice, given her no choice, and demanded obedience. It was her very nature to fight it.

He did love her. He hadn't realized what his heart had known long ago until he stood before his father. *She loves me.*

This was no place for a woman. On that he agreed with her. He was frustrated that she was even here instead of somewhere safe where she could dance to her hearts content. But he also wanted her close to him so he could touch her, smell her hair, make love to her.

Yeah, he had heard the vulgar comments, and while he could not fault any man for looking at eye candy, filthy talk in her presence was inexcusable. She had born it all and had fought back in her own way.

He should have told her in private without the camp hanging on every word about why she was being held and moved from base to base for her safety. Instead, like a fucking moron, he had blurted it out in anger.

He needed to talk to her. She would need time. He couldn't keep the memory of the look on her face when he called her a whore out of his mind. He saw her heart break, and it tore him up inside. He sat for a long time, speaking to no one, thinking about her.

When the drizzling rain started, he rose from his seat and walked toward her tent. Elyse was not there. A private walked up to him.

"Captain, Colonel Corrington would like to speak with you."

Elijah nodded and walked up to his father's office. Elyse was just walking out the door while replying to the colonel's question. "Yes, Colonel. I'm positive this is what I want."

Elyse turned and saw Elijah standing near the door. She stiffened, gathered her pride, raised her chin defiantly, and stepped around him. With Mountain and Arnold appearing to escort her back to her quarters, he watched her as she walked away.

"Come sit down, son. I know of no other way to say this other than to come out with it. Elyse called her father, and she's leaving as soon as the chopper arrives in the morning. She's going out to the aircraft carrier *Ticonderoga* to be with her father."

Elijah looked down, an overwhelming sense of sadness and loss gripped him. Nodding his head, he stood to leave.

"Elijah. This doesn't mean it's over. I know you love the girl, but she needs time to come to grips with all we have put her through. What I'm trying to say is women, bah. There is no explaining women. We have no idea how their minds work. Give her time, son. She will be back. Knowing

Elyse, she'll either sink that aircraft carrier and the Navy will send her back, or her father will talk some sense into her, and she'll come back on her own. Either way, you'll have a chance to make amends."

"What's the point, Father?"

"Don't be a fool. You don't want to live a life of regret knowing you let her slip away and didn't fight for her."

"I'm in Vietnam. I don't even know if I'll be alive tomorrow."

"That's no excuse, Elijah. I made mistakes myself. I almost lost your mother once because of my stupidity. And I was fighting in Korea at the time. Your mother never gave up on me nor I on her just because I might die in a war. As it turned out, she was the one who died. I've never regretted the time we had together, and I'll never love another. If you love her, you will fight for her. I just ask that you give her some time to be with her father. Send the team on a week-long R&R. If you want to go as well, that's fine, but Elyse needs time."

"Who will protect her while she's gone?"

"Her father. He was the biggest, badass Marine that I ever knew. He only retired when her mother died, and he had no one to take care of a tiny three-year-old girl. He did not want to risk leaving her alone in the world."

"Just give me one chance to talk to her first, Father. If she doesn't want to talk to me, I'll back off and give her the time she needs to be with her father."

"All right, son. You've got tonight. Tomorrow, she leaves. But, like I said, she'll be back. Mark my words."

LATER THAT EVENING the light drizzle turned to rain. Elyse still sat on her blanket outside. She got up to dance but her moves were slow and sad. The music playing on the radio was the duet they played on the piano together at the embassy in Saigon. Her heart ached. She fell to her knees and sobbed her misery, whore, he had called her a whore. He had defended her when someone else called her his whore. She did not know what she had done to deserve it, the pain in her heart was so great she couldn't bear it.

Elijah stood in the shadows watching her. Her dance was the saddest he'd ever seen. He knew he was to blame. He walked to her side and crouched down next to her.

"Elyse… Elyse I'm so sorry. I'm sorry, brat. I did not mean to call you that. It was cruel and untrue."

She sobbed even harder. He pulled her close and kissed her. "Please forgive me. I've made mistakes, Elyse. Lots of them. I hurt you, and that was never my intention. You mean too much to me."

She nodded and snuggled into his arms.

He laid her down and kissed her eyes, lips, and the tip of her nose. The rain came down harder, pooling to stream down his neck and back as he kissed her neck. It was only when the thunder rolled and lightning ripped across the sky that he pulled away.

Lifting her in his arms, he carried her inside and laid her back on her bunk. Stripping off his clothes, he pulled her nightgown over her head. He needed to feel her, her skin touching his, her lips on his.

"Tu es ma raison d'etre," she murmured in French. "You are my reason for being."

He smiled and brushed the hair from her eyes. Stroking her cheek, he deepened his kisses, moving to the delicate throbbing in her neck. He rolled so she sat astride him.

She placed feathery soft kisses on his lips and throat as he filled her. She arched with her head thrown back. He pressed his hands to grip her hips and thrust into her again and again. She bit her lip to keep from screaming her pleasure.

"Easy, Elyse, easy. Make it last," Elijah said.

She tried. She was well past the point of controlling it. Gripping her hips harder, Elijah knew this, so he increased the tempo of his thrusts. Her body exploded into thousands of sensations, and she screamed her release into his mouth.

He laughed and flipped positions with her as he plied her lips with soft kisses.

"You are so beautiful when you come."

She blushed. "I tried to control it."

He continued his sensual assault on her lips, neck, and breasts. "We have all night to practice." Looking into her eyes and cupping her face with his hands, he whispered, "I'm in love with you, brat. So very much in love with you."

Amazement and wonder filled her eyes, followed by tears of joy.

"I love you, too, Elijah."

"No tears, brat."

She laughed and cried at the same time. "Oh my God, Elijah, we're in love."

He brushed her hair back, looking into her amethyst eyes. "Now on to that practice I promised you."

❦

MUCH LATER, ELYSE ASKED, "ELIJAH?"

"Yeah?"

"My friends, the ballet company in Huế City. Where are they?"

For a millisecond, he debated not telling her. "Elyse, I'm sorry. They all died in the TET offensive."

"No, no, please… No."

Her grief ran deep. He held her close, offering words of comfort. She spoke of each friend and what they meant to her. How they made her laugh and cry, how they inspired her with their search for perfection as dancers, and how they shared the same love for ballet. Giang Ha, whose name translated to "river of sunshine," was her best friend. Bao was the lead male dancer who teased her relentlessly about her red hair, and all the others.

She was devastated at their loss and to know they would never dance again. Elijah knew beyond the shadow of doubt that the right decision had been made to evacuate Elyse from Huế City when they did, or she would have met the same fate as her friends or worse.

"Elijah, I leave in the morning. I must see my father. I must talk to him. Please come with me."

"Only if that's what you want, Elyse. You're still my responsibility, I'm more than willing to give you time and space to be with your father. I understand your need for your father's love and comfort."

314

"I don't want to be away from you Elijah. I love you. I need you. You give me strength."

⚜

THE NEXT MORNING, Colonel Corrington watched with smile on his face as his youngest son boarded the chopper with Elyse. He knew it would work out. He said a prayer and gave thanks to heaven above and to his own love. How he missed her. She had left him with five strong, stubborn sons each unique in his own way. He always tried to draw on what he believed his Elizabeth would have said and done for each of their sons. Elijah had a surprise coming. He didn't know his brother Donall was on the *Ticonderoga*. With a devilish chuckle, he picked up Soup, who was in his charge for the time being, and went back inside his office.

CHAPTER 36

Elyse and Elijah watched as their chopper approached the magnificent USS *Ticonderoga*, an aircraft carrier patrolling in the South China Sea. There were no fighter jets on deck at this time.

"They must be on a sortie," she guessed.

"It's either that or they're stowed below on the hangar deck," he replied.

Fascinated, Elyse watched as the chopper landed on the massive deck. Excitement bubbled forth as she found her father's familiar form on deck.

"Look, there he is."

AMBASSADOR ARTHUR BOOKER stood watching the chopper land, and his wee daughter on board. It had been Christmas time since he had last seen her. His thoughts returned to the day he stood in his old friend General Morgan's office and was told his child's chopper had crashed, and that she was not among the dead and was missing in the jungles of Vietnam.

His fear and grief for his only child was staggering. Just the thought of it brought tears to his eyes and a sickening feeling to the pit of his stomach. For three long days with no sleep or food, he waited for news of Elyse in the MACV command post. When the news came over the radio that a beautiful redhead had been found in the jungle he had openly wept.

Ambassador Booker turned to the man standing next to him. "Are you going to go say hello to your brother now or wait?"

"I think I'll wait and surprise him in a bit," Captain Donall Corrington replied. With that he left the group and went up into the bridge to watch from afar.

He turned to the ship's Captain and his officers standing at his left. "Are you ready, Captain Andrews? I'll apologize up front. She will absolutely rock your ship. You may want to double the *Saltpeter dosage."

Laughing, the Captain replied, "Saltpeter. That's an old rumor, my friend, that I can neither confirm nor deny. But, yes, we're ready. How much trouble can one woman be?"

The ambassador laughed. "You're about to find out, my friend."

❧

ELIJAH JUMPED DOWN and turned to lift Elyse down. He watched as her feet flew as they touched the deck.

❧

WITH A SHRIEK OF JOY, she ran across the deck only to be engulfed in her father's arms. Tears ran down her face as she hugged and kissed her father.

"Daddy, Oh, Daddy, I'm so happy to see you. Are you alright? Your injuries?"

"I'm fine, pretty much fully recovered. It's been too long, short stack. Way too long," he said, holding her close.

He looked up to see a tall, dark-haired, muscular Marine approaching them. He reached out to shake the Marine's hand. The men sized each other up and both were pleased. They shook hands.

"Very nice to see you, Sir."

"Elijah, you were a young boy the last time I saw you. I have a lot to thank you for."

Elijah was surprised. He didn't remember that the ambassador was

317

such a big man at six-foot-four. It was almost comical that his daughter was so tiny. Looking at Elyse and her father, he realized the only resemblance was the same amethyst eyes. Laughing, the ambassador noted Elijah looking between them.

"Elyse favors her mother. Spitting image other than the eyes, her mother's eyes were the color of topaz."

"Ah, figures," Elijah said.

The ambassador turned to make introductions to the ship's Captain.

"Captain Andrews, meet my daughter, Elyse, and Captain Elijah Corrington."

Captain Andrews, a well-seasoned Navy man, now understood the ambassador's apology.

He had never seen a more beautiful woman. She had fiery golden-red hair, mesmerizing eyes, flawless skin, and a body that should be illegal. *How the hell did Booker beget such perfection? What the hell am I going to do to keep order on this ship with three thousand men and this tiny temptation?*

He introduced his officers to them and thinking of the other Captain Corrington, he eyed Elijah with a smile and a wink to his officers.

Ambassador Booker eyed his daughter. She looked healthy and tan for all her bouncing all over Vietnam.

"What on earth are you wearing?"

Elyse laughed. "My trunk is missing, Daddy."

"They lost 'The Behemoth?" How is it possible to lose something so large?"

"I don't know, Daddy. No one seems to know where it is. Everything I own is now in a rucksack."

"Now that I find amazing. Why did you not tell me of your needs in your letter?"

She shrugged. "It wasn't important, Daddy. You have enough on your mind and most of my clothes would not be appropriate on base and would have been ruined anyway. Just give me my slippers and something to dance in and I'm good."

Elijah watched the exchange. So she did the same thing to her father. Her needs really were basic. It was that independent streak of wanting to do things in her own way and in her own time. He shook his head at Elyse being Elyse.

They were escorted to their staterooms to settle in. There would be no private time for them, as their quarters were on either side of the ambassador's own. Elyse looked at Elijah as she entered her stateroom. He looked around her room with a smile and warm expression.

"I still don't want you going anywhere without an escort."

She rolled her eyes. "You're going to have to trust me at some point, Elijah."

"It's not you, brat. It's the three thousand men who haven't been on shore leave in a long time."

"Fine."

❧

DINNER WITH HER FATHER, Elijah, Captain Andrews, and a few officers was lively and entertaining. Elyse wore her violet dress with the fringe and her black pumps, having lost the sandals in Saigon on their first date. She charmed the men with her easy nature and sweet smile. After dinner, she was escorted barefoot on deck by Elijah for a walk before turning in.

Elijah realized he had left his hat on the dinner table. "I forgot my hat, Elyse. Will you be okay for five minutes?"

"Of course, I will, silly."

She stood watching the calming ocean. The sun was setting in a riot of color. He came and stood next to her. "The sea is so beautiful tonight," she exclaimed.

"That it is," he replied. Turning, she put her arms around his neck and pulled him in for a sweet kiss.

Something was different. He tasted different, he felt... different.

Her eyes flew open. Gasping, she pulled away and put her hands to her lips. "You, you are not Elijah."

He grinned at her.

With a snarl she sent him flying with a sidekick to the chest to land on his backside. Elijah stepped on deck in time to see the kiss and Elyse's kick sending the man flying. There was only one man on Earth who could pull off that trick. *Donall.*

Striding to Elyse's side, he said, "Are you okay, brat?"

"He kissed me. I thought it was you."

319

He strode over to the man sitting on the deck laughing his ass off and reached out to pull him to his feet just to pull his fist back to punch him.

"God, Elijah. Relax."

"It was just one kiss. And for the first time, a woman has been able to tell us apart."

Turning to Elyse, he explained, "Elyse, this is my twin brother, Donall." Elijah pulled him in for a hug and a hair tousling.

"Twins?" Looking between the identical brothers, she realized they were the same, but different, with different mannerisms.

"Oh, good grief, Elijah. Twins. Why didn't you tell me?"

"How many more of you Corrington's are there?"

"Just five brothers," Elijah replied.

"That's it?"

Laughing at her, he said, "Five is more than enough."

"Oh, of that I'm sure. First Aiden, then Brendan, Collin, now Donall. All five of you are here fighting in Vietnam along with your father. Isn't someone supposed to stay behind to carry on the family name?"

"No one wanted to," Elijah replied.

She stuck her finger in Donall's face. "You kissed me."

"No, you kissed me." Donall countered. "I was just returning the oh-so-sweet kiss."

Elyse blushed but narrowed her eyes at him. "You have officially made my list."

Elijah laughed and clapped Donall on the back. "Welcome to Elyse's shit list, Donall. It's quite long: bugs, snakes, rats, bats, spiders, leeches, the Marine Corps, the Army, Aiden, Brendan, Collin, my team and, of course, Mac."

"And where's your name?" Donall asked.

"Oh, trust me, my name is at the very top."

"How's your chest?" Elijah asked.

Rubbing it, Donall said, "She caught me by surprise. I never expected it out of such a tiny pepper pot."

"Elyse is a black belt. You can thank her father for that."

"Why does everyone in your family call me 'a tiny pepper pot?'" Elyse asked.

Grinning, Elijah replied: "My Aunt Meg kept a tiny pot of jalapeños peppers growing outside the back door. They were tiny, sweet, and so hot they packed a wallop." Grinning, he added, "A good analogy, I'd say."

"Aunt Meg always said, 'Find yourself a pepper pot, boys, you'll never be sorry,'" Elijah and Donall said in unison.

"She's met Aiden, Brendan, Collin, and Mac as well? What did they do to make this list?" Donall said.

"Aiden kidnapped her, Mac couldn't keep his hands to himself, and Brendan…" A wide grin split Elijah's face. "Brendan was going to trade her on my behalf to the Montagnard's for four goats and some chickens."

Laughing outright, "Oh, this I've got to hear," Donall said.

"It was five goats, not four. A very generous offer for the Montagnard's I might add," Elyse said.

"I can still haul your sweet ass back and hand-deliver you to that one-hundred-year-old Chieftain." Elijah replied with barely contained mirth.

She wrinkled her nose at him. "Go for it, Captain."

"Still tempted, Miss Booker." Elijah replied with "Miss Booker" rolling off his tongue in a loving caress.

Elyse gave him an exasperated look. "You two can chitchat. I want to dance."

＊

SHE WENT TO CENTER DECK, turning on the radio she held in her hand. Just one dance, that was all she wanted. It was a dream come true to dance on an aircraft carrier.

Taking up her poise, the music started, and she began to move, her bare feet barely touching the deck as she raised her arms above her head. Twirling in a slow spin, the cool ocean breeze in her hair and she tasted the salt on her lips. The song was sweet and slow, and the tears rolled down her face. The moon had risen, and she heard the calls of the whales singing in time with the music. She stopped to listen, mesmerized by their song.

＊

Elijah excused himself to go to her, and Donall watched his brother before turning to go to the bridge. The ambassador and captain of the ship, along with some officers on duty, stood on the bridge watching her as she danced as well.

"Your daughter is *dansseur que pleure*?" Donall asked.

"Yes, a 'dancer who weeps.' She feels the music and moves of the ballet so deeply she sometimes cries."

"I recognize her, actually. I've seen her perform in Huế City many times. She's breathtaking. More so in person."

The ambassador's chest puffed up with pride. "Yes, she is."

Elijah wrapped his arms around Elyse's waist. She glanced back to look at him. "Just making sure you're Elijah," she said, before leaning into him. She sighed in her contentment. "The stars are so beautiful. I love you, Elijah."

"I love you, too, brat."

Dawn broke with Elyse on deck with her father as her escort. She had to dance before the deck hummed with the thunder of fighter jets taking off on missions. She would not be allowed on deck again until late evening or when the missions were completed with the pilots safely returned to the carrier.

It turned out to be one of her favorite places to dance. With the gentle rolling of the sea beneath her feet, the dolphins played off the bow of the massive carrier.

The sun sparkled like diamonds on the surface of the ocean. She understood the call of the sea to the hearts of men. She had felt it herself from time to time. Had she been born a son; the Navy would have been her preference for military service.

Wearing a white naval dress shirt found in the closet, with rolled-up sleeves and partially unbuttoned, and a shortened version of Elijah's boxers. Her hair hung down in all its glory, shining brightly as golden fire in the sunlight. She spun in her pirouettes across the deck and she leaped and jumped along the length of the runway.

⁂

THE MEN who came on deck to start their long day were stunned to find a beautiful woman with hair of fire dancing on the deck. They watched from afar, talking amongst themselves. Even out at sea they had heard of Elyse, the tiny ballerina who appeared on bases only to disappear and show up on another base. She was every bit as stunning as they had heard, and to see her dance was something they would never forget.

For most, it wasn't so much the ballet as it was just to watch a woman as she moved in the way only women could move.

⁂

FOR SOME MEN, such as Donall, it was both—not that he would ever admit his love of ballet to anyone. He was soon joined by Elijah. Donall, the elder son by seven minutes, said, "I knew you were on special assignment, little brother, but father never said anything about guarding a woman."

"It hasn't been easy. She has a fiery temper at times and is a frustrating ninety-eight pounds of sass, but I've fallen in love with her."

Donall looked at Elijah in surprise. "I don't believe it. You finally fell for someone?"

Elijah smiled. "I guess I was waiting for Elyse."

⁂

THE FLIGHT DECK was filling up with sailors ready to carry on their duties. Elyse finished to roars of approval. Curtsying, she made her way to her father's side, his pride in her apparent as he guided her toward Elijah and Donall.

"Good morning, gentlemen," she said.

"Good morning, Elyse," Elijah and Donall replied.

It was time for breakfast. The four went down to the mess hall. Only a few sailors remained, as most were now about their duties.

"The Navy is well fed." Elyse said, looking at the food provided. She helped herself to some fresh melons, scrambled eggs, toast, and orange juice. "What is it they say in that old song? 'The Navy gets the gravy, and the Army gets the beans.'"

"So, what does the Marine Corps get, Elyse?" Donall asked.

"C-rations," she replied.

Elijah chuckled. "That's about it."

They chatted about the war news and the duties of an aircraft carrier as they ate their meal.

"Speaking of duties," Donall said, looking at his watch, "I must leave. I have a sortie to run."

"What do you on this ship?"

"I'm a fighter pilot."

"You're bombing North Vietnam?"

"I go where they send me."

"Have a safe flight," she replied.

"Of course, I have the memory of your sweet kiss from last night to send me on my way," Donall said.

Elyse narrowed her eyes at him. "I think, Captain, you may want to remember landing on your ass instead."

Elijah choked on his coffee, and the ambassador pounded him on the back.

"Ah, there it is. That fiery spirit you warned me about, Elijah." Grinning, Donall took his leave.

Looking at his daughter for an explanation, the ambassador raised his eyebrows.

"Ahem, Donall misrepresented himself as Elijah, Daddy."

The ambassador nodded. "I see, and you were able to tell the difference?"

"Absolutely."

Elijah and the ambassador laughed.

"I have some paperwork to finish and calls to make. I'd like to spend some time talking after we have lunch today."

"I'll meet you at your quarters at noon. Elijah, please join us for lunch."

"Okay, Daddy."

"Yes, thank you, Sir," replied Elijah.

"You two have a good day—and Elyse? Behave." As he took his leave. Elijah's grin was ear to ear. Elyse narrowed her eyes at him.

"How were you able to tell the difference between us?"

"He tasted different," she said, smiling. "Nothing tastes like you, Elijah."

"We have the morning. How shall we pass the time?" Elijah said, as he smiled his wicked smile. "We, meaning you, will have to be very quiet."

Elyse blushed from the top of her head to the tips of her toes.

He laughed. "Let's see Donall off first. I think you'll enjoy that as well."

They went up to the deck in time to see the pilots come on deck. Introductions were made and all the pilots flirted with Elyse until it was time to leave. Elyse and Elijah were escorted to a safe place where they could observe without interfering in the mission. The pilots climbed aboard their fighter jets and one by one taxied to the runway. The rumble and thunder of the jets as they took off reminded Elyse of the day, she had danced on the runway at Tan Son Nhut. Once they were all away, they walked hand in hand to Elyse's quarters.

Once the door was locked, Elyse turned to Elijah, he pulled her into his arms for a kiss, unbuttoning each other's shirts and dropping them, he unhooked her bra and flung it away, kissing his way between her neck and breasts, he suckled each gum drop until Elyse groaned with need.

"Shh." He lifted her in his arms and carried her to the bunk. Stripping off the rest of his clothes he climbed into the bunk with her. Pulling her panties off he lifted her legs to his shoulders and entered her, her eyes widened in surprise at the new position. He never ceased to amaze her with each delight he introduced her too. Biting her lower lip to keep from screaming her pleasure, he rode her well till she could take no more and she exploded into a thousand sensations, she floated back to earth with Elijah breathless on her breasts.

They slept only to awaken to Elyse's father knocking on the door. With wide-eyed panic, they both flew from the bunk. "Elyse, are you in there? Are you ready for lunch?"

"Yes, just give me a few more minutes." Silently, she pushed Elijah into the closet, shoving his clothes in at him. With a twinkle in his eye, he pulled her in for another kiss. She kissed him back and shut the door. She spied another pair of boxers on the floor, his or hers? She didn't know, so she snatched them up, opened the closet door, and tossed them in. She glanced around looking for her pink panties. *Damn.*

"Where are my panties?" she whispered to Elijah.

An arm came out of the closet dangling her panties. Snatching them from his hand, she ran into the bathroom to clean up and dress, run a brush through her hair. Then she opened the closet door, kissed Elijah, and was on her way.

Elijah heard them talking in the hallway as she pulled her door shut. "You still have not learned to manage your time, Elyse."

"I'm sorry, Daddy. I dosed off."

Elijah shook his head in silent laughter. That was a first for him, almost getting caught by a woman's father. He dressed, whistling as he made his way to the mess hall. He realized his briefs were snug and shorter on his legs. Checking the fly, he saw that it was sewn shut. Damn, he had on the briefs he had given her, which meant she was wearing his. He laughed to himself. No worries. At least they were clean.

ELIJAH SAT DOWN NEXT to her. "Did you have a nice nap, Miss Booker?"

"Oh, yes, and did you rest, Captain?"

"Yes, indeed, I did."

The ambassador realized he had forgotten his silverware, so he got up to go get some.

"You're wearing my boxers," Elijah said.

"I wear your boxers every day," she replied.

"No, you're wearing mine, and I'm wearing yours."

"Watch the fly. It's open."

Her eyes widened as she looked down at the gaping hole.

"Elijah, we need to switch."

Smiling at her, he said, "I look forward to it."

"You're insatiable," she whispered.

"When it comes to you, yes."

"Shh."

Her father sat down just as Elyse poked her elbow into Elijah's ribs.

"Ow." He rubbed at his ribs with a grin.

The ambassador looked up from his meal. "What?"

"Nothing, Daddy."

ELYSE and her father strolled the deck. The fighter jets had long since returned to refuel and wait for further orders. They spoke of Huế City and the TET offensive, of their home in Saigon and his reasoning on why she was moving from base to base for her safety.

"You are still 'for sale,' Elyse. I have nowhere else to send you where you would have adequate protection. Even if I sent you back to the United States you would not be safe, and whoever you stayed with would also be at risk. You must trust me in this. I'm counting on you to stand strong and work with the Captain for your safety. It's my fault for not leveling with you in the beginning."

Elyse nodded her understanding. "I wish I would have been told and it's true I have not made life easy for Elijah, but I will try. I'm not a Marine, and it's so hard some days. It's hard to live amongst so many men, and to watch friends live and die. I do my best to make things a bit easier for them."

"Does Elijah know of the baby yet?"

"How do you know it's Elijah's baby?"

"I may be getting old, Elyse, but I'm no fool. I can see with my own eyes the attraction between the two of you. Am I wrong?"

"No, Elijah doesn't know I'm pregnant. I'm not sure how to tell him."

"Will he marry you?"

"I don't know. All I know is he mustn't be forced. I want him to come to me on his own despite the baby."

"I will be patient for now, Elyse, but be aware that my patience will come to an end and the Marine in me will kick in."

"Daddy, please."

"He deserves to know so he can make his own decisions. Does he love you?"

"Yes."

"You have two more days here, and then you must return to the base camp. This ship is heading back to Subic Bay, and then on home. I'll be returning to the hospital ship and then back to Washington for a meeting with the president. We are working to schedule the peace talks. It's imperative that we end this war, bring peace to this country, and send our boys home. You need to tell him about your baby soon, Elyse."

"I will."

He kissed her on the forehead. "You are so much like your sweet mother. Now go."

CHAPTER 37

Elyse strolled the deck with Elijah and Donall, her arms hooked through each of theirs. Donall explained the workings of the aircraft carrier. Her natural curiosity and quick mind brought forth intelligent and thoughtful questions. Impressed, Donall looked at Elijah, nodding his approval with their unspoken twin language. Offering a tour of the deck below tomorrow, Donall excused himself to return to his duties.

"Are they finished running sorties for the day, Elijah?"

"I'm not sure. I suppose you would like to dance. I'll ask the Captain if you can dance after dinner."

"Thank you, my father said we must return to the base in two days. This ship is heading home from deployment."

"I know." Stroking her cheek, he asked, "Will you be ready to return to base camp, brat?"

"Yes. I promised my father I would be strong. Anywhere you are is where I want to be. Elijah, we still haven't switched boxers."

Raising his eyebrows, he said, "You're right, I know the perfect place."

Elijah guided her to a broom closet of sorts with various items stowed away. Elyse stripped off his boxers and stood in her panties. Elijah stripped down and removed the ones he wore.

Looking down at him, she said, "Oh, we are not wasting that."

His wolfish grin confirmed that was his intention all along.

Elyse left the closet humming to herself. She still wore his briefs. In the end, they decided to wait. *Who would have thought it could be done standing up, leaning against a wall?* Her thighs were still quivering and her lips rosy from his kisses. She saw him stick his head out of the closet door making sure she entered her quarters before he left the closet and entered his own quarters.

Intent on taking a shower, she blew him a kiss and entered her quarters. She hummed another tune as she pulled off her shirt and briefs, pulling the pins from her hair she entered the bathroom. Standing in her bra and panties, she reached in and turned the water on and pulled back the curtain.

A wet naked man, towel in hand, stood in her shower. Elyse jumped back. Startled by her sudden presence, he caught her and threw her to the ground. Elyse landed and rolled to her feet. With a snarl, she proceeded to kick and punch him. Once she got him out of her bathroom, she continued her attack until they were out in the narrow hallway. Doors opened to see what the commotion was about. Elijah opened his door to see a thoroughly enraged Elyse side kick a naked sailor in the face.

He hit the wall with her last kick and sat there, stunned. With a heaving chest, she turned to see Elijah striding toward her.

"What the hell is going on?"

"He was in my shower."

"Are you all right?"

"Yes, I'm fine."

Glancing at the dazed man who still sat leaning against the wall shaking his head as others in the hallway moved to assist the incapacitated man. He walked her back to her open door. Looking oddly at the door, then up and down the hallway, he could see her discarded clothes on the floor inside the room.

"Uh, Elyse, these aren't your quarters. You're next door."

"What? Of course, they are," she said, grabbing her clothes off the floor, clutching them to her breast. He pulled her by the hand and opened the next door. A pile of her ballet outfits lay on the bunk.

Horrified, she whispered, "Are you telling me, Elijah... that I just pulled a naked man out of his own shower and kicked his ass?"

Donall appeared behind them shaking with silent laughter. Elijah struggled to contain his composure.

"Oh my God." Elyse's face flamed with embarrassment. "I have to go see if he's okay and apologize."

"No, no. You're going to leave well enough alone. We'll take care of him."

Elijah checked her shower. No one was in there. Once he determined her room was secure, he left and made sure she locked the door behind him. Elijah glanced at Donall, and they burst out laughing as they made their way up to the flight deck for some desperately needed fresh air.

Howling with laughter, hands on his knees trying to catch his breath. "Oh man, did you see O'Riley's face?" Donall asked. "I've never seen a more confused man. Do you think we should tell her he's second in command?"

"Nope."

"We'd better go see if he's okay," Donall said.

Commander O'Riley, the executive officer, stood with a towel wrapped around his trim waist. He was a tall, handsome man with light brown hair styled in a neat crew cut, in his late thirties.

Elijah and Donall saluted.

"Are you all right, Sir?" Donall asked.

"Elyse offers her humblest apologies, Sir. She thought she was in her own quarters and you were in her shower," offered Elijah.

O'Riley returned the salute, grinning through a cracked and swollen lip. "I have never in my life seen a more tiny, vicious wildcat. She was fucking beautiful. It was well worth it just to see that. Her apology is accepted."

ELIJAH FOUND the ambassador and explained what happened. Her father laughed till he cried. "The XO, Commander O'Riley? Oh, that's rich."

"I take full responsibility, Sir. I should have counted doors before she went inside."

"Don't be ridiculous. It's an easy mistake. I've done it myself on more than one occasion."

Wiping the tears from his eyes, the ambassador said, "Ah. That's my little girl. I'd better go notify the captain that my wee daughter just hauled his second-in-command out of his shower and kicked his ass."

⚜

"Oh my God, Elijah. How am I supposed to face the crew of this ship or that man?"

"Chin up, brat, if anything, they'll know not to mess with you. Let's go to dinner, and you can dance afterwards."

Elyse and Elijah walked into the mess hall, the grins on the faces of the men told Elyse they had all heard about it. Elyse blushed, still mortified. Her only saving grace in her mind was that at least she wasn't naked as well.

⚜

The next afternoon Elyse and Donall stood on deck. The sea was turning rough.

"It looks like bad weather is rolling in. Have you ever been in a storm at sea?" asked Donall.

"No, why?"

"It might be a rough night for you, landlubbers," Donall said.

Elyse laughed. "Landlubbers? What, are you a pirate? Yes, I can see it: a tall, dark, swarthy pirate. All you need is a scarf and a gold earring. Someday, Donall, you'll find a beautiful woman, sweep her off her feet, and sail off into the sunset with her at your side."

"Ah, Elyse, if I was a true pirate, I'd steal you away from my brother."

She laughed. "No, you wouldn't. I'd kick your ass and do everything in my power to return to him."

"Besides you don't have a pirate ship."

Donall grinned. "You've got me there."

Elijah came on deck and made his way to where they stood. "There won't be any dancing tonight."

"I know. Donall said us 'landlubbers' were in for a rough night."

He grinned. "Is he playing pirate again?"

Elyse laughed. "Something like that."

"Let's get you something light to eat before they close the mess hall. It's almost time to batten down the hatches, Elijah said.

They ran into the ambassador on the way to the mess hall. "Elijah, I don't have a strong constitution during storms at sea. I would appreciate if you would stay with Elyse during the storm. I don't want her unduly frightened or tossed about."

"Of course, Sir."

After a light meal, they returned to Elyse's room to ride out the storm. The room was quiet, well away from the thunder, lightning, and howling wind as the sea tossed the carrier about.

Elyse clung to the side rails as Elijah climbed into the bunk with her. Pulling her into his arms he held her tight. The ship rolled and Elyse wrapped her arms around his neck, looking up into his beautiful brown eyes. "You're such a handsome man. You take my breath away."

He smiled as he stroked her smooth cheek. "You're the beautiful one, and you take hot racking to a new level."

"What's hot racking?" Elyse asked.

"Men sometimes have to share a bunk, mostly on submarines where space is limited."

"Well, I for one, love hot racking," Elyse replied.

She ran her hands through his thick black curls, down his well-muscled bare shoulders to his back, down to his slim waist and lower to his hips to grip his perfect ass. She lifted her hips to wrap her legs around his back and pulled him in for a kiss.

THE CAPTAIN and his seasoned crew guided the massive ship through the storm and dawn brought calm seas and a glorious sunrise.

Elyse woke with memories of the previous night fresh in her mind. With Elijah's strong arms around her keeping her in place, she never knew a moment's fear as the ship was tossed about by the rolling seas. His lovemaking left her breathless, and her senses were heightened by the wild storm.

Elijah still slept with his arm across her side and belly in a protective hold. She lay on her side, her head resting on her hand and elbow. Taking one of her amber-colored curls, she tickled the side of his face. He made a face as she tormented him. He opened his eyes and rolled her underneath him. Her squeal of laughter at his quick-as-lightning move brought a boyish grin to his face.

"So, you think to torment me first thing in the morning?"

"I was just thinking about how amazing last night was."

"And you want a replay?"

"Always, my love."

He nuzzled her neck and kissed her lips. Brushing the hair from her eyes, he gazed into their amethyst depths. "We leave today, brat."

"Later, right now, I want you," she said, pulling him in for a kiss.

ELYSE PACKED HER BAG, while Elijah and the ambassador walked the flight deck deep in conversation.

"Captain, I want to thank you for taking care of Elyse. I know it has not been easy. I've spoiled her to a degree, but she is, as her mother was, fiercely independent, inquisitive, and has a unique thirst for knowledge. I know my daughter has her faults, but I believe she will eventually calm down. I'm also very much aware of your relationship with my daughter, and I would not want to see my daughter used and abandoned."

"I'll stop you right there, Sir. I'm in love with Elyse, I would never, ever use or abandon her."

"Just be firm with her."

"Of course, Sir. I tend to get a bit upset when she risks her life."

The ambassador grinned. "What did she do?"

"Played chicken with fighter jets while she danced on the runway, snuck out of her tent to dance before dawn, and our trip out here was precipitated by her going outside the base perimeter to swim in a lake."

The ambassador nodded. "I figured as much. She gave me a run for my money as a teen. Without her mother, she spent a lot time with men, mostly my friends and such. Her only real female influence was her Vietnamese nanny. When she was older, her ballet teachers and classmates. I was gone on business for lengthy periods of time. She spent a large amount of time alone. She's a good girl, Captain. Just a wee bit independent and headstrong."

Smiling, Elijah replied, "Oh, just a wee bit, Sir."

"Elijah, I'm going to tell you something, but you must promise to never tell Elyse."

His curiosity piqued. "More secrets? I don't like withholding information from her."

"Hear me out Captain. Have you ever wondered why Elyse has no real memories outside of Vietnam?"

"I did wonder when she said she had no memories."

"Elyse was kidnapped right from her bed and held for ransom when she was eight years old. She was released unharmed after I paid the ransom. I was fortunate that my wife was the only child of a wealthy family. They were gracious when she told them she had met and fallen in love with a simple Marine. She inherited a sizable fortune before her own death. Then again, if we never had that fortune Elyse would not have been kidnapped.

Elyse has no memories of the kidnapping or even her childhood before that. The doctors said it would come out in time when she was ready. Since that day Elyse has never known a time when she did not have armed guards at her side. She's never had the freedoms that you and I have known."

Elijah stopped short. "Never?"

"Not since she was eight, before then she always had an adult at her side. Except maybe the time when she was three, she rode her tricycle three blocks to the fair in the park. You might remember that, you're the one who found her."

Elijah gave him an incredulous look. "That was Elyse?"

The ambassador smiled. "She took a liking to you back then, followed you everywhere."

Elijah smiled as the memories of being a young boy of eight came surging like ocean waves back into his mind. "I couldn't shake her off. I seem to remember rescuing her from a few trees after she climbed them and couldn't get back down."

"She's always had a fondness for heights. Always gave me a heart attack. If you can't find her, look to the highest point available."

They both stopped short, looking at each other, they simultaneously turned and looked up to the top of the flight tower, past the radar equipment, up to the crow's nest at the very top. Not seeing Elyse up there, they both breathed a sigh of relief.

"I wouldn't have been surprised," The ambassador said, as a flash of amusement crossed his face.

Chuckling, Elijah replied. "Me neither,"

"I always found it amazing, even back then, that she was one of the few people who could tell the difference between you and Donall."

Elijah gave him a wry grin. "She still can."

"I'm going to assume part of her troublemaking has been ditching her guards?" asked the ambassador.

"Yes, Sir."

"It's mostly my fault. I struggled with my own insecurities and in turn was an over-protective father. Then she grew up and joined the ballet, moved to Huế City. Even then, I built the American compound for her safety. She doesn't know that I own it. I hired private guards to watch over her. She'd ditch them at every opportunity she had. Then no one could be trusted when we found out about North Vietnam's interest in her. The only people I could trust completely were Marines or Army, and why not the son of my best friend? So, you see Captain, I do not excuse my daughter's rebellion, but I want you to understand why she is the way she is. That, and she has a hell of a lot of her mother's spark."

Elijah gave him a half smile. "We're in a combat zone, I can't allow her the freedom she craves, but someday she'll have it."

The ambassador nodded his head. "Agreed, I'll send some packages to the base for her. Keep her busy, and you'll keep her out of trouble."

They were approached by an ensign. "Telegram's for you, Sir."

He handed them to the ambassador.

The ambassador opened the first and quickly read the telegram and handed it to Elijah to read.

"I had bought a cottage in a small community north of Boston, Rockport. My original plan was to hide Elyse there. As you can see, they found it, killed the guards, and ransacked it looking for her. The police are treating it as a simple murder, burglary, but we both know better. She never would have been safe there."

Elijah nodded in agreement. The ambassador turned away to read the second telegram. Taking his cue, Elijah excused himself.

The ambassador read the second telegram from the Pentagon. *A bill? Removal of tank from swimming pool… One-thousand-five-hundred-thirty-six dollars and seventy-five cents. Replacement of mess hall tent… Seven-hundred- sixty dollars…. Total due: Two Thousand….*

"Elyse." he bellowed.

ELYSE WAS PACKED and ready to return to the base. Elijah was giving his goodbyes to Donall, while she talked with her father.

As he enveloped her in a bear hug, he said, "No tears, short stack. I'll see you soon."

"I love you, Daddy."

"I love you, too."

Then Elyse gave Donall a big hug and a kiss on the cheek. "Take care of yourself. No playing pirate on the high seas."

"Are you sure you don't want to sail away with me, Elyse?"

"No, I'd either sink your pirate ship, or you'd make me walk the plank."

"You love him, don't you?"

"With all my heart."

"Then I'll be happy for my little brother and will search for my own pirate's wench."

"You will find her, Donall, you will. One question: which is better? To soar through the skies or sail the seven seas?"

Smiling, he replied, "I'm a fighter pilot. We don't soar. We scream through the skies. But to answer your question, I've never been able to decide which is better. That's why I love my job. I get the best of both worlds."

Thanking the Captain for his hospitality and blushing, she held out her hand and said goodbye to Commander O'Riley.

He held her hand, gave her a wink, and said, "You pack a wicked wallop, Elyse." He then shook Elijah's hand. "Take care of your wildcat, Captain."

Elijah grinned and put his arm around her shoulder as the chopper touched down on deck.

Walking to the chopper with a look of trepidation, she scowled at Elijah's outstretched hand. "Fine." Sighing, she took his hand, and he lifted her into the chopper and jumped in after her.

ONCE THE CHOPPER WAS GONE, the ship's Captain clapped the ambassador on the back. "Well, Art, she didn't sink my ship, and I didn't have to keel-haul you or Captain Corrington. I guess the worst she did was terrorize Commander O'Riley, and he swears it will be a cherished memory."

"We got off lucky, Joe. We got off lucky."

THE CHOPPER RIDE BACK to base was uneventful.

"We'll have a day or so alone before most of the team arrives back from their R& R in Taiwan. Sarge and Doc went to Hawaii to meet with their wives, so they'll be back around the same time."

"What do they do in Taiwan? Wine, women, and song?"

Elijah laughed, remembering a few of his own exploits in Taiwan. "That's pretty much it, Elyse."

They landed on base to cheers from the troops that Elyse had returned. Soup raced to the helipad and was scooped up by Elyse. His sloppy kisses were sweet, and both Elyse and Elijah laughed at the pup's excited antics.

The colonel hugged Elyse and clapped Elijah on the back. "Welcome back. Life on base has been quite dull without you, Elyse. How's Donall?"

"You didn't tell me he had transferred to the *Ticonderoga*, Father," Elijah said.

"He wanted to surprise you."

"Oh, he surprised us all right."

"How so?"

"Let's just say Elyse took him to task for trying to impersonate me."

The colonel chuckled. "Up to his old tricks, eh?"

Elyse giggled. "He won't try that one again."

CHAPTER 38

The chopper landed with mail and care packages from home for the troops. They handed out two additional big mail bags and a large package. All were marked for Elyse. Thinking someone had made a mistake, they opened the bags, but every single piece of mail in the two mail bags were addressed to Elyse. They hauled the mail over to Elyse's tent. Elijah was heading that way himself. He knew the ambassador was sending a package but was stunned and more than curious as to who had sent all the letters.

Elyse opened the bags. "Where on earth did all of this come from?"

She chose a letter that was addressed to her, in care of one of the Armed services radio stations that continued the radio dedications to her. Opening the letter, she read the contents. Written by a lonely soldier far from home, he had seen her dance, and he just wanted to tell her how she had brightened his day.

She handed the letter to Elijah for him to read and grabbed another letter with similar sentiments. Tears came to her eyes. Some letters were sweet, with poems or offers of marriage, while some were on the risqué side. Some made her laugh out loud, they were so bad, and some made her blush head to toe.

Elijah was flabbergasted. "I'd say you have a fan club."

"Me? I'm a simple ballerina. This is insane."

"Elyse, you have to understand you're a distraction for these men. So many are still teenagers. Most are barely out of their teens. You're something to focus on other than war, death, and their fears. It's a good thing, but if you want it to stop, I can make it happen."

"No, it's okay. I guess I'm just a little embarrassed. Can I respond to them?"

He brushed a wayward curl from her face and caressed her smooth cheek. "No, we can't afford to give away your location."

Disappointed, she nodded her understanding.

"What's in the box?"

Elyse grabbed it, and with a squeal of delight, realized it was from her father.

※

THE BOX from the ambassador included a large stack of beautiful materials: cool muslins, dotted Swiss, cottons, scissors, lovely threads, patterns, and enough supplies to make some lovely clothes.

Elyse prided herself on her seamstress abilities. Granted she had no sewing machine, but she did pretty well sewing by hand. Sifting through the material, she chose her first pattern for a simple dress and a lovely cream-colored, soft, cotton with a tiny, pink rosebud pattern.

Excited, she spread the material on the bed and laid the pattern on top. It took her five days to sew. Wanting to surprise, Elijah she hid the project away whenever Elijah came into her tent. The dress was perfection: slinky straps, slight cleavage, short with an empire waist that flared out when she twirled. A perfect summer dress—soft, feminine, and it made her feel pretty.

Once the dress was finished and on, she was ready to meet Elijah at the mess hall for lunch. She walked out of her tent to whistles from Arnold and Mountain.

"Elyse, you look beautiful. Where did you get your new dress?" Arnold said.

"I made it," Elyse replied.

"That's cool that you can make clothes," Mountain said. "My mom does that too."

THEY WALKED over to the mess hall. Elijah stood twenty feet away with his back to her as he conversed with a group of officers. Big smiles and whistles told him Elyse was behind him.

Elijah turned around to see her. She was perfection. With a glowing smile on her face, she posed for him. She twirled so he could see the dress fan out around her. He smiled at her, she looked beautiful, feminine, sexy.

IT HAPPENED SO FAST no one had time to react. A fight broke out just to the left of Elyse. One man hit another man so hard he flew backwards into Elyse, knocking her into a large mud puddle. Stunned silence followed.

ELYSE WAS SHOCKED. One minute she was posing in a pretty dress for Elijah, the next she was sitting in a mud puddle. She looked down at her dress covered in thick mud. It was ruined.

They all reacted at once, jumping to come to her aid.

"No. Back off." The tears flowed as she sat in the mud. "I just wanted to feel pretty again, to feel like a woman. I'm tired of men's underwear. I'm tired of being treated like a Marine. I want a bubble bath. And perfume, nail polish, pretty clothes again. I want to feel feminine, soft and smooth. I want a pink ruffled tutu, flowers in my hair, and delicate lace. I'm tired of green and camouflage, I want to wear makeup and to have clean feet, and chocolate cake."

Standing up in the middle of the mud puddle, she angrily wiped the mud and tears from her face. "I am done with the whole lot of you. For seven months I have been dragged through this war. I am tired of being ugly and dirty. I just wanted to be pretty."

She lifted the edge of her ruined dress. "I really did feel pretty for a few minutes, but you men wouldn't even allow me that." She stepped up out of the filthy puddle, turned, and walked toward her tent.

ELIJAH'S HEART broke for her as he watched her walk away. The silence from the men all around was deafening.

"Son of a bitch," Elijah said, glaring at the two fighting men who stood in silence. In a quiet, deadly voice, he said, "You two assholes had better come up with a really good plan to make amends to Elyse—and that's a direct order." With that, he followed after Elyse.

THE TWO MEN watched as he caught up with her. They looked at each other, feeling pretty low. They had just hurt the one person who was always there for them.

"What the fuck is a tutu?"

"I have no clue. How the fuck are we going to fix this?" Looking around at all the men standing there, he asked, "Does anyone know what a tutu is?"

They all shrugged their shoulders and shook their heads.

ELIJAH CAUGHT UP WITH HER, putting his arm around her and pulling her into him.

"It's okay, sweetheart. I don't ever want to hear you say you're ugly. Whether you're wearing my boxers, a pretty dress, or are naked in my arms, you're beautiful. Someday soon, we'll have a normal life, and all of this will just be a memory. You'll have all the pink, girly things you could ever want or need."

"You saw it? The dress, before it was ruined?"

"Yes, I did, it was beautiful and sexy."

"I made it to please you as well."

"You did, brat. You did."

"Let's get you another shower, and then I'm going to kiss every inch of your body."

Smiling at him, she asked, "Every inch?"

"Every sweet, delectable, pretty inch."

❧

THAT EVENING, they had dinner in the mess hall. Elyse and Elijah had finished their meal and sat chatting with the team. At a signal from Sarge, the team moved away from the table. Cookie came out of the kitchen and placed a large piece of chocolate cake in front of her. Elyse looked up at Cookie in surprise.

"We love you, Elyse," Cookie said.

❧

ONE BY ONE, they came, placing small items in front of her: vials of perfume, a small bouquet of wildflowers, lingerie, oriental fans, different items they had bought and meant to send home to their loved ones.

Elyse fought to control her tears. She stood up and through misty eyes spoke to them. "I am touched, but I am nothing. It's you who are everything. It's you in the trenches and fighting every day, risking life and limb. It's you who are important. My tantrum this morning was just that, a tantrum. I can't accept the things you spent your hard-earned wages on to buy for your wives and lovers at home." She smiled. "Except the cake. I will do hand-to-hand combat over anything chocolate. You are sweet, impossible, and I love you all very much."

❧

THE TWO ONCE-FIGHTING Marines stepped forward. A tall, skinny, blonde man, with intense blue eyes named Oakly said. "You have it all wrong, Elyse. It's you who is everything to us. You're the one who is always here for us. The one greets us when we return from missions and makes us feel better. My girlfriend has tons of perfume and girly trinkets. All of our loved ones have enough, and then some. You have nothing. We're sorry we ruined your pretty dress. You're beautiful no matter what. The only thing none of us can figure out is what the fuck a tutu is."

344

Elyse giggled through her tears. "It's a ballet skirt. You've all seen ballerinas with those skirts that stick straight out. That is a tutu."

Grinning, they nodded their understanding.

Picking up a slinky black negligee, Elyse raised her eyebrows at them, and they grinned back at her.

"Maybe you can model that for us?" called out one man to boisterous laughter.

"In your dreams, boys."

Cookie brought out enough cake for anyone who wanted a piece. How he pulled it off, Elyse didn't know. She sat back down and looked at Elijah.

"Did you know they were doing this?"

"No, I didn't, but I wholeheartedly approve, especially that little black negligee," Elijah replied.

Elyse gave him a sultry look. "And you call me naughty?"

Elijah grinned his wicked grin.

CHAPTER 39

Elijah sat in the grass watching over Elyse as she showered, trying to remember a ditty she sang for him earlier in the day. She never ceased to surprise him with some of the things she came up with. He watched as she lathered her hair. He had timed her once. Ten minutes to wash and rinse her hair alone. He smiled. Even on his filthiest days, the longest shower he'd ever had in 'Nam was five minutes, and it was ice cold.

He glanced away from Elyse to see his team running full speed toward him. He jumped to his feet. Looking over to Elyse, he saw that she was still washing her hair and unaware that the team had entered the off-limits area. He ran over to them.

"What's going on?"

"ARVYN just landed. They're with the colonel now." Sarge replied.

"What the hell are they doing here? How many?"

"A general and six troops."

A string of profanity came out of his mouth. "We have to hide Elyse. There's no way we can make it to her tent without them seeing her."

Getting his bearings, he spotted the closest perimeter guard post bunker. He was pointing toward their objective. Elijah turned and raced to Elyse. He opened the wooden shower door, reached in, and snatched a naked, soapy Elyse right out of her shower.

Elyse, eyes closed as she washed her hair, barely had time to give a muffled shriek as his arms wrapped around her body and he covered her mouth with his hand. "Hush, it's me," he said.

Grabbing a towel, he threw it over her, carrying her in his arms he hauled ass across the field to the bunker with the team running behind them.

He made it to the bunker just in time. He tossed her in and jumped in after her as the team leaned against the sandbags of the bunker trying to act nonchalant. Johnson, lit a cigarette, jumped to the top, and pulled a worn deck of cards from his shirt pocket, just as two of the ARVYN troops walked by nodding their greetings.

"Sarge, send Arnold to follow them," Elijah whispered. "See what they're up to."

Sarge nodded to Arnold, and he left following after them.

"Elijah, what the hell are you doing?" Elyse whispered. "I am covered in soap and sitting in a bunker, naked. Are we under attack?"

"Shh, brat." he whispered back.

"Two more heading this way, Cap," Sarge said. "One of the men appears to be the general, himself."

"Sarge, get a positive ID on him."

"Evening, Sir." Sarge said, as the two men walked up to the team.

"Good evening, Sergeant. A beautiful night for a stroll." Stopping in front of them, the general pulled a cigarette from his shirt pocket and lit it. In broken English, he continued, "How goes the fighting, men?"

"Bloody as hell," Doc replied.

"You men ever hear of an American woman? A—how do you say it? —ballerina who dances on bases?"

"Fuck no," Sarge replied. "That's a bunch of bullshit the brass made up to boost morale. There's no such woman."

"Hell, I'd love to see a prime piece of ass on this base," Mountain said. "I'd be fucking that."

Henson laughed. "Yeah, you and the whole base."

The whole team laughed at the comment.

ELIJAH HELD his breath while holding her on his lap. He had put his hand over her mouth again to muffle her outrage. She stared into Elijah's eyes. He couldn't contain the grin on his face at the team's comments. Elyse narrowed her eyes at him.

❧

THE GENERAL LAUGHED. "If she exists, let us pray her virginity survives intact. Have a good evening, men." He moved along at a leisurely pace, stopping to chat with another group of troops further down. Elijah exhaled and uncovered her mouth.

"Mountain and Henson," she whispered, "I'm going to box your ears as soon as I get out of here."

They grinned, and Mountain whispered back, "You know we love you, Elyse."

Sighing, she replied, "I love you guys, too."

Turning back to face Elijah, she said, "That's the general my father and I had dinner with in Huế City. What's going on, Elijah?"

"That's the man who is auctioning you for the North Vietnamese. He's searching for you."

Elyse scowled. "Let me at him." Elyse let loose a string of profanity.

Elijah chuckled. "My ferocious little firecracker, do you even know what those words mean?"

Elyse gave him a look of chagrin. "No."

"You probably shouldn't repeat what you hear out of the mouths of Marines." Elijah replied with a grin.

"That bad, huh?"

"Yeah," he replied.

Pulling her close, he realized she was shivering from the cold, still wet and slippery with soap.

"You're going to have to act like you and the team are on perimeter guard duty," Elijah whispered up to Sarge. "We can't risk moving her. We'll have to stay in here until they leave. Send Mountain as soon as Arnold gets back to find out what he can from the colonel. I need blankets, food, water, and my weapon. Did you get his name?"

"It said 'Nguyen' on his shirt, Sir."

348

"Have the colonel call Mac. Tell him that's our man. He'll take care of it from there."

Arnold returned. "They're asking questions, searching for Elyse, Sir. They've probably been checking bases the ARVN army aren't assigned too. Hopefully, none of our own troops give it away that she's here."

"Shit." Sarge said. "Most of our men can't stand the ARVN. Our troops are smart, they won't risk her safety."

"Someone throw their shirt down for Elyse," Elijah said. "It's cold and damp down here. Get those blankets and be careful."

Henson handed his shirt down as Mountain left to relay Cap's message to the colonel and get the necessary supplies. When he returned fifteen minutes later, he pulled blankets from under his shirt, dropped a few C-rations, and handed a canteen of water down to Elijah along with his weapon.

"The colonel called Mac, they got it covered," Henson said.

The team set up their perimeter guard position and settled in on top of the bunker to wait. Elijah wrapped a blanket around Elyse's shoulders after she put Henson's shirt on. She straddled his lap, aware of her nakedness under the shirt.

"Why is this general doing this," she asked, "and why do the troops hate the ARVN?"

"Most are decent men just fighting for their country, but not all are trusted because of a few bad apples. As to the general, maybe greed and corruption? I don't know. I can't answer for another man's failings."

"Why me, Elijah? What's so special about me that they want me on the auction block?"

"You're beautiful. You're the beloved Prima ballerina of the South Vietnamese people, and you're the daughter of the US Ambassador. Capturing you would put leverage on your father during the peace talks, but we all know you would never have been seen alive again. That, and the millions of dollars North Vietnam would receive to fund their war."

"This is all very frightening."

He brushed the hair from her eyes. "I know." He pulled her in and kissed her lips, following the natural path down her neck.

"Elijah, the team. They're right above us."

Elijah grinned. "I know, it's kind of hot."

"You're bad."

"There's something about you and bunkers."

"What if someone comes?"

"We have the team."

"That's who I'm talking about...." Elyse felt herself melting at his sensual assault on her neck. Her half-hearted protests died on her lips.

"We're probably in here for the night. We might as well make it enjoyable," Elijah replied.

❦

THE ARVN CHOPPER FLEW LOW, hugging the hills and valleys, as its pilot took evasive maneuvers trying to outrun the two unmarked gunships on its tail chasing it through the mist laden valley, pushing and taunting until the chopper was deep into NVA territory. On board, General Nguyen realized his cover had been blown. The Americans must know he was responsible for the auction of the American ballerina. He and his six men screamed as the American choppers flew side by side and sprayed their chopper with bullets from their M-16 guns.

The American pilots chattered back and forth, intent on the kill. They pulled back and fired their missiles into the ARVN chopper then watched as it fell from the sky, twisting and churning in a ball of fire to crash on the ground.

❦

ELIJAH LEARNED LATER that day the generals ARVN chopper had been shot down with no survivors. Elijah smiled and raised his coffee cup in a silent toast to Mac.

CHAPTER 40

Being a base camp, they sometimes had members of other branches of the military show up looking for a hot meal and a clean bunk to rest in. This particular day, a company of army rangers landed at the base. They were led by a tall, handsome, blonde captain by the name of Bjorkland.

Captain Bjorklund presented himself to Colonel Corrington and explained his mission and his needs for his men. He explained that there would be another chopper along shortly with some brass on board. Once the captain left his office, the colonel instructed his aide to find Captain Corrington and have him report to him immediately. The Marine Corps and Army did not usually get along, and today would be no different.

Elijah reported to his father right away.

"Elijah, restrict Elyse to her quarters for the duration of their visit here. I would prefer them not to see Elyse and have friction between the Army and the Marine Corps over her."

Elijah agreed and went in search of Elyse, which was not an easy task. Half an hour later, he found her in the rec area.

SHE DANCED ON A BUNKER, a flower lei she had weaved that morning on her head, Elijah's shirt tied in a knot below her breasts. She wore a sheer, pink ballet skirt and matching panties, and her long hair swirled as she spun. She heard an unfamiliar voice.

"I must be in heaven and you are definitely an angel."

She opened her eyes to see a tall, handsome blond soldier standing just below her.

Elyse laughed. "No, no angel."

"Just a flesh-and-blood woman, and this is the furthest from heaven there is."

"Then the question is Miss?"

"Elyse."

"So, you're Elyse, a real woman. Most of the troops believe you to be a fantasy. The jocks on the radio do not do your beauty justice. Why are you here?"

Elijah walked up from behind the captain, shaking his head at her. He stepped around the captain and lifted Elyse down from the bunker.

"Elyse, return to your quarters."

She opened her mouth to argue the point but thought better of it at the look in Elijah's eyes. She acquiesced. Elijah motioned for Johnson to escort her.

Once she was away, Elijah turned to Captain Bjorklund and introduced himself. "I'm Captain Corrington, Captain…?"

"Bjorklund, that's quite a lovely surprise to find on a base camp, Captain. Who is she and why is she here?"

"I would appreciate it if you and your men would steer clear of Elyse for the duration of your visit here," Elijah said.

"Kind of sounds like you've already staked your claim, Captain."

Elijah smiled. "Elyse is here under the protection of the Marine Corps. She belongs to no one but herself."

The captain smiled. "So, she's available?"

"No, she is not available. She is off limits."

❧

ELYSE WAS WALKING BACK to her tent with Johnson when she noted the men new to the camp.

"Who are they, Andy?"

"Army Rangers. Best to avoid them. They look like trouble."

THE RANGERS sure as hell noticed Elyse. Their whistles and wolf calls caused the Marines to stop what they were doing and stare them down. There was definitely friction between both sides.

One of the Rangers pinched Elyse's bottom. Her screech of outrage and slap to the nearest man was all the incentive they needed. All hell broke loose with Marines and Rangers in a fistfight with Elyse standing right in the middle of it. Elijah and Captain Bjorklund entered the melee trying to break up the fight and ended up in their own battles as Elijah fought to make his way toward Elyse.

ELYSE STOOD in the middle of the chaos she had unwittingly created. She knew about the bad blood between the two military branches, but this was insane. From the looks on their faces, they were enjoying it. *They're killing each other.* She pulled a sidearm from a nearby man, raised it to the sky, and pulled the trigger, emptying the clip. Every single man hit the ground.

"Enough. What is wrong with you? I could have sworn you were all Americans on the same side. Each and every one of you should be ashamed of yourselves, brawling in the street like common dogs. Get up and behave yourselves." Elyse said.

ELIJAH LOOKED at Elyse from his vantage point on the ground and grinned. She was magnificent with her eyes flashing and her hands on her hips.

Elijah rose from the ground. The other men followed suit, looking a bit sheepishly at each other and avoiding eye contact with Elyse. Elyse disappeared from his sight with so many coming to their feet. Marine and Ranger alike kept their distance from the tiny woman. Not one would want to mess with the visibly angry woman.

❦

"Ten-Hut." Colonel Corrington and the Army brass along with Marine Corps brass had entered the area. "Who threw the first punch?" the colonel asked.

❦

Elyse wove her way through the group of Marines and Rangers standing at attention. She stopped next to Elijah and gave him a sideways look with a hint of sass and a slight smile on her face. She turned and addressed the colonel.

"I did, Colonel. I'll take the blame for this. Someone pinched my bottom, and I slapped him. Each side sought to defend me. If I would have realized the friction between the two groups, I would have tempered my reaction."

❦

An army one-star brigadier general spoke. "Elyse should be moved under the protection of the Army. Clearly, a mere simple woman can't comprehend that she is not only a temptation, but a distraction to the men of the Marine Corps. They are in danger because of her."

❦

Elyse raised her eyebrows, and with hips swinging and eyes flashing, she moved to stand in front of the general.

"A simple woman? I hardly think so, General?"

"Anderson."

"General Anderson." She leaned in. "Are you telling me Army Rangers are immune from temptation? From women? And moving me under the protection of your Rangers they would fare better? Let's just see about that."

Looking into Elijah's eyes with an unsaid apology, she sashayed over to stand in front of a ranger. Staring up into his eyes with a wicked smile on her face, she leaned into him showing a goodly amount of cleavage. She moved between the Rangers, looking each one in the eye, and stopped at Captain Bjorklund. She had said it all with the promise in her eyes, parted lips, and the way she moved her body, running her hands down her curves. They were not immune. She knew it. They knew it.

Only the growl from Elijah stopped her. She came to stand before the general again.

"Your Rangers squirm as we speak. They're men, and they react as any man—Ranger or Marine—would. Men are men, there is no changing them, General Anderson."

"It generally is not my way to flaunt myself or purposely tempt men. Every Marine on this base would give his life for me. They are like big brothers to me; I have no interest in any of them but one. They are "safe" from me, and they know it. I hardly think the Marine Corps feels it's necessary to be rescued by the Army from me."

She turned to address the Rangers. "I'm sorry for your discomfort, but it was necessary to prove my point. Please forgive me."

She turned back to address the brass again. "I am where my father, US Ambassador Booker, and my godfather, General Morgan, thought I should be. I am not a pawn to be used in a tug of war. I'm a flesh-and-blood woman, and I'm staying right here under the protection of Captain Corrington.

"If anyone chooses to argue the point, I'll just make a phone call to reinforce my father's wishes, along with my own. I choose to be here. Enough said. Now I expect all of you to put your differences aside and behave yourselves."

She turned and walked back to Elijah. "Don't let it go to your head, Captain."

HE GRINNED DOWN AT HER. Only Elyse would not only defend men she had just chewed out for fighting but go toe-to-toe with the top brass. She was a force to be reckoned with. Ninety-eight pounds of sass with some C-4 thrown in. She had just been upgraded from a firecracker.

COLONEL CORRINGTON DISMISSED THE TROOPS, thinking to himself, *maybe they should sic Elyse on the VC. The war would soon be over.*

ELIJAH LOCKED eyes with Captain Bjorklund. He was grinning and shaking his head. He came over and shook Captain Corrington's hand.

"Captain, I think you have your hands full. Elyse, it has been entertaining to say the least."

Elyse reached out her hand to his. "Captain. No hard feelings, I hope."

He took up her hand and kissed it. "Oh, something's hard all right, but it's not my feelings." With a grin, he walked away. Elyse stifled a giggle.

ELIJAH LOOKED at Elyse and shook his head. "I have no idea what to do with you."

"What? Would you rather have given me up to the Army? Do you feel safe from me, Captain?" With a smile, parted lips, and a promise in her eyes, she turned away.

"Where are you going, brat?"

"Back to my quarters as ordered, Captain. Would you care to join me?"

With a grin, he followed her, watching the swing of her hips as she made her way back to her tent.

CHAPTER 41

He watched her in the distance. Even from here he could see and feel her joy. She made life here in 'Nam bearable. Radio in hand, she leaped from inner bunker to bunker, her fire-red hair flying in circles as she pirouetted, her laughter carrying in the wind to Elijah's ears.

Elijah saw her fall. Her bloodcurdling screams sent shivers down his spine and resonated throughout the camp. He was on the move at her first scream. The Marines who were closest were there first. Their shouts for a medic had him racing through the camp even faster. A sandbag had slipped as she landed causing her to lose her balance. She never saw the knife sticking up until she landed on it. Someone had jammed their Ka-bar knife through the roof of the bunker and had left it there.

Elijah and Doc climbed to the top of the bunker, along with the four Marines and Mountain already up there. Elyse was impaled by the knife through the backside of her upper thigh. One of the Marines had pulled his belt off and applied it as a tourniquet. They lifted her off the knife and laid her on her side. Elyse had long since fainted. The deep, bloody gash on the back of her thigh was bad, once they got the bleeding under control, they lifted her down, and Elijah carried her to her tent with Doc and Bradley, another medic at his side. Once in her tent, they laid her, stomach down, on her bunk.

"THAT GASH IS PRETTY BAD, CAP." said Doc. She's lost a lot of blood. She'll need lots of stitches. It may have even nicked an artery, and I'm pretty sure that's going to cause an infection." His thoughts were on the baby. "She needs a doctor."

"Get on the phone with headquarters," Elijah said. "Get someone up here now."

Doc sent Bradley to go make the call.

Elijah placed a cool cloth on her forehead. Elijah eyed the slippers on her feet. He unwound the ribbons and removed the slippers, her toes and arches were taped with duct tape, bloody, and bruised. He didn't think the blood had penetrated her slippers, but he remembered she had told him how painful it was to dance on her toes. He shook his head. His tiny dancer, what was he to do with her? For all her strength, she was so fragile. He gently removed the tape and washed her tiny feet.

THEY WERE EXPECTING a doctor within the hour. He was coming up from one of the field hospitals. The chopper landed, and the doctor was rushed to Elyse's bedside. He shook Elijah and Doc's hand and introduced himself. 'Captain Monroe." He looked toward his patient. "A woman? This is a surprise."

THEY USHERED Elijah out of the tent and the Doctor, Doc, and the other medic Bradley, went to work on her leg. They cleaned the wound and sewed thirty external stitches with many more inside. They gave her antibiotics through an IV, along with a tetanus shot, and wrapped her leg in clean bandages. Doc also informed the doctor of Elyse's pregnancy, so he checked the baby as well.

Elijah and the team paced outside as one hour turned to two and two to three. His nerves were shot. For hours now, he'd fling himself into a chair only to jump up and start pacing back and forth again. The Colonel and others stopped by to check on her progress.

❧

Doc finally opened the door. "Cap, you can come in now."

Elijah nodded to Bradley as the medic left and he rushed inside. The doctor acknowledged him with a nod. "She's sedated with morphine, Captain." Giving instructions to Elijah and Doc for her care, he said, "She and the baby will be fine. Keep her resting in bed for at least a week to ten days. You can remove the stitches at that time. Watch for fever and infection." With that, the doctor took his leave.

❧

Elijah stood as if turned to stone. "Baby? Did he say baby?" Shocked, he looked at Doc. "Did you know?"

"Yes."

His voice barely above a whisper. "Why didn't you tell me?" Elijah asked.

"It wasn't my place. That is between you and Elyse," Doc replied.

Elijah nodded, his thoughts racing through his mind. *A baby.* Absolute joy coursed through his veins and for the first time in his adult life tears filled his eyes. Turning away from Doc, he looked down at Elyse. He smoothed the hair back from her face and placed a butterfly kiss softly on her lips. *Brat, you never cease to surprise me.*

❧

An hour later, Elyse opened her eyes, feeling an unfamiliar fog in her brain. She looked over, Elijah sat on a chair next to the bed, elbows on his knees, he held his head in his hands.

Her voice was a raspy whisper. "You look like hell, Elijah."

Startled, he jumped, then leaned toward her, touching his forehead to hers. "How are you feeling?"

"What happened?"

"You don't remember?"

"No."

"You fell on the bunker and landed on a knife and cut the back of your thigh pretty badly."

Fear filled her as her eyes teared up. "Will I be able to dance again?"

"Of course, but you need to trust me on when. That's all I ask is for you to trust me."

"I do trust you, Elijah, but sometimes you're over-protective."

Smiling at her. "Obviously with you I need to be. We'll discuss dancing when you're better. As it is, I don't think you'll be doing any dancing for a while. For now, you need to heal your wound."

Elyse's eyes welled again.

"Please don't cry, Elyse. Don't cry, sweetheart."

"I want to go home, Elijah, but I want you with me. I want to go home. Please take me home."

"I can't Elyse. You know I can't, or I would just to see you safe and away from all of this. Please be patient. I'll figure something out." He placed feathery soft kisses on her lips and brow. "I promise. Now, my love, be a good girl and rest."

Elijah watched her as she slept. He wondered if she was trying to get up the nerve to tell him about the baby. He had no doubt in his mind that they would make a beautiful child. He had no idea how to ease her obvious discomfort about telling him.

SARGE CAME to see him a day later. "Cap, I have something to show you." He took him over to another bunker. We found another Ka-Bar knife. I've inspected all the bunkers. There's another one further down. "Elyse's accident was no accident."

"Who would want to hurt Elyse? And why?"

"I don't know, I just don't know," Sarge replied, "I can tell you one thing for sure. If she would have landed on that knife with one of her feet, her dancing days would have been over."

"That means this is a personal," Elijah replied, the worry lines etched deep in his face.

GUARDS around the base were doubled, and the team were now three on and changing every four hours. Elijah had a bunk brought in, so he could stay with her at night. She was not to be left alone under any circumstances.

ELYSE LAY in her bunk on her side of the room. Elijah laid in his, softly snoring. She watched him as he slept. He was beautiful, rugged, handsome, and sexy. She wondered if their child would favor him or her. He opened his eyes, and she smiled at him.

"This twin bunk thing isn't working out so well," Elyse said.

He returned her smile. "I can't touch you, brat."

"I know, but I still need your arms around me so I can hear your heart beating in your chest."

He got up and pushed the bunks together and climbed back into bed after adjusting the mattresses. Careful of her IV, he pulled her into his arms. She lay her head on his chest, sighing peacefully, she drifted off to sleep.

ELIJAH BROUGHT ELYSE HER MEALS, carried her to the powder room, and even allowed visitors with team members present. She played checkers and poker with his men, and one evening, Elijah brought in a chess set. He beat her soundly the first game, and she returned the favor in the next round.

Colonel Corrington and Collin came in to visit and told her stories of Elijah's childhood adventures. Elijah arrived soon after, Elyse pointed her finger at him, laughing. "You were just as much a little stinker growing up as I was."

Elijah grinned at her. "There were five of us. What trouble one didn't think of the other four did. You, my love, managed, and still manage to get in trouble all on your own."

2

She stuck out her tongue at him.

The talk turned to birthdays. "Donall and Elijah's birthday is next month," the Colonel said.

"Oh." Elyse said. "I guess mine is next month as well."

"When is your birthday, Elyse?" Elijah asked her.

"The twenty-third. And yours?"

He grinned that wolfish grin. "The twenty-third as well."

"We have the same birthday?"

"I'll be twenty-seven."

"I'll be sixteen." Elyse said.

Elijah looked positively ill. She let him suffer for a full minute.

"Just kidding. I'll be twenty-two."

He gave her a "I'll get you for that" look. She merely smiled at him.

Elyse asked: "So, tell me, Colonel, you have five sons, four of whom have Irish names. Elijah's name is Hebrew. Why?"

"My wife was full-blooded Irish, a black-haired, blue-eyed beauty. Our first son, Aiden, was born from her first marriage. Her first husband, a soldier, died in an accident on base."

"When we married, I adopted Aiden and raised him as my own, though it was our wish that he use his father's surname, Yarusso, which was the only right thing to do."

"My stubborn wife wanted Irish names for our sons. Elijah was our surprise. We didn't know she carried twins, and I finally got my wish to name a son after my own great grandfather, Elijah. Mickal, his middle name is Irish, and Elijah fit with her alphabetical theme."

"And no daughters, Colonel?"

"There hasn't been a daughter born into my family for five generations."

Elyse raised her eyebrows. "Then who was this Auntie Meg I've heard about?"

"My wife's elder sister. A retired WAC, she moved in after my wife's death, and she helped raise my boys, and took charge whenever I was deployed. I'll always be grateful for that old bat. God rest her sweet soul. She could wield a wooden paddle with the best of them."

Elijah and Collin grinned like little boys.

Elyse smiled. "I'm sure you both deserved it."

THE COLONEL CAME ALONE one afternoon and told her a family secret. He had once come home from one deployment to find all his boys knitting as punishment for some offense. Aunt Meg had made them all learn how to knit. In the end, it calmed them and kept them out of trouble, though not always. "We always had boxes full of hats, scarves, mittens—you name it," he said with a laugh. "All of my boys were proficient at knitting and not a one would admit to it. I suspect at least a few of them still knit in secret."

Elyse covered her mouth to stifle a giggle.

ALL WORKED to cheer her up. She would have a scar, a nasty one, and she worried she would never dance again.

A few days later, she was finally out of bed. She had tried to get out a few times during the week and had promptly been caught and carried back to bed with stern warnings to stay in bed or her stitches wouldn't hold, and then she'd be in real trouble.

DOC CAME in to change bandages and check her wound daily. During one such morning, Elyse apologized to Doc for dragging him away from his medical books and other wounded Marines to care for her. Looking at her delightful cheek peeking out from beneath pink panties, he grinned at her. "It's a tough job, Elyse, but someone has to do it. Let's get those stitches out."

Elyse laid on her tummy. Elijah sat on a chair looking into her eyes and holding her hands. Doc was efficient and moved quickly to remove the stitches.

"It's healing nicely, Elyse," Doc said. "The scar won't be as bad as we thought."

Elyse breathed a sigh of relief. "Thank You Doc."

"You'll be able to slowly work the muscles by next week," Doc replied.

CHAPTER 42

It was a lovely morning. Doc finally cleared her for dancing, so she headed off to a nearby field. The music was perfect, still somewhat limited in her movements, she swung herself in circles just enjoying the moment and the warmth of the sun. She slowed to the rhythm of the song, moving sweetly.

Noticing something in the grass that clicked when she stepped on it, she stopped cold. Looking down at her foot, she broke out into a sweat. *Stay calm, stay calm.*

She looked over to where Johnson and Henson sat. Her fear was so great she didn't dare speak. *They will see. They will help.* They were laughing about a joke Mountain had told them that very morning. Looking up at Elyse, they saw her stop and watched her for a minute.

"What's up with Elyse?" Johnson asked.

"She's not moving." Henson replied.

Both men jumped to their feet. Making eye contact, they saw the fear on her face.

"Elyse, what's wrong?" Johnson called to her.

Walking closer, they looked down at her feet and saw it. A mine. Elyse had stepped on a mine.

"Holy shit." Yelling for more help, they called to her. "Don't move, Elyse. Don't move."

The area in front of the field filled with Marines.

"Someone go, get Cap." shouted Henson.

※

ELIJAH HAD JUST STEPPED from the shower. After pulling his trousers on, he rubbed the towel over his thick, black hair. He thought Elyse had to be almost done with her morning dancing. She would shower, and then he'd take her to breakfast. A breathless Marine ran toward him.

"A mine, Elyse stepped on a mine."

"What?" Sheer terror filled his mind as he pictured the worst. Elijah was off at a run toward the fields.

※

STEPPING GINGERLY THROUGH THE FIELD, looking for mines as they went, Henson and Johnson made their way out to where Elyse stood.

"Don't move, Elyse. Cap is on his way," Henson called out to her. "You're going to be fine."

※

ELYSE STOOD STONE COLD, waiting. It seemed to her that everything and everyone was moving in slow motion. Then she saw him just behind Henson and Johnson, making his way toward her. She locked eyes with his and drew strength and courage from his steady gaze.

"Deep breaths, brat. Stay calm and don't move." Elijah said as he came up behind her.

Henson and Johnson were on their knees brushing the dirt and grass away from her feet.

"Pressure plate mine, Cap, we need something to counter the weight," said Henson.

"Johnson, get some rocks from the edge of the field," ordered Elijah.

Johnson backed up and sprinted to the edge of the field, returning a few minutes later with two large rocks in hand.

"Johnson, give the rocks to Henson and back off. There's no reason to risk both of your lives," Elijah said.

Johnson balked.

"That's an order, Johnson."

Johnson backed off.

Elyse stared straight ahead.

"You're doing great, Elyse. We've got this. Just breath. We're going to counter-balance your weight and the three of us will dive away together because it will explode," Elijah said.

"No Elijah, like you said there's no reason for you to risk your life as well," Elyse replied.

"Elyse, I can't let you do this alone."

"I can dive, further, and faster than you can. This time you need to trust in me and let me do this. Back off. I'll dive straight into your arms."

Elijah knew she was right, nodded his head and slowly backed away.

"Okay Elyse," said Henson. "I'll put the rocks down and dive that way toward Johnson, you dive to Cap. We got this. On three, one, two... three."

They dived.

Elijah watched as she seemed to move toward him in slow motion, she dove into him as the mine exploded behind them. He pulled her to his chest. She collapsed against him as he rolled to cover her body with his.

She didn't speak. She just held onto him tightly, her breathing slow and even.

"It's over. You're safe," Elijah said.

She finally spoke. "You're sure? I'm not dreaming?"

"I'm sure."

"You're okay, nothing hit you?" she asked, as she ran her hands over his back.

He smiled at her, "Yeah, I'm okay too."

Her breath came raggedly, and she started to shake as tears rolled down her face.

Looking over at Johnson and Henson, also uninjured, she sat up, reached out to them and pulled them in to give them a hug. "Thank you, boys. Thank you."

Sweeping her into his arms and standing up, Elijah carried her back across the field. Troops were already at work sweeping the field for additional mines and booby traps. Henson and Johnson watched Cap carry Elyse away.

"You ever defuse one before?" Johnson asked as he stood, reaching out a hand to pull Henson to his feet.

"Not with someone standing on it."

"Me neither."

"Holy fuck."

"We got lucky."

"I need a beer."

"Me too." With that, they followed Cap off the field.

Elijah stopped at the edge of the field looking at Sarge with a grim face. He nodded at him. Shifting her slight weight in his arms, he strode off toward her quarters.

⚜

ELIJAH SLAMMED THE TELEPHONE DOWN, his frustration growing by the minute. Turning to the colonel and Sarge, he said, "There's nowhere we can move her to. With this mini Tet Offensive going on, bases across South Vietnam are under attack again. It's too dangerous. We'd be taking her from the frying pan right into the fire. We're going to have to stay right here and hope we aren't also subject to attack by the VC—or whoever is trying to kill her."

"I agree," the colonel said. "Elyse's safety is of the utmost concern. We've doubled the guard, and still someone mined the field where she dances. They found three more mines when they swept the field. This was done by someone on base, I'm sorry to say. An individual or a group of Marines."

"I'll keep the team on three for four-hour shifts. We can't trust anyone else with her safety. I'll be staying with her at night, but we still need an adequate number of guards overnight." Elijah replied.

"She's not going to like this, Cap," Sarge said.

"She has no choice," Elijah replied.

⚜

Elyse walked into the crowded mess hall. She had just ditched Mountain, Johnson, and Arnold. She crossed the hall to the kitchen and called out, "Cookie, are you in there?"

Cookie came out of the kitchen with a large jar of pickle juice. He handed it to her with a shake of his head.

"You're kind of weird, Elyse."

"I know, Cookie, I know. I got caught sucking on rocks and eating dirt yesterday. I don't know what it is, but I'm craving it."

With that, she unscrewed the lid and proceeded to guzzle the whole jar of pickle juice down while Cookie watched with an amused look on his face. Wiping her mouth with the back of her hand, she burped. Blushing, she said, "Pardon me."

Cookie laughed. "That had to feel good."

She sighed. "Now they've got me belching like a Marine as well. Same time tomorrow?"

He nodded. "If we get more in." Cookie glanced up and then over to Elyse.

She turned around to find the entire team and Elijah standing behind her with scowls on their faces and hands on their hips.

"Damn."

"Elyse," Elijah said.

"Oh, come on. I cannot go on with the seven of you hovering over my every move. I'm fine, give me some breathing space."

"Elyse, we've been over this numerous time's now. You go nowhere without me or the team. No more ditching them. Until we know who is out to do you harm, you need to behave and do as your told. I told you yesterday no bunker dancing or dancing in the field until this is resolved. Give me your slippers, brat."

Elyse, her irritation shown on her face as she handed over her slippers.

"Could you possibly be any more annoying?" She asked.

"Probably," Elijah replied, with a smile.

"Can I at least stay here? They have chocolate pudding."

Smiling, Elijah stated: "I'm not sure how well that goes with a gallon of pickle juice but, yeah, you can stay."

CHAPTER 43

Elyse walked back to her quarters with her entourage trailing behind. Off to the right just before the rec area was another outdoor area that some of the troops liked to lounge in. A group of FNG's sat on a log watching another Marine cut a chunk off of a big block of some plastic material.

When he pulled out his lighter and lit the small chunk on fire, the group scattered. Elyse's curiosity was piqued, and she made her way over to the man. She sat on the log and watched as he pulled a "Jiffypop popcorn" container out of his rucksack and proceeded to shake and heat his popcorn over the fire.

"Aren't you afraid, little girlie?"

"Afraid of what?"

"Didn't you see those cherries scatter like cockroaches?"

"That's C-4 you lit on fire."

Smiling, he said, "Yeah."

"Without a blasting cap, it can't explode," she stated.

"Pretty much," he replied.

"Then there's nothing to be afraid of."

He grinned and nodded.

"What's your name?" she asked.

"It's right on my helmet."

"Well, I'm hardly going to call you 'Killer.'"

"Then look at the name on my shirt."

"No, your given name."

"You sure are a nosy dame."

Elyse laughed. "Dame?"

"Dame isn't okay?"

She shrugged her shoulders. "I've been called worse."

"Rick. My name's Rick."

Mesmerized, she watched as the tinfoil top of the popcorn container expanded more and more. He removed it from the fire after a final shake. Tearing open the top, the tantalizing smell of popcorn hit her nose. He offered her some popcorn, and she took a handful.

Popping a few kernels into her mouth, she calmly stated, "Someone at home loves you Rick."

"And how do you know that?"

"You can't get this popcorn anywhere in Vietnam. I've lived here since I was ten and have never seen it before, so obviously it was sent by someone from home."

Taking off his helmet, he poured some of the popcorn inside and handed it to her. "Like I said, nosy."

"Elyse, come on," Mountain called to her. "We need to get back."

With a sigh, she handed him back his helmet. "Thank you, Rick."

"Wait." He shook some more of the popcorn into his helmet and handed her the tin container.

Smiling, she thanked him. "Rick?"

"Yeah?"

"You're right. I don't care for 'dame' either."

"Nah, thank you, I can't remember the last time someone called me Rick."

She smiled at him as she turned away.

HE SMILED and nodded his head. Watching her as she walked away, he didn't see the Marine come up to him until the carton of cigarettes was thrown to the ground in front of him. "*Frag Corrington and the whole damn team. I want them all dead."

"What have they done to you?"

"Nothing. I want the woman. You can have her when we're done, or I can slit her throat. It makes no difference to me."

Picking up the carton of cigarettes, Rick stood up. Pulling his knife, he pushed the man back into a sandbag wall. Shoving the cigarettes into his chest and the knife to his throat. "Touch that woman, and I will slit *your* throat. Understood, pal?"

Fear lit his eyes as the man gulped, nodded, and made his retreat.

❦

ANOTHER HOT ONE. The air was thick with humidity and the sweltering heat of the sun. When Elyse lay on her back on the blanket in the shade. She could see the bubble of her belly. Someone was bound to notice soon. She had better start practicing "I'm just fat" as a response. She thought of Elijah and wondered what his response would be when she told him she carried his baby. She had heard horror stories of women abandoned and shamed. *Don't be ridiculous. He loves you.... He will treasure this child as much as you do. You should have no fear or worries. Tell him... tonight... Do it tonight.* Elyse smiled, her mind settled at last.

She felt the need to dance. She hadn't for a while. Her wound was almost fully healed now, and she felt much better. She was strengthening her muscles daily and wanted to dance, but Elijah had yet to return her slippers after the knife and mine incidents. She made a mental note to ask him later. Maybe it had been enough time.

Evening came and the setting sun cooled the heat of the day a bit.

A dark, moon-less night. The occasional flare lit the night sky as guards watched the perimeter for enemy attacks. Elyse walked to the powder room with Arnold. It was pitch black as Arnold stood waiting for her outside the powder room.

❦

SHE HEARD A STRANGE NOISE. Thinking it was a rat, she hurried herself along.

Elyse stepped out of the powder room, looking around for Arnold. "Bobby? Where are you?"

This was highly unusual. She normally ditched them, not the other way around. She turned and walked right into four men. She only recognized one, Smith, the man who called her Elijah's whore. She knew she was in trouble as they circled her.

"Evening Elyse, you out here all by yourself?" Smith said.

She went into her ready stance. "What do you want? My guard is right behind you."

Smith laughed. "No, he ain't sweetheart, he's lying over there behind the head where I dragged his dead body."

Sweet Jesus. Bobby. She moved first, landing a kick in the face of one of the men, she heard the crack as she broke his nose. With a howl of pain, the man cupped his nose as the remaining men jumped her at once.

Hand over mouth, they dragged her down the hill with rape on their minds. They tore at her clothes, touching her breasts, as tears ran down her face and sheer terror filled her mind.

Screaming for help behind her captor's hand, she prayed for Elijah to come. They forced her to her knees and slapped her when she refused to open her mouth. She kicked and struggled as best she could, while trying to protect the baby in her belly.

⁂

ELIJAH SAT with the other officers. He was waiting for Elyse to come back from the head with Arnold. Soup stood, and the hair on his back rose. He started with a low growl and then began barking loudly. He bit at him, and Elijah knew something was wrong.

"Elyse."

Soup took off like a bat out of hell with Elijah and ten men following. They could all feel it. Something was very wrong. Near the head, they found Arnold, alive but unconscious.

Elijah signaled to Doc to take care of Arnold. They heard the voices coming from the bottom of the hill.

"You fucking bitch. I'll cut your throat. Open your mouth."

❦

ELIJAH and the other men crawled to the edge of the hill and saw two men held Elyse by the arms, while another man stood behind her with a handful of her hair and held a knife at her throat. The fourth man, his fly unzipped with his swollen member in his hand, approached Elyse. Elijah's head nearly exploded with rage. He was on them in a heartbeat, throwing them off of her, fists flying. The Marines surrounded and subdued three of Elyse's attackers.

Knife still to her throat, Smith wrenched Elyse to her feet. With his hand still in her hair, he tightened his grip, yanking her head back against his chest as he backed up.

"Let her go, Smith," Elijah said. Hi voice rough and grating, his cold eyes, calm.

"Corrington, I got your little whore here. She was just showing us what she's been giving you."

He let go of her hair and cupped a bare breast, stroking her with his thumb he pinched her nipple as she struggled against him. He pushed the knife closer to her throat until a bead of crimson blood appeared and rolled down her neck and she ceased her struggles.

"I gotta tell ya, Captain, she's the sweetest piece. I've been fucking your whore every night since I got here."

The surrounding sky lit up with the ethereal glow of green and red flares as Smith's hand roamed her breasts and slid lower to her belly. Elyse was wild eyed as fear and revulsion gripped her senses.

"Get your filthy hands off of her, Smith. I'm telling you one last time, let her go," Elijah said.

Seeing his own death in Elijah's eyes. "No fucking way," Smith replied, he raised the knife to stab her. A shot rang out, and the bullet took his hand with the knife at the wrist and left him with a bloody stump. Screaming, he loosened his hold, grabbed his wrist with the other hand as Elyse slumped to the ground.

❦

ELIJAH LET his comrades take care of him with Marine justice, while he went to Elyse. She was on the ground half-naked, gagging and vomiting, trying to crawl away, sobbing her revulsion at what just happened. Elijah slowly approached her. She screamed, still trying to crawl away.

"Elyse, it's me, baby. It's me."

※

SHE RECOGNIZED HIM AT LAST. "Oh, God, Elijah."

He went to his knees and pulled her into his chest wrapping his arms around her and she clung to him.

"I prayed for you to come." Her sobs broke his heart. She vomited and cried for a long time.

Jumping to her feet, she raced toward the closest showers with Elijah in pursuit. Running into the showers she frantically turned the water on. Grabbing the soap, she scrubbed her skin to get Smith's touch off of her. Crying, she scrubbed harder as Elijah stepped into the shower with her. She collapsed against him.

"Get his touch off of me... please... get his touch off of me," she sobbed. Elijah sank to his knees with her in in his arms.

"Bobby," Panic in her voice, she cried out. "Bobby. He's dead, Oh God." She tried to rise.

"No, no, no, he's okay, he's okay," Elijah said, as he cradled her in his arms until her tears subsided.

He eventually reached up and pulled the string to shut the water off. They lay there in the shower for a long time with Soup curled in by her knees.

"Elyse, did they get inside of you?"

"No, no they didn't."

Elijah breathed a sigh of relief. As bad as this was, it appeared they were not successful in their rape attempt. Elijah and his men were lucky they got there when they did, thanks to Soup. Elyse's little dog had earned his place in their hearts and on the foot of the bed.

"Elijah, they said they put the knives in the bunkers and the booby traps in the field hoping I would be injured or killed. Why? I do not understand why."

"Some people are just evil. They have twisted minds."

Elyse shuddered and snuggled into Elijah. She had quieted and shed no more tears. "Elijah, I have something to tell you. I was going to make tonight special for us, to tell you... to tell you we made a baby at Khe Sanh."

❦

ELIJAH WAS QUIET FOR A MINUTE. Then he kissed her eyes, her lips, her cheeks. Determined that there would be no secrets between them. "I already knew we made a baby."

"How did you know?"

Love shone in his eyes. "After your accident, the Doctor told me we were going to have a baby. Do you know the joy and happiness I felt then and now? The woman I love beyond all else carries our child."

He held her close, his own tears running down his face. Instead of their own expected deaths at Khe Sanh, they had created a life.

"Our baby will be beautiful," Elyse said.

"I know it will," he replied.

"Elijah, I am only ever safe in your arms. This is the only place I am truly safe. Make love to me. Wipe tonight from my mind. Replace it with only you. Please, make love to me."

He lifted her into his arms and carried her to his tent. He removed the remnants of her wet clothes and his own. He was able to lose himself in her eyes. He loved her and told her so. That she returned his love made his heart sing. He loved her until they fell into an exhausted sleep.

Elijah woke in the morning with Elyse on his chest watching him. Her eyes held a hint of sadness.

"I know it's kind of strange, maybe most women would not want to be touched after an attack, but it was important for me to be with you last night," Elyse said.

"There's nothing strange about wanting to feel the touch of the man who loves you beyond all else. You'll get past this."

"They said I had been asking for it," she whispered, the horror of it still fresh in her mind.

"You did nothing wrong, if anything, the fault is mine for allowing you to go the powder room with just Arnold."

"No Elijah, it's not your fault. I blame no one but those filthy animals. I want to see Arnold, to make sure he's okay."

"I'll send him in to see you later," Elijah replied. "For now, I want you to rest."

AFTER SHE FELL ASLEEP AGAIN, Elijah reluctantly pulled himself out of bed. He had some business to attend to. He dressed, kissed her, and told her to stay put. She half-murmured an agreement. He slipped out of the tent. His men were up waiting for him.

"How's Elyse?" said Doc and Sarge in unison. The rest of the team stood behind them, anxious worry on their faces.

"She's strong, resilient, and she's going to be fine," Elijah replied.

"Doc, she is, however, pretty bruised and battered. I want you to check her out after she wakes up." He left Mountain, Doc and Johnson behind to guard her.

ELIJAH, Sarge, Henson and Arnold walked over to where Elyse's attackers were being held. Arnold apologized for his failure to protect Elyse. He had a knot the size of a baseball on his head.

"All is forgiven. Nothing you can do with a rifle butt to the head. She wants to see you to make sure you're okay," Elijah said.

Astonished, Arnold replied. "She's worried about me. Why?"

"They told her you were dead," Elijah replied.

Arnold stopped, pain and rage clear on his face. "Just give me five minutes with one of them for what they did to her, just five minutes, Cap."

Elijah clapped him on the back in support. "No, Arnold, we'll let the Corps decide their punishment. Go see Elyse after she's up and about. You'll both feel better."

They watched as the men were loaded onto the chopper, and the bird lifted off.

Elijah found Elyse still in her quarters. Arnold had just left, they had cried and clung to each other grateful that each other was alive and going to be okay.

"You are forbidden from any physical labor or exercise," Elijah said.

"What? No way."

"Don't argue with me."

"Elijah, I'm pregnant, not incapacitated. Physical exercise is good for me. I don't want to be fat and fluffy. I need strong muscles to carry our child and to give birth. I know when enough is enough. I don't want any more fainting spells."

"Fainting spells? You had fainting spells?"

Elyse squirmed. *Damn.* "I'm fine. Really. They were early on before I knew."

"I think you've kept a lot from me."

"Absolutely," Elyse replied.

ELIJAH TOOK her to the mess hall for breakfast, pancakes, and bacon. Elyse slipped Soup some bacon, too. She asked Cookie for a bottle of ketchup, and Elijah gave her an odd look. They sat down at the table with the team. As she proceeded to pour ketchup on her pancakes, Elijah and the team looked on, looking at each other and back at her pancakes.

Taking a bite, she exclaimed, "Oh my Gosh, that is so good. I knew it would be." Looking up at the men, she said, "What?"

"Nothing," replied Sarge. They watched in fascination.

"Did your wife eat like that?" Sarge asked Doc.

"Yeah, Chow Mein and French fries. Chinese restaurant in town made a fortune off of me," Doc replied with a laugh.

"Dairy Queen for us." Sarge said, laughing.

Elijah looked on. "So, this is normal?"

They nodded.

"Yeah, gets worse," Sarge replied.

SHE SET HER FORK DOWN. Looking at Elijah, he nodded his head in agreement.

"I know some of you already know but, we're going to have a baby," Elyse said.

The team's face's lit up with big smiles that radiated across their faces. Wallets came flying out as Mountain, Arnold, and Henson each tossed Johnson five dollars in scrip. Elyse looked at Johnson and raised a delicate eyebrow. He grinned a shit-eating grin at her.

Shyster. She thought.

"You guys had a bet going?" Elyse asked.

"Yeah, we did." chuckled Mountain.

Addressing Sarge and Doc, she asked, "And you two?"

"We've got, what, five kids between us. I have three and Doc has two. Do you think we don't know when a woman is expecting?" said Sarge.

Doc smiled. "Maybe three, got a letter from my wife, she's late. Just might get that little girl we've wanted."

Sarge laughed. "Mine too. Might get that little boy we wanted. Nah, it's going to be another little girl, I just know it."

Elijah laughed, "Sounds like you two were busy in Hawaii."

"Not as busy as you are, Sir," replied Sarge.

Elyse's felt her cheeks pinken as the Team and Elijah burst out into laughter.

"I'm pregnant. It's going to get a little weird here, but at least I don't have to keep ditching you guys to hide my searches for food anymore."

"Well, at least you're not eating dirt or sucking on rocks," Arnold said.

Elijah looked at her. "Say what?"

"Um… I've been eating dirt."

"It's the minerals. You have a mineral deficiency. You need prenatal vitamins," replied Doc.

"Aren't you supposed to be like, eating pickles and ice cream?" Mountain asked.

"Pickles. That sounds groovy with pancakes."

Elijah grinned. "Pickles and pancakes?"

"And ketchup," Elyse replied.

"I'll get you some pickles." He left and returned with a bowl of sliced pickles.

She poured the whole bowl of pickles over her pancakes and took a bite. "Oh my God, that's orgasmic."

Seven sets of eyebrows shot straight up.

CHAPTER 44

Elijah went to see his father. "Father, I need to speak with you."

The colonel dismissed the aides in the office. "What is it, Elijah?"

"Elyse is going to have a baby."

"When?"

"In approximately five months, Sir."

"What are you going to do about it?"

"I have no idea."

"You have no idea?" he roared. "Think of her reputation. If you're not man enough to handle this, then step aside. A husband will be found for her. This may be nineteen-sixty-eight, free love and all of that flower power hippy shit, but my first grandchild will not be born out of wedlock. We can find a Navy man who's willing to overlook her indiscretions."

Elijah paled. Her indiscretions? He had not considered repercussions, and yes, Elyse would be blamed. That they would take Elyse from him and marry her off to someone else. Someone else who would raise his child.

"Elyse will need to be moved to DaNang or a smaller facility, where she'll receive proper medical treatment. I told you before to think long and hard about your life and if you wanted Elyse as part of it. Now is the time to make your decision. You've got twenty-four hours to make up your mind. You're dismissed, Captain."

ONCE ELIJAH LEFT HIS OFFICE, the colonel called one of his aides in. "Get me Ambassador Booker on the line." Five minutes later the call was connected. "Art, it's Reggie. My fifty bucks is on Elijah. He finally admitted Elyse is pregnant. We're going to be grandfathers in about four-five months."

"I'm certain he will do the right thing. I'm trying to decide where we should move Elyse to. She needs medical attention. DaNang is too big. I know of a small hospital. It's also a nice R&R spot for the troops."

"Good. I'll keep you posted."

ELIJAH WAS MORE confused than before he spoke with his father. The thought that he could lose Elyse hit him like a ton of bricks. Marriage was a big step, and a baby even bigger. Would she even want to marry him? After all that had happened, he wanted Elyse to have a say in her own life and who would raise her child. But Elijah was horrified that someone else could be forced upon her. He could not comprehend life without her.

And just like that his mind was made up. It was only ten minutes before he returned to his father's office. He burst into a meeting. "Pardon me, Sir. Elyse is mine. She will be my wife, and I will raise my child. No one else."

Colonel Corrington opened a drawer and slid a box across to Elijah. "Here you go, boy. It was your mother's. She would want you to have it for Elyse. I've carried it with me since the day she died."

Elijah opened the box to find his mother's rings. He remembered them well. Gold, delicate filigree, a solitaire diamond on the engagement ring. Perfect for Elyse.

Now for the battle plan. He was going to need some help. First, he needed permission from Ambassador Booker to marry his daughter. He had to make a phone call. Twenty minutes later, he exited the office again with a grin on his face as permission was granted. He knew he could count on Collin and the Marine Corps for a plan of action. He slid the box into his pocket and went in search of Collin. They came up with a plan that they would implement tomorrow, Elyse and weather permitting.

⚜

THE NEXT MORNING, Elyse moved about her quarters, humming a tune, straightening up as she went. Her eyes came to rest on a guitar standing in the corner of the room. The man who had owned the instrument had been KIA. Her eyes welled up at the loss of such a talented musician. Pulling the guitar from its place she sat down to play. She strummed the strings, playing the cords of a favorite tune. Her melodic voice, sweet and clear as she sang the melody of "Where have all the flowers gone."

⚜

ELIJAH STOOD JUST OUTSIDE of her tent with Henson and Johnson. His mouth dropped open in surprise when he heard her sweet voice and the soft strumming a guitar. *She said she sang like a cow.* The song ended, and he heard her weeping then. Looking at Johnson and Henson, he asked, "Where did the guitar come from?"

"Aitkin's was KIA the day before yesterday. His buddies brought it over to her this morning. He wanted her to have it," replied Henson.

Elijah nodded. "They've left her quite a bit, haven't they?"

Johnson replied, "Did you see the sketchbook Mastel left her? The drawings of her are stunning, she never even knew he was drawing pictures of her, or that he was such a good artist."

"No, I haven't seen it," Elijah said.

Johnson grinned. "She was a little annoyed when she saw the nude. Said she'd box Mastel's ears if he was alive."

"The nude?" Elijah asked.

"Yeah, she figured he guessed at what she looked like under her clothes because she never posed for him."

Elijah thought back to every time he had ever seen the skinny kid, pencil and sketchbook in hand, always drawing. It didn't surprise him that Mastel had been drawing Elyse all along.

"This has to be painful for her," Johnson said.

"It is, but she's the strongest woman I've ever known," Henson replied.

Elijah nodded his agreement and calling out to her, he entered her quarters.

⚜

"ELYSE."

She stood up, gently placing the guitar back in the corner.

"I could have sworn you said you sang like a cow?" Elijah said.

She smiled at him. "I don't like to let people know I can sing. I'm always afraid they will ask me to sing for them. I'm a bit shy about it."

He spotted the sketchbook where it lay on her bunk. "May I?" he asked, and she nodded her head.

He flipped through the pad, amazed at the artistry of the kid who had drawn the almost lifelike pictures of Elyse. One of her lying on her stomach on top of a bunker, book in one hand, apple in the other. Another of her in the mess hall, sadness in her eyes as she stared off into space. The sheer joy on her face, another of her with tears flowing down her face as she danced. The different poses all captured her beauty and emotions to perfection.

"They're like a snapshot in time, the artwork is so beautiful." she whispered, the sadness and pain in her voice almost unbearable.

"If we would have known of his talent, we would have assigned him to a base camp in the rear. They have need of artists," Elijah responded.

He stopped on a drawing. In the drawing Elyse lay on her back, hair splayed out around her. Her finger in her mouth with a come hither look on her face, bountiful naked breasts and smooth belly graced the page. Elijah's breath caught in his throat.

"That one is pure imagination," Elyse laughed.

"I know it is, your nipples are much larger in real life." he replied. Dropping the sketchbook on the bunk, he pulled her into his arms and placed a kiss on her lips.

"We're moving you tomorrow. You'll have today to say your goodbyes and pack up your things." He handed her back her slippers. "Be a good girl. Stay close to your guards. Stay off of the perimeter bunkers. Stay inside of the perimeter. Stay out of the lake. Keep your clothes on. Stay

383

off of the new towers. Absolutely no bunny rescues, no joy rides in tanks and, finally, no fleecing the camp of their hard-earned wages."

Elyse laughed a light lilting laugh of amusement.

"Have I covered every possible scenario of trouble that you could get into?"

"Sir, yes, Sir." She said, saluting him.

"Good. I have some things to prepare. Meet me by the rec area at noon."

"Elijah, wait."

"Yeah?"

"Happy birthday."

"It's our birthday today?"

She nodded.

"Happy birthday, Elyse." Nodding his head toward her small desk and the stack of money. "Where did you get all of that scrip?"

"Oh, I won that yesterday playing poker."

"Poker? I thought I had warned everyone in camp."

"You did. I've been told they won't play with me unless its strip poker. I've told them, repeatedly, I might add, the most they're getting out of me is Old Maid. I won the money off of the new officers."

"What do you do with all of these ill-gotten gains from gambling anyway?"

She gave him an impish grin. "They're not ill-gotten gains, I won them fair and square. I have no real need for it. I've been sending most of the money to Sister Mary at the orphanage in Saigon."

He stroked her soft cheek. "You never cease to surprise me, brat."

ELYSE ENTERED the rec area early. The men were happy to see her and talked her into some dancing. A favorite of Elyse's, they were soon singing and dancing

Elijah came in and watched for a while. The men were quite good. Though the colonel bemoaned the fact his beloved camp was becoming "American Bandstand," they all had fun blowing off steam. Elijah signaled Sarge. He was ready. Mountain and Arnold carried an empty litter into the area and laid it on the ground. The marines lined up on either side of the stretcher. He walked toward the middle, signaled them to start the music and crooked his finger at Elyse.

"Come here, brat."

Elyse watched him move to the center of the sandy area and sit down on the stretcher, his long legs splayed wide open.

"What's he doing?" she asked a nearby Marine who smiled and shrugged in reply.

Elijah crooked his finger toward her again and pointed down for her to sit in front of him. She stepped out and moved to meet him, sitting down in front of him she turned half-way around to look at him.

"What is this? What are you up to?" she asked.

"I had heard you've never been on a roller coaster. I can't bring you to Coney Island to ride the roller coaster there right now, so I brought a roller coaster of sorts to you."

✤

CARNIVAL TYPE MUSIC played in the background as the Marines stepped forward and lifted the stretcher into the air. They shook it and with their own sound effects to create a rumble they slowly started to move forward. Passing the imaginary roller coaster cart forward from man to man they picked up speed. The tallest men angled and lifted them higher and higher until they were at the very top of their reach. Then down as fast as they could run.

Elyse squealed and screamed in delight as she hung on for dear life. Through banks and wild turns, they wound their way left than right through the rec area. Up another hill and then down again the imaginary roller coaster came to a crazy stop. Breathless from laughter, Elyse and Elijah were unceremoniously, but gently, dumped into the soft sand.

A laughing Elijah rolled to one knee, pulled a box from his pocket, and said, "You have turned my life into a hell of a roller coaster ride. Marry me." He opened the box and the simple solitaire diamond ring within sparkled in the sun.

Stunned, Elyse was in tears. She rose to her knees to cover his face with kisses "Yes, Elijah... Yes."

He put the ring on her finger, and it fit perfectly. He kissed her and the crowd cheered their approval. Elijah held her close, she was his. He swung her up into his arms and stood to spin her around. Elyse laughed wrapping her arms around his neck. He was hers.

Congratulations were in order. A relieved but laughing Colonel Corrington was first in line. He kissed Elyse on the cheek and pounded Elijah on the back. Collin and the team were next, and so on.

They walked back to the tent arm in arm and spent the rest of the afternoon in each other's arms, kissing, touching, exploring. They spoke of their future together and their baby. They made plans—so much to think about. And the wedding? How was that going to work? Where? When?

CHAPTER 45

Elyse put her slippers and a few things into one of the extra rucksacks Elijah had found for her. That made three rucksacks filled to the brim. That was it, that was all she owned. Somewhere in the world was a huge trunk with all of her clothes, toiletries, and shoes. She missed her soap the most. The military issued man soap she had dried her skin.

Elijah came up behind her and wrapped his arms around her waist. "What are you thinking about, brat?"

She sighed. "Girly soap."

"Girly soap?"

"Yes, girly soap. Smells of lavender, makes your skin so soft you could slide on it."

"That sounds interesting."

Elyse laughed. "You'll have to try a bath of your own to see."

"Oh, no, no. Someday I'll try a bath with you and your girly soap."

"For now, I smell like a man with manly soap, manly deodorant, and manly boxers. Soon they'll think I'm a man, and I'll be drafted."

"You'll make a terrible Marine. Can't follow orders."

"Oh, but I'm a good student."

"Yes, you are."

"I really liked what you taught me yesterday."

"We've got ten minutes. I'll teach you something new. It's called a quickie."

Ten minutes later, they walked out the door.

"You're an excellent teacher, and my thighs are still quivering."

***

ELYSE STOOD LOOKING at the chopper on the helipad with a wary eye. She handed Mountain one of her rucksacks. Hefting it up over his shoulder, he asked, "You pack bricks?"

She gave him a "you're a smart ass" look.

She shook her head at the chopper. "Doesn't anyone have a Jeep? A bike? A moped? One of those bouncy trucks? Can I walk?"

Elijah gave her an indulgent smile. "No, Elyse. Give me your hand. Trust me, I'll take care of you."

She looked him in the eye, then down at his hand. Squaring her shoulders, she took a deep breath, slapped his hand down, and walked on her own the short distance to the chopper and climbed in.

Elijah watched her and smiled, *that's my girl*. He trotted over and climbed in after her.

The chopper lifted off and headed east toward the South China Sea. Looking out over the base camp, Elijah spotted her old orange bra, flying high over the base camp. Scowling, he pointed at it.

She smiled and shrugged. "I left them something to remember me by."

***

BASE CAMP FIVE, Vung Tao: Early August

It was small, but it had a hospital. It was also an R&R spot for troops, complete with a pool, volleyball court, a big PX, and a non-denominational church.

***

ELIJAH WAS happy Elyse's pregnancy would be monitored. They could even have a small wedding ceremony here. He was pretty sure they'd be here till the baby was born. It was right on the sea, so Elyse could walk the beach and swim as well.

Elyse was thrilled. Maybe she could buy shoes and girly soap at the big PX. She frowned.

"What's wrong?"

"My purse. I lost my purse in the chopper crash. I have no money left since I sent the last of it to Sister Mary."

Elijah laughed. "I've got you covered, brat."

"Elijah, you don't understand. I have a lot of money in my account. Maybe my father can access it since my savings book was in my purse. I'll have to write him."

"No worries, I'm sure your father can deal with your checkbook."

"Checkbook?" She laughed. "Women aren't allowed a checkbook. It's just a savings account."

Elijah raised his brows. "Why not?"

"Society doesn't allow women checking accounts, credit cards, or even a mortgage for a home on their own. They, for the most part, are treated as second-class citizens. Like we don't have brains to make good financial decisions. What do you think this whole women's liberation movement is about? That, and we don't want to be objectified. I'm surprised you don't know that."

"I must have had my head in the clouds," he replied.

Elyse laughed. "Head in the clouds, it's more like eyes on my chest."

Elijah couldn't keep the twinkle out of his eyes. "Well, you know, eye candy."

Elyse rolled her eyes. "That is exactly what I meant."

⚜

THEY PRESENTED themselves to the commandant, Colonel Berg. A good friend of Colonel Corrington, and he greeted them warmly. He had his aide show them to Elyse's quarters inside of a one story building right next door to the hospital. An unfamiliar Marine stood guard outside her door. Elyse opened the door and entered. Elijah tried to follow her in there, and the guard blocked him. "I'm sorry, Sir, Miss Booker's quarters are off limits to you."

Elijah raised an eyebrow and Elyse stifled a giggle.

"By whose orders?"

"Colonel Berg's, Sir."

"Your quarters are in the officer's tent, Sir."

Elijah groaned. Nowhere to have privacy with Elyse. It appeared someone was giving them a nudge to get the nuptials over and done with ASAP.

They received a quick tour of the base. Elijah made mental notes of what areas would be off limits for Elyse. It was compact but comfortable. He wondered who was behind the stunt of restricting him from Elyse's quarters. No matter, his own men would still be there standing guard when Elyse was inside her quarters.

They walked down to the beach. The ocean was beautiful and had white sandy beaches. It would be another perfect spot for Elyse to dance.

ELIJAH LOOKED AT HIS WATCH. Elyse was scheduled to meet the doctor later that afternoon. It would be nice to know exactly when to expect the baby. They were in the process of returning to Elyse's quarters when a chopper flew in. Hanging from the cable was a massive trunk.

"Look, my trunk." Elyse shouted, practically jumping up and down.

Elijah's mouth dropped open. He looked at Elyse, raising his eyebrows. "Do you think you could have found a bigger trunk, brat?"

She shrugged and gave him an impish smile. "Girl."

Four Marines struggled with the huge trunk.

Elijah questioned one of the Marines, "Where's that trunk been since January?"

"I guess it was up on the roof of the embassy, Sir," the Marine replied.

The annoyance on Elyse's face was priceless. "All this time, they had left it up on the roof?"

The Marine shrugged.

Two more men jumped in to help carry the trunk the ambassador had once affectionately called "The Behemoth" to her quarters."

Elijah grinned, shaking his head. "Six Marines, brat. It took six Marines to carry that monster. What's in it?"

Elyse was thrilled, laughing. "Everything a girl might need. No. Oh no."

"What's the matter now?"

"The key, the key was in my purse. What new torment is this?"

Shaking his head, he said, "Don't worry, we'll get it open for you. All I can say is I'm glad it was misplaced. I cannot imagine hauling that beast from base camp to base camp. Go ahead and shower, I'll return soon with someone to get it opened."

Elyse explored her quarters and the big comfortable bed. It had a nice bathroom with a cast iron clawfoot bathtub and shower. A small sitting area with a beautiful view of the ocean from the window. She wondered if she could sneak Elijah in. He would never disobey orders so that wouldn't happen. However, she was not a Marine. She could easily sneak out.

Elyse showered and put on a clean shirt and boxers. A knock sounded at the door, and Elyse bade the man to enter with the tools to open the trunk. Elijah lounged in the doorway under the watchful eye of the guard, his own gaze rested on the comfy bed.

Soon the trunk was opened, and the man left. Elyse's squeal of delight at rediscovering her clothes amused Elijah. *Women.*

"Elyse, I will return in one hour to escort you to the doctor."

She kissed him goodbye, and he left.

⚜

ONE OF THE niceties of a base like this was they had ice cold beer readily available. He sat outside on a patio area drinking a beer. He could almost imagine he was back home in California. He had a tiny house, more of a shack really, right there in Bodega Bay, right on the ocean. He wondered if he had told Elyse about it. Elijah finished his beer and left to get Elyse.

⚜

ELYSE PRIMPED in front of the mirror. She was a little nervous. Elijah had never seen her as she really was. A little make-up, she applied some pale pink lipstick. A dot of perfume and she was ready. She heard the knock on the door. Here goes, I hope he'll still love me.

391

Elyse opened the door. Elijah's mouth fell open. He looked her up and down, stunned. She wore a soft, pink, floral dress—short but not too short —pink sandals, light makeup, and heavenly perfume. Her hair flowed down to curled at her waist. She was classy, graceful, and beautiful.

"Brat, you're breathtaking."

"You like it? This is me."

"I love it, you were beautiful before, and you're even more beautiful now."

She smiled and relaxed. With a nod to the guard, Elijah took her by the arm and escorted her to the hospital next door.

※

STILL A MARINE BASE, it could service about two hundred men for R&R. They normally stayed about a week before rotating back to their primary base. She turned quite a few heads as they strolled over to the hospital. Dr. Isaacs was a kind middle-aged man, drafted and uprooted from his own practice and family in upstate New York. There were nurses on sight as well. It was nice not to be the only female on base.

The doctor examined Elyse while Elijah waited in the waiting room. When the exam was over, and Elyse was dressed, he called Elijah into his office with Elyse.

"Your baby is fine. You can expect your baby around early January."

They were both relieved. Elijah shook the doctor's hand and murmured his thanks. Elyse was to return once per month for a check-up.

They took their leave and walked the beach hand-in-hand as they carried their shoes. Elyse was hungry, so they went up to the mess hall to find food. Some of the team members were in the mess hall and they called out to her.

"Elyse, you're beautiful. It's nice to see you with clothes on," Mountain said.

Elyse laughed, and Elijah scowled at them. This base even had identifiable food. Elyse was thrilled and starved. After lunch they found the patio crowded, so they borrowed a blanket, grabbed another beer for Elijah and a lemonade for Elyse, and went back to the beach.

They talked for hours. Elyse was excited to learn about Elijah's tiny house in California. She was born in San Diego, so it was a no-brainer to return to California. Elijah's third tour of duty would end in January as well. His future military plans were still undecided. He would have to think long and hard about whether to move his family from base to base. He had grown up a "Marine brat" and did not necessarily want that lifestyle for Elyse and the baby, or more deployments.

THEY LAY on the blanket together, with Elijah placing petal soft kisses on her lips, eyes, and her long, elegant neck. Elijah groaned. "Damn, you taste good. I want more, I'm going to burst."

Elyse giggled. "I know you won't defy orders and crawl through the window, but I can sneak out to meet you."

"Yeah, you're pretty good at that."

Elyse laughed at him. "You have no idea how good I am at it. I had been sneaking out since the second day at Khe Sanh."

"You were sneaking out at Khe Sanh?"

"Every day until the siege started."

"Why, you little shit. Please no sneaking out to dance here. I'll take you to dance wherever and whenever you want to go, but no ditching your guards. Promise me."

"I promise, though I will sneak out to meet you if you want."

"Tempting, very tempting."

"Let's get married now. Then we won't have that obnoxious guard keeping me from that comfortable looking bed," Elijah said.

Excited, she replied. "Really? They'll let us get married here?"

"Let's see what the chaplain and colonel can come up with. Meanwhile, I'd better take you back to your quarters while I still have my wits about me."

CHAPTER 46

Elyse could hardly believe it. Tomorrow was her wedding day. After three long agonizing nights alone in her bed, she could hardly wait. Elijah told her he had a surprise for her, and he'd come by for her in an hour. They planned dinner with the Colonel afterwards. She wanted to look her best, so she chose a low-cut, teal green dress for dinner, complete with snappy sandals, and her hair twisted up into a bun.

She was ready. A knock on the door told her Elijah had arrived. Elyse opened the door, and Elijah sucked in his breath. He had never seen a more beautiful woman. She dazzled him with her smile.

"Good evening, Captain."

"Miss Booker, stunning as usual. I can't wait to devour you."

"Shh." She laughed. "The guard might hear you."

They walked down the hallway hand in hand, but as soon as they were around the corner, Elijah pinned her against the wall and kissed her until she was breathless.

"Ah, damn."

"Behave, what's my surprise?"

He laughed. "Okay, brat, I'll take you to your surprise."

They went to the colonel's personal quarters.

"I thought dinner was afterwards?"

"It is, patience."

They knocked, opened the door, and entered the colonel's quarters. A man stood next to the window admiring the ocean view. He turned at their entrance.

"Daddy."

"Elyse."

She ran to him, and he engulfed her in his arms. Tears came to his eyes at the sight of his beautiful child. How he missed and worried about her. He held her from him.

"Let me look at you, short stack. You're just as beautiful as ever. I have a surprise for you as well, Elijah. Reggie get out here."

Elijah's father and brothers, Aiden, Brendan, Collin, Donall and, of course, best friend Mac, stepped from the other room. Elijah was surprised. It meant a lot to see them all there for the wedding tomorrow.

Elyse giggled. "Oh, good grief. All of you at once, I'll never survive this."

She hugged and kissed each brother and the colonel. Eyeing Mac, she held her hand out until he rolled his eyes, grumbled about wee card shark fairies, and pulled the ten dollars he owed her in scrip from his pocket. He handed it over as she laughed and hugged him.

A knock sounded on the door and it was opened to find the team standing there all spiffed up in their service uniforms, Elyse laughed and hugged each man.

"You guys shine up just like a new penny." Elyse said.

"Not as shiny as you Elyse," Henson shyly replied.

***

DINNER WAS A FABULOUS AFFAIR. Elyse was in stitches. All fifteen men were enchanting, gallant, and fun to watch as each interacted with the other. The conversation turned to the two women who would have loved to be there: their mothers. Both Elyse and Elijah felt a moment's wistfulness.

"It would have been their greatest wish to see our families united," the Colonel said.

"I'm sure they are watching from heaven," Ambassador Booker replied.

"Michelle and Elizabeth were the best of friends for many years. What drew them closer together was that their children had the same birthdate and similar names," explained the Ambassador to the group.

"Since we are now free to discuss within our families and circle of good friends, Colonel Corrington said. "Operation Amethyst is still a clear and present danger. We wanted the two of you to meet as adults. We had hoped that the two of you would be drawn to each other like you were as children. It was unfortunate that Elijah was unable to make the party at the embassy last December."

"That's right, I had forgotten I was supposed to attend a party at the embassy when I was in Saigon. I was called back to my unit the morning of the party," Elijah replied.

"Once we learned of North Vietnam's interest in Elyse, we had planned with General Morgan's help, that Elijah and his team were to be assigned as Elyse's handler and guards well before you two met in the jungle. The original plan was to send Elijah to Hué City to pick up Elyse and escort her to Saigon," the colonel said.

"That she had to evacuate Hué City in a hurry and then having the chopper crash was every father's nightmare. That it was Elijah that found you anyway was an act of fate probably instigated by heaven," the ambassador said.

Elijah and Elyse were incredulous. Their fathers had planned this all along.

"So, we did know each other as children?" Elyse asked.

"Yes, we did, my love." Elijah replied.

"I have no memories of it, but I did have an odd dream the other night," Elyse said. "I dreamed I was small, riding a tricycle, and there was this boy who looked like you, Elijah. We were at a fair, standing in front of some amusement park ride and then the boy took my hand and walked me home."

Elijah glanced over at the ambassador who nodded his approval. "Elyse, that was no dream, it was a memory," Elijah said.

"I was lost?" she sniffled. "And you found me?"

He brushed a wayward curl from her eyes. "Yeah, I found you," Elijah replied softly. "It appears I have always been meant to rescue you from mischief."

Elyse narrowed her eyes. "Here's your last chance Captain, you can either haul me back and throw my sweet ass back into that ditch, or trade me for your five goats to the Montagnards."

⚜

BRENDAN AND ELIJAH's booming laughter lit the room as the Ambassador and Colonel raised their questioning eyebrows. Each brother told what they referred to as their own "Elyse story" leaving the men in stitches and Elyse giving them all the evil eye.

The team laughed, "Oh we got way more than that," Henson said. "Did you know she fits perfectly inside a seabag?"

Elyse's face broke into a beautiful smile. "Now you know why you've all made my shit list."

⚜

AFTER DINNER, the men enjoyed a beer or two. Elyse excused herself for a few minutes. While she was gone, the ambassador happened to glance under the table. Elyse's shoes.

He smiled, shaking his head. "I'd hang on to those if I were you, Elijah."

Elijah looked under the table with a questioning look to the ambassador.

"Since the day she was born, I have never been able to keep a pair of shoes on her feet."

Elijah smiled. "She's been barefoot since the day I met her."

"Did she ever once complain about not having shoes?" the ambassador asked.

"No, not really."

"My daughter has lost most of the shoes I have ever bought for her except her ballet slippers."

Elijah grinned. *Brat.* "Yeah she lost the one pair I bought her in Saigon." And here he had always felt guilty about her lack of shoes.

Elyse returned. Sitting down, she caught the end of their conversation.

"I hate shoes, only ever wear them for decorum's sake, and pants too, never wore them."

"Are you telling me I've been searching since January for something you wouldn't wear anyway?" Elijah said, exasperated.

Elyse laughed outright. "You should have asked me. I've spent ninety percent of my life in ballet outfits, and the remainder in dresses, and sometimes shorts. I don't wear pants, they're hot and itchy."

He pulled her close and kissed her lips. "Brat, what am I to do with you?"

Elyse smiled. "Marry me."

"Tomorrow, brat."

***

IT WAS GETTING LATE. Elijah and Elyse rose to take their leave.

"Collin, I'll meet you on the patio in half an hour," Elijah said.

Aiden, Brendan, Mac, and Donall had spotted some pretty nurses earlier by the hospital, excusing themselves, they were off on a conquest.

***

ELIJAH PULLED her into a quiet area between the buildings. Elyse leaned against the building, as Elijah stood in front of her arms on either side of her, boxing her in. Brown eyes stared into amethyst eyes, he leaned in and kissed her petal soft lips.

"I remember the first time I saw you, in the ditch, half-naked. Your eyes mesmerized me then, and they mesmerize me still. I'm a lucky man. Tomorrow you will be my bride, and I will never know another moment's peace. I love you, Elyse."

She smiled at him. "I love you too." She reached up, pulled him close, she kissed him, caressing his lips with her own, leaving him breathless and wanting more.

He sighed. "Tomorrow can't come soon enough." He left her at her door, making sure she was safely inside with the door locked.

***

398

Elyse could see something was on her bed. She went to investigate. There it was, her mother's wedding gown. It was breathtakingly beautiful. She stroked the beautiful brocade of the bodice inlaid with tiny seed pearls. She teared up, missing her mother more than ever. She hung it up, put on a nightgown, and climbed into bed. She lay there thinking of Elijah, his handsome face, his beautiful brown eyes, his… ass. He really did have the hottest ass. Elyse blushed at her own thoughts. She closed her eyes and slept.

***

Outside on the patio, Elijah and Collin talked of family and sacrifice with beers in hand.

"Yes, it's hard to give something up even for a short time," Collin said. "Especially when it's forced on you, like my wedding night when you and our brothers stole my bride for three hours."

Elijah looked at Collin, and the shit-eating grin on his face. His eyes narrowed.

"Three nights for three hours, little brother."

"You bastard. You put the colonel up to posting the guard at Elyse's door and forbidding me access to her quarters."

Collin threw back his head and let out peal of triumphant laughter.

Elijah threw the first punch. They were well-matched. Always had been. Their fighting lasted a few minutes. When they were done, they finished their beers and walked back to the officer's tent. Elijah lay in his bunk thinking of Elyse in that big bed.

"Collin, you really are a nasty son of a bitch."

Collin chuckled and rolled over in his bunk. At some point in the middle of the night the remaining brothers and Mac stumbled into the tent. Their loud snores soon filled the tent. Elijah covered his ears with his pillow and cursed them all.

CHAPTER 47

Elyse woke up to Elijah sitting in a chair by her bed.

"Hi."

"Hi, brat."

"Did I do it again?"

"Yes."

"The guard let you in?"

"He's gone."

"What time is it?"

"Not too bad this time. It's only eleven."

Elyse groaned. "I need to get up."

"Slowly. You're beautiful."

"So are you, but you're not supposed to see me until the wedding."

"I wasn't going to leave you unprotected."

Once Elyse was out of her sleep fog, he sent in a surprise for her. Noona, her much loved, old Vietnamese nanny, was brought out of a comfortable retirement by the ambassador to help her prepare for her wedding day.

Noona prepared a bath for Elyse and then laid out her wedding undergarments. Elyse climbed into the tub. *Oh, this is heavenly.*

She laid in the tub until the water cooled. Once dressed in her undergarments, a white lacy bra, new orange panties. She applied light makeup and Noona brushed her hair until it shone. She put her hair into a beautiful upsweep with a simple veil. She was almost ready and on time. Noona answered when a knock came at the door. Elijah handed the lady a small present.

"For Elyse. Make sure she wears it. Is she almost ready?"

"Yes. Half an hour, Sir."

Elyse unwrapped the present. Inside was a gold necklace with a dark, teardrop-shaped amethyst stone, the same color of her eyes. "Oh, it's so beautiful."

NOONA HELPED her put it on, and then she donned her mother's dress, an off-the-shoulder, scalloped lace creation. The bodice was low-cut and enhanced Elyse's curves. Elyse was the same size as her mother, curves and all. The dress fit perfectly, even with the slight curve of her belly. Low-heeled shoes completed her ensemble. With a final a dot of lavender oil behind her ears and a teary hug from Noona, she was ready. There was another knock on the door, and the ambassador entered the room. He stopped short, swallowing the sudden lump in his throat. "You are as beautiful as your mother was on her wedding day."

Elyse gave him a nervous smile.

"Are you ready?"

"Yes, Daddy."

"And you're sure this is the right man?"

"Oh, yes."

He handed her a small bouquet of lavender-colored flowers. "These are from the team."

Elyse was thrilled. She hadn't thought of flowers.

"What are you missing, short stack? The ambassador asked as he looked down.

ELYSE LOOKED DOWN; her bare feet peeked out from under her dress. *Shoes. Damn.* With a sigh she slipped her feet into white heels.

"It's time, Elyse." He kissed his daughter's forehead. "Your mother would be so proud of you, and you know I'm proud of you as well."

SINCE THE CHURCH was so small, they decided to have the ceremony outside. Everyone on the base was welcome to attend. All were dashing in their dress blues, they stood in the front next to the chaplain. Elijah, Aiden, Brendan, Collin, Mac, and Donall, as his best man stood as Elijah's witnesses. The team; Sarge, Doc, Mountain, Arnold, Henson and Johnson, as Elyse's best friends, stood as her witnesses.

ELIJAH WATCHED Donall twist Elyse's wedding band, trying to get it off the tip of his pinky finger. "You'd better be able to get that ring off your finger. Otherwise, I'm sure someone's got their Ka-Bar knife here."

Donall grinned. "No worries, little brother."

A Marine started strumming a song on his guitar. All the men turned as one to the center to honor the bride.

Soup ran down the aisle with purple flowers stuck in his collar and he jumped up and sat on the colonel's lap.

Elyse appeared on her father's arm, a stunning vision in white. With a full skirt, low bodice, and flowers in her hand, she had never looked more beautiful. They made eye contact, and Elyse gave him a brilliant smile. Her father handed her into Elijah's arms, kissing his daughter he turned away teary eyed, and sat down next to Colonel Corrington.

They turned to the chaplain and a few minutes later they were pronounced husband and wife. Elijah pulled Elyse into his arms and kissed her passionately. Waiting patiently, the chaplain cleared his throat, and they finished the kiss much to the delight of the guests. They ran down the aisle laughing as they went. Afterwards, the base provided a feast for all paid for by the ambassador.

Elyse was breathless from laughter. The men all took advantage of the situation and kissed the bride, starting with the brothers alphabetically, Mac, and then the team. More than one man prolonged his kiss and seemed intent on not only outdoing his brothers but annoying the groom as well. The last man pulled her into his arms, kissing her soundly, he only stopped when he felt the hand tap on his shoulder.

Elijah irritated now. "Who the fuck are you?" he demanded.

The man saluted and grinned at him. "Corporal Lee, Her Majesties Royal Australian Army."

"An Aussie? You've got a lot of balls."

"Thank you, Sir," he replied.

Elyse giggled outright, placing a gentle hand on Elijah's arm, they moved away to mingle with their guests. The beer and wine flowed as steaks sizzled on the grills to be enjoyed by all.

THE DOOR OPENED, and a woman stepped inside the mess hall. She was blonde and beautiful with long legs that just kept on going. She was tall for a woman, her husband often called her his "tall glass of water." Her emerald green eyes adjusted to the light as she searched for him.

HE SPOTTED her from the bar, his gaze caressing every curve, her soft creamy skin, high cheek bones and full pouty mouth. And with long cat-like strides, he crossed the room to stop in front of her.

"Hello, beautiful."

"Collin," she cried, as he pulled her into his arms.

"God, I've missed you." His words smothered as he kissed his wife, cradling her in his arms.

"WHO'S COLLIN MAULING OVER THERE?" Sarge asked Brendan.

"Belinda, his wife," Brendan said, with a whoop.

"COME ON, I have someone for you to meet," Collin said to Belinda. He brought her over to Elijah and Elyse. Belinda hugged Elijah and Collin made introductions. "Elyse, this is my wife, Belinda."

"Elyse, I've heard so much about you. Welcome to the family. It's so nice to have a sister and someone to stand with me against these wild Corrington's."

The women hugged, teary-eyed, and spoke softly with each other.

⁂

THE AMBASSADOR and Colonel Corrington watched the exchange. Catching each other's eye, they grinned.

"That will be a strong alliance. The boys have no clue what they're in for," the colonel stated.

The ambassador grinned. "The family will change. The boys will have more order in their lives. It'll be different though, not like the military. God help them."

"I've never told my boys their mother died in the same car accident as Michelle, though I suspect Aiden knows."

"I've never told Elyse either. Someday maybe we should."

"Now they're in heaven, and I'm sure they are happy."

With a toast to their wives, they raised their glasses.

"And now we'll be two doting old grandpa's together." the ambassador said.

"I'm rather fond of being called Pops," replied the Colonel.

"Pops?" The ambassador let out a guffaw. "Was thinking about Gramps for myself."

"I'm retiring when the new administration takes over in January. It's time for a new man and fresh perspectives for the peace talks. I cannot continue to risk my daughter and grandchild," the ambassador said.

"I was thinking the same thing. I want to spend my old age with my new grandchild," the colonel replied.

"Just keep in mind, no way am I sitting in some park playing chess with your sorry old ass," the ambassador stated.

"Battleship?"

"Now you're talking."

⚜

THEY BARELY HAD a moment alone before Elijah said, "I have a surprise for you."

"What is it?" Elyse asked.

"If I tell you it's not a surprise."

They escaped from the patio, and Elijah took her over to the volleyball area. The net had been removed, and the area was decorated with white lights. Elijah took off his boots and socks and encouraged her to do the same. Elyse, being the wicked girl she was, kicked off her shoes.

The music came on over the PA system, and they danced barefoot in the sand. They twirled and swirled, just the two of them. She lay her head against his chest and inhaled the manly scent of him.

At the end of the song, he lifted her up in his arms and carried her toward her quarters.

⚜

THEY HAD WATCHED from the doorway, waiting for the perfect time.

"You know he's going to kill us, right?" Donall said.

"I'd be more worried about what Elyse will do," Aiden replied.

"I've already had my revenge," Collin said. "But I'm game."

Brendan laughed. "Is his team ready?"

"Yup, and in place," replied Collin.

"And look at this nice straight jacket I got from one of the nurses over at the hospital," Mac said.

"Where are we going to take her that she'll be safe?"

Donall grinned. "Why the last place he'd ever look." With devilish grins and mischief on their minds, they implemented their ambush.

⚜

ELIJAH NUZZLED his brides throat placing kisses on her lips as he walked along. Hearing a noise behind him, Elijah spotted two of his brothers shadowing him. Knowing full well their intentions, he took off at a run, throwing her over his shoulder, he raced toward Elyse's quarters.

Elyse gasped. "Elijah, what the hell…"

Then from over his shoulder she spotted Donall and Brendan giving chase. "Oh, my God, run faster." Then she saw the team coming up on them from the left. Squealing, she shouted, "Team on the left."

Aiden and Collin came up on the right side, and Elyse squealed, "Right side, Elijah. Right side."

Mac came at him head on and took him down at the knees. Elyse flew up out of Elijah's arms and Sarge caught her. Tossing her to Donall, who caught her in mid-air, throwing her over his shoulder he made for the Jeeps with the laughing team on his heels.

The remaining brothers and Mac tussled with Elijah and put the straight jacket on him and tied his feet. Laughing, hooting and hollering, they ran for the jeeps and climbed in and raced off leaving Elijah in a cloud of dust, tied up and bride less.

Rolling to his knees and coming to his feet, Elijah cursed them long and loudly.

THE COLONEL, ambassador, and Belinda, along with the other guests exited the party upon hearing the ruckus outside and cheered them on. Laughing, the colonel and ambassador untied Elijah from his straight jacket.

"I'm going to kick each and every one of their asses." Elijah shouted.

The colonel laughed. "I seem to remember you doing something similar to Collin on his wedding night." Pointing to the lone remaining Jeep, he said, "Go find your bride, Elijah. Save your revenge for their wedding nights."

"Oh, trust me, it will be epic," Elijah growled, and took off running for the remaining Jeep.

Belinda turned to the colonel. "That's not very nice, Dad. You just sent your son on a wild goose chase."

The Colonel grinned. "Still a Marine, darlin'."

Elyse stood on the bar with her hands on her hips, her eyes narrowed at the men standing before her. Pointing her finger at them, she said, "I am not a football to be tossed back and forth. You are all on my shit list."

They all laughed, and Aiden said, "Come on, Elyse, we've all been on that list for a long time anyway."

Her laughter rippled through the hall. "This is a double shit list."

"Ooh," they all said at once.

She smiled. "Come on, boys. How's he going to find me?"

"He'll check out a few bars in town and realize that we're not going to risk your safety and that we doubled back and brought you back to your own wedding party," Aiden replied.

"That's really sneaky," Elyse replied.

They grinned at her.

"A drink, Elyse?"

She raised her eyebrows and looked over the brothers, and Mac oddly. "You don't know?"

Mac said, "Know what, wee fairy?"

"Elijah and I are going to have a baby."

They whooped and hollered. Grabbing her off the bar, they all kissed her before depositing her back to sit on the bar. She laughed as they handed her a soda. They toasted the baby, it's beautiful mother, and the poor sucker in town searching for his bride. She laughed and sipped her soda.

"He'll be all right, won't he?"

"He'll be fine," Collin said. "He's a smart guy. We give him an hour tops before he figures it out."

Belinda rolled her eyes.

Elijah was halfway to town when it dawned on him.

"Assholes." He did a U-turn and headed back to the base.

He walked into the wedding party to laughter and good-natured claps on the back. Nodding his head and laughing, he saluted his father with a grin.

The ambassador looked down and laughed, "I see she's corrupted you already?"

Elijah looked down and grinned, he had forgotten he was barefoot.

He only had eyes for his bride after that. The crowd of admirers around her at the bar parted to let him pass, and he stopped in front of her.

Her eyes held his gaze. "What took you so long, Captain?"

She squealed as he scooped her off the bar and carried her out the door and across the compound to her quarters. He opened the screen door and carried her down the hallway, just to see a guard at her door.

"Oh, hell no, Collin," Elijah said.

The guard smiled and opened the door for them. One last little dig from Collin.

"Congratulations, Captain and Mrs. Corrington."

As Elijah laid her on the bed, she laughed. "What was that all about?"

"I'll tell you tomorrow."

Elijah looked at his bride, so soft, she smelled so good, now to get her out of that dress.

Elyse stood. "You'll have to help me."

He unzipped the back of her dress, placing light fluttery kisses on the back of her neck as he did so. With one tug from his hand, the bodice came down, and she stepped out of the dress. Elijah pulled the pins from her hair, and the red tendrils swirled down to dance against her waist. He picked up a strand and breathed in its scent, feeling its soft textures between his fingers. He kissed her lips, his lips burning with their intensity. He picked her up and laid her back on the bed. Never breaking eye contact, he stripped off his uniform.

"You know what they say?" Elyse said.

"No, what?"

"There's nothing like a Marine in uniform."

Elijah grinned. "Is that what they say, Mrs. Corrington?"

"Oh, yes, Captain Corrington."

Elijah climbed into bed with Elyse and pulled her into his arms. He looked into her eyes and kissed her parted lips. "I love you, Elyse. From the moment you fell into my ditch, you were meant to be mine."

"I didn't fall in. You pulled me in."

"Semantics, Elyse. Semantics."

They made love slowly, and every nerve in Elyse's body tingled, each kiss and touch made her quiver. Elijah spotted the bottle of champagne icing in the bucket on the nightstand. Opening the bottle, he took a long swig.

"You can have a sip, brat. The rest is for me."

Elyse took her sip right from the bottle and handed it back. Elyse squealed with laughter as he trickled the cold champagne over her nipples, down her smooth belly to her most intimate parts. He licked the champagne off her, and they made love late into the night. Eventually they slept, only to awaken and love each all over again.

⁂

ELYSE WOKE MID-MORNING STARVING. Elijah nuzzled her neck, and she laughed.

"Food, I need food," she begged.

He reluctantly went in search of breakfast. He encountered some good-natured teasing along the way, but he just smiled. "Yeah, yeah."

When he headed back to their quarters with a tray full of food, he ran into Brendan, who had red, blurry eyes and was nursing a massive hangover.

Elijah, who was in a devious state of mind, pounded his brother on the back and shouted, "Good morning, Brendan" in his ear.

"Shut up, Elijah." Brendan said, pressing his fingers to his temples.

Elijah assumed a good portion of his team, Mac, and his brothers—hell, everyone at the wedding—would be nursing hangovers today as well.

⁂

WHEN ELIJAH RETURNED to the room, Elyse was in the bathroom.

"I'm in here."

He brought the tray in with him and set it on a side table. Elyse had drawn a bath. She helped him to undress, and he climbed into the hot tub. Leaning back, he groaned in appreciation. She sat on a little stool nearby nibbling on toast with strawberry jam.

"This is yummy. Wherever did you get it?"

"Secret strawberry jam stash," he replied.

She giggled and licked the jam from her fingers. Elijah opened one eye to watch her. In a split-second, he pulled her into the tub, robe and all. Elyse squealed in protest. Elyse peeled off her soaked robe and grabbed her girly soap.

"Let's see if you slide."

Elijah raised an eyebrow. "Yes, let's."

An hour later, they emerged from the now-cold tub and curled up together on the bed and napped.

ELIJAH TWIRLED Elyse's hair after he awoke from his nap.

Amber, he realized. *It's the color of amber.* Soft curls that swirled around her waist when it fell from her bun. He looked at the ever-so-slight swell of her belly. He was amazed a child slept there. He thought about Khe Sanh. In the dark bunker, he could only feel her and not see her. But they had created a life in the middle of that dark chaos. Her breasts were now exposed to his gaze, He remembered the day her bra broke open while she sat in his lap fighting for her freedom. The memory of that moment warmed many a lonely night for him. He thought about how much she defied him in outright disobedience, sneaking out of the back of the tent countless times.

Spoiled brat. God, he loved her. Her independence, her fighting spirit… She had the will to fight and was as determined to win as any Marine. She never ceased to surprise him, but her safety and the baby's safety were utmost in his mind now. He would not budge on that.

SHE WOKE with his hand between her thighs and his mouth on her breast. She moaned deep in her throat.

"You are so bad."

So many new sensations, so many things she had no idea existed before Elijah. She wanted to learn it all.

410

"Show me more, Elijah."

He left her breathless, sated, and starving. Elijah again went off in search of food. He returned a short time later with sandwiches, potato chips, and wedding cake. He had rushed her off to bed so fast the previous night, they never had any of the cake. They picnicked in the middle of the bed, they laughed, they spoke of future plans, they argued about baby names… and they loved again.

CHAPTER 48

Elyse was sore from lying about. She needed to stretch her muscles, so she cajoled Elijah into getting dressed and taking a walk on the beach with her. She put on his boxers and his tank top. He gave her a questioning look.

"I'm more comfortable dancing in these."

He grinned ear to ear. "I'm going to need to buy more of those."

HE LOUNGED on the blanket watching the surf roll in and out and watching Elyse stretch. She pirouetted with graceful arms above her head. She moved as one with the ocean. She was a creature of the Earth, his very own swan song. He knew when this tour was done there would be no more tours. He didn't want to be away from her for even a moment. His life had been turned upside down ever since he pulled a half-naked woman into the ditch. Now she was his wife and his child grew inside her belly. A familiar barking broke his train of thoughts. Soup was running up the beach with Donall not far behind. The dog ran to Elyse first, and she scooped him up in her arms.

"THERE YOU ARE, little man. Where have you been?"

She kissed and cuddled him. She set him down so he could greet Elijah and receive more kisses and belly rubs. Donall sat down next to Elijah. Elyse waved and continued her dance.

THEY WATCHED HER IN SILENCE, while the dog laid down on the blanket to sun himself.

"Father sent me to talk to you. Command feels Elyse is safe here. Orders just came down from headquarters. The Marine division commander has use for you and your team in the Mekong Delta to conduct long range reconnaissance of the VC into South Vietnam from the Ho Chi Mein trail. You, and your team, have been reassigned back to your unit. The rest of your platoon will link up with you there. You have one week left here. I'm sorry, Elijah. You're not so far away that you can't get away from time to time to come see Elyse."

ELIJAH KNEW HIS DUTY. He would do as ordered, but Elyse... this was not going to go well. Donall stood and picked up Soup. "I'll keep him with me until I ship out at the end of the week. I don't think he's housebroken yet." He patted Elijah on the back and took his leave.

A FEW MINUTES LATER, Elyse sat down on the blanket with Elijah. He stared off into the darkness of the sea. His sadness went deep. Now he understood what some of his men were going through when they spoke of wives and lovers at home.

Five months. He would just have to survive five months—four and half really—just when the baby would be due. He wondered if he would live to see his child.

"Elijah, what's wrong?" Elyse said.

"Nothing, brat."

He would tell her tomorrow. He kissed her and with every second his need for her grew. He lifted her into his arms and carried her to their quarters. Once inside he laid her on the bed, stripped and joined her on the bed. He took her swiftly, once finished, he lay still inside her.

"Elijah, what is wrong? tell me."

"Tomorrow, brat. Tomorrow."

He loved her again. This time slowly. Every touch and every curve was burned into his memory. He would live each day to its fullest. She had taught him that, and that was the best he could hope for. She had taught him so much about living. He buried his face in her hair and slept.

ELYSE WAS WORRIED. *What did Donall say to upset Elijah?*

Come hell or high water, she was going to find out. She slid out of bed, dressed, and slipped out the door. Elijah would not be happy with her leaving, but she had to find out what was going on. She searched out Donall and found him on the patio drinking a beer with Soup on his lap. She stood in front of him.

"What did you say to Elijah?"

"Elyse, does Elijah know you are out here alone?"

"No, and I intend for him not to find out. What did you say to Elijah?"

"That's best left for me to tell you, brat," a familiar voice said from behind her.

"Oh, shit."

ELIJAH HAD AWOKEN to no Elyse in his bed. She was nowhere in the room. He had dressed, worried that she was out and about with no guard. This place had many men on R&R, and most of them were out getting drunk every night. He had no wish to see her attacked by unscrupulous men again. He knew where she would go. He was out the door in the blink of an eye.

There, on the patio, she stood in front of Donall. He suppressed the urge to turn her over his knee right here and now. With a nod from Elijah, Donall took his leave.

"Elyse, I told you tomorrow was soon enough."

"It is tomorrow, Elijah."

"Why are you out here with no guard after midnight? Do you want to be attacked again?"

"No, of course not."

"Then why don't you behave?"

"You're changing the subject, Elijah. I want answers."

"I'm being returned to my regular duties. You're staying here."

"No. No, Elijah… They can't do this." Her eyes welled up with tears.

"They can and they did."

"They used you. This is not fair. When?"

"One week."

"One week? That's all the time we have?"

"Yes, I sought to save you the pain until tomorrow, but being the impetuous brat that you are, you forced the issue."

"I had thought that this would be it. That they would let us leave to go back to the world. Then we could live our happily ever after," Elyse whispered.

"Tomorrow is not promised to us, brat, and sometimes life doesn't give us that happily ever after. But I promise you I will do my best to stay alive," Elijah replied.

She gave him a weak smile. "I need to lie down," she whispered, and then she fainted.

Elijah caught her in his arms as she fell. She was in shock. He lifted her into his arms and carried her to their quarters. Laying her on the bed, he put a cool washcloth on her forehead. She woke slowly.

"Lie still, Elyse. You fainted."

"Hold me. Please."

Elijah climbed into bed and pulled her close. She cried and eventually slept, but it was fitful sleep full of nightmares of the horrors of war.

Elijah lay awake for a long time. They had both been lulled into a fantasy while the bloody war raged on all around them. He knew better and should have warned her it was a possibility he would be sent back. He cursed himself for his stupidity. He pulled her closer and slept off and on.

415

When a nightmare would make her squirm, he would kiss her and speak into her ear until she calmed again and fell back asleep. He would have to keep her busy for the next week.

Elyse woke with a headache from crying. She hid her head under the pillow, while Elijah searched for aspirin for her. When there was none to be found, he'd have to go over to the hospital to get some. On the way back, he ran into the ambassador and his father. They were leaving the next day and wanted to see Elyse. He explained her headache.

"Yes, she knows now."

"I'm sorry, Elijah," his father said. "I had no choice."

"I know, Father. I will follow my orders, but I'm worried about leaving Elyse with unfamiliar guards."

"Choose two of your men to stay behind with Elyse, and I'll have them reassigned to her protection."

Elijah nodded his head. He addressed the ambassador. "Why can't she return to Saigon with you, Sir?"

"It's not safe there since the TET offensive. Too many spies. She's protected here with a hospital, her own guards and, more importantly, she'll be close to you. We'll do our best to get you free time to visit her."

"And if I die who will take care of my wife? My child?"

"Don't worry, Elijah. If something happens, and it won't, I'll give up my ambassadorship and return stateside with Elyse. We will do our best to take care of her until you return to her side."

They agreed to meet later for lunch, and Elijah was on his way back to Elyse's side.

ELYSE TOOK the aspirin and felt well enough within the hour to dress. Her own shorts were too snug now, so she was stuck with a choice of sundresses or Elijah's boxers. She would save the boxers for dance. She looked refreshed, but her eyes had a sadness about them. Elijah wanted to wipe the sadness away.

They walked into the mess hall to the cheers of the men and amazement that the Captain had let her out of bed. They now called her Mrs.

Cap. Elyse giggled. Elijah thought it was good to see some of the sadness gone from her eyes.

Sitting down at a table with the team and some others, Elyse noticed a few of the team members were sporting black eyes.

"Fighting again, boys?" Elyse asked.

Donall grinned. "It seems the team took exception to being called bridesmaids by some of the Aussies."

Elyse bit her lip and stifled a giggle. "I'm sorry. It never occurred to me."

"We were honored to stand as your friends with you," Sarge replied.

They were soon joined by Collin, Belinda, the Ambassador, and Colonel Corrington. Mac sat down next to Elyse. Elyse looked at him through narrowed eyes, and Mac grinned as she drew an imaginary line on the bench between them.

"Relax, wee fairy, I remember how sharp your elbows are. My poor ribs will never recover," Mac said.

"You, and half of the Corps." Elyse replied.

At Elijah's questioning look, Elyse said. "They like to hover just over my shoulder trying to catch a peek."

"Why did you not tell me, I would have taken care of them for you," Elijah said.

"You would have spent your whole day doing nothing but taking the troops to task. She smirked, they're harmless and I can take of them myself. They learn pretty quickly."

CHAPTER 49

Elyse rolled over to find Elijah still sleeping. He had such a boyish face when he slept. When awake, his eyes were intense, almost like he could see into the depths of her soul.

Four days. They only had four days left, and then he would be taken from her to walk the rice paddies of the Mekong Delta searching for the Viet Cong. A dangerous job. She would not embarrass him by crying. She had to be strong for him. He was a Marine through and through, and he needed to know she was strong and waiting for him to return to her. God willing, he would survive. If he didn't, she didn't think she'd be able to carry on, but she had his baby growing inside her, she must be strong, her chin lifted defiantly… She must.

"Why the defiant chin, brat?"

"You're awake. Look, it's like my belly grew overnight."

It did indeed. He kissed her belly. "We should settle on names before I leave."

Elyse's face fell. It was going to be so hard to watch him leave and she said so. He pulled her into his arms and kissed her. "I know, it will be hard to leave you behind. Let's make the most of each day that we have left."

a

THEY HAD breakfast on the beach, they swam in the sea. They sat on the blanket and argued about names for their baby. They made up and settled on names to be kept secret until the birth. They would contact Elijah as soon as she went into labor, and they prayed he would be able to come back for the birth. He promised to return as often as possible.

They went to the mess hall for more food. Elyse was always hungry, and her pregnancy was now visible. It would be four-and-a-half months till the baby was due and four-and-a-half months till the end of Elijah's tour of duty.

They entered the mess hall. Some noted her growing belly, which they nicknamed Lil' Cap. They asked when the baby was due and she told them the doctor said early January. Elyse blushed anew when she realized they were counting back to conception. Elijah took it a step further, raising a few eyebrows,

"Khe Sanh." He smiled, winked, and sat Elyse down at a table to eat. They finished their lunch and stood to leave. Elyse stopped short, a look of wonder on her face.

"What is it, Elyse?"

"The baby. It's moving."

Elijah took her by the arm and escorted her outside. Outside, she took his hand and placed it on her belly.

"There, do you feel that?"

He didn't, but his smile was a mile wide. They went back to their room and made slow, easy love. They slept and loved some more. He took her to dance on the beach at midnight. The moonlight cast an ethereal glow on Elyse as she moved. She swayed and twirled to the music, her dance a little more tempered with her growing belly. God, he loved her. This is where he would want to spend eternity, on the beach watching Elyse dance.

They slept, made love, fought over stupid things, and the remaining days passed in a blur. Elyse cried the last day. She hugged and kissed each man on the team with a tearful goodbye.

She said she wouldn't cry, but it was so hard to be strong and brave. Elijah held her in his arms, kissed her tears, told her she was his brave little fighter and he would be back before she knew it. They made love, at times frantic, and at other times, slow and easy. The night passed, and soon it was time for him to go.

SHE STILL SLEPT, and he watched her for a little while longer, sliding the thick strands of her hair through his fingertips. He felt its softness and silky texture and inhaled her fragrance. He kissed her lips one more time, whispered, "I'll be back, wait for me, brat." And then he was gone.

Elijah nodded to Arnold and Mountain left standing guard at her door. Outside, the remainder of the team waited for him. They headed to the helipad.

ELYSE WOKE WITH A START, looking around the room in confusion. He was gone. "No." She threw on her clothes and raced to the helipad, the pink sky of dawn silhouetted the choppers in the distance as they faded out of sight.

"No. Elijah, Elijah…." she cried. "Come back to me, Elijah. Come home." She fell to her knees and whispered, "Elijah."

ELIJAH WATCHED the camp fade from view. He saw Elyse running to the helipad and watched until she faded from sight. He inhaled, the pain in his heart unbearable. He took off his helmet. Inside he found an envelope. Inside she had placed a lock of her amber-fire hair tied in a tiny, purple ribbon. He touched it, smelled it, and smiled. He wondered where she had cut it from. *Disobedient brat. I told her to never to cut her hair.*

EIGHT WEEKS LATER, the end of October, Elijah rested against a tree, his exhaustion complete. Filthy from the mud and grime of the rice paddies of the Mekong Delta. His soaked to the waist, he couldn't remember the last time he had felt completely dry. He pulled off his boots, stripped off his wet socks, dried his feet with his towel and put on a dry pair. He took off his helmet and pulled out the now well-worn envelope. He could still smell her scent on the tendril of hair. He wondered how she fared and if she thought of him as often as he thought of her.

He would have to tell Elyse, his heart ached for her, but he had to stand above the emotion of the tragic loss. He couldn't send such sad news in a letter. They had lost one of his team today, and Elyse would be devastated by his loss. The brave man had sacrificed his life saving so many, including himself.

Elijah made the decision he would tell her in person to help alleviate the pain of losing a good friend. Soon, he'd be able to see her again.

CHAPTER 50

Seven weeks out from her due date and Elijah's return. Elyse, with Soup at her side, sat at the helipad staring off in the direction the chopper flew the day they took him away from her. "Please come home to me, Elijah," she whispered.

The troops had given her a baby shower of sorts last week, which was amusing for a bunch of Marines. They gave her tiny, camouflage blankets embroidered with Lil' Cap. The men's thoughtfulness brought tears to her eyes. They were kind and gracious and all of them were there for her to offer a helping hand when needed.

THANKSGIVING DAY DAWNED WITH LUMINOUS, fluffy clouds with shades of pinks, orange, blue, and soft lavender spread across the sky as the sea rolled in and out. Seagulls squawked and hovered overhead. Elyse danced on the beach. It was her favorite place, and it reminded her of Elijah the most.

Mountain stood in his usual spot watching his charge. He heard a noise and turned to see the Captain coming down the path, his finger to his lips. With a smile and a nod, he dismissed Mountain.

ELIJAH SAT in the sand watching Elyse. Her grace and beauty and some-what slow movements touched his heart as only she could. When she turned he saw her very large round belly. He stood and walked toward her.

"Do you dance for me, brat?"

She stopped and breathed out his name. "Elijah."

He took her into his arms and kissed her long and deep. She touched his face, his hair, and whispered, "Is this a dream?"

"I'm here, brat."

"They did not tell me you were coming."

"I told them not to. I did not want you disappointed if I couldn't make it."

"You're back for good?" she asked, hopeful.

"It's only for a week."

She touched her belly. Elijah dropped to his knees to kiss her belly and promptly was kicked in the face. He laughed at the sheer strength of the baby.

"The doctor said it's going to be a big one."

"Yeah, I was almost ten pounds."

Elyse laughed. "Now you tell me."

They walked back to their quarters arm in arm. Elijah grabbed his rucksack and other things he left at the entrance to the path. Elyse looked into Elijah's eyes. She saw exhaustion and the stubble of his beard. He had lost weight as well. Rough campaign.

She drew a bath for him and cajoled him into it. He sank into its warmth and sighed. He opened one eye and looked at her sitting on the stool next to the tub.

"No," She giggled. "We won't both fit now."

He laughed as she dribbled soapy water from the sponge over his chest. Her eyes welled up with tears. She couldn't believe he was here.

"Don't cry, Elyse. I'm here now."

He finished his bath and rose from the tub. She dried his back, and he took the towel to wrap it around his lean, muscled waist.

She led him back to the bed. He laid down and watched her as she moved about the room. She headed into the other room to change because she was embarrassed by her new shape, when he stopped her.

"Where are you going?"

"In there to change."

He was out of bed lightning quick. "Never, ever hide from me. You are never to be embarrassed of your body. You are beautiful just as you are." He undressed her and led her to the bed and made long, slow love to her. He cradled her in his arms afterwards. How he had missed her, her scent, her hair and soft touch. He slept finally, now at peace.

He woke to the feeling of something kicking and pushing on his back. Elyse slept with her belly up against him. He rolled over and lay there watching the movement in Elyse's belly. He put his hands on her stomach and was rewarded with a resounding kick.

"He moves a lot now," Elyse said.

"You think it's a boy?"

"I'm almost positive."

Elijah smiled. A son would be nice but, then again, a little girl would be nice as well. A baby girl hadn't been born into the family for five generations. A healthy baby was all he prayed for. He worried about Elyse. She was so tiny. If the baby was large, she would have a rough time giving birth.

"Why are you frowning, Elijah?"

"Are you able to birth a large baby?"

Elyse laughed. "I have wide, curvy hips. The Doctor said I was perfect for birthing babies."

"They don't look wide to me."

"Bone structure. Wide on the inside, Elijah. I'll be fine."

"Are you scared?"

"I don't know what to expect. I know there's pain. The doctor said childbirth is the worst pain there is so, yeah, I'm a little scared."

He kissed her. "I will do everything in my power to be here when the time comes."

ELYSE WAS SUPPOSED to help prepare the Thanksgiving feast. Two hundred hungry men who hadn't had a real Thanksgiving in a long time was her motivation. Elijah escorted her to the mess hall where she was greeted by all.

"Good morning, how's Lil' Cap today?" said Grant, one of the cooks.

"Growing bigger every day."

Most had never met Elijah before. They pumped his hand and complimented him on having such a beautiful, warm-hearted, generous wife. He smiled and thanked them. She hugged and kissed the team—even the three *FNGs—and bade him to go sit with his men who were astounded at the size of her belly.

Looking around, Elyse asked, "Where's Johnson?"

The team went silent. Cold dread filled her heart as Elyse turned to Elijah for an explanation.

"Elyse, sweetheart, Johnson was killed in action a few weeks ago."

"No. Not Andy." She stumbled as though she had received a physical blow to her heart, and she burst into tears. She sobbed against his chest. "He was so young Elijah. So special, I could tell him anything and he was always there for me."

Sarge, Doc, Henson, along with Elijah had dreaded this very moment. Mountain and Arnold sat in quiet misery mourning the loss of a good buddy. The three new replacement troops, Tatum, Marcus, and Caldwell had never known Johnson still felt the anguish of those around them, went off to get a beer and a shower. The rest of the team told Elyse about Johnson and how he had given his life protecting them by throwing himself on a grenade that had landed in their trench.

Once she recovered and with a heavy heart thinking of Johnson and all that he had meant to her, she worked to prepare the meal. In Andy's honor she sang, "One hundred bottles of beer on the wall, one hundred bottles of beer…" She wiped her tears with her hands as she chopped vegetables. When she finished her work, Elijah took her out to the patio to rest.

Elijah was impressed. She had built a life here while waiting for him. It sounded like she spent her days working to make the troops comfortable while they rested and relaxed. She understood them, and they loved her for it.

THEY SPENT most of their time on the beach or in the bedroom loving each other and simply being together. They spent a few hours one afternoon decorating the mess hall for Christmas. A small artificial tree was decorated with whatever they or the troops could find for ornaments and lights. This was their Christmas together. A month early, but no matter. They sang Christmas carols, and Elyse baked cookies for them. The aroma of fresh baked cookies wafted from kitchen as Elyse carried a plateful out to the team. The men gleefully grabbed cookies off the plate she placed in front of them. Taking a bite of their cookies they glanced at each other. When she walked back into the kitchen, looking at each other, they spit the gross cookies out. When she returned a few minutes later, commenting that there were still cookies on the plate, Elijah looked at the team with a silent order to have another cookie and they did, washing them down with massive amounts of coffee and hot chocolate. Elyse stood by watching Elijah as he ate his third cookie. With a beaming smile on her face, she returned to the kitchen. The team shook with laughter.

"What are you morons laughing at?"

"Cap, we only have to do this once. You've got the rest of your life, Sir." said Henson.

Narrowing his eyes at them, he said, "Is that so?" He called out. "Elyse, have you got another plate of cookies for the team?"

They groaned.

With a grin, Elijah said, "I'm just making sure your one time is memorable."

Elijah set a chunk of a cookie in front of Soup sitting on the bench next to him. The little dog looked up at him and whimpered.

"Eat it, and that's an order."

AT SUNRISE, Elijah took her to dance at the shore. She wore a soft cotton shift, pale orange in color. She showed him the deep pockets she had sewn into the dress so she could carry her own things. It molded to her large belly and breasts as she danced. That she moved so brought a tightening to his chest. Even though she was unable to leap and jump as she once had, her ever-present beauty and grace reminded him of why he loved her so much. She tired easily and sat next to him to rest. Elijah pushed her down on the blanket and covered her face with gentle, fluttering kisses.

"Your belly is so big you're going to teeter-totter over."

She sighed. "Last year at this time, I danced as the Sugar Plum Fairy. This year, my belly is so round, I *am* the sugar plum."

He grinned, leaving a trail of kisses on her belly. "My very own sugar plum. I'm going to gobble you up."

"I want lots of children, Elijah, a whole houseful." She said.

"You realize it may be a house full of boys?"

Elyse smiled. "I've had training. I've lived with Marines for close to a year now."

He grinned at that.

"Elijah, have you ever seen snow?"

He smiled at her question. "Yes, I have. Up in the mountains back in the world. Why do you ask?"

"I was thinking about it the other day and wondered what snow is like."

"Cold. Bone chilling cold, but magical. I've seen snowflakes so big they stick to your mittens and eyelashes."

"I've never had mittens."

"Someday, brat, I'll make you some fuzzy red mittens and take you there. We'll take our baby sledding and have a snowball fight."

"It sounds wonderful. I'm tired of being hot and sticky."

"Well, let's swim and cool you down."

"Sounds perfect to me."

❧

ELYSE WANTED to finish decorating the mess hall. She had found a silver garland and red bows tucked into a corner in the supply room. Grabbing the stepladder, she moved it around the hall hanging the garland and attaching the shiny, red bows. Up on the top rung of the ladder, she struggled to reach and attach the very last bow.

"Woman, are you out of your fucking mind?" Elijah bellowed.

Teetering as she almost lost her balance, he snatched her down and set her on her feet.

"My brat, forever the daredevil.

She looked up into his eyes and her own welled with tears. "Do you know how much I have missed you scolding me?" she whispered.

His anger disappeared, and he pulled her close. "I shudder to think what you have done while I've been gone."

"I did set the kitchen on fire."

He shook his head. "I suppose you have a perfectly good explanation?"

"Of course."

"No more climbing on ladders or stools or doing the things you used to do. I need to know you're safe while I'm away."

"I'm safe, Elijah. Just counting the days till our baby arrives and the day when you never have to leave me again. Now that you're here, I don't want to let you go."

"I feel the same way, my love."

※

ELYSE WAS thirsty and experiencing mild contractions. At 03:00, she roused Elijah from his sleep. "I need to walk, and I want some milk."

So, he escorted her to the mess hall where she proceeded to guzzle a half-gallon of milk down. She bent over with hands on her knees as a strong contraction took hold of her belly. She practiced breathing deeply, and it passed.

Elijah, white-knuckled and pale, asked, "Is the baby coming now?"

"No, I don't think so. My body is preparing for birth. The Doctor warned me it might do this for the next six weeks or so."

Elijah wanted to get the doctor, but Elyse refused to wake the exhausted man from his sleep. So Elijah insisted on rousing Doc from his slumber to check her out. Doc confirmed Elyse's suspicions, false labor.

※

OFF AND ON ALL DAY, she would stop and breathe as the contractions came and went, and then continue on. The Marines on base watched, some

428

with bittersweet memories of the births of their own children, and others whose wives were expecting a child had their thoughts drawn home and wrote letters or called their families.

The single men were clueless and downed their beers, thankful it wasn't them. It was an exciting and terrifying time for Elijah. Elyse handled it and calmed his fears. After one strong contraction that left her breathless, Elijah said, "Enough. You need to get off your feet."

He wouldn't be moved by her protests. "Don't argue with me, Elyse. You are going to lie down and rest." She laid in his arms, grateful for this time together, and they drifted off to sleep.

TIME PASSED BY QUICKLY, and soon Elijah had to leave again. He kissed her, held her close, and kissed her belly.

"I'll be back soon."

Elyse struggled to hold back her tears, but he was a Marine and must do what he must do. She could only pray for his safety and swift return.

CHAPTER 51

After mail call, Elijah stood looking at the package he held in his hands. Three tours of duty in Vietnam, and this was his very first care package. All of his family was here fighting, none had ever received packages from home.

Taking it back to his quarters, he sat looking at it for a few minutes. He smiled as he opened the box, which was filled with Elyse's God-awful cookies, many little treats, packets of grape Kool-Aid, nuts. Wherever did she find macadamia nuts? They were his favorite. He also found a wrapped present in green-and-red paper.

Reading the letter, he laughed out loud. She said her belly was so big she could no longer see her feet. She had dropped a spoon the other day and had to step two feet away to see that had landed right beneath her. She spent her days visiting the troops in the small hospital, reading to them, and helping them to write letters home to their loved ones. She also still worked in the kitchen.

She could no longer dance. She was just too big and uncomfortable. She could neither sit nor stand for long periods of time and looked forward to the day when the baby would arrive and when he returned to her side. She also revealed that she had forgotten to put sugar in the cookies she had made him when he was there at Thanksgiving. Why didn't you tell me? So, the two dozen in the box were fine.

Elijah grinned and reached for a cookie. *Only you, brat, sugar cookies without sugar. Pretty damn good,* he thought, and then he had another.

She told him she had sent care packages to all of his brothers, Belinda, the Team, and Mac as well, and Elijah smiled. He had once called her selfish. It was the furthest thing from the truth. He knew it then and now. She had also just received a letter from his father who was going to come to Vung Tao at Christmas time and spend a few days with her.

Elijah opened the present. She had made him a Hawaiian-style shirt. He grinned. He had once told her he wanted to take her to Hawaii. God, he missed her. He put the shirt on and pulled out the well-worn envelope to smell her lock of hair. He fell asleep dreaming of making sweet love to her.

CHRISTMAS DAY AT DUSK, Elyse sat by the helipad, an unopened Christmas gift from Elijah and Soup sitting in what was left of her lap. The Colonel had handed it to her this morning.

"Elijah sent this and asked me to give it to you today."

"Thank you, Dad." Her eyes welled with tears as she accepted the gift, holding it close to her heart.

With a busy day behind her, she finally had some private time to open the gift. She found a note inside. Reading it, she sobbed. It read, "Brat, someday we'll have a Christmas with real snowflakes and fuzzy red mittens. Merry Christmas my love, Elijah."

Fuzzy red mittens. The gift was fuzzy red mittens and white paper snowflakes. She knew he had made them, and she bawled like a baby. She ached to feel his arms around her again. The baby kicked at her ribs and somehow jammed its little foot up under her rib cage, pushing on her belly to release the little foot. "Okay, baby. It's okay. Mommy will think happy thoughts for Daddy. Merry Christmas, Elijah, wherever you are."

Rolling to her hands and knees, she was stuck and could not get up. She was defenseless. Soup took advantage and licked the salty tears off of her face.

Laughing, she said, "Soup, you little stinker. Stop."

Mountain and Arnold appeared at her side.

"Boys, now I've done it. I truly cannot get up."

Laughing at her, Arnold replied, "I don't know, Elyse. I think we might need a winch this time."

Her muffled cursing filled with laughter put a smile on their faces, and they lifted her to her feet.

Mountain and Arnold heard the whistle overhead, and they hit the dust, pulling Elyse to the ground with them as fifty round mortar bombs screamed overhead, hitting a chopper sitting on a helipad not too far away from them. Arnold grabbed Elyse by the arms, pulling her back to her feet.

"Come on Elyse, go, go." Mountain yelled.

"Wait, wait, My mittens. Get my mittens," she cried.

Mountain grabbed the present, and they were off at a run as fast as Elyse could go. The base was on fire, the night sky lit up as flares flew lighting the perimeter fencing with an ethereal green glow through the blackness of night. Marines returned fire defending the base against the attacking VC forces as they attacked by land and sea.

Mountain saw VC making their way up the pathway from the beach. They would be overrun soon.

"Run, run. Inside the building. Now." Mountain screamed.

They made it inside of her quarters and barricaded the door with the bed up on its side along with other various furniture.

Elyse shaking in fright, scooped Soup up and held the quivering pup in her arms to calm him and herself.

The battle raged on and came closer and closer to them. At the sound of gunfire in the hallway, they pushed her into the bathroom and into the relative safety of the bathtub, and there they made their last stand.

❧

THREE WEEKS AFTER HIS RETURN, Elijah was exhausted. This latest mission had cost him six good men. He was tired and longed for Elyse. He wanted to lay his head on her breast and sleep. He missed her tinkling laugh, her arguing, her body, everything.

The baby would be coming soon and his tour was almost up. Officially a short timer. God, he was tired of war. The chopper set down on the ship. A private waited to escort him to the ship's Commanders office. There was a grim look on his face, and he wouldn't look Elijah in the eye. It appeared that the entire crew and Marines on board were preparing for combat. With a look to the team, he asked, "What the hell is going on?"

Five minutes later, he emerged from the commander's office. Falling to his knees, he roared out his pain and rage. "Elyse. Oh, God, Elyse."

They had found her after the base was overrun by the VC, and they had taken her. Elijah went into cold killer mode. He was going to track them down and get his wife back if it killed him. The baby was almost due. He couldn't imagine her trekking through the jungle in her ninth month. His face hardened. "Elyse."

⚜

ELYSE STRUGGLED with her hands tied in front of her and a gag in her mouth. Her captors pushed her relentlessly. They screamed at her, not realizing she spoke Vietnamese. She understood everything they said about her. She was tarnished now, married, expecting a child. They were to meet up with an NVA company and they weren't sure if North Vietnam would want her anymore. If they couldn't put her up "for auction," the VC planned to set an example and use her for revenge. They planned horrible things to do to her and her baby. She was terrified as they pushed her deep into the night jungle and further away from Elijah.

Elijah, please come for me. If she died like this, the way they planned, he would be destroyed, and his soul would turn dark. She prayed, for herself, for their child, for rescue, and if it was God's plan that she and her child die this way, she prayed for Elijah.

Dawn came and Elyse and her captors came to an area deep within the jungle, they brushed away the grass to show a hole in the ground.

A spider hole. Cold dread filled Elyse as she realized they might never find her within the underground tunnel system. A VC guerilla behind her pushed her, and she climbed down the hole praying she didn't get stuck with her large belly. *You can do this Elyse.* She crawled behind the men in front of her, occasionally kicking at the man behind her when he would

433

prod her with a stick to move faster through the tunnel. They finally came to a large room, climbing down from the tunnel Elyse turned around and laid the man behind her flat with a kick to his face.

"I may be nine months pregnant asshole, but I can still defend myself," she hissed in English. Grabbing her by the arms they dragged her into a smaller room and over to a wall where they placed handcuffs on her and then chained her to the wall. Elyse sank to her knees thankful she could sit and rest. Her back was starting to hurt, and she worried labor had started.

Looking around the room she realized this was where they kept their American prisoners. She prayed the men who had passed through here before her had survived, perhaps even escaped their VC captors. A man brought her in a small bowl of rice and a cup of water. Elyse ate the rice only because of her child and drank the water. Exhausted, she leaned against the wall and closed her eyes to rest as contractions started in her belly.

❧

Elijah and his team jumped into the chopper, their plans in motion. He would travel to the base first, and then they would meet up with the rest of the three battalions as they moved northwest following their trail in pursuit of Elyse's and her captors.

The chopper landed at the base. His father, Brendan, and Collin were there. Colonel Corrington had been there during the attack, visiting his daughter-in-law for Christmas. He was wounded, but because the small hospital was overwhelmed with casualties, he would wait to fly out to the hospital ship with the remaining injured. However, he refused to leave until Elijah arrived. Brendan and Collin were part of the first wave of troops who landed after the attack.

Elijah raced to her quarters with Collin and Brendan at his side. He had to see. Was she really gone?

The door and bed up on its side were both riddled with bullet holes. The room spoke of a struggle with furniture upended everywhere. The baby bassinet lay on its side, its soft blankets, tiny gowns, and cloth diapers, all once lovingly folded inside, now spilled out onto the floor. Blood covered the bathroom floor and spattered the walls. The fuzzy red mittens and paper snowflakes still lay in their gift box on the floor.

Soup, injured, crawled out from his hiding spot and whimpered his joy at seeing Elijah. Picking the little dog up, he petted and comforted him. "Have someone see to his injuries," he told Sarge.

Doc stood in the doorway, unable to hide his shock and anguish.

"Sir," Doc said.

Elijah unable to breathe as his mind processed the horror of the room looked up. "Mountain and Arnold?" Elijah asked.

"Both alive, barely. They'll survive." replied Doc.

Elijah breathed a sigh of relief. Doc spotted something on the floor, leaning over he picked it up and stuffed it into his medical bag.

THE TROOPS HAD CAPTURED a prisoner during the assault and Elijah rushed to question the man. The man was a local and VC spy. He had told the VC where she was and led them right to her. The man sat on the ground his arms behind him, tied to a wooden board.

"WHERE IS MY WIFE? Where are they taking her?"

The man laughed in the face of Elijah's rage. "You can do nothing for your American whore. They take her now to the Ho Chi Minh trail They will fillet her like a fish and hang her and her child as motivation to the VC and as revenge to American aggression."

Elijah stared at him, horrified. He pulled his sidearm and pressed the muzzle to the man's head.

"No, Elijah. We know how desperately you want too, but you can't," Collin said. "You'll do Elyse no favors by pulling that trigger."

After taking a deep breath, Elijah dropped his arm. With a nod to Collin and Brendan, they made their way back to the main group.

As the sun came up, they rushed to the choppers to meet up with the troops who trailed Elyse and her captors. They were there within an hour. Elijah glanced over at another chopper as it landed next to them. Filled

435

with Montagnard's, they exited the chopper and were off at a run heading into the heavy jungle.

Elijah pointed after them. "The Montagnard's?"

Brendan grinned, "Yeah, the old chieftain feels beholden to you. He found a young bride soon after your encounter. He's quite smitten with her and felt it was you turning him down on trading for Elyse that helped him to find his new bride."

"They're the best trackers in Nam, they'll find her." said Brendan.

Elijah nodded his head, his heart heavy with worry. "We need all the help we can get right now," Elijah said. *I'm coming for you brat, hang in there. Live.*

Elijah and the Marines headed into the jungle following the Montagnard's trail.

ELYSE WOKE WITH A START, Elijah's voice in her head. *Live.* Startled, she looked around, he was not there with her. She pulled a bobby pin from her hair and went to work on the handcuffs. Memories flooded her mind… *she was a little girl of twelve again, at her father's side. Handcuffs on as she worked to free herself in less than two minutes under his gentle tutelage.* Her hands now free, she realized she would have to pretend she was still shackled to the wall. *Thank you, Daddy.*

A man stood in the doorway, flashlight in hand, back lit by the glow of the light from the larger war room. He moved closer and Elyse gasped, General Nguyen.

"I thought you were dead, you bastard," Elyse hissed in Vietnamese.

"You should tell your American pilots to make sure all on board are dead when they shoot down an Allies chopper," General Nguyen replied. He moved closer, and the raw burn marks and scarring on his face and neck were visible in the poor lighting. Elyse gasped at his gruesome face as he reached out grabbing her by the hair, pulling her to her feet.

Looking at her large swollen belly, he said, "I see the Marines, did indeed, use you well, Miss Booker."

Elyse put her sharp elbow into his ribs, turning she put her knee to his groin. "It's Mrs. Corrington to you, you bastard."

He loosed his hold on her hair and she retreated to the wall.

"American whore, you will pay for everything you have done," he ground out.

"What have I done to you?" Elyse asked.

"As usual, Americans taking what rightfully belongs to Vietnam, A Prima ballerina, the title belongs to the Vietnamese, not an American whore."

Elyse gasped. "I earned that title it wasn't just given to me."

"It belongs to Vietnam."

"And this is why you betray your country? Because of a ballet title? I was proud to dance for South Vietnam," Elyse said.

"There is no South Vietnam, it is just Vietnam," he screamed at her. "One country, once we expel the American invaders. You over-value yourself Miss Booker. You were just the icing on the cake in my decision to work toward uniting my country. We leave here in an hour to meet the NVA, they will decide your fate. You will end up servicing the troops once your child is born and taken from you, or they use you as leverage against your father. It matters not to me as long as I never see you dance for Vietnam again."

Elyse gasped, sinking to her knees as a contraction ripped through her belly.

General Nguyen stepped closer to grab her hair again and pull her back to her feet,

"That's right, deliver your devil's spawn now, I'll take it and nail it to a tree for the Americans to find."

Elyse looked at him in horror, pulled her pocketknife hidden deep within the pocket of her dress, and drove it straight into his heart.

"Not my baby, asshole."

He crumpled to her feet and breathed his last breath.

Elyse looked down as a puddle of water formed at her feet. *My water broke, oh no baby, not here, we need to get out. We must survive, for your daddy, for us.*

Quietly stepping over the general's body, she slipped from the room with his flashlight. Grabbing hand grenades from a box she found in the corner, and stuffing them in her deep pockets, she climbed up the ladder and into the tunnel system. Throwing two of the grenades down into the war room where the VC had gathered, she crawled away as fast as she could."

⁂

ELIJAH RAN the small piece of material through his fingers, a pale orange cotton. His hand shook as he lifted it to his nose, smelling the delicate fragrance of her perfume. Elyse. She had been marking the trail with pieces of her dress. It had been awhile since the Montagnard's had found the last piece.

His stomach rolled at the thought of them catching her marking the trail and the danger she was in by doing so, but he was grateful for each and every piece they had come across. Nodding to the smiling Montagnard warrior at his find, Elijah and Collin walked over to the spider hole where they had found the material.

Looking down the hole Elijah dropped his weapon and started to remove his flak jacket.

"No, Elijah, you're too big, you'll never fit through the tight tunnels," Collin said.

"That's my wife down there," Elijah cried, frustrated, and filled with fear for Elyse.

"Let the tunnel rats do their job, there's no one better than them. They have the experience and knowledge. If Elyse is down there, they will find her."

⁂

ELYSE CRAWLED THROUGH THE TUNNEL, the explosions from the hand grenades shook the earth and sent choking dust through-out the tunnels. She paused as another contraction took hold of her, breathing slowly, she moved on once it passed. Remembering her conversations with Marines, the tunnel rats, and all the stories told to her about the underground tunnel systems used by the VC, she made her way through the system, only pausing when contractions stopped her movement.

Terrified that she would be trapped, and her child be born underground, she steeled her resolve, only allowing thoughts of Elijah to enter her mind. She got stuck, only once. *Great, this is just great. Why couldn't I be one of those women who have a cute little basketball? No, Elijah had to plant a big old watermelon in my belly.* Rolling to her back she scooted through until the tunnel widened enough to let her crawl. She came to a ladder, climbing up she found the exit blocked. Moving the wooden barrier, she pulled herself up and out of the tunnel. Breathing the fresh air in large gulps, she said a prayer of thanks, and looked around the jungle. Another contraction started, and she breathed through it. Ripping another piece of cloth from her dress, setting it by the spider hole she rose to her feet, turned and came face to face with an NVA soldier.

❧

THE TUNNEL RAT, Corporal Richmond, climbed out of the spider hole to face Elijah and the group of Marines gathered around him. Looking at Elijah, shaking his head.

"Well?" Elijah said.

"This chick, who is she? Corporal Richmond asked.

"Elyse, my wife, she's nine months pregnant."

"She's not down there now. She was, I found these. He handed Elijah a piece of Elyse's dress and a pocketknife. "Now let me tell you what else I found. About twelve dead VC, and a dead ARVN general by the name of Nguyen. Had that knife buried in his chest. The VC, looks like she got them with grenades. I don't know any chicks, nine months pregnant, or not, who could have done what that chick did."

Collin whistled. "Don't mess with Elyse."

Elijah paled, *his mind wandering back to the day before he had left her at Vung Tao.*

He had placed her pocketknife back in her hand. "You may need this someday, brat." *"I thought you didn't arm women?" she had asked with an impish smile. Not wanting to explain his actions, he had pulled her into his arms and kissed her senseless distracting her from her questions.*

"Nguyen, we shot his chopper down months ago. He must have survived," Elijah said.

"I'm guessing she went out through the tunnels at the other end," Richmond said.

439

"Spread out, find the other end to this tunnel system. Sarge, get on the horn with Brendan and his team, update him. She's got to be close by," Elijah said.

*

ELYSE GLARED at the soldier as he gestured with his rifle for her to move. *Damn.*

She moved ahead of the NVA soldier until they came to a camp of NVA soldiers. A man strode toward them and stopped in front of Elyse. A small Vietnamese man, barely taller than her, as was the norm for the people of Vietnam.

"Miss Booker, I presume. *Danseuse qui pleure*, the pride of the South Vietnamese Royal Ballet, though an American. I never quite understood why they chose you over a Vietnamese woman for Prima Ballerina, though I understand your ballet dancing is exquisite. Your father, Ambassador Booker, must have had great influence over their choice of you. I'm Colonel Dao, we have been searching for you for close to a year now."

Elyse carefully chose her words. "It's Mrs. Corrington, as I told General Nguyen, I earned that title. My father had nothing to do with it."

"None of it matters to me, it is my superiors who have interest in you. They may not be able to sell you now, but they will use you to extract concessions from your father, the ambassador.

My father." Elyse stopped. *They have no idea he's retiring. They'll kill me if they find out this is all for naught.*

"Where is General Nguyen? I am quite surprised to find you without your VC escorts."

"They're dead," Elyse said.

"Dead? By your hand?" He looked at her belly. "Impressive, Mrs. Corrington."

He nodded his head to the soldier standing behind her and the soldier dragged her over and tied her to a tree.

"Please, I'm in labor. I must have my hands free to deliver my baby," Elyse begged Colonel Dao.

"It is best, Mrs. Corrington, if you rid yourself of the child now. My superiors will not be pleased if you are encumbered with an American monster."

Elyse cried, "No, please, my baby is an innocent in all of this. Please."

They stuffed a dirty rag in her mouth, silencing her plea's for mercy.

She watched the NVA as they worked, laying booby traps and mines all around her. The Colonel stood above her, staring down at her with cold black eyes. "The Americans are close, , as we speak, NVA forces lay in waiting to launch an ambush. We will leave you here and return once the Americans, a Marine company I believe, are dead. If we are not success-ful, you will die here, along with your baby, and anyone who tries to get past the surprises we left for them."

Hearing the far-off sound of small arms fire, the colonel bowed to her. "And so, it begins."

THE FIREFIGHT WAS FIERCE, the NVA company, even with their ambush plans were ill-prepared for the onslaught of a Marine battalion. Twelve hundred men strong, they swept through the jungle in search of a tiny woman, their ballerina, and the enemy forces that held her captive.

ELYSE LIFTED her head after what seemed like hours. The baby would arrive soon and die, stuck in the birth canal. Her arms tied high above her head, she couldn't remove her panties or do anything to help the birth. She wept, for her baby, for Elijah, the fear in her great as the firefight came closer and closer. Lying low, she tried to move to the other side of the tree as an occasional bullet zinged overhead but, could not. Soon all was quiet, only the sounds of the jungle and her muffled crying and screams of pain could be heard.

SHE LIFTED her head when she heard a noise. The old chieftains face poked through the foliage and he grinned at her. Startled, Elyse jumped,

441

and looked around. *Montagnard's, if they're here, Brendan is close, and so is Elijah.* Sheer joy coursed through her and she cried in relief. *No wait, booby traps.*

Then she spotted Elijah. Tears coursed down her face as her eyes met his. Shaking her head, she silently screamed, *"No, no. Don't come near me, you will die."* She signaled with her eyes for them to look up in the trees, and various spots throughout the clearing, where the booby traps were set.

One by one, the Marines cleared the traps as Elyse labored alone, breathing and resting between each contraction. A Marine, an elite combat engineer, swung by a rope and made it up in the tree just above her head. He worked his magic to clear a swinging bamboo booby trap. Finally, he was able to get close enough to reach down and pull the gag from her mouth.

Looking up into his eyes, she said, "Hello, Rick."

"You remember me, little girlie?"

She smiled. "Popcorn."

A contraction took hold of her, leaving her moaning.

"Don't you worry, little girlie. Just give us a few more minutes, and you'll have your Major by your side."

There was almost no time left, the baby would come soon.

Elijah watched her from his position, each contraction was agony for both of them. Elyse screamed, but he could not go to her yet. They maintained eye contact, and he called to her, offering words of encouragement. "I'll be there soon, brat. Breath, baby, breath."

The amount of time it took for Rick to dismantle the next trap above Elyse was agonizing. Then she was free. Elijah cut her bonds, and she fell into his arms. Her swollen belly contracted again, and she cried, "I knew you would come. I knew."

He kissed her, cradled her in his arms and buried his face in her hair. "Elyse. God, Elyse. I thought I'd lost you."

"We need to move you out of here. Do we have time?"

Nodding her head, she said, "Yes, I'll let you know when."

"Elijah, Mountain and Arnold?"

"Sustained severe injuries, but they will live," he assured her.

Relief and tears filled her eyes. With Doc at her side and Elijah on the other, they put her on a litter. Sarge, Henson, Collin, and Brendan carried the litter and moved her out of the clearing. She continued to labor with each contraction coming harder and faster. Her screams were agonizing to hear. She had a death grip on Elijah's hand. They passed many Marines on the way toward the Dust-off chopper, most of whom knew Elyse. They called out their encouragement as she passed by.

"You got this, Elyse."

"Hang in there."

"Stop. Stop. The baby's coming." They quickly found a clearing and set her down. They got Henson on the line with the doctor on the hospital ship, while Doc prepared to assist her on the ground.

She struggled to sit up. "Elijah... this... this is all your fault. You should have kept your hands to yourself."

"Sassy. Even giving birth, you're sassy." Elijah said.

The laughing team, Collin, and Brendan moved to stand guard, with the company surrounding them in a wider perimeter, their backs to them to offer privacy. Doc instructed Elijah to sit behind his wife and brace her. Doc followed instructions over the radio, the baby was soon crowning. It wouldn't be long.

"Okay, Elyse, push. Push Elyse."

She rested between contractions.

"Here we go again. Push." Doc said.

Elyse was exhausted at this point and could not muster up the strength.

"She must push, Cap," Doc told him. "She cannot give up now."

Elijah nodded, and in his sternest, now-you're-in-trouble voice, he said, "Brat, you must push. Give me our child. Now, Elyse. NOW. Push, push..."

She pushed once more, screaming in her agony... and the baby was out.

A strong cry resounded in the clearing, and Doc cut the cord and handed Elyse her baby. She held him up for Elijah to see his new son. The boy squalled his outrage at his parents. With tears streaming down their faces, they laughed and welcomed their son to the world. Elyse kissed him all over his little face and laid him on her breast, shielding him from the jungle insects.

Softly, she spoke. "Name your son, Elijah."

"Andrew Finn Corrington." Elijah announced as he brushed the hair out of her eyes and kissed her lips. She looked into his face in surprise. Her eyes teared. "Andrew."

Drinking in the sight of him, she noticed the Major insignia on his collar. Looking up at him, she said, "Major? Why didn't you tell me?"

Smiling at her, he said, "Later, brat."

"Elyse we are not done yet. You must deliver the afterbirth," Doc reminded her.

She nodded. It would be more discomfort, but at least the worst of it was over.

When it was over, Doc handed her what he had taken from her room, the Lil' Cap blanket. She wrapped her son and crooned to him to quiet his cries. He had thick black hair on his crown and eyes that shone with a hint of amethyst. He was beautiful.

Elijah kissed his wife, while Brendan and Collin gave each other a high-five. With a laugh, Collin said, "We're uncles."

POPPING A CAN OF BLUE SMOKE, the Marines guided the dust-off chopper in, and it landed.

Elyse gave Elijah that "oh hell no." look. He smiled.

Elyse said her goodbyes with hugs and kisses. They loaded her on the chopper as Elijah held his son a moment longer. When she was settled, he handed the baby in. He turned, pounded Doc on the back, shook his hand. Then he said his goodbyes to his brothers and his team and jumped on the chopper. The baby squalled as they took off.

"Maybe he's hungry, Elijah. I think I should feed him." Unbuttoning the top of her dress, she pulled her bra aside and bared her nipple to his little mouth. He latched on with vigor.

Elijah laughed. "Yeah, he's a Corrington."

The chopper landed on the deck of the hospital ship. On board already were Colonel Corrington, Ambassador Booker, and Soup. Orderlies carried Elyse on the litter, while Elijah carried his tiny baby.

He looked down at his son. Andrew had his fingers in his mouth and quizzical expression on his little face. Elijah sank to his knees, as tears ran down his face. He did not think he would live long enough to see his child.

ELYSE LOOKED BACK. She signaled to the orderlies to stop and help her up. She walked to Elijah and went down on her knees and kissed him, sweetly and gently. He pulled her to him with his free arm. He thanked God for Elyse, his son, and his life. The little bundle between them started his squalls again and tooted.

"I think the little bugger just shit on me," Elijah said. Elyse giggled, and they rose to their feet as one.

"Get back on the litter, Elyse."

"What? I'm fine."

"Elyse don't argue with me. Get back on the litter."

MID-FEBRUARY 1969

Elijah and Elyse lay on a blanket on the beach in front of their tiny home. Soup ran back and forth with the ebb and flow of the tide. Andrew, wrapped in his receiving blanket between them, was having none of it. He kicked and wiggled till he was free. A fat, happy baby, he did not like to be restrained. Conceived during a siege, born in the jungle, they nicknamed him Bunker as an endearment and it stuck.

ELYSE LAY ON HER TUMMY. A stack of mail in front of her as she read the letters. Elijah shook a giraffe shaped rattle in front of the baby and smiled as the baby smiled a big toothless grin back at him.

"How's Mountain and Arnold doing?" he asked.

"Good, they're still in the hospital in Taiwan. Mountain expects he'll be able to go home within a month or so. The same with Arnold," Elyse replied.

"It's odd that you got letters from the team all on the same day. And the letter you received from Johnson's parents last week."

Elyse gave him a sad smile. "He had a lovely family. As to the team, I threatened them with bodily harm if they didn't write to me. Henson is home now. He said he got the nerve up to ask Angela out on a date. Both Sarge and Doc are at DaNang. Their tours are up within the week. Both are waiting to be sent home."

"Who are the other letters from?" Elijah asked.

Elyse's hands shook as she looked at the return addresses on the letters. She opened the first envelope and inhaled sharply. "New York. They've invited me to audition for a role in the ballet troupe."

"and the other?" Elijah asked.

"Paris."

Elijah leaned over brushed the hair from her eyes and placed a feathery soft kiss on her lips. "See, I told you so. You're not so small that they don't want you."

Running her hands through his thick black hair, she pulled him closer. "I love you."

"I love you too brat. Now go for your walk."

"You're sure you'll be okay?"

"You just fed Bunker, and I think I have the diapering down to a science. We'll be fine. Go."

"Be careful so you don't pin your sleeve to his diaper again," Elyse replied, with a devilish grin.

"Go, brat," Elijah chuckled.

ELYSE ROSE TO HER FEET. Walking to the water's edge. She pirouetted and leaped into the air and landed with a splash in the surf. Spotting a seashell in the sand she picked it up and slowly she meandered up the shoreline.

The End

Dedication

Between, August 5,1964 and May 7,1975,

9,087,000 military personnel served active duty during the Vietnam era.

2,709,918 Americans served in Vietnam.

58,272 died. 8 of those were nurses who died.

2338 are listed as MIA (Missing in Action), 766 were listed as POW (Prisoners of war).

303,704 were wounded.

To this day, many Vietnam veterans still suffer from PTSD (Post Traumatic Stress Disorder), the lethal effects of Agent Orange, and their physical wounds.

All gave some. Some gave all.

This book is in no way meant to trivialize or glamorize their sacrifice but to honor the men and women who served in South Vietnam.

Welcome home.

I would like to take this time to thank the organizations and people who made this book possible.

The Vietnam Veterans of the American Legion Post 39 for sharing some of their memories of the Vietnam war.

Captain Thomas C Billig IV (US Army, retired) For your time, patience, and guidance.

My Husband, family, and friends. Whom I tormented endlessly.

Glossary

Military

Bird - Helicopter

CO - Commanding officer

Dust off choppers - Medical evacuation helicopters

KP - Kitchen Police

R&R - Rest and relaxation

KIA - Killed in action

MP - Military Police

Saltpeter, Potassium Nitrate - folklore indicates saltpeter reduces libido

SOP's - Standard operating procedures

Twenty clicks - 12.43 miles

French

Ta beaute m'a coupe souffle. - Your beauty my breath

Tu es aussi avengle qu'une chauve sauris. - You're as blind as a bat

Galician (Gaelic)

Mo ghra fior Fein- My own true love

Spanish

Lobo - Wolf

Vietnamese

Khong xau. - Not bad

ABOUT THE AUTHOR

Leesa makes her home in Twin Cities metro area in Minnesota with her husband and their two dogs Rosie and Jax.

When she isn't writing, she enjoys gardening, painting, and reading romance novels. She and her husband also enjoy movies, traveling, and entertaining their two grown children, along with their spouses, and seven beautiful grandchildren.

Leesa's favorite romance authors are Kathleen Woodwiss, Christine Feehan, and Johanna Lindsey.

The book's inspiration came one night from a dream about the characters, a song, and the story around them.

f facebook.com/Leesa-Wright-Author-116720209702749

🐦 twitter.com/Leesaauthor

📷 instagram.com/Leesawright.author

Made in the USA
Monee, IL
02 July 2020